Music from Home

Geraldine O'Neill

POOLBEG

Published 2013
by Poolbeg Press Ltd
123 Grange Hill, Baldoyle
Dublin 13, Ireland
E-mail: poolbeg@poolbeg.com
www.poolbeg.com

1

A catalogue record for this book is available from the British Library.

ISBN 978-1-84223-513-3

Typeset by Patricia Hope in Sabon 11.5/15

Printed and bound by CPI Group (UK) Ltd, Croydon, CR0 4YY

www.poolbeg.com

About the Author

Geraldine O'Neill was born in Lanarkshire, Scotland.
She has lived with her husband, Michael Brosnahan, in
County Offaly in Ireland since 1991.
She has two adult children, Christopher and Clare.
Music From Home is her tenth book.

Acknowledgements

Many thanks to Paula Campbell, and all at Poolbeg – especially my editor Gaye Shortland – for their work on this book.

Thanks also to Mandy, Sallyanne and the staff at Watson Little.

I am grateful to two lovely men who helped with my research about the Italian communities in Manchester and Stockport – Michael Lowry and Tony Rea. Michael kindly gave me information about his Italian background and gave me access to books etc. He also introduced me to Tony Rea, author of *Manchester's Little Italy*. Tony patiently and diligently guided me around Italian culture and customs during the 1960s in Manchester.

A sad farewell to my great-uncle Kevin O'Reilly from Daingean, who was very handy with the pen himself. Kevin not only read all my books but delivered the post in several of them.

My deep gratitude to my parents, family and friends, and all the people who support my writing in so many ways.

Thanks to Chris and Clare for their love, support and valued advice.

And my loving thanks to Mike. In all the years since we were students, I couldn't have asked for more care, encouragement and love. I am grateful for all the small and the bigger things you do which make it easier for me to write.

Music From Home
is dedicated to my dear friend,
Helen Fahy

*Oh, the comfort, the inexpressible comfort, of feeling safe
with a person, having neither to weigh thoughts nor
measure words, but pouring them all right out, just as they
are, chaff and grain together, certain that a faithful hand
will take and sift them, keep what is worth keeping, and
with a breath of kindness blow the rest away.*

– DINAH CRAIK (1826–1887)

In family life,
love is the oil that eases friction,
the cement that binds closer together,
and the music that brings harmony.

EVA BURROWS

Chapter 1

Manchester

February 1968

The evening light was fading as the green Volkswagen Beetle turned the corner and rattled down the cobblestones into Chapel Street. It came to a halt in front of Leonardo's Restaurant.

Maria Conti climbed out of the back seat, still dressed in her navy school uniform, knee-length socks and dark winter coat. Her friend, blonde-headed Stella, was seated in the front alongside her mother.

"Thanks for the lift, Mrs Maxwell. My father said he will drive us on Friday."

"It's a pleasure, dear," Jane Maxwell told her. "Give Leo my regards."

Maria leaned back into the car for the bag with her ballet shoes and clothes. "I'll ring you when I get back home later tonight," she told her friend.

Stella looked over her shoulder. "Enjoy your lovely Italian meal. You're lucky having a dad who can cook. Ours can't even boil an egg without burning the pan."

Mrs Maxwell raised her eyebrows and smiled. "But Leo is not a typical man, dear."

1

Maria laughed. "I'd better not go mad and eat too much or James Granger will complain he can't lift me!"

"James Granger will always find something to complain about," said Stella. "He's the biggest moan on two legs and looks a total twerp in ballet tights!"

Mrs Maxwell tutted loudly. "Don't talk about poor James like that. His father is one of the top consultants at Manchester Infirmary."

Stella rolled her eyes in Maria's direction. "Who cares what his dad does? That doesn't make James a good ballet dancer or stop him being an idiot."

"There are times," her mother said, "when I wonder about you, Stella."

Maria waved the car off then turned to face the brightly lit restaurant. As she walked towards it, her heart lifted as always when she heard the low strains of violin music and breathed in the scent of tomatoes and thyme and strong Italian coffee. She opened the door and went into the empty, rosy-lit restaurant.

She loved it at this time of the evening, when the place was lulled into quietness with the sound of taped classical music and the vague hum of activity coming from the kitchen.

The music always warmed her as some of the violin recordings were those played by her mother, Anna, who had died when Maria was nine. When she was younger, Anna had learned to play the piano and basic traditional tunes on the fiddle at her home in County Offaly in the Irish Midlands. When she came to Manchester and met Leo she had given up music entirely, but he encouraged her to take up violin lessons and Anna discovered a very different kind of music which she came to love. Within a short time she had studied and listened to the famous violinists and composers and she then set about learning to play their works.

It was a comfort to Leo that she had in fact been practising her violin when she had the final asthma attack which robbed him of the love of his life. It was after that, when he needed something to fill the huge void in his life, that he set himself the goal of opening his own restaurant which would have traditional English dishes alongside a small menu of carefully chosen Italian food. To achieve his dream he took every extra shift he could get in the hotel to earn money to add to his savings, most of which had come from the unexpectedly good insurance payment he received when Anna died.

Maria went straight to the table she liked by the window. She dropped her bag on the floor, shifting it under the table with her foot. Then she went across to the small cloakroom and took her school coat off and placed it on one of the hangers. She smoothed her long dark hair down then made her way towards the kitchen, wondering which staff would be on for the night. There were usually three in by now, not counting her father who always worked front of house, but helped in the kitchen when they were busy. Two or three of the waiting staff would be due in soon.

"Ah, Marietta!" Franco, the restaurant chef and her godfather, greeted her warmly, calling her by her pet name. He put his meat cleaver down on the worktop and came towards her, arms outstretched, as though he hadn't seen her for an age. "And how is the little ballerina?"

"Hungry and tired after going straight to ballet from school," Maria said, making a face. "But I suppose I'll survive."

Franco hugged her and kissed her on both cheeks, as he had done since she was a little girl. Although Franco came from Florence and Leo from a small village near Lake Garda, they were like brothers. They had first met when they were both lodging in the same house in Ancoats – the area of Manchester known as 'Little Italy' due to the number of Italians living there. Leo went straight into hotel work, while Franco started off working in a local shop owned by Italians. The landlady was an old widow called Mrs Nardini, who loved having the boys to look after since her family were all grown up and married. She made them Italian dishes which reminded them of the mothers they had left back home, and hot chocolate, and on special occasions gave them small glasses of Italian liqueurs. When Franco was in the house during the long winter evenings, he asked Mrs Nardini to show him how to do some of her basic

3

pasta and pizza recipes. He progressed to cooking several evenings a week, until, encouraged by Leo, he started going to nightclasses to learn English cooking skills as well, and gain certificates which would help him find work in a restaurant.

A year or so later after arriving, Franco was working in the busy restaurant in the city centre while the ambitious Leo had moved to become restaurant manager in the Palace Hotel. They often sat up late at night drinking coffee and helping each other with their command of the English language, although Leo always had a better grasp of it than his friend and was more confident in conversation with the customers at work. On those nights they also shared their hopes for the future, and it became understood that when Leo was in the position to open his own restaurant, Franco would be in charge of the kitchen.

The two men had spent many nights discussing how the restaurant would be run, when it was only a dream. It was decided that the main part of the menu would be English to suit the local customers they expected to frequent it, but they hoped that requests for Italian food would gradually increase as their customers became braver in trying out their pasta and meat dishes.

Years later when Leonardo's was opened, their careful approach had worked and, as the diners got used to the smell of the Italian herbs and sauces, a number of them were known to order only from the Italian section. The restaurant had also become a favourite place with the Italian community, who booked it for weddings, funerals and christenings.

Maria wandered around the kitchen now to have a quick word with Vincent, the quiet sous-chef, and Johnny, the local boy, who was the new commis chef. Although Johnny's family were Manchester born and bred, he had grown up in Ancoats and something of the culture had rubbed off on him. His open appreciation of the Italian music and food had won Leo over, and he had chosen him from several other candidates when interviewing for the vacancy of apprentice chef.

From what she already knew about males, Maria could tell that the confident Johnny had an eye for the girls. He was

4

always laughing and teasing the waitresses, young and old, and she knew he would have been more forward with her if her father hadn't been the boss.

"Where's Dad?" Maria asked now.

"Leo had to go out." Franco's voice was low. "But he said he will be back very soon . . ."

Maria's eyes narrowed as she wondered where he had gone. There were several places she hoped he *hadn't* gone.

"He said you should start eating without him." Franco indicated the stack of menus. "What do you fancy? You must be hungry after all that dancing."

She lifted one, then without opening it asked, "Have you any lasagne on tonight?"

"But of course. Whether it is on the evening's menu or not, I always have a dish made especially for you."

Maria smiled. "Ah, Franco, you're always so good to me!"

He winked at her. "The staff fight to take it home when you are not here."

Johnny came to stand at her elbow, holding up a jug. "Orange juice?" He looked her directly in the eye and then winked.

"Yes, thanks," she told him, deliberately moving her gaze away from him.

"I'll go and get on with a bit of studying," she told Franco. "I have a History test in the morning."

"Good girl. You are sensible using all those brains you have. You want to get a big important job when you grow up, and not slave in a hot kitchen."

"When I grow up?" Maria laughed, heading back into the restaurant. "I'll be sixteen in a few months."

"Almost *sixteen*? Sixteen?" He shook his head. "That's impossible."

She went back over towards the table at the window and lifted her bag, searching inside for her book on the Tudors and her pen and notepad. It could be worse – at least it was an interesting period with all Henry's wives and the scandal surrounding them. The only pity was that the exam questions would focus on the more boring aspects like Cardinal Wolsey and the Dissolution of the Monasteries, and her interest and knowledge of these was sketchier.

She sat for a while, jotting down the main points and dates, and then covering the pad and trying to memorise them. The class exam was the first big one since entering fourth year – the O-level year – and would give an indication of her chances when sitting the main exams at the end of the year. Maria still wasn't sure what she wanted to do, but her father was encouraging her to study hard in case she needed the results for teaching or some of the other professions. A good and steady option her father often suggested was working in a bank. One of their neighbours was a manager in the local Barclays Bank, and he had told Leo that if Maria got decent A-level results he would put a good word in for her. Maria wasn't sure about this, as it seemed to her a rather boring, colourless job, but she couldn't come up with any suggestions that her father felt really happy about.

When she told him she might like to work in the restaurant, he had raised his eyebrows. "Young people think working in a restaurant is all about meeting people and having a good time, but the real work is in the kitchen and after all the customers go home. I tell you, there are much better things for you than this life, Maria, if you have a good education."

"But you've been happy working in the restaurant, and I love it here too. It's a beautiful place and it feels like my second home."

"I am happy you feel like that," he said, "and I love the restaurant and I love my work – but it is all I have ever known. If you work hard at school, you'll have opportunities I could never have dreamt of when I came to England as a nineteen-year-old boy. You don't have to work these long hours. I had no choice – for Italians it was restaurant work, play music or sell ice cream." He squeezed her hand. "I have worked over the years, happy to know that you will have much more choice than I did. And it was your mother's wish that you would go to college . . ."

As always, that had ended the conversation. She didn't want to let either of them down. She decided she would just have to concentrate harder on her studies.

She was engrossed in Tudor London when Franco appeared at the table with her lasagne, and a small dish with crispy fried potatoes and vegetables. He gave his usual little bow. "Just as madam ordered."

Maria thanked him as she put her school books on the windowsill and he arranged the dishes in front of her. She unwrapped her knife and fork from her red linen napkin and then she looked up at him and asked if he knew exactly where her father had gone.

Franco's eyes slid from hers towards the window. "I'm sure he did say, but as usual I do not remember. Some people he had to meet." He threw his hands up and smiled. "Ah, Leo is a busy, busy man!"

She knew of course that he was covering up for her father. Franco wouldn't want to cause trouble between his boss and his daughter. Maria understood exactly how things were. Like most people, Franco had a great affection for her father. The chef might not always approve of his boss's behaviour, but he gave his loyalty nonetheless.

There was something about Leo Conti that drew people in. His dark hair and handsome looks made him stand out from the other men and made his slightly under-average height pass unnoticed. But it was his bright, intelligent eyes and warm, caring manner that won everyone over and made Leonardo's Restaurant the great success it was. He had a great sense of humour which men of all backgrounds warmed to, whilst women of all ages were charmed by his good manners and the genuine compliments he gave without seeming in any way forward.

Maria thought of asking Franco if her father had started disappearing from the restaurant in the afternoons again, but something stopped her: the usual feeling of betraying the person closest to her heart, the person she most depended on. Besides, she couldn't be sure that Franco wouldn't warn her father and then he would take more elaborate steps to cover up anything that might concern her.

This was the problem when there was just the two of them. When there was no one else to safely share her fears with.

She finished her main meal and was staring out of the restaurant window into the darkness when the kitchen doors swung open and Johnny came through with the dessert menu.

"I shouldn't have anything more," she told him. "I'm already full."

"You should have whatever tickles your fancy," he told her, winking. "You don't have to worry about getting fat. You've got a lovely slim figure . . ."

She felt her face start to flush and in order to distract from it she rolled her eyes to the ceiling as if she didn't care what he thought. Secretly she liked the compliment and, although she didn't fancy Johnny in the least, she knew the girls at school would think him good-looking and funny.

After a few moments she felt awkward with Johnny just standing there, gazing openly at her. "If you come back in a few minutes," she said, "I'll have made my mind up."

She was debating whether to have an Italian dessert or ice cream when the restaurant door opened. She looked up as her father came rushing through.

"Maria, I'm sorry I'm late, but I had some important business to attend to."

His eyes were shining, and she could see he was more animated than usual – obviously happy with his afternoon's business.

He kissed her on the cheek and then pulled out a chair opposite her and sat down. "And how was the ballet lesson?"

"It was fine," she told him, trying to keep a light note in her voice.

He touched the side of her face. "You don't seem so enthusiastic?"

She smiled and pushed her long dark hair behind one ear. "Well . . . I really don't know if I will keep the classes on much longer."

"If that's what you want." He nodded his head slowly. "Only you can decide."

"I know I haven't got what it takes to be a professional dancer and, even if I had, I don't think it's what I want to do. I don't feel the same passionate way as Stella does about it, and I don't enjoy all the practising." She sighed. "The other thing is, I don't want to become panicky about my weight as lots of the girls do . . ." Maria was talking too quickly now and knew she was making more of the ballet thing than she needed to, in order to cover up her anxiety about where he had been.

"No, no . . . we certainly don't want problems like that." A smile broke through the seriousness of his face. "And what would Franco have to say if little Marietta stopped eating all his lovely dishes? I think he would say forget the stupid ballet lessons."

"He would, wouldn't he?" Maria was smiling now in spite of the little knot of anxiety. Whatever worries she felt about him, she could never get beyond the fact she adored him and wanted him to be happy.

"You must make your own decisions. Hobbies are meant to be enjoyable and if they stop being that then maybe it is time to stop." He thought for a moment. "What about the horse-riding?"

Her face lit up. "That's different! I still enjoy it every bit as much as I did when I started. It's good fun and relaxing and I don't have to enter competitions or anything unless I want to."

There was another reason that kept up her interest at the riding school – one she had not yet shared with her father. Paul Spencer. He was a couple of years older than her – eighteen this year – and she saw him at her classes every Tuesday evening and Saturday morning as his family owned the stables. His father – a short, wiry man – had once been a jockey, but Paul had obviously inherited his striking good looks from his tall, dark-haired mother.

"Well," Leo said, "I do think you need to have some interests outside of your studies, and only you can decide what those are to be."

Her father was always fair with her and gave her a lot of leeway – the only thing he was inflexible about was her education.

The kitchen door swung open and Franco came into the dining room. "A cup of coffee, Leo?" he called.

"Come here, my friend, come here!" Leo said, beckoning him. "I have some good news. I was just about to tell Maria about it, and I'd like you to hear it too."

As he came towards the table, Franco took his white chef's hat off and scratched his dark curly head.

"We were just talking about horses," Leo said, "which is a wonderful coincidence, because that's what my news is about."

Maria felt her throat tighten. "What do you mean?"

Her father threw his hands in the air and laughed. "I have bought a horse!"

Franco looked as shocked as he did. "For Maria?"

There was a moment's silence.

"In a way . . ." Leo was making a juggling gesture with his hands now. "But it's not for her horse-riding lessons. Not yet." He patted her on the shoulder as though to reassure her. "I've promised her that I'll buy her a good show-horse if she is still riding at eighteen and very serious about it. It's not something you buy for a fad."

Maria and Franco waited.

He grinned at one and then the other. "I've bought a *racehorse*! A fifty percent share in a beautiful yearling – a filly!"

"That's some news," Franco said. "You're a brave man, Leo."

Maria's heart slowly sank. It was all she had dreaded and worse.

Leo's voice was high and excited. "And I know you will both love her! She's a terrific runner. She has a pedigree as long as your arm." He held both arms out as long as he could reach to illustrate the point. "From a terrific sire and dam who have won a great many races. She won her maiden race in record time and by fifteen lengths. Winning is bred into her." He looked at Maria and his face suddenly became serious. "I bought her on the condition I could name her," his voice was cracked with emotion, "and she will be called . . . Bella Maria . . . after the most important lady in my life – my beautiful Maria!"

"Lovely," Franco said. "That is lovely."

Maria nodded her head, not knowing how to react to the

news. She could see so many pitfalls – mainly financial – but she did not want to spoil his obvious pleasure.

"The name your mother and I chose for you is also the name of my mother and of Our Blessed Lady." He shrugged and then held his hands up and joined them together as though he was praying. "It might just help her to look upon us more kindly and make our Bella Maria a lucky winner!" He laughed, his lively, dark eyes darting between them. "Well, Maria, what do you say? Having a beautiful, winning filly called after you? Won't all your friends at the stables think that is really something?"

Maria swallowed hard. "It's really nice of you . . ."

"I knew you would be delighted with the name. It's a great honour for a girl to have a boat or a horse named after her."

"It certainly is," Franco said, standing up. "Congratulations, Leo, but I must get back to the kitchen or you will not be able to afford to feed that horse."

Leo laughed and shooed his friend away.

When Franco had gone, her father suddenly seemed to notice her serious face. "Are you all right? You are happy about the horse?"

His concern made her feel guilty. "I don't mean to put a dampener on it, Dad. I'm just a bit worried about the cost of it. It's a very expensive thing to own, isn't it?"

"It is, but I will be sharing the costs. Now, don't you worry about anything. Your father has this whole thing worked out."

Maria forced a smile on her face and tried to look happy. Tried not to think that buying a racehorse meant he was back involved in gambling. Because that meant that he had learned nothing from his narrow escape a couple of years ago when they almost lost the restaurant.

Chapter 2

Johnny came back to see what Maria wanted from the dessert menu but her appetite had disappeared. Anxiety about her father always did that to her. She told him she would just have a plain ice cream and remained resolute and straight-faced while he tried to persuade her to pick something fancier.

"Are you feeling all right?" her father asked. "I thought the news about the racehorse would make you happy . . . I know how much you love horses."

Maria looked at him. He had the open, innocent face of a young boy, looking as if he truly believed that she should be happy. How could he not realise how unsettling the situation was for her? Did he not remember the nightmare he had put them through two years ago when the bank was threatening to close Leonardo's down by refusing to extend his business overdraft? When he had to beg them to give him another six months to get his finances back in order?

Their financial predicament had come as a terrible shock to her, because up until then she had happily never given money a single thought. She could remember back to when her mother was alive, and money had not seemed a problem then either. Her mother had never had a permanent full-time job – Maria only remembered her working a couple of mornings a week in the local florist's and maybe the full week leading up to Christmas and Valentine's Day and busier occasions like that. This had led Maria to believe that they had enough money for her mother not to need to work. Looking back now, Maria wondered if her mother's asthmatic condition meant she did not have the stamina for it, because she had often heard her father saying that she should take things a little easier, and make sure she rested when Maria was at school.

Maria could recall a few occasions when her mother had had a bad asthma attack, and the doctor had to be called for, and on one occasion an ambulance came to the house and she was gone for several days. If her mother had been unwell at other times, she did not make a big issue of it to her, and was always discreet in her use of her inhaler and medication. She had appeared as active as most of the other mothers, she had kept the house perfect and cooked and baked, and she walked Maria to school every morning and then collected her afterwards. She took time to help her with her homework and, in the lighter evenings when her father was at work, she would walk her down to the local park with some of the other mothers and children to play on the swings and slides.

Her father had worked long hours in the hotel and travelled home on the late-night bus. Apart from special events organised by the Italian groups that Leo was a member of, or Christmas staff nights at the hotel, they rarely went out. When she thought about it now, her parents did not then have an over-lavish way of life – they didn't have a car or a television or phone up until a few years before her mother died. They had gradually built up towards those luxuries that were now taken for granted as part of her life. And she was sure they had been happy back then, and she could recall no incidents or arguments regarding her father drinking or gambling. And although she knew that it would be easy to remember her mother through rose-tinted glasses, her one solid memory was of lying in bed, her parents downstairs, and hearing the distant sound of her mother playing the violin. She knew that her father, relaxing with a glass of Italian wine, had asked her to play for him, and that sound had always told her that everything in their home was safe and well.

Later, after her mother died and her father had bought Leonardo's, she had believed that they were comfortably off. She knew they were not in the same league as Stella's family with her father's solicitor's firm and their much bigger house, but compared to some of her other school friends, they were doing fine. Her father employed Mrs Lowry and her husband on a regular basis to take care of Maria and the house and garden. Leonardo's was always busy and her father was easily making what it cost to pay for their nice home, television, phone, any clothes she needed and all the little extras like her riding classes and ballet.

She had never paid any attention when her father was talking business on the phone or to any of his friends, and he did not expect her to be involved. Naturally, he told her when the restaurant had a particularly good night, and how pleased he and Franco were with the takings around Christmas and holiday times. Money therefore, to her, was something that was always there and not an issue until the first financial bomb had gone off, and Leo had sat her down to explain that he had been so busy that he had not been keeping an eye on his home accounts and had overspent in certain areas. She had not understood everything that followed, but got the gist that he had used money from the house to subsidise the restaurant which had to be paid back in six months, and that was why they would not be having their annual trip to Italy or the piano he had hoped to buy her that Christmas.

He had not mentioned gambling in his talk to her, but it was clear from his many phone conversations and from general chat to the men in the restaurant, that it had, over the years, begun to feature more in his life. And, she was aware that his drinking had increased both at home and after work, which was bound to have had an impact on the gambling.

Later in the year, he had told her how relieved he was that finances were back on track and her concerns about money had begun to fade away again. But they had only faded, they had never completely gone, and the experience had left her wary about what she now saw as a weakness in her beloved father. And she realised now that her wariness had been warranted.

14

After all the hard work and cutting back, the restaurant accounts had eventually come out of the red and back into the black. And now he was obviously back in the racing and gambling world again. She wondered if he thought she didn't understand all that had happened – and what might happen yet . . .

"I'm okay – I just have a bit of a headache," she told him now, reaching for her schoolbag. "I think maybe I should go home now." She often stayed for a few hours in the evenings until the restaurant started to get busy and then her father would run her home, or, if he was very busy, he would call her a taxi.

Leo took one of her hands in his and when she looked up she saw the concern and love in his eyes and all her anger began to seep away. She now felt guilty at spoiling his excitement about the horse. Maybe she was worrying too much. Maybe buying the horse had nothing to do with his gambling problem. She wondered perhaps, if all his attention were to be focussed on looking after the horse, consulting with the trainers and the stable staff, he might not have the time or interest to bet on the others. Surely he wouldn't have the time between the restaurant, horse and home to be part of the gambling group as well? She wanted so hard to believe that.

Her father was still looking at her with concern. "I'm fine," she reassured him. "I'm just a bit tired after school and ballet and studying."

"I think an early night might be a good idea with your exam tomorrow." Leo looked at his watch. "I've just got a few things to check in the kitchen and then I'll run you back to the house. I'll ring Mrs Lowry and ask her or Michael to put the heating on for you."

"Thanks." He was so loving and caring that she couldn't stay angry with him for long. She smiled and thought she should say something to take the frown of concern away. "I'm looking forward to seeing the horse."

His handsome face lit up. "It's a dream come true," he told her. "How many people have the good fortune to own a horse? Such a beautiful, vibrant animal! And I have a strong feeling that Bella Maria is going to be a winner for us. Exciting times are ahead!" He took her face in his hands and kissed her on the forehead.

Leo went off into the kitchen singing and moments later Maria could hear the distant sound of laughter and congratulations. For the moment her father was happy, and she loved seeing and hearing him like that. His handsome face did not wear worry well.

She stared around the rosy-tinted restaurant for a few minutes, her eyes flitting over the carefully ironed wine-coloured tablecloths, the shiny silver cutlery and the candlesticks. Then she turned her gaze to the window and looked out onto the cobbled street, wondering what their housekeeper would make of her father buying the racehorse.

Mrs Lowry was an Irishwoman in her late sixties, who lived in a small house a few streets away from the Contis' larger Victorian detached house in Heaton Moor on the outskirts of Manchester. She had baby-sat Maria when she was a toddler on the occasions her parents went out, and then became a full-time minder when Maria's mother died, to allow Leo to work. The elderly lady now came in a few times a week to tidy the house, do the washing and anything else that was required and have a meal ready the evenings that Maria wasn't at Leonardo's. Rose Lowry's husband, Michael, did the gardening and any odd jobs that Leo was too busy to attend to. The couple kept the Conti household running and gave Maria a steady home routine.

As Maria waited for her father to drive her home, the evening waiting staff came in, each one stopping to have a word with her. By the time the last one disappeared into the kitchen her face was aching from smiling so hard, pretending everything was fine.

All the way home Leo talked about Bella Maria, and the good friend he would share the horse with – Charlie Ford – the butcher who supplied the meat to the restaurant.

"Being a butcher sounds like a simple occupation," he explained, "but there's a lot more to it than meets the eye. Charlie is a very successful businessman. Do you know he has a chain of seven shops in the Manchester and Stockport area now?"

No, Maria said, she hadn't really thought about it.

"And every one of those shops is doing very well. He is not only doing well for himself, he is giving employment to over fifty men. Isn't that something to be proud of?"

Yes, she agreed, it was definitely something to be proud of.

"You see, Maria, to be a good businessman you have to be willing to take a risk. But you must weigh up – very carefully – all the pros and cons. And Charlie has done precisely that with every shop before he opened it. He told me that he did his homework on each area and made sure that there were big customers there like hotels and restaurants, hospitals and even convents – all those sorts of places. Then he made sure that his meat was the very best and that his shop was the cleanest. And he never lets his standards down. The way he starts off is the way he keeps going." He took his gaze off the road to look Maria in the eye for a moment. "That tells me that Charlie is a man who knows his business. And I believe that he will put the same care and attention into Bella Maria – I know he will! He has put the same effort into finding the right horse as he put into his business, so I know it is a safe bet, and I'm honoured that he thinks I'm a suitable partner for it."

Maria could hear pride in her father's voice at being included in this venture. He had always given his heart and soul to Leonardo's and she felt that maybe it was a good thing that he had something else to take up his interest. So, as she looked back at him, and in spite of all her misgivings, she found herself nodding and smiling as though everything in her world was fine.

Chapter 3

When they arrived at their house in St Aiden's Avenue, Leo accompanied Maria inside as usual to check all was okay. Mrs Lowry had left the place shining, with a warm fire crackling safely behind a fireguard in the sitting room.

"I won't be too late tonight," Leo promised as he headed back out the door after pulling all the blinds down. "And make sure you have all the phone numbers beside you, keep the blinds down and don't answer the door to anyone."

Maria rolled her eyes. "You say that to me every night, Dad. I'm not stupid."

"You can't be too careful. You just never know who could be watching the house and noticing that a young girl is at home on her own."

The area they lived in was a good one with much bigger houses than their own, and burglaries were not unheard of. When Maria turned fifteen, she had insisted that Mrs Lowry go home in the evenings, as she felt much too old to have a baby-sitter. After several arguments about it, Leo had furnished her with list of phone numbers – of the restaurant, of people like Mrs Lowry whose phone bill Leo paid as she only needed it to talk to him, of their next-door neighbours, the Coxes, and the

18

number of Father O'Donnell, the Parish Priest from the local Catholic Church, in case of emergencies.

After she had settled in and was changed into her pyjamas and dressing-gown, Maria curled up in the armchair by the fire, lifted the phone from the Italian marble-topped side table and dialled her friend Stella's number. It gave only two short rings before it was answered.

"I was just waiting until Mum went to make the supper, then I was going to ring you," Stella told her. "She's in the kitchen. Hang on a second until I close the doors . . ."

Maria felt a little stir of anticipation as she wondered what news her friend had that she didn't want to be overheard. She could hear Stella's footsteps going down the hallway of their big Edwardian house, closing the doors which led into the main reception rooms and the kitchen. Then she heard her friend coming back to the phone.

"Guess what?" Stella's voice was low and excited.

"What? I've no idea . . ."

Her voice went lower still. "Tony rang me." Stella's voice was a bare whisper.

Tony O'Brien was one of the riding instructors at the stables.

"Did he ring the house?"

"Yes. Luckily I got to the phone first and I just said it was you."

"You're terrible," Maria gasped. It annoyed her that her friend lied to her mother so easily and never gave a thought to involving her in the deception. "One of these days you'll get both of us into trouble."

"He's asked me to go to the pictures on Thursday – tomorrow night. He's going to speak to Paul Spencer tomorrow morning and arrange a double date for the four of us!"

"Oh, no! Don't let Tony ask him! I'd be mortified if he says he doesn't want to go! Ring Tony back and say you two can just go on your own."

"Don't be stupid, Maria. Everyone knows that Paul fancies you. Tony told me that the first time we were riding together."

"I'm not too sure about that. He's never given me the

impression he was going to ask me out. He's always quiet when we're together."

"It's just because he's shy," Stella said. "Some boys are like that. They just need a bit of a nudge. I bet he'll jump at the chance of a date with you if it's all arranged." There was a sudden pause. "Hold on . . ."

There was silence on the line then Maria could hear a muffled conversation going on in the background. A minute or so later her friend came back on the phone.

"My mum drives me completely insane."

"What's wrong?" Maria couldn't imagine anything ever really being wrong in the Maxwell household. Stella was lucky: she had two ordinary parents, and two younger brothers – Thomas aged twelve and George aged ten – who at times she adored and at other times drove her mad. And although she complained about her mother and father being strict at times, Maria couldn't see what her problems were. Her father was a solicitor with a busy practice, and her glamorous mother helped out in the office a few afternoons a week. The Maxwells had no money problems and Stella appeared to have everything she wanted, as she was the most fashionable girl in their year.

"She's on at me all the time about practising my ballet and studying to make sure I get the grades I need for college. She never lets up. She said I should consider giving up horse-riding until after my exams, but I know she's only saying it because she doesn't want me to see Tony."

"Have you told her that you're going on a date with him?"

"Are you joking? She would have a fit if she knew. She's seen us talking and joking together at the stables and she said the way I was carrying on it was obvious that I fancied him. She said I was demeaning myself and our family name by having anything to do with a boy like that."

Maria's brow wrinkled. "But most people think Tony's a nice lad. What's he ever done that she doesn't like him?"

"*Maria*," Stella's voice was now an urgent whisper, "surely you know that my mother is a complete and utter snob? She doesn't think a riding instructor is a suitable boyfriend for me.

20

She calls him a *stableboy*! She acts as if we're landed gentry or something from the Victorian age. She's told me that she doesn't want me seeing anyone until I'm old enough to pick the right type."

"And who does she think is the right type?"

"Let me think now . . . Prince Charles might just satisfy her . . . or maybe James Granger because –"

They both chanted together in whispering voices: "His father is a top consultant!"

"Oh, my God! Can you imagine it?" Maria said, putting her hand over her mouth.

The two girls went off into a fit of giggles.

Then Stella said, "She's really got a bee in her bonnet about Tony. She's been going on about him to Dad as well, and I even heard her moaning to her friend Diana on the phone about me. Thank God, Diana is more modern, and I hope will have told her to stop interfering in my life."

From what she had just heard, Maria didn't think there was any chance of her mother stopping interfering as long as Tony was around. "So what are you going to do about the cinema tomorrow night?"

"I'll say I'm with you. It's not really telling a lie – I just won't mention the fact that Tony and Paul will be there too."

"No, Stella," Maria said in a serious voice, "I'm not going. I really don't want to go on a date with Paul when he hasn't even asked me."

"Listen," Stella said, "just answer me this – do you like him or not?"

There was a pause. "You know I do . . . but I want *him* to ask *me*."

"How many times do I have to tell you! Tony is doing it on his behalf because he's too shy."

"It's not the same as him asking me properly."

"Right, Miss Fussy-pants," Stella hissed, "I'll speak to Tony tomorrow and I'll tell him that Paul has to phone you or you won't go."

"Good – and I'm not being fussy!" Maria laughed to keep

21

things light. Stella would quite happily steam-roll over her if it suited her own agenda, but she wasn't going to allow it.

After the phone call Maria went into the kitchen and boiled milk to make a mug of cocoa to have while she was studying. As she walked back into the sitting room, slowly and carefully in case she spilled the hot drink, she had an uneasy feeling and her mind kept flitting back to the conversation with Stella – the part where she had said that her mother didn't think Tony was good enough for her. She wondered now, if she did actually go on a date with Paul Spencer, what his family would think of *her* . . .

It was something she had never considered before. She had always been proud of her father and Leonardo's. Her father had always instilled in her the belief that it didn't matter what people had – what mattered was whether they were decent people or not. She had presumed that most families worked on those same values and had thought, from the odd comments that Stella had recently made, that her mother was joking. She wondered now if all her friends' families thought along the same lines. It was obvious that the Spencers were wealthy – Stella said they were much wealthier than her mum and dad, and Maria knew they were definitely much wealthier than her father. They not only owned the stables but a big farm with hundreds of acres and she had heard Stella's mother going on about how successful a businessman Paul's father was, and that he was often on the radio and television commentating when there were big races on. Jane Maxwell said that the Spencers had money coming in from all angles.

More sensitive to financial things after the racehorse shock, she could now recall a number of conversations where Mrs Maxwell made reference to families being well off and that sort of thing. If what Stella had said was true, it made her now wonder if the Maxwells and the Spencers knew anything about her father. A cold shiver ran through her now. She wondered if they could have heard rumours about his drinking and gambling? Could they have heard about the difficulties he got in when he almost lost Leonardo's? They had met him on a number of occasions when he dropped her off at the stables and he always had a friendly word with whichever of the staff were on duty and she had always thought that they all liked him. But maybe that was because he was paying for riding lessons for her. Going out with the Spencers' son might be a whole different matter.

She settled down with her cocoa and her schoolbooks and tried to push the uncomfortable thoughts from her mind. But every so often, try as she did to ignore them, they came flooding back. This sudden new feeling of people judging her intensified the anxiety she already felt about her father and Bella Maria.

Around ten o'clock she gave up trying to concentrate and closed her books, hoping she would wake up early and have time to look over her notes again in the morning. She went upstairs to her bedroom and was grateful to slip in between the fleecy sheets warmed by the electric blanket that Mrs Lowry had switched on for her earlier. She read a magazine for a while then she turned her bedside lamp off. As always, she kept the landing light on and a small night-light in the corner of her room.

She lay for a while in the dim light, trying not to think of the situation with Paul Spencer. There was no point, she reasoned, in worrying what the Spencers would think if they started dating. Even though she was sure he liked her, there was a definite shyness to him, and there was no guarantee that he would agree to join them at the cinema.

She would just have to wait until tomorrow to find out what was going to happen.

She closed her eyes and buried her face in the pillow. She was sure that tomorrow was going to be an absolutely awful day, with exam questions she didn't know the answers to followed by complete humiliation when Paul Spencer turned her down.

Chapter 4

Diana Freeman stood in front of her open mahogany wardrobe in her satin nightdress, unable to decide what to wear. Then she went barefoot across the floor to look out of the tall sashed window of her Edwardian semi-detached once again. As she stood, she raked her fingers through her damp auburn hair to separate the ringlets, so that it would dry straight.

She thought how choosing clothes was becoming increasingly difficult. Especially in the last few years when the fashions had changed so dramatically and become much more casual. She couldn't decide whether – at thirty-eight years old – she should now be moving into a more formal style of dressing, or whether she could still get away with following some of the latest fashions.

And of course she had to consider the impression it gave to her customers. If she dressed too young it might put off some of the older ladies, and if she dressed too old the younger women would automatically assume the shop was too old-fashioned for them.

It was the same dilemma when ordering stock for the two businesses she owned – La Femme in Didsbury, near where she lived, and her second shop, Gladrags, in Heaton Moor which she had opened three years ago. The problem was deciding which way she wanted her businesses to go. The tried and tested ladies' shop was still working for her established customers, but the bigger chain stores and boutiques were now luring away less dedicated customers with their bright and brave shorter skirts, trouser suits, and tights in every colour and design.

When she first opened La Femme in the early sixties, it had started off as more of an accessories shop with hats and gloves and fancy umbrellas, and basic stock such as dressing-gowns, nighties, petticoats, stockings and suspenders. Gradually, as her business grew, she broadened out into selling blouses and ladies' cardigans and then suddenly her wholesalers were offering her a whole new range of clothing that she hardly recognised. Formal hats were apparently only being worn for weddings and functions now and were being replaced with jaunty caps and the more practical tights were the preferred legwear for women of all ages and had now overtaken stockings and suspenders. Every time Diana checked with her suppliers, they told her that there was a revolution going on in the clothing industry and, if she wanted to keep ahead in business, she would have to stock what the modern woman wanted.

She rifled through the hangers in her wardrobe now and decided on a sleeveless geometric-print dress in shades of pinks and blues with a three-quarter-length belted blue jacket. It was suitable, she thought, for getting in and out of the car and if the jacket was too warm in the shop, she could change into one of the cardigans she kept there. She laid the dress and jacket on the bed alongside her little pile of fresh underwear and tights and then went over to the dressing-table to finish drying and straightening her shoulder-length hair.

As she sat at the mirror she wondered again if she should have her hair cut shorter. Was thirty-eight too old for long hair? She had read numerous articles that said that after a certain age women should have their hair shorter and lighter in colour. She had always felt that longer hair suited her and had serious doubts about having it chopped off and, when she discussed it with her hairdresser Valerie, she had assured her that both the length and the brownish-red colour were still perfect. Apart from a subtle rinse every few weeks to tone in the few grey hairs that had started appearing, she said that Diana would easily get another five years out of her colour or style without worrying about it.

Later, when she was dressed and sitting at the mirror brushing on brown mascara to accentuate her green eyes, Diana wondered at the effort she expended on both her appearance and her work. Between the two shops she often worked six days of the week and, while she had staff helping in both places, she was the one who filled in if anyone was sick or on holiday. But what else was she supposed to do to fill her time? It wasn't as though she had a husband or family.

She was downstairs in the hallway, just lifting her handbag, when the phone rang. It was Jane Maxwell.

"Hi, Diana – I won't keep you chatting as I know you'll be heading to work. Just checking if you managed to order those charcoal slacks for me and the lace tights for Stella?"

"Hi, Jane – yes, they both arrived late yesterday afternoon in the Didsbury order. I was going to give you a call from the shop this morning when I picked them up. I'm going in there first today and I'll bring them over to Gladrags with me after lunch."

"You're a star!" Jane said. "I can always rely on you." She paused. "How did the weekend in London go?"

"The show was great, and I enjoyed catching up with my friends."

"And – any suitable husband material in the big smoke? Did anyone catch your eye?"

Diana rolled her eyes and gave an inward sigh. "No, and I wasn't looking for anyone. It was my friend's husband's fortieth birthday."

"You never know the time and the place when you could meet Mr Right."

She wished now she had never confided her interest in meeting someone to Jane Maxwell. But she was in a difficult spot with Jane having become a friend as well as one of her best customers. She had been a loyal customer when Diana had her first shop in Didsbury and had been the person who told her when the shop came up for sale near the Maxwells' house in Heaton Moor. She had also helped with an opening night and encouraged all her local friends to shop in Gladrags rather than travel into the shops in Stockport or Manchester.

"I did tell you about that magazine article I read, where it said that older people meet their husbands and wives through friends, golf or joining nightclasses?"

"Yes, I think you mentioned it a few times recently . . ."

"Good advice – and you know I always have my eye open for any of Richard's colleagues who might suit you."

"I'm really sorry, Jane," Diana said now, "but I need to hurry. I told the girls I'd be in the shop for half past nine and it's nearly that already."

"Oh, you'd better rush," Jane said, "and if I don't make it into the shop to collect those things today, I'll pick them up tonight or tomorrow night at your house if you don't mind throwing them in the back of your car. Stella is driving me mad asking about the tights."

By the time she parked her black-and-white Mini outside La Femme, her uncomfortable conversation about finding a man with Jane Maxell was gone from her mind. But the minute she stepped inside the shop it was brought back with a vengeance as Pippa – curvy with red, curly hair and the youngest of her two staff members – came rushing towards her from behind the counter.

"You're not going to believe it – Elaine got engaged last night! Isn't it fantastic?"

Diana felt her face stiffen for a few moments, then she quickly recovered and smiled. "Oh, that's wonderful news!"

Then Elaine, the tall thin manageress, came out from the small staffroom at the back of the shop and Diana went forward to give her a hug.

"Congratulations! I'm so delighted for you and Peter." She then stepped back. "Now – let me see the ring."

Elaine held out her left hand to show a sparkling trio of small diamonds.

"Oh, it's beautiful – simply beautiful. Well, well . . . what a surprise!"

"Have you set a date for the big day yet?" Pippa asked.

Elaine nodded, her face flushing. "We're thinking of the summer."

Pippa's eyebrows shot up. "Gosh – that soon?"

"I know it's a bit quick," Elaine said, "but we both decided that there's no point in waiting. We're sure about our feelings and neither of us are getting any . . ." her eyes dropped to the floor, "getting any younger."

She looked up at Diana, who was still smiling, but she was embarrassed about making the gaffe about the age thing since Diana was older than her. There was also the issue about engagements that Pippa knew nothing about.

"Quite right," Diana said. "There is absolutely no point in waiting when you've made up your mind."

"It's Peter's age as well," Elaine said. "Don't forget he's older than me. He'll be forty next year . . ."

"Of course," Diana said. "You don't want to waste time. No point in dragging things out . . ."

Elaine caught her eye and for a moment there was a silence, and then Diana turned back to Pippa.

"I think this calls for a celebration! Take ten shillings from the till, please, Pippa, and pop down to the baker's and get some lovely cream cakes for us, and a small bottle of fresh cream for the coffee. I'll put the kettle on!"

"Oh, lovely!" Pippa said, pleased with the impromptu treat, and rushed to get her coat.

When Diana was in the staff room boiling the water, Elaine came to the door.

"That's really kind of you," she said.

Diana turned towards her, her hands resting on the end of the small table. "Not at all. I'm genuinely delighted for you both."

Elaine shrugged. "Hopefully it will all work out . . ."

"Why shouldn't it? Peter is a lovely chap and I think you'll make a great couple." She smiled and raised her eyebrows. "Most engagements work out, Elaine. Don't take mine as an example."

"I wasn't thinking of that . . . honestly."

Diana shrugged, knowing that Elaine was lying. "Well, it's a long time ago – over two years."

"Is it that long?"

Diana nodded. When her engagement to Brian was broken off, it had such a devastating effect that Elaine had to take over running the shop for a fortnight. And, besides, they had discussed her broken engagement too many times since for her employee to really have forgotten.

She looked at Elaine's serious face now and felt guilty for dampening her spirits. Like herself, Elaine had almost been resigned to being single when Peter came on the scene, and she had been let down so often in the past that she was careful not to presume her new romance would develop into something more serious. But now it had.

"So," Diana said, "what are the plans? Any ideas about what kind of wedding dress you would like or where you're going to have the wedding reception?"

Elaine's face brightened. "We have a few ideas for places in Manchester or Stockport, and there's a wedding dress I've had my eye on in a shop here in Didsbury." She laughed. "I've been looking at it for the last couple of months, just on the off-chance he proposed."

"Is it in the window of Bridal Heaven?"

"Yes."

"The one with all the little pearls at the neck and cuffs?"

"Yes, that's it!" Elaine's voice was high and excited.

"It's gorgeous, and it would be absolutely perfect for your height and colouring. Have you tried it on yet?"

"Oh, no . . . I would have been terrified that it was tempting fate to go into the shop before I was properly engaged. I thought I would ask you to come with me when I do. You've got a good eye and I'd really value your opinion."

Diana looked at the gold, French-style clock on the wall. "Why don't we have our coffee and cake and then leave Pippa to hold the fort while we go down to Bridal Heaven and let you try it on?"

"Really? Oh, that's so good of you!"

Later, as she walked towards her Mini carrying the bag with Jane Maxwell's slacks and tights, Diana thought how different things would be in the Didsbury shop now that Elaine was going to be a married woman. Up until now, only single women had worked there, and it had been a consolation to her not to have to listen to conversations about married life or babies at work. She had enough of it in her social life as all her best friends had gradually one by one tied the knot.

A further consolation had been the fact that Elaine too was over thirty. At thirty-three she was five years younger than Diana, but with Elaine's quieter demeanour and her own bubbly personality and modern dress, they had seemed of an age. Whatever way she looked at it now, Diana felt over the hill. A perennial wallflower. A spinster for life.

And all because she had wasted her best years on Brian Taylor. Seven whole years. Seven whole years during which she could have found someone else.

And she had spent four of those years engaged. And during all that time he had managed to evade making any concrete plans for a wedding or plans for a family in the future. Diana now knew that she should have realised there was something seriously wrong but she had been so besotted by him that she was prepared to wait until he was ready.

Now she knew that a man like Brian would never have been ready. And she would continue to pay the price for having believed in him.

Chapter 5

There was an uneasy silence in the big Victorian hall as Maria sat alongside fifty other girls all dressed in identical navy uniforms waiting to do their final exam paper, History. The only sounds were the footsteps of the two female teachers as they walked up and down the aisles placing the salmon-coloured examination papers – face down – in front of each student.

She worked a pen between her fingers as she frantically tried to recall the main points of the Tudor period she had spent the past few weeks studying. Then, as the last paper was placed on a desk at the front of the hall and the teachers moved back to their tables, her gaze moved towards the tall windows and she said a quiet prayer.

"You may turn your papers over now," Miss Hartigan said. "And may I remind you to read every question very carefully?"

At that point, Maria's eyes slid across the row to meet Stella's for a few moments. During the English Literature exam the previous week, Stella had been delighted to spot a question about *Othello* that she could answer easily. It was based on one of Iago's soliloquies and she launched straight into her answer. It was only when a group of the girls were discussing the papers after the exam that she realised she had written about the wrong soliloquy.

Stella rolled her eyes now and pulled a face. Maria gave her a sympathetic smile, then they both turned back to their exam sheets.

On first inspection, Maria found only three questions – out of the five she had to pick – that she felt reasonably confident about. A sense of panic came over her which she had to fight back. As she read the other questions again, her throat ran dry and her hands started to shake. Her eyes flitted from one half-read question to another, the words making no sense to her. All she knew was that if she could only answer three of the questions she would fail the exam. She closed her eyes for a few seconds to try to still her breathing and then, when she felt a little calmer, she read over the questions again.

This time, she was relieved to find that certain sections of the questions were beginning to sound more familiar to her – and then her memory cranked into action, flooding her with related facts and dates. She took several deep breaths and then, remembering all the exam preparation that Miss Hartigan had given the class, she went back to the question she felt was the easiest to answer and started writing.

The silence continued for the next two hours. Maria kept her head down for most of the time going from one question to another. Every fifteen minutes or so she checked the time on her watch, and every half an hour Miss Hartigan or Mrs MacGregor told them how much time had elapsed and how much time they still had to go.

During the last half hour, Maria became aware of some of the other students leaving the hall. As she did with every exam, she wondered if they had been so well prepared that they could write all the correct answers quicker than her and without the nerves she felt, or whether they were giving up having answered all they could.

Then, when she was in the last fifteen minutes of the exam and only starting her final question, she felt the panicky feeling starting to return. Her heart quickened as her hand flew across the page while she tried not to let her writing descend into a complete scribble.

Then a bell rang and suddenly Miss Hartigan was telling

everyone to finish the sentence they were on and put their pens down. Maria wrote her last line and sat back in her chair – her head feeling light after all the intense concentration.

Minutes later the girls were all outside in the yard, huddled in groups, heatedly discussing the exam paper amid yelps of delight as correct answers were confirmed and excruciating moans when mistakes were realised.

"How did you feel you got on?" Stella asked, with a serious face. "Every time I looked over at you, you were busy writing."

Maria shrugged. "I haven't a clue. I just wrote anything that came into my head. What about you?"

"I don't know either . . . but I keep remembering things I should have written." She bit her lip. "I don't think it was as bad as the English one, but it was hard enough."

"Thank God we have the afternoon off," Maria said. "I'm going to catch the bus home and have a rest doing absolutely nothing. I couldn't pick another book up if you paid me."

"What about tonight?" Stella asked. "Have you heard anything from Paul?"

"Not a thing, but I'm not bothered because I didn't really expect to hear from him." She made a small, dismissive sound with her lips as though it meant nothing to her.

Stella looked annoyed. "Tony told me that he definitely liked you, and I know he wouldn't say it if it wasn't true." She spoke as though she knew Tony really well.

Maria checked her watch. "I'm going to run for the two o'clock bus."

"Phone me the minute you hear anything."

Sitting alone at the back of the bus, Maria took out her History exam papers again and as she went over them she realised that she might not have done quite as badly as she'd thought. In fact, the three questions she had been fairly sure of at the start of the exam she now felt were definitely okay, and the other two she now thought she had answered fairly well. She had been rushed with the last question but, even so, after listening to what the other girls had said about it, she felt she had done enough to scrape a pass.

She was fairly sure now that she had passed all the exams.

She knew this should have made her hugely relieved – happy even – after all the studying and worrying. But it wasn't enough. There was still something there niggling away at the back of her mind. Paul Spencer.

As the double-decker bus wound its way out of the city centre and into Longsight and then further along to Levenshulme her mind kept working its way back to him and the awkwardness she felt about this set-up date. She stared out of the window, trying to find things about the people or places she saw to distract her thoughts. There was definitely a degree of pressure because Stella and Tony were involved. If Paul didn't ring, she would feel she was letting them down because Stella needed her company at the pictures to keep her mother happy. On the other hand, there was a part of her that felt manipulated by her friend and she didn't like it.

When her stop came she got off the bus and crossed over to walk down Heaton Moor Road. As she came up towards the railway-station building, Jennifer Cox, the eighteen-year-old girl from next door, came out. When she saw Maria she gave her a big cheery wave and Maria hurried to catch up with her. As they walked along Jennifer informed her she had a half-day off work from her office and had spent a few hours shopping in Manchester. She showed her the two new LPs she'd bought, one by The Beatles and the other by The Kinks.

They chatted about music and then Maria told her about her exams. Having company until she reached her own street distracted her and she didn't have time to think of Paul Spencer until she was walking up the front steps of the house.

She was only in the door five minutes when the phone rang. Her heart raced as she went to pick it up.

Her father's voice came on the line. "How did the exam go?"

"It was difficult," she told him, "but I think I did enough to pass."

"Good girl! I'm sure you did. Are you coming to the restaurant tonight?"

"No. I'm supposed to be going to the cinema with Stella, but she might not be able to make it. If she doesn't I think I'll just have a quiet night in. I'm tired after all the studying." Then, knowing what was coming next, she said, "I went to one of the cafés beside the school with the girls for lunch, so I'm just going to make something like beans on toast."

"That's not very much," Leo said. "If it's not too busy here around five or six, I could drive home with some lasagne or some chicken for you –"

"No, honestly, I'll be fine with a snack. I've had enough to eat already."

"Okay, okay – just make sure you keep the doors locked and draw the blinds and curtains when it gets dark." He paused for a moment. "Do the windows look as if they've just been cleaned?"

Maria held the phone away and rolled her eyes.

"Can you just look over at the window and tell me if the window-cleaner has been?"

She turned her head to check and then clamped the phone back to her ear. "I don't think so," she said. "There are a few smudges on the glass."

"Well, you know Mrs Lowry worries about these things, and she phoned to say he is due sometime today if he hasn't been already. If he comes to the door you can tell him that Mrs Lowry has his money and will pay him when he gets to her street."

She was upstairs changing out of her uniform and into slacks and a brightly patterned sweater when the phone rang again. She rushed into her father's bedroom and picked it up.

"Have you heard anything from Paul or Tony yet?" Stella asked.

The fact that she had mentioned Tony made Maria realise that Stella wasn't convinced that Paul would phone either.

"No, I haven't," Maria said, sinking down on her father's bed. "And I don't really care. I'm not in the mood for going out after the exam."

"*Maria!*" Stella hissed. "Thanks a lot! You know I can't go if you don't go."

"Why don't you find someone else to go with?"

"Oh, yeah . . . *who*? Who else can I ask at this late date?"

A noise from downstairs suddenly caught Maria's attention. "I've got to go."

"Maria," Stella's tone suddenly became softer, "if you hear from him, ring me straight away."

"I've got to go, there's someone at the front door." Then, while Stella was still talking, she placed the phone back in its cradle.

She went downstairs quickly, expecting to see the window-cleaner or a neighbour, and was surprised when she opened the door to see two men in dark suits standing on the doorstep – one tall and bald and the other smaller and stockier with dark hair. It crossed her mind even before they spoke that there was something rough-looking about them, even though they were decently dressed.

"Excuse me, Miss," the shorter one with the thick dark hair said, "we're just checking the official registered owners of the houses in the area."

She noticed his eyes sliding past her, his gaze directed into the hallway, and she instinctively closed the door a few more inches.

"Would this be the property of Mr Leonardo Conti?"

She glanced from one to the other. "What is it that you're actually doing?"

"It's a survey of sorts . . ."

"For an estate agent," the taller, bald man added. He smiled. "We're checking how many reception rooms, bedrooms and bathrooms are in each house. You don't need to worry, we don't want to come inside and we've been to all the other houses in the street."

She paused, calculating. "Three reception rooms, four bedrooms and two bathrooms," she said, and went to shut the door.

The short man moved quickly to stick his foot in the gap to stop her closing it. "And just to confirm before we go, Miss – it is indeed the property of Leonardo Conti? The same gentleman who owns the restaurant in Manchester?"

The gesture made her suddenly feel intimidated. "Yes!" Her

answer was snappy and her eyes moved down pointedly to his foot.

"Thank you," he said, smiling broadly.

As soon as he removed his foot she banged the door closed and slid across the heavy bolt which she seldom used. She then moved quickly into the dining room which faced towards the street and went over to the window. She could see the two men walking down the path, out of the high wrought-iron gates and into the leafy street. She watched as they went along, straight past all the other houses, until they disappeared off into the distance.

She gave it a couple of more minutes and then she went back to the front door, unlocked it and stepped outside. She locked it again from the outside and, holding the key tightly in her hand, ran down the path and turned into the gateway next door.

She rang the bell and a few moments later Jennifer came to the door.

"Hi," Maria said, "I'm just checking if two men in dark suits called at your house a few minutes ago saying they were doing some kind of a survey?"

Jennifer shrugged. "I didn't see anyone, but then I had the record player on fairly loud upstairs –but if you come in I'll ask Mum."

As she called out for her mother, Maria followed her into the hallway, wondering if she was doing the right thing. She wasn't too keen on involving Mrs Cox who was inclined to be both nosey and a bit of a brag, always going on about their cul-de-sac being in the best area of Heaton Moor. She was also inclined to make comments about the late hours Leo kept and how his car often woke her when he was coming home from work. She had recently made a few little digs about how much the Italians liked to drink. But, Maria supposed, if anyone knew anything about the callers it was likely to be her, since little escaped her notice.

Mrs Cox emerged from the kitchen at the end of the hallway and came towards them, drying her hands on a tea towel. When Maria explained the situation, the older woman's face grew serious.

"I saw the two men you're talking about when I was in the dining room five minutes ago, but they never called here."

"Maybe they called before going into Maria's house and you didn't hear them," Jennifer said.

Mrs Cox shook her head. "I was in the dining room polishing the good silver cutlery for the last half an hour and, even if I wasn't looking out of the window, that doorbell is a good loud one, and I definitely would have heard them."

Jennifer raised her eyebrows. "It's a bit strange, isn't it? Telling Maria that they were doing a survey of all the houses and yet they didn't call here."

"I wouldn't normally have given it a second thought," Maria told them. "People call at the door often. But I just felt there was something funny about them." She then went on to explain how one of the men had stuck his foot in the door to stop her closing it.

"That doesn't sound like the sort of thing that an estate agent would do!" Mrs Cox's voice was indignant. "And I would think his company would not be impressed with that kind of behaviour. In fact, if you only knew the name of the company, I think your father should report him."

She went over to the door, looked out at the street and spotted an elderly neighbour, Mr Sweeney, out sweeping up some leaves. "Hang on," she said, "I'll just check if Joe saw anything – he's been in the garden for the last hour or more."

Maria and Jennifer went out of the house and down the path. They stood at the gate chatting about music and the latest episode of *Coronation Street* until she came back.

"They didn't call to Sweeney's house either," she told them. "It all sounds a bit fishy if you ask me . . ." She looked at Maria, her eyes narrowing. "Your father hasn't put the house up for sale or anything like that?"

Maria felt a wave of shock. "No . . . not at all. He wouldn't do anything like that without telling me. Why would we want to leave here?"

Mrs Cox nodded her head. "I didn't think it, but you never know. I've seen it happen before." She pointed down the street. "The Atkinsons from Number 17 were there one day and gone the next without a word to anyone. They just decided to move to Penrith to be nearer their daughter and put the house up for sale and didn't even tell their next-door neighbours." She gave a sigh. "Not a word to a soul. Then there was the young Cullen family at Number 6. When Sally had the baby she lost her job, and then the talk was that they got into financial difficulties and weren't managing to keep up with their mortgage payments." She shook her head. "This is what happens when young people get big ideas and think they can just walk into the most desirable areas without having the money to back it up. If people would only know their place in life instead of trying to keep up with more professional people, they wouldn't get into all this sort of nonsense."

Maria suddenly felt that there was some point being aimed at her father, and it made her feel defensive. "Well, our family have been living here since before I was born – and before some of the other families in the street – but I think it's a shame when any family hits hard times."

"So do I," Jennifer added, making eyes behind her mother's back.

Maria saw her neighbour's face tighten, and she knew her remark had hit home as the Contis had been there five years before the Coxes.

Mrs Cox shook her head and smiled. "You're both young and naïve in the ways of the world. When you have your own houses and families and responsibilities you'll soon know what it's all about."

There was a slight awkwardness so Maria turned towards the gate. "Sorry for being a nuisance . . . I've probably made the thing about the two men more dramatic than it was."

"You can't be too careful," Mrs Cox said. "So we'll keep an eye out for anything further going on."

After she let herself into the house and carefully locked it behind her, Maria sat at the kitchen table debating whether or not she should phone her father and tell him what had happened. One half of her knew she should, but the other half was reluctant in case he came rushing home and refused to leave her on her own again. She was just thinking that maybe she should talk to Mrs Lowry about it and get her opinion, when her heart suddenly leapt as another loud rap came on the door. She moved quickly out into the hall and into the dining room so she could look out of the corner of the bay window to check who it was. Her first thought was that it was the two men back again and, if it was, she had no intention of opening the door to them.

Her heart was racing as she pulled the curtain back a little to allow her to see who it was. She could just see the bottom of a man's dark trousers and shoes. It was only when he moved back down a step that Maria realised it was only the window-cleaner.

She went out to speak to him and had just finished explaining to him about Mrs Lowry having the money when she heard the phone start to ring. She closed the door and went in quickly to answer it, but it stopped. She was halfway up the stairs when it suddenly rang again, startling her.

She ran down into the hallway and picked the receiver up.

A voice said, "Hi, is that you, Maria?"

After all the shocks she'd had this afternoon, this was the biggest one. "Yes," she said, "it is."

"It's Paul . . . Paul Spencer."

There was a little pause during which her stomach did a somersault.

"I hope you don't mind me ringing you?"

"No . . . not at all." Then, there was another pause which made her feel so nervous that she suddenly heard herself saying, "Is there anything the matter?"

"What do you mean?"

She swallowed hard. "With you ringing me . . ." As soon as the words were out of her mouth, she made a fist with her hand and pressed it to her lips to stop herself from saying something else that was stupid.

Paul gave a little cough to clear his throat. "I know it's short notice . . . but I wondered if you'd like to go to the cinema with me tonight? It would be a kind of double date with Tony who works with me at the stables and your friend Stella."

Maria had to take several deep breaths to steady her breathing. "That's nice of you to ask," she said, "but can I just check that you

40

haven't been railroaded into this by the other two. Are you sure you definitely want to go?"

"No, no . . . I haven't been railroaded into anything . . ."

She thought his voice sound taken aback or maybe even slightly anxious, but she didn't know him well enough to work out which it was.

He cleared his throat again. "I'd really like you to come to the cinema with me tonight."

She held her breath to stop herself from saying that she would have preferred to have been asked out on her own, as it might just put him off her entirely or set a bad tone for their first date. And maybe, she thought, it might be easier in some ways if the four of them went together. Besides, she didn't really want to mention the date to her father and if Stella was with her she wouldn't have to. It wasn't that her father would have a problem with her going out with a boy – in fact he often joked about it – it was more she didn't want to make a big deal of it in case it came to nothing.

"Okay," she said, "that sounds great."

"So, you'll go?"

"Yes."

"Fantastic!"

She couldn't believe how delighted and relieved he sounded and she felt instantly better about it all.

"I've been thinking of asking you out for a while," he went on, "but I never seemed to get the opportunity and, to be frank, I didn't have the courage to just phone out of the blue. It seems so stupid but if it hadn't been for Tony I probably would have dithered about for ages."

Stella had been right, she thought, feeling guilty for misjudging her friend.

"Where will we meet?" she asked now.

"I think Tony and Stella have worked out all the arrangements. Tony is borrowing his friend's car, so we'll drive over to the cinema."

"Okay," Maria said, "I'll ring her after this."

There was a pause.

"Great, I'll see you tonight then," he said.

She couldn't think of anything else to say, so she just said, "Yes, see you tonight."

After she hung the phone up, she clapped her hands together and laughed with delight.

"I'm going on a date!" she said aloud. "I can't believe it – I'm going on a date with Paul Spencer!"

When she calmed down, she dialled Stella's number. Mrs Maxwell answered the phone.

"Hello, Maria, I'm afraid Stella is busy with ballet practice at the moment. Can she ring you back when she's finished?" Then she said, "Oh, hang on a moment. She's just come down the stairs. Stella, it's Maria . . ."

There was a pause.

"Hi, Maria."

"It's all on for tonight!" Maria's voice was high and excited. "Paul phoned."

"Great. I'll meet you in the café opposite the cinema at six o'clock"

Stella seemed unnaturally calm and quiet, making Maria wonder if she was still annoyed with her for the curt way she ended their last phone call.

"Is everything okay?"

"Yes, thanks, I was just in the middle of practising some barre work for my ballet exam."

Stella's parents were so convinced of her talent that her father had converted one of the spare bedrooms in their large house into a practice room for her with a barre, mirror tiles on one wall and a special wooden floor. Stella often asked Maria to come over to practise their exercises with her, but she only went occasionally as Mrs Maxwell said she thought they only distracted each other and never got around to any serious work.

Stella suddenly raised her voice. "My mother doesn't approve of me stopping dancing when I've just warmed up. She thinks I'm so immature and stupid I still need her to tell me absolutely everything I should do."

Maria heard a door banging in the background and realised

that her friend and her mother had obviously been rowing. "She hasn't heard about you and Tony, has she?"

"You are joking!" Stella whispered in a scathing tone. "She wouldn't just be banging doors, it would be more like World War Three if she knew. She said I couldn't go to the cinema if I didn't get all my ballet work done and some studying too! She's driving me mad!" There was a slight pause. "Hang on – just let me check that the kitchen door is shut."

Maria waited, her high spirits about Paul Spencer now dampened by the atmosphere she could detect in Stella's house. She couldn't imagine anything like that happening between herself and her father, and felt uncomfortable on her friend's behalf. She wondered now if Mrs Maxwell would be annoyed with her for distracting Stella from her dance practice, and maybe be annoyed they were going out to the cinema later tonight.

When Stella picked the phone up again, Maria said quickly, "I just wanted to know what the arrangements are for tonight. I won't keep you back in case you get into trouble."

"I'm not in any rush," Stella told her, loud enough for anyone around Maxwells' hallway to hear. "Go on. Tell me what Paul Spencer said."

Maria went on to relate the conversation word for word.

"I told you he liked you!" Stella said triumphantly. "So now do you believe me?"

Maria gave a self-conscious giggle. "Well, I suppose so . . ."

Stella lowered her voice. "Okay, the plan is that you and I will meet in the Plaza café at six o'clock, so we've plenty of time to chat about things before the film."

"You mean that we're meeting up on our own before Tony and Paul arrive?"

"Precisely."

"Okay," Maria said, glancing over at the clock. "It's half past three now and I'm going to go and have a bath and wash my hair."

"See you later, alligator!"

"In a while, crocodile!" Maria laughed. "And don't break your leg dancing!"

Chapter 6

When she was putting the towels in the laundry basket, Maria thought that she should phone her father to say she was definitely going out to the pictures in case he rang her. It was then that she remembered about the two men. She bit her lip, debating whether to mention it to him on the phone now, or leave it to a more suitable time. He would definitely be worried, she decided, and especially when she told him about the man jamming the door open with his foot. There was also the possibility that he would drive home to investigate the matter further and she did not want that when she was virtually on her way out to meet Stella.

Her father might even ring Mrs Lowry and ask her to start coming over every evening. And although she was very fond of the housekeeper, she definitely didn't want to be baby-sat at almost sixteen years of age. It was best, she thought, for the time being to say nothing about the callers.

She had a quick chat with her father and told him about her cinema plans, and he told her that the restaurant was busy for a weeknight but he hoped to be home reasonably early. Afterwards she tidied up the kitchen then went back upstairs to her bedroom to put her make-up on and spray herself with Madame Rochas, a birthday present from the chef Franco and his wife Bernice.

As she slid her arms into her coat, she wondered if she had gone a bit mad with the perfume as it seemed more potent than usual. She rubbed at her wrist and neck with a tissue and consoled herself that a walk out in the fresh air would tone the scent down by the time she met up with Paul Spencer.

As she walked along Heaton Moor Road, her mind full of the evening ahead, she spotted Mrs Lowry coming out of the fruit and vegetable shop on the corner with a bag in each hand. Maria went towards her, always delighted to see the housekeeper.

"Hello, love," Mrs Lowry said, giving her a big smile. "You're looking very well dressed tonight. Are you off out somewhere nice?"

"I'm just off to the cinema with some friends."

"Ah, it will do you good to have a night off – you've been studying hard for the last few weeks. Have you found everything okay at home after I've been in? Is there anything else that you noticed needed doing?"

"It's all fine, thanks." Then she remembered. "Did the window-cleaner call for his money? Dad told me to remind him this afternoon."

"He did indeed," Mrs Lowry said. "How's your dad doing? I haven't seen him for a while – I've only spoken to him on the phone."

"He's fine, thanks."

"I hope he's not killing himself at the restaurant? All those late hours he does . . ."

Maria felt a little catch in her throat. "No . . . no. He tries to finish earlier during the week. I was on the phone to him just before I came out and he said he's hoping to be home in a couple of hours."

"I'm glad to hear it. No one could ever accuse your father of being a lazy man."

For a moment she considered telling Mrs Lowry about her father buying Bella Maria, but something stopped her. Time was one thing, because Stella might already be in the café waiting for her, but there was also the fear that Mrs Lowry might disapprove of him getting further involved in horses and gambling.

She might voice the same fears that Maria herself had. And the housekeeper might even say them to her father.

They chatted for a little longer then Maria said she'd better go as her friend was waiting for her. As she hurried towards the Plaza Café, she thought back to the last time she had been worried about her father – weeks before he ran into all the trouble with the bank.

It was during a particularly bad period, when Leo was not coming home after the restaurant closed at the weekends and some weeknights and was instead drinking and taking part in late-night card games. The housekeeper would be there when Maria came back from her after-school classes or the restaurant, depending on what evening it was, and then they would have supper together and she would see Maria off to bed. Then she would sit watching the television and knitting or sewing until Leo returned. Sometimes he came home as he should around eleven o'clock but there were occasions he didn't arrive home until the early hours and he was usually the worst for drink. Mrs Lowry tolerated his lame excuses about problems in the restaurant for a while but she eventually told him that if his erratic hours continued, he would have to find a new minder for Maria. She explained as inoffensively as she could that, whilst she loved being with Maria, she needed to get to bed before midnight as she was up again at seven o'clock to get her sons out for work in the morning.

Leo had apologised profusely and told her he would organise things at the restaurant to make sure he was home earlier and had more evenings off. Things improved for a while but, bit by bit, he started sliding back to his old ways. One night he came in drunk and fell over the hall table, waking Maria up and causing Mrs Lowry to have the big showdown with him that had been coming for a while.

Unknown to the two adults, Maria was sitting in her dressing gown at the top of the stairs and listening to every word. She heard Mrs Lowry tell Leo that he was going to come to a bad end if he didn't stop all his drinking and gambling. She heard her father's weak apologies and then she heard him break down crying, saying that he felt lonely since Maria's mother had died, and how he couldn't sleep at night, and how the only time he relaxed and forgot about losing his wife was when he had a few glasses of wine or was watching a race or playing cards.

"That's not an answer to it, Leo," the housekeeper said, but Maria heard a kinder note in her voice. "And the restaurant won't run itself if you're at the bookies every afternoon and playing cards in bars in the evening. And you're going to run into an accident in the car one of these nights when you've been drinking too much. Then what will Maria do?"

Maria closed her eyes. The thought made her feel sick. Losing her father was her worst nightmare.

"You're right," he said. "You are correct. I will be more careful for both our sakes, and I will try to spend more time with Maria. It's just that I find it very lonely without Anna . . . and I still have nightmares about the way she died, gasping for breath . . ."

Maria's hands flew to her mouth. She knew her mother had died from an asthma attack, but she hadn't really thought about what that meant. She hadn't thought of her struggling like that . . .

"I know it's very hard for you, Leo," Mrs Lowry had continued, "and believe you me, I know what it's like to feel that way. I lost my only daughter to cancer when she was fifteen years old. It's something you never really get over, but you just have to make yourself."

"But how?" Leo had asked. "Do you think I haven't tried? Do you think I want to feel this way?"

"Keep thinking of Maria and you won't go wrong. Anna's gone a few years now, God rest her soul – and maybe it's time that you found yourself another wife and a new mother for Maria. I think it's what Anna would have wanted."

Maria's heart had raced at Mrs Lowry's words. How could she say or even think such a terrible thing? She didn't want someone strange coming into their lives, trying to replace her mother, and neither did her father. They had got used to things, and were happy enough on their own, apart from her father needing to cut down on his drinking and gambling which he had just promised he would.

She moved forward to grip the bannister, listening carefully for his reply.

"Another wife? How could I even think of replacing Anna?"

Maria was glad her father's voice had sounded so incredulous.

"Think about it, that's all I'm saying," Mrs Lowry had said. "It's not normal for a man to be on his own, and you might be more inclined to come home if you had a nice woman waiting for you. And you're a fine-looking man – there's many a woman out there who would be happy to look after you and Maria."

Maria's heart had leapt into her throat. How could Mrs Lowry betray her mother's memory by suggesting her father could love someone else?

Then there had been a silence that made her feel sicker. What if her father took the housekeeper's advice? Supposing he brought someone back to the house who thought she wanted a new mother?

"But I'm not ready to meet anyone," her father eventually said. "At this moment in time, the only female I want in my life is Maria."

Maria's shoulders slumped forward in relief, and she leaned her head on the bannister railings. Thank God, she thought . . . thank God he doesn't want another woman.

"Well, you know your own mind," she heard Mrs Lowry say. "Just make sure that you're good and sober for her and not throwing all your money away on the horses and cards."

Maria knew the housekeeper was right, and was speaking to her father as if he were one of her sons, but listening to her telling him off made her feel sad for him.

"Have you any family who could come over from Italy to help you for a while?"

"Well, you know my two brothers recently moved to America." Her father's voice was weary. "And my older sister looks after my parents. I have a niece I could ask, but I'm not sure how she would find Manchester . . . if she could settle here." There was a silence and then he said, "I have many, many good friends here in Manchester and I know they would help me out, but I know Maria would prefer you. You have been with her since she was a baby and I know the feelings you have for her."

"I know, I know," Mrs Lowry said. "And it's not just her I think the world of – sure, you're like one of my family, Leo – and better than some of them."

His reply was so low that Maria could not hear it.

"And I don't really mean it about you getting somebody else to look after her," Mrs Lowry continued. "I just wanted to give you a bit of a fright, so you would get things on more of an even keel, and not have me sitting here late at night worrying about you."

"You have my word that things will improve," he had told her. "I know I need to improve in a few areas of my life, and I will start with this. From now on I will be home as soon as the restaurant closes."

"Well, that's fine," she said. "And I do understand that Fridays and Saturdays are always that bit later. We'll say no more about it. Now, I need to be getting home, I've a busy day ahead of me."

"I'll just check Maria is okay, and then I'll walk you down to the end of the road."

"She's fine," Mrs Lowry said. "I checked on her not five minutes ago and she was fast asleep."

Before either of them could see or hear her, Maria crept silently back to her room.

It was from that night onwards that Maria began to feel anxious about her father. And while she was very fond of Mrs Lowry, she hoped she would not make any further suggestion that her father go out and find himself another woman. They were doing okay on their own. She had her friends at school and Mrs Lowry and Franco and all the other people in the restaurant. They didn't need anyone else in their lives.

The wake-up call from the bank came shortly afterwards, and things then changed in the way her father had promised, and had continued nicely up until now.

Chapter 7

Maria always felt self-conscious before walking alone into any café or restaurant other than Leonardo's. Her face was flushing even before she pushed the glass door open, although she immediately began to relax when she caught sight of the confident Stella standing over by the jukebox. Her friend's arm was leaning casually over the top of the machine, and she had one long wing of blonde hair falling down over her face. She stood half-posing in her new jeans and leather jacket – the jacket which she had fought over for weeks with her mother.

It was amazing how nothing ever seemed to rattle Stella. She was confident about almost everything, always saying she didn't care what people thought of her.

Maria hadn't seen her friend in trousers for a week or two and noticed, with a start, how much looser they seemed than before. Stella was obviously losing weight again. Maria wouldn't say anything because, the last time she brought up the subject, Stella had been very defensive about it, saying that all dedicated ballet dancers had to watch their weight, that it was part and parcel of their life. But, looking at Stella now, she was looking too thin, almost frail.

Maria came up behind her and tapped her on the shoulder. "Do you come here often?"

50

Stella swung around and they both started to giggle.

"Do you want a Pepsi?" Maria asked.

"Yeah, that would be great. I'll just finish picking my five records and then I'll grab us a booth at the back." Stella always preferred the seats at the back of the café as they could watch everyone who came in and out without being seen too obviously themselves.

When they were both settled with their bottles of Pepsi and pink-and-white stripy straws, Stella leaned across the table and whispered, "Can you believe we're going to the pictures with Tony – and Paul Spencer? It's brilliant, isn't it?"

Maria pulled a face and then rolled her eyes. "I'm quite nervous about it, aren't you?"

"Not really – they're probably a lot more nervous anyway. I read in a magazine that boys are less confident than girls." She laughed. "We're not the ones who have to worry about making the first move . . ."

"Oh, don't!" Maria said.

Stella laughed, knowing she had hit a raw spot. She turned to the side and then slid her arm up on to the back of the leather seat. "This will be Paul pretending he's leaning his arm on the back of your seat in the cinema, and next thing he'll casually lean on your shoulder . . . and then he'll make a grab for one of your –"

"Don't dare say it!" Maria leaned across the table and pushed her friend's arm in a playful manner. "If he even tries anything like that on a first date he'll be in so much trouble."

"Won't you let him kiss you? Seriously, Maria – surely you won't mind him kissing you?" She lifted her Pepsi bottle and took another sip.

Maria shrugged. "I haven't even thought that far."

"You don't need to worry – you've been out with other boys before. What about Kevin Andrews? You went out with him for a few months last year."

"That was different – he seemed much younger. I felt a lot younger than I do now. And I suppose I only saw him the odd weekend because he lived in Buxton. When I think back, we only saw each other half a dozen times. Not exactly a serious boyfriend."

Stella's brows came down. "You did at least kiss him, didn't you? I'm sure you told me you did."

"Yes, of course I kissed him!" Maria felt a sense of indignation, as though her friend thought she was a complete child. How could she tell her that up until recently she wasn't that interested in boys? That her schoolwork, her hobbies and the restaurant had all kept her busy enough. And each summer, when Stella and her other friends were out and about meeting boys, she and her father had spent a month in Italy with her elderly grandparents.

"Kissing a boy is no big deal," Stella said. "It's deciding when to let them go a bit further is the problem. Especially when they're nineteen years old and really good-looking, like Tony."

A tinge of alarm ran through Maria now. She always felt awkward when Stella alluded to sex. It was something she herself had no personal experience of, and their discussions nearly always ended up in a row because one minute Stella would talk as though she knew everything about it and then, if Maria showed any kind of shock, the next minute she would back-pedal and say she had picked her up all wrong. The last time they had the conversation Stella had really had a go at her, saying she was suggesting she was some kind of a harlot.

Maria thought better of continuing the conversation and side-stepped it by laughing and saying, "I've not even thought about anything like that – I've been too busy worrying about not having anything to talk about."

"You've loads to talk about – horses for a start."

"That's all I've ever spoken to him about before. The conversation we had on the phone this afternoon was the very first one we've ever had without mentioning horses. We can't just say 'Hello' tonight and then go straight into talking about horses again."

Stella's shoulders started heaving and she had to cover her mouth.

"It's not funny," Maria said, laughing in spite of herself.

"You've chatted to Tony loads of times. What do you talk about?"

Stella looked thoughtful. "Lots of things . . . music, television, football . . . all that sort of thing."

"*Football*?" What do you know about football?"

"Well, I don't actually have to say much on the subject. Tony just yaks on about it and I just pretend to look interested. Most of the time we just have a laugh together. He's really funny."

"The thing is," Maria said, "you know him much better than I know Paul Spencer."

"Well, don't forget that Tony is a few years older than us, and he's very easy to talk to. And he might only be a riding instructor – as my dear mother keeps reminding me – but he is intelligent in his own way." She narrowed her eyes in thought. "Paul is definitely more the shy type, but he can't be *that* shy if he got the courage up to ring you himself."

"I suppose that's true . . ."

"I must be honest, Maria, I was terrified he would back out of tonight because he wasn't brave enough to phone you –" Stella suddenly stopped and craned her neck, looking towards the door. "I don't believe it . . . here they come, half an hour early! They must be really keen."

Maria's heart started to race, and she wished she'd had time to go to the ladies' to check her hair and make-up. She grabbed her friend's hand and whispered, "Do I look all right? My hair's not all messed up or anything, is it?"

Stella gave her a brief glance. "You look fine. Stop worrying. Just act natural and relaxed." She gave a wave now to attract the boys' attention and then, when they spotted her, she swept a hand through her blonde hair and gave them a big sultry smile.

Amidst her panic about how she looked, Maria registered her friend's sexy hair gesture. It was one of the film-star poses that Stella often did for a laugh at school to entertain their friends when they were fooling around at break times. The one she had just demonstrated was a Brigitte Bardot gesture, but this time there were no giggles – she was doing it for real.

Tony came straight up to the table and slid into the leather couch on Stella's side, grinning and bumping his hip against hers to get her to move along and make room for him. Maria half-turned to see Paul standing at the table next to her. When she looked up at him, he smiled and raised his eyebrows and she tried to look casual as she quickly moved to the inside to let him sit beside her.

Tony clapped his hands and then rubbed them together. "Well, girls," he said, looking at one and then the other, "you're certainly looking good tonight without the school uniforms or the riding gear."

"The cheek of it!" Stella said, giving him a playful shove. "We could say the same about you two."

"Oh, it's a long time since I wore a school skirt!"

They all laughed.

Tony looked at his watch. "We've three quarters of an hour before the film starts. Do you fancy another Pepsi, girls?"

Maria looked at him and thought his manner – albeit pleasant and cheery – was that of someone who was now in complete control of the group. She presumed it was because he was older than them that it was the natural thing to do, but something told her that Tony would be like that with fellows his own age. Paul Spencer was only a year or so older than her and Stella, and obviously had a different personality altogether. So far he hadn't said a word.

Stella held her bottle up and made a little face. She looked over at Maria. "Do you want another one?"

Before she could say anything, Tony put his hands flat on the table and said, "Maybe you'd like to chance something a bit more exciting? A shandy or a Babycham maybe?"

Maria caught her breath at the suggestion of them going to a pub and looked across the table to see Stella's reaction – but Stella just smiled and shrugged.

"Is there anywhere around here that would let us in?" Paul's voice was doubtful.

"With your height, no one's going to question you."

"I was thinking of the girls. They're quite a bit underage."

Maria knew she should speak up now because she could tell

54

Paul felt the same as she did but she didn't want Stella to accuse her of being a killjoy. She was actually surprised that her friend wasn't speaking up because the Maxwells were stricter than her father about everything. Over the last few years Maria had been allowed a glass of wine with their meals at the weekends as her father said he would rather she learned to drink carefully than feel she had to sneak it behind his back. Maria had no great interest in it at all and would have been happy with a Pepsi.

"They don't look underage for anything tonight," Tony said, winking at the girls. He turned back to Paul. "I'm sure we'd get into The Staging Post without any trouble. I've been in there a good few times and never seen the staff question anyone. The old fella at the bar is easy-going and at this time it's empty so he'll probably be glad of the custom. They have a small room at the door – you three could go into and I'll go to the bar."

Stella caught Maria's eye now and gave her a big smile. Then she put her arm through Tony's. "I'm game for it if the rest of you are."

"Great stuff!" Tony looked at the other two.

Maria suddenly felt a hand on her arm. She glanced up and saw Paul was staring at her with a concerned expression on his face. "Are you okay about going into a pub? We won't be there long."

Maria's mind worked quickly. What was the worst that could happen? She supposed it would be getting put out of the pub for being too young or her father finding out. Neither were the end of the world for her. She shrugged and smiled. "If you all want to go, then I'm okay too."

As they left the café, Tony caught Stella's hand and they walked ahead, laughing and carrying on, leaving Paul and Maria to follow. Maria felt awkward and shy for a few moments until Paul started chatting.

"I hope," he said, "that you didn't think that the pub idea was all planned out between me and Tony? If I'd known I would have mentioned it to you on the phone."

Maria looked at him. "So you didn't know?"

"When Tony suggested it in the café, it was the first time I'd heard of it. I don't mind myself, I've been in pubs before – but I just wanted you to know that I wouldn't have gone about things the way he has."

"It doesn't really matter," she said, picking her words carefully, "but I think it sounds as though Tony made all the decisions for the four of us."

"He's a decent enough guy, and a great worker – but it's a work friendship and we have our own very different ways."

Maria nodded and smiled. She could tell that he didn't want to run Tony down, and she liked him more now for the careful way he had explained it.

The pub was exactly as Tony described it, although Maria thought it felt dampish and smelled strongly of beer and cigarettes. It made her think that it was usually frequented by older men. It was entirely different to Leonardo's, with its lovely cooking smells, where most people drank wine with their meals although some of the customers did smoke after they had eaten.

Tony ushered the two girls into the room at the front, which was just big enough to hold four small round tables, each with four tapestry-covered chairs. He held a chair out for Stella and then rushed over to do the same for Maria while Paul was taking his coat off. Maria felt he was making an issue of this to show that he knew the correct way to treat ladies, even though he might not come from the same moneyed background as his boss's son.

"Right, girls," Tony said, leaning on the back of Stella's chair, "what will it be? Babycham, Cherry-B, shandy, lager and lime?" He listed the drinks like an expert then smiled indulgently at them both as he awaited their decision.

Maria looked over at Stella. "What are you having?"

Stella thought for a moment. "I think I'll have a . . . gin and tonic."

"And I'll have the same, please." It wasn't worth it, she thought, to make an issue of having something like wine or sherry just because she'd tried it before. Besides, she heard all the girls at school going on about gin and tonic as it was seen as one of the more sophisticated drinks, and she reckoned that's why Stella had picked it.

"Starting off with the hard stuff!" Tony laughed. "I like your style." He went over to the bar and, just as he had said, the man serving never came to look at them or check on their ages.

They chatted away – sometimes all four of them, and sometimes the two couples. Tony held court for a lot of the time, making jokes about the friend's car he had borrowed, which he described as a "bit of an old banger".

When they were chatting on their own, Paul asked Maria how her exams were going and then told her that his parents had been in Leonardo's on several occasions and thought it one of the best restaurants in Manchester for a nice, relaxed night out. He said his mother particularly liked the Italian food, and was trying different things from the menu each time they went. Paul then asked her what sort of music she liked and they discovered they both liked The Rolling Stones and Bob Dylan. At one point Maria had to stop herself from smiling when she realised they hadn't talked about horses once.

When they were all halfway down their drinks, Paul checked if they would all have the same again.

"Shall we have a Babycham this time around?" Stella suggested.

Again Maria agreed. She had found the gin and tonic a strange-tasting drink at first, though she had gradually got used to it, and thought the bubbly drink might be more to her liking.

She watched Paul go to the bar with a small degree of trepidation in case the barman refused to serve him as he was more than a year younger than Tony and, even though he was almost eighteen, he was still at school. For all he seemed quietly confident, she felt he was acting more relaxed than he really felt.

When he came back with the drinks Tony launched into a funny story about one of the adults who came to the stables who had bought a new horse that wasn't as docile as the seller had promised and had all sorts of problems with it. As they were all laughing, Maria wondered – since they were talking about people buying horses – whether it was a good time to mention that her father had actually bought a racehorse, but something held her back.

Fifteen minutes before the film started, they finished up their second drinks and then made their way towards the cinema,

Stella and Tony once again leading the way and the two others following behind.

A string of cars came loudly past them, so Paul put his arm around Maria's shoulders to draw her close enough to hear. "I hope you didn't feel too awkward in the pub?"

"It was fine," she told him. "I enjoyed it."

"Good. It's not the best place I've been in, but it filled the time in nicely." He let his arm slide off her shoulders now as they walked along, then, when they came to cross the road further along, she smiled to herself when he put his arm around her again. She wondered if he would kiss her in the cinema.

Maria and Stella stood to the side in the foyer as the boys went to join the short queue for tickets. "Well," Stella whispered, "how are things going so far between you and Paul? I looked back earlier and I thought the pair of you looked very cosy."

"He's been really nice. He's quiet but . . . nice. How are you and Tony getting on?"

"Oh God!" Stella smiled and closed her eyes for a few moments, and when she opened them, they had a dewy look about them.

Maria couldn't tell if her friend was overcome by emotion or whether the two drinks had had an effect on her.

"Tony is fantastic," Stella said, her eyes shining. "Everything about him is just fantastic. He's been everywhere and done everything." Her face grew serious. "He lived in Epsom, just outside London for a while, you know – he was working in one of the really big stables. He has a lot of experience with horses."

"Paul says he's one of the best riding instructors in the Manchester area."

"He is, and Spencers' Stables are lucky to have him. He says he loved the life in London – going to parties and concerts. He came back because his family are here, but I think he finds it a bit quieter than he expected." She dropped her voice now. "He's asked me if I'll go to an all-night party with him in Manchester a week on Saturday."

"An *all-night* party?" Maria's eyes widened. "What did you say?"

"That I'll think about it. I'll have to work hard to get into my mother's good books before then."

"Do you think she'll let you go to an all-night party?"

Stella laughed. "Are you joking? Can you just imagine my mother or my father's reaction if they knew? They'd have a complete fit and I'd never be let outside the door."

Maria looked baffled. "So how can you go?"

"I just need to come up with a good, believable excuse. I wish you didn't live so close or I could say I was staying the night with you."

"Hoi – don't drag me into your lies!" Maria said, her tone half-joking and half-serious. "I don't want your mother blaming me and then I'd get into trouble with my dad. It wouldn't work anyway, because your mother would only phone the house to speak to you. She always does when you stay overnight."

"I thought I might say I'm staying with one of the girls from my ballet class who lives the other side of Manchester," Stella went on, as if Maria had never spoken. "I could say we're going to a specialist ballet shop or something. Or I might just say it's the girl's birthday and her mother has invited me to stay overnight."

"But she'd still phone!"

Then, as the two boys came towards them with the tickets, boxes of popcorn and bottles of Coca-Cola, Stella said, "Whatever happens I'm going to the party with Tony, and I don't care how I do it."

Chapter 8

When they were part-way through the film, Maria wished she had checked with Stella what they were going to see. Had she realised what an emotional film *Imitation of Life* was, she would never have agreed to go. Her mind had been so taken up with her exam and then all the drama with the two men in the afternoon, that she hadn't thought to check. Usually, she and her friends went to see Elvis films or light-hearted ones like *Mary Poppins*. But even when she was younger, she had always found certain films like *Heidi* or *Little Women* – which dealt with losing people – too sad to watch with any enjoyment.

The storyline about the two mothers and daughters was okay to begin with but, as the film went on, she found herself becoming increasingly tense as she watched the heart-rending scenes between them. She tried not to become involved in the story, because it made her think of her own mother and intensified the loss she kept in a small dark place at the back of her mind. She tried to think of other things like the exams she still had to come, her ballet exercises and horse-riding manoeuvres. She also managed to distract herself for a while when Paul put his arm around her shoulders again and left it there. She closed her eyes and leaned back against his arm, surprised at how relaxed she felt with him. Every so often he would bend his head and whisper something about the film in her ear or tighten his arm to pull her closer to him.

Then, during a silent part in the film she heard Stella giving a slightly stifled giggle. She leaned forward slightly and looked along the row past the boys to see what was the cause of the mirth, expecting to see something funny. Instead, she was shocked to see in the dim light from the screen that Tony had his hands under Stella's sweater as they kissed and, instead of fighting him off, Stella was laughing about it.

Maria sank back into her seat, totally thrown by her friend's behaviour. It wasn't that she was totally naïve or stupid. She knew that girls her age got married and had sex, and certain types of girls had sex before they were married. And of course she had heard heated whispers about young couples 'petting' and 'heavy-petting', and had a good idea what that involved, but she had never imagined that her closest friend had any experience with anything like that up until now.

But even if Stella had a steady boyfriend and had said they were getting closer physically, Maria would not have imagined that she was the type to behave like that in the public arena of a cinema. Granted, they were in the back row and no one else could see them, but that wasn't the point. She and Paul were right next to them and that should have been enough to make them contain themselves. An uncomfortable feeling crept over her as she wondered what they would have got up to had they been totally alone. What would Stella get up to if she went to the all-night party with Tony the next weekend?

As she sat staring at the screen, Maria started to wonder what Paul made of their behaviour. He surely couldn't be oblivious to it as he was sitting right next to Tony.

She was startled out of her thoughts when the film suddenly shuddered to a halt and then the lights and the adverts came on, loudly signalling the interval. An ice-cream seller came down the aisle to the front of the auditorium with a tray full of packaged ice-cream tubs, wafers and a variety of ice lollies. Paul asked Maria what she would prefer, and then tapped Tony on the shoulder to check with him and Stella.

When Paul stood up to go down to join the queue, out of the corner of her eye Maria could see Stella straightening her jumper and then discreetly adjusting her bra underneath. She could feel her face burning up with embarrassment for her friend – and for herself – because she didn't know what she was going to say to her. What on earth would happen, Maria wondered, if anyone who knew them saw Stella's low behaviour? She wondered if Stella would even care. It was as if within a few moments, Stella had changed into this totally brazen person who could now do or say anything.

After a few minutes of talking exclusively to Tony, Stella leaned forward.

"Are you enjoying the film, Maria?"

Maria barely turned her head. "Yes – it's okay."

"The girl is a real bitch to her mother, isn't she?"

Maria nodded.

Tony said something, and then he and Stella went back to their own conversation and Maria was grateful when she saw Paul coming up the steps carrying the ice creams.

He handed them out and then sat down and turned to Maria. "Are you enjoying the film?"

"Yes, thanks." She concentrated on carefully opening the wrapper on her Choc Ice as she didn't want to appear foolish by scattering any small, loose pieces of chocolate all over her clothes, and was grateful to find it was intact. "But I suppose I find it a little bit sad."

"In fairness, there's a good story to it, not like some of the light, silly films you get." He opened his ice cream then turned towards her. "To be honest, I didn't really care what kind of film we came to see tonight . . . I was just so pleased you had agreed to come with me. Actually enjoying the film is an added bonus to having your company."

Maria looked up at him and their eyes met. He smiled warmly at her, then he put his arm around her and kept it there. They didn't speak for a few minutes as they sat eating their ice creams, but Maria didn't feel it was an awkward silence.

Then, when the lights dipped again just before the film resumed, he bent his head closer to her. "How do you feel about us going out again on Saturday night – just you and me? We could go for something to eat in Manchester or we could see if there's a different film in the cinema there –whatever you like . . ."

Maria caught her breath. It was more than she had hoped for. "Yes," she said. "That would be nice. I don't really mind what we do."

"Maybe eating out would be a bit boring for you, what with going to your dad's restaurant so often?"

She shrugged. "I like trying different places."

"That's great. We can chat about it later or when you have your lesson on Saturday morning. But I'll probably ring as we might not get much chance to talk at the stables."

Then her heart quickened as he drew her towards him and lightly kissed her on the forehead. He did it in a natural and easy way, as if he had done it a hundred times before.

She would have to tell her father this time. She had no reason not to – it wasn't as if she was in the same situation as Stella with a difficult mother and it would be uncomfortable trying to keep up the pretence of being out with friends again. Besides, she thought too much of her father to do that to him. It would be only fair to tell him.

She settled back into the film again, feeling much more relaxed now that Paul had made his interest clear to her. She realised then that the fear had been lurking at the back of her mind that he might have only come out tonight to support Tony out of friendship. But that obviously was not the case, and she felt a certain satisfaction in the knowledge that they were comfortable enough together to go out on their own without having to rely on Stella and Tony for company. It wasn't that she had any problem with Tony, because up until tonight she had found him friendly and entertaining company – it was the fact that as a couple they had been embarrassing to be around.

She also realised that if, at the end of the night, another double-date had been suggested, she would have told Stella she wasn't interested. The more she thought about it, the more determined she felt that she would not be used to cover up for her friend's shady relationship with Tony.

When the film ended the four of them came out of the cinema

and then had a quick discussion as to how the boys would walk the girls back home, since they lived at opposite ends of Heaton Moor.

"Okay," Tony said after some thought, "if we give ourselves half an hour to see these lovely ladies home, then you and I can meet back at the car."

Stella's face was suddenly serious. "I think I'd be best walking home on my own. If I'm seen with you, my parents will guess we've been at the cinema together and there will be war."

Tony slid his arm around her. "Okay then, I'll drive you home and drop you off in the next street so no one will see you. You can just say you walked home as normal." He glanced over at Maria and grinned. "Are you in the same boat? Will Paul get hit over the head with a rolling pin by an angry mother if he's seen walking home with you?"

Maria's heart missed a beat.

Stella looked at Tony with wide eyes. "I thought I'd told you about Maria's mother . . ."

There was a moment's silence then Maria said, "I lost my mother when I was young."

"Oh, God . . . I'm so sorry. I didn't mean to put my foot in it."

"It's okay, really. I'm used to this happening, so you don't need to feel bad." She managed a smile. "But my dad's fine. He won't mind a friend walking me back."

"She is so lucky having a father like Leo," Stella said, "and being able to go anytime to a fantastic restaurant like Leonardo's. It's got to be the best place in Manchester."

Maria knew her friend was going a little overboard to compensate for Tony's gaffe, which made her feel slightly worse. She looked at the sky. "I think," she said, "it might start to rain soon, so we'd better get moving."

Tony looked at Paul. "I'll drive down Heaton Moor Road when I've dropped Stella off and wait for you there."

Maria and Paul set out.

"I hope that blunder of Tony's didn't upset you too much?" Paul said as they walked along the main road.

"No, I'm used to it," Maria said. "And I know people who mention my mum feel worse than I do when they find out." She glanced at him. "You didn't look surprised. Did you already know about her?"

"Yes . . . I somehow knew it from before, but my mother reminded me about it when I said we were going to the pictures tonight. I think your father told her when you first started riding lessons."

Maria wondered what his mother's reaction had been to them going out together.

Then, as if he had read her mind, he said, "She was really pleased when I told her we were going to the cinema tonight. She said you were a lovely, well-brought-up girl."

She felt a sense of relief. "That's very nice of her to say."

Paul looked straight at her now. "I don't think she would have said the same thing about Stella, if she'd seen her with Tony tonight."

She hadn't been sure whether he had noticed all the behaviour in the cinema. "In fairness, Stella is not normally like that. But I have to admit I was surprised by her tonight."

"I could tell you were as uncomfortable as I was. First, it was the way Tony railroaded everyone into going into a pub, then all the carry-on in the cinema. I think I should have had a word with him about it all, but it was awkward. I've never really socialised with him before so I don't know if this is the way he usually goes on. As I said, our friendship is mainly based on work."

"Well, I definitely thought I should have said something to Stella but, again, it wasn't the right time to say it tonight. It would have ended things on a sour note. As soon as we're on our own, though, I'm going to say something."

"Well, I'm glad we feel the same about things."

He reached out now, took her hand and held it lightly as they walked along. They chatted about random things and, when the topic came around to talking about school, he told her that he hated it. Maria was surprised and asked him why.

"I suppose I've never really fitted in with the mainstream type of guys. I don't like rugby or football or any of those team sports, so it's not that surprising. I have a couple of friends, but they live a bit of a distance away so I only really see them in school. Part of it's my own fault too, because I'm so involved in the stables and the horses. It's a huge family thing – we live and breathe horses. That's why I've become sort of friendly with Tony – we have the whole equine thing in common."

"And is this what you want to do full-time when you leave school?"

"Definitely," he said. "I'd have left school long ago if I'd had the chance, because I know exactly what I want to do – which is eventually run my own stables and stud farm – but my mother and father really wanted me to do my A-Levels, so I'd have something to fall back on in the future. Thankfully, I'll be leaving school next summer and then going on to do some sort of equine course."

"Well, I suppose you can see their point about getting qualifications. At one point I told Dad I wanted to leave school to work in Leonardo's – learn the management side of the business, that sort of thing, but he wants me to stick in at school. I don't mind really, as I quite like school."

"Lucky you!" he said, laughing.

"Well, I'm in a different position from you because I enjoy the company at school because I spend so much time on my own at home when Dad is working. Though I've really got used to it now, and I quite like my own company. I like listening to music and reading and watching telly." She laughed. "I'm spoiled not having to share things with anyone else – I'm lucky it's always my choice! I know Stella complains about having to take turns with her younger brothers in choosing what she wants to watch on telly!"

He tilted his head to the side. "Have you any idea what you want to do when you leave school?"

She shrugged. "Not a clue. I'm hoping that I'll get careers advice next year which will give me some ideas."

"You do loads of things outside of school, don't you?"

"Mainly the ballet and horse-riding, but I'm getting fed up with ballet."

He gave her hand a squeeze. "I hope you're not getting fed up with the riding lessons?"

"No, no – I really enjoy it. It's far more fun than ballet, and I always feel great after it."

"I hope a little bit of that has something to do with me being there?" He gave a small, self-conscious laugh.

"You never know . . ." She looked up at him and then she laughed too.

"Well, it's good that we know a bit about each other and what we like and don't like. And horses are obviously a big part of it."

"Talking of horses . . ." Maria took a deep breath, "I haven't told anyone else yet – not even Stella – but we're going to be more involved in horses in a different way because my dad has just bought a half-share in a racehorse."

"Really?" Paul came to a standstill. "Wow! That's fantastic!"

She then went on to tell him about Bella Maria and how her father had just told her about it recently.

"I'd no idea he was so involved in racing," said Paul as they walked on. "You know my dad was a jockey, don't you?"

"Yes, of course," she told him. "Everybody knows your dad was really famous."

"He had to give it up after a serious accident in one of the big races when he hurt his back. He was thrown off the horse and then got trampled."

"That sounds terrible – I'm surprised it didn't put him off horses for life."

Paul shrugged. "It's part and parcel of being a jockey. He knew all the risks, and it certainly hasn't put him off. He knows he'll never race professionally again but he still loves being involved in the whole racing world. But isn't it great your dad has bought a racehorse? That's a complete departure from running a restaurant."

Maria bit her lip. "To be honest, I'm a little bit worried . . . Dad enjoys watching horses racing, but I'm not sure he has the necessary experience to actually own one. Up until now he's been more involved in betting on horses."

"As long as he has a good trainer he doesn't need to worry about having experience himself. That's not what the owner does – that's the trainer's job. The trainer will take care of everything like the exercise routine and organising all the training schedules, and he'll take the responsibility for the horse's health."

As she listened to the list of things that Paul said the horse would need, Maria's heart sank. She started to work out in her head all the things that her father would have to pay for like a trainer and stables for the horse. Those things would not come cheap.

Another thing occurred to her. "Will my father have to find a jockey for the races as well?"

"Yes, but there will be other people involved and don't forget he'll be sharing all the work and the cost with someone else." He seemed to sense her anxiety. "You don't need to worry – if he's been interested in racing for a few years he'll know all this. Regular punters know everything there is to know about horses and trainers and jockeys."

"I hope he does know what he's taking on," Maria said.

"He will have worked out all the costs – don't forget he's been running his own successful business for years, so he must be doing something right."

"That's true, and he's definitely a hard worker. He throws his heart and soul into things. I remember all the time he used to spend at the restaurant when it first opened. We spent more time there than we did at home. It's only in the last few years that he's been able to take it a bit easier."

Paul's face became serious. "Well, my mother has often said that my dad's accident made them look at life differently. They both said that they actually enjoyed all the time he had at home when he was recovering from the accident and wasn't allowed to drive or even walk very far. She said they had been worried that he would be bored out of his mind, but after a while he got used to it. They started doing more things together like going to concerts and doing a bit of gardening, and then Dad started reading again and even watching television. Things he never had time for."

Maria thought about her father now. He rarely had time to relax at home. Most evenings or afternoons he was at home he spent them working on the restaurant books at the big dining-table or on the phone to suppliers. She wondered now how much of his time Bella Maria would take up and whether her father fully understood the huge commitment both time-wise and financially he had signed himself up for.

When they turned down the avenue the Contis lived in, the noise from the busier roads faded almost into silence.

"We're nearly at my house now," Maria told him, "and I'll be fine walking the last little bit on my own if you want to head back to catch up with Tony."

"There's no rush," he said, and tightened his grip on her hand.

As they slowly walked along the tree-lined street, he commented that it was a nice street with well-kept houses and gardens, and it crossed her mind that her house was very obviously not in the same league as Spencers' huge rambling house with all the acres of land surrounding it.

"That's our house at the top of the cul-de-sac," she told him. Then she noticed a light on in her father's bedroom. "It looks like my dad is already home." She wondered what had brought him home earlier tonight. He hadn't mentioned that he would get away before his normal time. Maybe tonight was exceptionally quiet, Thursday was one of the nights that could never be anticipated. Some weeks it was busy and others it could be deadly quiet.

Paul slowed to a halt. "Will it be a problem if he looks out of the window and sees me?"

"No, I don't think so . . . He's never been funny about my friends."

"What about boyfriends?"

Maria looked at him. "He's never really met any. I haven't really had a serious enough boyfriend for him to meet. Anyway, it's handy that he already knows you and your family and likes you."

"Will it sound too corny if I tell you that my mother really likes you?"

He caught her eye and they both laughed. Then, before she realised what was happening, he had swept her up in his arms.

"Do you mind if I give you a goodnight kiss?"

She stared up at him, her heart racing at his closeness. "No," she said lightly, "I don't think I mind . . . very much."

He guided her back a few feet into a gateway with deep bushes and overhanging trees where they wouldn't easily be seen, and she thought that he must have spotted this as they were walking along and planned to stop there. The idea made her smile.

At first his lips were soft but the longer they kissed the harder his mouth began to feel on hers, almost as if he was going to crush her and, after a while, she felt that she was kissing an entirely different boy to the one she had imagined. She had presumed Paul Spencer would be hesitant and shy, and not this confident boy who seemed to know exactly what he was doing.

Then, when he pulled her so close to him that she could feel his heart beating, it occurred to her that he was every bit as keen on kissing her now as Tony had been with Stella in the cinema. The only difference was that they were kissing in private and not in the back seat of the cinema where anyone could see them

When he eventually stopped kissing her, he continued to hold her in his arms. Every so often he would hold her out at arm's length, and say, "You know you're gorgeous, don't you?" Then at one point he said, "I've fancied you for ages."

She looked at him and said, "What took you so long asking me out?"

"I suppose I'm a bit shy," he said. Then, he gave her a really tight squeeze and gave her another kiss. "But now I've finally got the courage up, there'll be no holding me." He looked deep into her eyes. "I've really, really enjoyed tonight . . . and I'm glad that the next time we go out, we'll be on our own."

She looked back at him and said, "So am I."

There was a pause.

"I think," she said, "it might be best if I went – I've still some homework to do for the morning."

He dug his hands deep into his coat pockets. "And so have I – bloody Geography if I remember correctly. I hate it and I'm less than useless at it."

The way he said it made her start to laugh and that was when he took his chance for one final, very careful kiss. "Okay," he said, walking backwards and grinning at her. "I'll ring you!"

They looked back and waved at each other a few times and then Maria went running up towards her house. She had hardly placed her key in the lock when the door was pulled open, almost sending her off her balance.

"Maria! I've been here worrying about you for the last two hours! What has been going on? What secrets have you been keeping from me?"

Maria looked back at him with startled eyes.

"I thought I could always trust you, but it seems that I have to be told the truth by other people."

Her mind worked quickly as she tried to work out who might have been talking to him about her. And then it dawned on her that Stella's mother might have spotted her with Tony and saw fit to tell her father that she was also out and about with a boy tonight.

"Are you talking about me being out tonight?" she asked.

"You tell me, Maria!" he said. "You tell me."

Chapter 9

It was only when Maria got inside the house that it started to become clearer what her father was talking about and she began to understand why he seemed so upset.

He was pacing up and down in front of the blazing sitting-room fire. A bottle of whisky and a glass with golden dregs were on the side table. "Why didn't you tell me about the men who called to the house this afternoon? I rang you before you went out tonight and asked if everything was okay and you chose not to tell me the truth."

Whilst she was still concerned at causing her father to be so upset and angry, a small part of her was relieved that it was nothing to do with her being out with Paul tonight. She was also grateful that he hadn't seen them together and come rushing down the street all upset as he was quite capable of doing when he was worried.

"Oh, Dad," she said, "I'm really sorry, but it wasn't like that. I wasn't deliberately not telling you, I completely forgot about it." She felt so guilty lying to her father.

"Forgot?" His brow was wrinkled in confusion. "How could you forget such a serious thing?" He jabbed his finger in the direction of the house next door. "Our neighbours thought the situation was serious enough to ring the restaurant to tell me that two men had come to the door and been menacing and threatening towards you!" He took a deep shuddering breath. "I think, Maria, that anyone would think there was a serious problem."

Maria's shoulders slumped now as she thought how it must look to him and tears sprang into her eyes. "Oh, Dad, I didn't mean to give you such a fright. I'd no idea that Mrs Cox would ring you – if I'd thought for a minute that she would, I would have told you straight away."

He looked at her for a moment and then he suddenly rushed over to her and threw his arms around her. As he hugged her close she was aware of the smell of drink from him.

He kissed her several times on the forehead then moved to view her at arm's length. "Okay," he said, "let us have no more difficulties between us – and tell me right from the beginning exactly what happened."

She explained, as best she could, everything from the time she opened the door to the two men until they walked away down the street. She repeated, several times, the words they had said to her and then, in as great detail as she could remember, she described how they both looked and the sort of clothing they were wearing.

"And they told you that they were conducting a survey about houses?"

Maria nodded. "They said they were going around all the houses in the area."

He started pacing up and down the room again. "Mrs Cox has asked everyone she's seen in the street this evening, and they didn't call at anyone else's door." He closed his eyes and then hit the palm of his hand off the side of his head. "I can understand that people have do these surveys and they might get fed up in the middle of it and abandon it – that I understand – but the one thing I have great difficulty in understanding is why the man tried to push the door open when you were closing it."

Leo's voice was rising now, in an angry way Maria had never heard before.

"Why he should stick his foot in the door and frighten you!

What professional man working for an estate agent would behave in such a way? And what decent man does that to a teenage girl?" He brought one hand down on the open palm of the other in a slicing manner. "None! No man I know."

His eyes narrowed. "But I will find out. One way or another – I will find out."

Maria's eyes widened. "How?"

"The police. I'm going down to Stockport Police Station first thing in the morning to report this incident and find out if there have been others. It could be one of those scams that you read about in the newspapers where they keep someone talking at the front door while someone breaks into the house through the kitchen door at the back. I am not going to let this rest until I find some answers."

Maria noticed his hands shaking now and she went over to put her arms around him, trying hard to think of something that might reassure him. "Dad – Dad – don't get so upset about it. Nothing terrible happened to me. I'm okay!"

Leo threw his hand up in the air. "But, Maria, it changes everything – I'm afraid now to leave you in this house alone. I'll have to get Mrs Lowry to come and sit with you every night."

"You can't do that, Dad!"

He put both his hands on his head now. "No, no – she's too old to protect you. I'll have to find someone more suitable."

"*Dad!*" Maria almost shouted. "You're overreacting, Dad – you really are!"

He suddenly froze. "Am I? Am I really?"

"I'm nearly sixteen years old! I can look after myself."

His voice dropped to a whisper. "But how can I be sure you are always safe?"

"You can't. No one can ever be one hundred per cent sure of anything. We just have to do the best we can. From now on, if I'm on my own, I won't open the door unless I know who it is. And, if anything worries me when I'm in the house on my own, I'll phone the Coxes or the Grants and ask them to come around. They're only seconds away."

Leo nodded slowly, but didn't look convinced. "We shall see."

There was a silence then Maria said, "I have some homework to do so if it's okay I'll go up to my room."

"Of course – of course. Would you like something to eat? I brought a nice pizza back from the restaurant."

"I'm fine, thanks."

"Maybe a sandwich?"

"No, honestly. It's late and I'm not really hungry. I'll do a bit of homework and then I'll go to bed."

Leo beckoned her towards him, and then he folded his arms around her. "You know you are the most important person in my life – don't you?" His eyes were still grave but his voice was much calmer now.

"Yes," she replied, "and you are the most important person in mine."

"Sleep well," he told her, "and we'll work out how to solve this problem in the morning."

Maria went out into the hall, took her coat off and hung it on the stand by the front door, then she picked up her bag and walked slowly upstairs. Inside her room, she closed the door and stood for a few minutes with her back against it. What she really wanted to do was go and lie on the bed and rerun the whole evening with Paul in her mind – every minute of the time they spent together. But instead, she was now swamped with anxious feelings about her father – and about herself.

She gathered herself together and moved to her desk by the window where she did her studying.

She had some algebra she needed to do for her next lesson, but it was the last thing she felt like doing. She would catch up on it at some point tomorrow before the class. Thank God, she thought, that she had the weekend ahead to look forward to.

She got changed into her pyjamas and then went into the bathroom to wash and brush her teeth. She was coming back to her bedroom when she decided she would go downstairs for a glass of water, and use it as an excuse to reassure her father once again, for she knew he would not be able to relax for thinking about it. She also thought that if he was calmer she might mention about Paul Spencer walking her back from the cinema.

She would make it sound casual, and would let him think she met Paul there if he didn't specifically ask if she had arranged to go there with him.

She went down the stairs barefoot, her feet making no noise on the thick stair carpet. She was just about to knock on the sitting-room door when she heard her father's voice and realised he was on the phone.

She waited for a moment and listened to see if he was nearly finished. Then she heard him say, "Thank you, Franco. It was good of you to lock up tonight when I had to leave at such short notice. You are a good friend, and you know how much I appreciate you."

He was quiet for a while, and then she heard his voice again.

"I hear what you say, Franco. And no, I won't do anything to put me or my daughter at risk. But, sooner or later, I will find out who the men are who came to my house and frightened Maria."

Maria felt a shiver run through her. The slur in his voice told her that in the short time since she had been upstairs he had drunk a lot more whisky. She knew he drank glasses of red wine in the restaurant and wondered now if the whisky had become habitual when she was in bed.

"Oh, I have to do this," her father said now. "But, Franco, if I discover that it is related to the loan company I used for the interim payment on the horse, then I will be very angry. Very angry indeed. You and I both know that it is not the way people should do business. "

There was a silence again and then she heard her father say, "It will be sorted first thing in the morning. I've decided if I have to extend the mortgage on the house to pay for it, I will. I had hoped not to do that, but I need to pay these people off. I'd rather my bank owned the house than have some loan shark think they have a claim on it."

Maria stepped backwards until she was touching the bannister and then quietly crept back up the stairs.

Chapter 10

After the *Ten O'Clock News*, Diana had washed and dried her supper dishes and then wiped down the top of the cooker which had some small splashes from her scrambled eggs. Then she had brushed and mopped the black-and-white tiled floor. She'd finished off by polishing her glass-topped kitchen table with Windolene.

She'd then gone into the sitting room and settled down to look over her order forms for the coming month. Apart from all the new fashion lines they included the usual women's perfume she stocked which was otherwise only available in select department stores in Manchester.

Finally, propelled by guilt, she lifted her diary. It was a particularly nice hard-backed diary, a gift from Sandra, an old school friend in Washington, and every alternate page featured a painting from a special collection in the capital's main art gallery. Diana had promised herself that she would do a daily entry in the diary to prove to herself that her life was improving after her relationship ended with Brian. But, after starting off well, her entries had dwindled down to just a couple a week.

She ran through her day in her head, trying to think of anything noteworthy to put in, and found precious little. Eventually, she wrote down that she had gone to Benediction at the local church.

She wasn't overtly religious, but her Catholic mother had taken her regularly as a child, and she found herself drawn to the short peaceful evening service with its incense, candles and the Blessed Sacrament on the alter in its golden sunburst monstrance. She knew quite a few of the other people from going to Sunday Mass and, besides, she had little else to do mid-week and it passed the longest part of the evening. It was usually eight thirty by the time she got in and made supper while watching television or listening to the radio.

Apart from the church entry, she made a note of what she had worn to work that day and at the top of the following day's page she jotted down the suit and sweater she planned to wear to work the next day. She tried to wear something different every day for about ten days before repeating the cycle, and writing it down ensured she didn't wear the same things too often.

Then, she sat for a while leafing through the diary, looking at the beautiful paintings. She paused at Robert Henri's misty *Snow in New York*, and studied it for a few minutes, and it set her mind to wondering about holiday plans for the coming year. There were so many places she would love to visit and New York and the National Gallery of Art in Washington, DC, were top of her list. She had an open invite to Sandra's home close to the centre, but Sandra had three young children and a husband with a busy law practice. She had told Diana to come with a friend and see the sights but, so far, a suitable friend to travel with had not materialised. Of course she did not tell Sandra this – instead, she explained how busy she was with the two shops and attending fashion shows in London, and that America would have to wait.

She flicked on through the pages of paintings until her gaze fell on her favourite one, *La Coiffure* by Henri Matisse. If she was brave enough, she would have loved a print of the beautiful nude for her bedroom or even her bathroom but she felt it would look weird to have a painting like that in a single woman's house. Maybe, if some kind of miracle happened and she met the right man, she might just hang a print of it on her bedroom wall. Meantime, like her trip to the Art Gallery, it would just have to wait.

She closed the diary, put the order sheets back into the folder, and then went out into the hallway and down to the kitchen to make sure the blinds were closed and to lock the back door. She came back to the sitting room and went around the lamps switching each one off and, just as she touched her hand to the main light switch, the phone suddenly rang out, startling her.

She put her hand to her throat to still her breathing and then, when she had composed herself, she lifted the receiver. As soon as she heard the voice, she closed her eyes.

"Diana, it's me . . . please don't hang up."

"What is it? What do you want?"

"You know what I want. You know why I'm ringing."

She sank down onto the arm of the sofa. "I don't know what you want me to say."

"Have you given my proposal serious thought?"

"No, Brian," she said, "I haven't."

"Please! You must at least give me a chance."

"There is no point in us trying again."

"It's not just *trying again* – this time I want us to get married straight away. We can do it quietly if you prefer – any way you want. We can go travelling together for a month afterwards like we always said we would."

"I can't . . . I can't do it."

"Please, please, think about it. Apart from that one . . . that one indiscretion . . ."

"An *indiscretion?*"

"Come on, Diana, give me a break. You know what I mean."

"I take it that you are referring to the weekend with your so-called business colleague when you say 'that *one* indiscretion'? I take it you are deliberately ignoring the other episode with the magazines?"

There was an uncomfortable silence before he spoke again.

"How many times do I have to say that was normal curiosity? It meant nothing and had absolutely nothing to do with the mistake I made later."

"To me they were very much linked," she said.

"I cannot keep apologising. You know how sorry I am, and

you know how much I have tried to make it up to you since. It's all in the past and we have to look forward. That's what I'm trying to do if you will just give me another chance. Everyone knows that we are perfect for each other. We *are* perfect for each other." There was another pause. "Diana, are you even listening?"

"Yes, and I'm trying to imagine what people will think if I suddenly tell them that we are to be married within weeks."

"It will be a nine-day wonder," he said. "And then everyone will get on with their own lives. It doesn't matter what they think."

"But I know what happened."

"It has nothing to do with our life up here. What happened was down in London and it's over. It will never happen again. I promise you with all my heart. I do understand that it may take a little time for it to fade . . . but it will. I've told no one, and I know you haven't either."

She presumed he took the silence that followed as an indication that she was actually considering his proposal when he said: "Why don't we have a holiday away together in the next few weeks to talk things over? To make concrete plans for the future. I know I dragged my heels before, but I was stupid, I hadn't worked things out. If we could just take the time now to talk properly and sort things out. Somewhere lovely on our own. We can go anywhere you want. You name it and I'll have it booked in the morning."

Her mind went back to the places and the paintings that she would like to see. Brian would, of course, be her ideal companion. Apart from being wonderful entertaining company, he was confident driving up and down the country, and had no problems booking trips further afield and negotiating airports. He spoke French well and, when they visited Paris a few years ago, he had studied it all beforehand and was as good as any tour guide.

It would be so easy to say yes to him. To say yes to the big house he owned, to the good salary he earned, and to become part of his lovely extended family. Brian's parents and his two sisters and even a special auntie were devastated when their engagement was broken off, and it was only recently that they had stopped sending letters and birthday cards as though she were still part of the family.

It would be so easy to fall back into it all again – having someone so handsome and presentable by her side, as her husband – as the father of her children. Especially when no one else had come along in the interim to fill the gaping hole he had left in her life.

But she knew she couldn't go back there. Despite all his promises and his very good intentions, it would all end the same way. It was inevitable. She could not let loneliness and her yearning for a marriage and a family take her back down that dark and dangerous route again.

"I'm sorry, Brian," Diana said, "but you're wasting your time. I have no intention of marrying you or going on holiday or anywhere else with you. The problem that broke up our engagement has not gone away, and you're deluding yourself if you think so. It might disappear for a short time, but it would only come back again."

"It won't come back, because I refuse to allow it," he told her. "I only want you."

"Well, that," she said, "is something you cannot have."

Chapter 11

After a fractured, dream-filled night, Maria woke in the morning with a dull ache in her chest.

She went downstairs in her pyjamas, filled the coffee percolator, switched it on and put a slice of bread in the toaster. Then, she went into the sitting room and made straight for the drinks cupboard to check the whisky bottle. It was no great surprise to her to see that it was almost empty.

She then went over to the white marble mantelpiece and lifted the Italian Rococo-style frame that held her parents' wedding photo. Her eyes went straight to the small, neat figure in white lace. It was rarely she allowed her thoughts to dwell on her mother as it always resulted in sadness.

It didn't matter this morning as she was already sad and her mind full of shadowy images of her mother from the dreams. When her vision was too blurred with tears to see the image properly, she held the heavy frame to her chest and said a silent prayer. She didn't pray to her mother too often, as there were more occasions than not when the situations she had asked for intervention in showed no noticeable change for the better. This only made Maria question her Catholic religion and the afterlife it promised, and made her worry about her mother's fate if that didn't actually exist.

The smell of fresh coffee and toasted bread came through the open doors from the kitchen. She took one last look at the picture then kissed the pristine, suited image of her father and her white-veiled mother and carefully put it back in its place.

There was no doubt that her parents had loved each other with a great passion. Her father told her that on a regular basis when he recounted the story of how they met and married. He described the beautiful, gentle Anna Donovan who had come to work in Manchester. A year or so later she was disowned by her family when she told them she was getting married to a foreigner – an Italian – Leonardo Marco Conti.

The resulting rift was so bad that Maria had only met her grandparents once, at her mother's funeral when she was nine years old.

Some time afterwards, Maria – trying to make sense of it all – asked her father for more information.

"I know my mother always told me she wouldn't go back to Ireland on the boat because she had a stormy journey one time which terrified her – and she said she had always been too frightened to go on the plane."

"That's very true," Leo said. "And it wasn't just Ireland – if you remember she wouldn't fly to Italy with us either because she was so afraid." He shrugged. "Some people are like that with travelling. Franco hates flying as well."

"But why didn't my Irish grandparents come to stay with us here?" Maria had persisted. "Lots of my friends have grandparents who live in London and Scotland and they come to stay regularly. And I have two uncles – why didn't they come to visit us?"

"I don't know much about them – they were a lot younger than your mother. I do know that you have an uncle around the same age as you, and that he wasn't well when he was born and your grandmother couldn't leave him."

"Why didn't my mother talk about them? I used to ask her things about them but I could tell she didn't like it."

Leo had shrugged and looked away. "Your mother was

waiting until you were old enough to explain. I think she was hoping things would change . . . that someone might get in touch with her."

"It all sounds peculiar to me . . ."

Leo had then taken his young daughter's hand. "Maria, I don't want to lie to you. I'm afraid there is more to the story. There was bad blood between your mother and her family because she married me."

"But why?"

"Because," he told her, "they did not like that I was an Italian."

Maria could only think to say once again, "But why?"

"They did not like to have a foreigner marrying into their family."

"But that's ridiculous! Did they ever meet you?"

"No. I did offer to go over to Ireland with your mother after we were married, but she wouldn't because of the travel." He shrugged and held his hands out. "I can't answer that, Maria. Your mother got upset if I talked about it, so I just left it."

"It's awful that the first time you met her family was at the funeral, isn't it?" Maria's voice was incredulous.

His eyes suddenly filled up. "Sadly . . . yes."

Maria eventually gave up asking questions about her mother's family because it was quite clear that it upset her father and perhaps made him feel guilty for the estrangement from the Donovan family.

The Christmas following the funeral, Maria received a card from her grandparents, saying that they hoped she might visit them some time when she was old enough to travel to Ireland on her own. The words 'on her own' underlined how deep the grudge was towards her father. After everything that had happened, they expected her to turn her back on her father and ignore all the hurt they had caused her mother.

She showed the card to Mrs Lowry and talked it over with her. They both agreed it was best that the soft-hearted Leo knew nothing about it, so Maria ripped the card into tiny pieces and burned it before her father came home.

After that, she thought only of her mother in terms of their own little family and blocked out any thoughts to do with her relations in Ireland.

She finished her breakfast now, leaving the mug and plate in the sink as Mrs Lowry was due in at lunchtime and tiptoed upstairs to get ready for school without disturbing her father. She would catch the bus today as she did not want to see his morning-after face and bloodshot eyes, and she did not want him to start interrogating her again about the two men. She had no real worries about them – from what she had heard of her father and Franco's phone conversation last night, the men's reasons for calling yesterday had nothing whatsoever to do with her.

She felt anxious enough already about her father buying the horse, and her fears about his irresponsibility with money had once again been confirmed. She now knew for certain that he had bought a horse he could not afford – and that he had taken out a loan to pay for it. And she now reckoned that, in the process, he had somehow got himself involved with people who were checking out the house they lived in.

Chapter 12

When the bus pulled up at her stop, Maria boarded it and went into the lower deck to sit at the back. She stared out of the window, hoping that no one she knew would sit beside her. She tried to relax and relive all the lovely memories of the previous night with Paul Spencer, but they were overshadowed by this new worry at home.

Apart from being tired after her disturbed night, she had a dullness in her head and an ache low down in her stomach which she recognised as symptoms of an approaching period. She usually got these signs a day or two before she bled but, knowing her luck, it would probably arrive today when she had no sanitary towels in her bag.

As she walked along the avenue towards the main building of the school, Maria barely glanced at the groups of pupils she passed. Her first class was Maths and it was in a smaller building at the end. As she got closer to it she spotted the half dozen or so girls she was friendly with, in a huddle beside the wall. There, in the middle of them was Stella. She was, Maria thought grimly, probably regaling them all with the story of the night before.

"Maria! Maria!" Stella called excitedly when she saw her friend.

Maria walked slowly towards them.

86

The tallest of the girls, Amanda, came to put her arm around her. "We've just been hearing all about your night out with the two fabulous boys!"

"Lucky things!" another girl said.

Maria rolled her eyes. She didn't feel like playing to the gallery. "It wasn't that big a deal – it was just a night out at the pictures."

"Listen to her!" Stella said, nodding around the others. "It was much more exciting than that!" She laughed. "We were in a café and then a pub, even before we went to the cinema, weren't we?"

"Yes, Stella – we were." Maria's tone was flat, but she couldn't help it.

"I was just telling everyone that Tony is a bit like James Dean, isn't he? And I was saying how good-looking Paul is as well. He's the typical tall, dark and handsome type."

"They both sound absolutely gorgeous," Amanda said. "Like film stars."

Maria wrinkled her brow. "I wouldn't go that far . . . but they're nice enough."

"I thought you really liked Paul?"

"I didn't say I don't like him – it's just a bit of an exaggeration to say he's like a film star."

The girls looked from one to the other, then the bell rang for the students to line up in the various classes. When the group began to disperse, Stella approached her.

"You don't seem yourself this morning, Maria. I was just wondering if everything was okay after we left you with Paul last night?"

Maria fiddled with the fastener on her schoolbag "It was fine, thanks."

"Did he ask you to see him again?"

"Yes . . . we're going out together on Saturday."

Stella's eyes lit up. "Is it the all-night party too? Has Paul asked you to go to that with him?"

Maria looked at her coldly. "No, it's not the all-night party. And if Paul asked me to go to it with him – I wouldn't."

"But why not? It would be great if we all went out together again."

"Well, I don't think it's great. First, I'm not going to put myself in the position of being with a boy all night, and secondly I think you and Tony would be better off with your own company."

"What's wrong with you? Why are you being so snappy with me?"

"Because I think the way you behaved in the cinema was totally embarrassing."

There was a hush, then Stella spoke slowly and quietly. "What do you mean?"

"I think you know perfectly well. It's up to you what you do privately, but if anyone sees you then you'll get a terrible reputation."

"What do you mean?" Stella repeated, her voice rising.

Maria clenched her jaw, annoyed at being forced to spell it out. "The way you were letting Tony touch you . . ."

Stella looked as if she had been slapped. "That's a complete exaggeration – I don't know what you think you saw, but it was nothing serious. It was harmless, light petting – which is normal for a lot of couples."

"But it was your first date, Stella, and you were in a public place. What is he going to expect at an all-night party with no adults around?"

"Tony's not like that."

"I think you're being a bit naïve. He's a few years older than you and he's been around a lot more."

"You sound as though you have a very low opinion of the two of us!" Stella's tone was wounded.

Maria looked her square in the eye. "That's not true – I just think you need to be more careful."

"Miss Maxwell and Miss Conti!" one of the male teachers yelled. "Kindly discontinue your conversation and pay attention. Your class has gone into the building without you and you didn't even notice."

They moved quickly towards the door without saying another word.

Several times during the morning, Stella brushed past her in the class without looking in her direction, and each time Maria pretended that she hadn't noticed. Then, when the Maths class was finished and they were heading out into the yard at the morning break, Stella announced to no one in particular that she was going down to the art block as she needed to get some materials for her craft project. Maria let her go off on her own without saying anything, when she usually would have followed her and sorted out their differences.

If it was possible, Maria now felt worse than before she had said anything to Stella. She now had two situations weighing on her mind. Certainly, her father buying the horse was more serious, but the situation with Stella was serious enough in that she had to say something to her friend or it would eat away at her. She knew she had probably handled it clumsily but, the way she felt she didn't really care.

Having skirted around each other for most of the day, Maria was surprised when Stella came up to her place at the back of the room when the last class – French – had finished that afternoon. She perched on the desk beside Maria while she finished packing her books away.

"It's your dad's turn to pick us up for ballet today, isn't it?" Stella was smiling as though nothing had been said earlier on.

"Yep." Maria rearranged the books and pens in her bag to give the other girls time to leave the classroom. If things had been more normal between them now, she might have said to Stella that she was thinking of giving up ballet lessons. She would wait now.

"Listen, I've thought about what you said – and you're right. I know you were just being a good friend, speaking truthfully to me . . . and I'm glad you did say it, because you are the one person who knows the type of girl I really am and I wouldn't want you to think badly of me."

"I don't think badly of you and I don't want anyone thinking that I'm some kind of judge and jury."

Maria's shoulders relaxed for the first time since leaving the house that day.

"It's nice of you to say that."

They both started moving towards the door.

"I've gone over and over it in my mind, and I think it might have been what we drank in the pub." Stella shrugged. "I think it must have gone straight to my head and then I didn't realise that I'd got a bit carried away with Tony. You see, I'm not used to drink at all. I know you're more used to it, because your dad lets you have a glass of wine, but my mother and father are more old-fashioned and strict and they wouldn't let me touch it. You know what they're like – they only let me have a tiny sherry or a shandy if it's Christmas or some kind of special occasion."

Maria smiled, in spite of the memories of last night. "I suppose it's something that can take a while to get used to . . ."

She wished her father hadn't got too used to it though. She wished she could confide in Stella or one of her other friends, but she felt it would be betraying her father. Everyone loved him and up until this he had an unblemished reputation in both his business and personal life, and Maria desperately wanted people to keep holding him in that high esteem. She didn't think she could bear it if she told her friend about her concerns and then Stella told her parents and the secret gradually dribbled out. It was the same with Mrs Lowry. She might start worrying about him again and repeat all the nonsense about him getting married or something like that. Besides, she hoped there was every chance that her father might soon get over this stupid drinking phase without anyone else needing to know about it.

"I'm going to be more careful in the future," Stella said now, "if Tony suggests going into pubs or anything like that."

"What about the party tomorrow night?"

"I've decided not to stay all night," Stella told her. "I think it's too risky and, anyway, my mother won't let me stay out all night unless she thinks I'm staying at your house. If I say it's one of the other girls from the ballet class, she'll insist on meeting them and speaking to their mother or father."

There was a small silence during which Maria wondered if her friend wanted her to lie for her and pretend she was staying at her house. But it passed without anything more being said.

"For some reason," Stella said, "my mother believes she can't trust me to behave like an adult. She is so old-fashioned and fuddy-bloody-duddy!" She then gave an embarrassed laugh. "Well, maybe if she saw me the other night with Tony, she might have a good reason to think like that."

Maria laughed now too and they both linked arms and walked down towards the gate where Leo was waiting for them.

He was cheery and normal and, as soon as the girls were settled in the car, he swung around towards the back seat where Stella was sitting and said, "Did Maria tell you our good news?"

Stella looked at her.

"No, Dad," Maria said. "I forgot all about it . . ."

Leo shook his head and smiled. "We've bought a racehorse, Stella. Isn't that something?"

"Wow!" Stella said, looking really impressed. She nudged Maria and looked at her with wide, reproachful eyes. "How could you forget something as exciting as that?"

"I meant to tell you. My mind was full of the exams and everything."

"That is understandable," her father said. "Your exams are much more important."

Leo smiled warmly at her, but she recognised a hurt tone in his voice because his achievement of owning a racehorse meant so little to her. She listened now with some discomfort as he went on to tell Stella all about Bella Maria and how she would be running her first race in York in two weeks' time.

Stella was impressed. "That's fantastic! Imagine having a horse called after you!"

"Well, my lovely daughter is the most important female in my life."

"Well, she's very lucky. Most girls I know would feel very honoured to have something named after them. If it was me I would be bragging about it to everyone." She turned to Maria. "You're too modest for your own good."

When she saw her friend's earnest face, Maria just gave a self-conscious shrug.

"Everyone has a different nature," Leo said philosophically, and she felt a stab of guilt for not being more grateful.

"Actually, Leo," Stella said, "I bet some of the people at the stables would love to go to watch her race."

"That's a great idea," Leo said. "Why don't you girls organise a group to come and support Bella Maria sometime?"

Maria sat in silence, staring straight ahead. She could not imagine anything worse.

"Maybe we could hire a small coach like we do for the show-jumping events," Stella suggested. "We'll tell the instructors, and I'll bet Paul Spencer's father will be going anyway, because he used to be a jockey."

"He goes to most of the races," Leo said. "I have often seen him there."

Stella leaned forward and prodded Maria on the back. "You should tell Paul about it when we have our lesson tomorrow morning."

Maria looked over her shoulder and shot her friend a warning glance, but Stella just smiled back at her. A day's outing to the races with Tony there for a bona fide reason would be right up her street. It dawned on Maria that it was pointless being annoyed as Stella would have no understanding of the anxiety she felt about Bella Maria. Stella constantly commented that she envied her perfect life with only one indulgent, easy-going parent to deal with.

"I'll pick you up at half past six," Leo said, "and I'll make sure that Franco has a nice big pizza and chips ready for you both."

Friday was always cheese and tomato pizza or fish for the girls in the restaurant, due to the Catholic Church rule on abstaining from meat that day.

Maria smiled at her father. He was so good in so many, many ways. "Thanks, Dad."

"You think I'm going to run a restaurant and not feed my own daughter?" he joked.

The warm look in his eyes tugged at something deep down inside her, and she had to turn her head away.

They got out of the car and ran up the stairs of the big old house in Didsbury. They went along the tiled corridor and, just as she put her hand on the heavy interior door of the ballet practice room, Maria turned towards her friend.

"This is the last thing I feel like doing today . . . I wish I hadn't come."

"What's wrong with you?" Stella asked, pulling her to a standstill. "It's ballet – the best class of the week. And it's Friday – and we're going straight from here to Leonardo's." Her brow wrinkled. "Are you not feeling well or something?"

Maria shrugged. "I just feel everything is changing . . ."

"How? Are you still annoyed at me because of last night? Is it to do with me and Tony?"

"No . . ." There was a sigh in her voice and she suddenly felt her eyes starting to fill up. "I don't know what's wrong with me . . . I'm just being stupid . . . it's probably just my period coming."

"When are you due?"

"This week some time. I'm never exactly sure of the date – it changes every month."

Stella clicked her fingers. "That's exactly what it is. I bet you'll be fine by tomorrow." She grinned. "And don't forget you have your date tomorrow night to look forward to."

Maria thought of Paul Spencer and was grateful when she felt her spirits lift a little.

Chapter 13

Diana Freeman had just carried a mug of cocoa and a plate with two digestive biscuits into the sitting room when she heard the heavy thud of the brass knocker on the door. She glanced at the clock and wondered who was calling at eight o'clock at night. She put the mug down on the small side table by her chair at the fire, and went out into the hallway.

She was startled for a moment when she saw a face looking in through the stained-glass panel at the side of the door, and then she heard a voice calling and she realised it was Jane Maxwell.

She unbolted the door.

"Sorry for calling so late," Jane said, when the door opened. "I hope I'm not disturbing you. You don't have company or anything?"

"No, no, it's okay. Come in." Diana led the way down to the sitting room, trying not to read anything into Jane's comment about her having company.

"I didn't get a chance to pick up the slacks and tights as I ended up having to go into the office for the last few days. Richard's full-time secretary has had dreadful trouble with a wisdom tooth she had taken out. By the sound of it, I think she has an abscess or something like that."

"No problem," Diana told her. "I was just having cocoa and some biscuits, if you'd like to join me? Tea, coffee, cocoa?"

"I don't want to put you to any trouble."

"It's no trouble at all."

Jane looked at the mug and smiled. "The cocoa looks lovely."

"It won't take two minutes to boil another cup of milk. Actually –" she lifted her untouched mug, "you have this one and I'll make myself another."

Jane sank down on the poppy-decorated green sofa with the metal legs. "If you're sure I'm not intruding, that would be absolutely lovely." She glanced around her. "Your place is bright and modern compared to ours, so full of colour. I'd love to have some of these new-style pieces."

"Lots of the furniture shops in Manchester have this sort of thing in now."

Jane shook her head. "It would look ridiculous in our house – our stuff is so ancient. I wouldn't know where to start modernising it. And I don't think for one minute that Richard would be keen on me making any big changes. He's an old-fashioned man at heart and likes having the same things he grew up with around him."

"There's a lot to be said for the old solid stuff too and all the memories they bring. Right – I'll go and make that cocoa. Help yourself to a magazine while I'm in the kitchen."

Jane took the current issue of *Vogue* from the glass-topped coffee table and placed it on her lap, then she lifted the mug of hot cocoa and took a sip. "God, this is so lovely. And even lovelier to have it in such peaceful surroundings."

Diana smiled at her and went into the kitchen thinking that the way Jane openly enjoyed how she did things was probably the main reason she liked her. There were so many of her married friends who treated her as an afterthought, as though she had little in common with them after Brian had gone. And whilst Jane's favourite topic was how to find a suitable man, which was annoying, most of the time she was actually good company and brightened things up.

A short while later Diana came back in and sat in the chair opposite her guest. "So, you've had a busy day in the office?"

"Dreadful," Jane said. "Then an evening arguing with Stella again about that awful stableboy she's mad about."

"Oh, dear!"

"She just won't listen. She thinks we're old fuddy-duddies who don't understand." Jane threw her hands up. "Me of all people! I'm as open-minded a woman as you will find, but Stella just doesn't get it about mixing with the wrong sorts early on. I've seen it before so many times. I had a school-friend, Astrid, who actually ran away from home to marry a lower-class boy when she was only sixteen. A gorgeous girl with fabulous blonde hair who could have had any boy. We all thought it was terribly romantic at the time, but she ended up with a shabby small wedding and six children, living in a council house – bedraggled, poorly dressed and old before her time."

Diana took a drink of her cocoa. She had heard this several times before.

"And the thing is," Jane went on, "I was going out with the chap's friend, and every time I think of her I think how it could easily have been me. It took me a few years to get the notion out of my head. I think it was only when I saw Astrid with her first baby in a small damp room that the reality of it all began to dawn on me." She lifted her eyes to the ceiling. "Thank God I was so terrified of my parents that I didn't follow her down the same route. And I feel I have to keep on at Stella to make sure she doesn't latch on to this Tony fellow." She paused. "What do you think, Diana? Am I making too much of it?"

Diana stared at her for a few seconds. "Me? Oh goodness . . . I have no experience with teenage girls. I wouldn't like to pass any opinion on it. I will just say that I've always found Stella to be a very nice polite girl."

"Oh, but she has her moments too. What's the saying – street angel and home devil? Something like that." She took a sip of her cocoa. "God, I know it's awful to say it, but I wish Stella was more like her friend, Maria. Have you met Maria Conti? Beautiful, dark-haired, half-Italian girl. Extremely well-mannered."

"No, I don't think so."

"Her father owns Leonardo's restaurant just off the city centre. He's an Italian chap – very attractive for a foreigner." Her eyes narrowed in thought. "Actually, he's a widower . . ."

Diana shrugged and turned to her plate on the side table to take another digestive. She could tell that Jane was adding him to the list of single men. "No, it doesn't ring any bells."

"She's Stella's best friend. Now, there's a girl who has her head screwed on the right way. She's started to go out with Paul Spencer, the son of the people who own the stables. And she's not a pushy sort – she's the kind of girl who does all the right things without even knowing it."

Diana looked over at her now. "Would it be worth having a word with Maria? Maybe she might have some influence on Stella."

"I don't think so. Stella is so hotheaded I think it might cause a fall-out between them, and Maria is too good an influence for her to lose."

"She sounds like another lovely girl."

Jane took another drink of the comforting cocoa. "Maria Conti has something more about her that's hard to describe. The nearest thing I could describe her as is classy – and yet I wouldn't say her father came from the wealthiest of backgrounds. The Italians rarely do – they come over to Britain looking for a better life. And Leo has certainly done that. He has a thriving business and a very nice house and car." She suddenly caught herself. "Not that I'm saying you have to have money to have class."

"Of course not," Diana said. "I know you're not the sort of person who would judge people by how wealthy they were . . ."

"I suppose the point I'm trying to make is, there's Stella who has had every advantage in life and doesn't seem to appreciate it – seems hell-bent on doing whatever she wants. And then there's Maria Conti, who seems to float along in life, always instinctively knowing the right thing to do."

"That must say something about her upbringing," Diana said. "Do you mind me asking – what happened to her mother?"

"Poor woman, I remember it well." She put her head to the side, calculating. "I suppose it must be six or seven years ago now. An asthma attack. I think she must have had a weak heart as well."

"Dreadful . . . and she must have been so young."

"She was Irish, so I can't imagine that her background was a lot better than her husband's. Although she did seem well educated and I believe she was a good musician – I never heard her myself, but the priest mentioned it at her funeral. She was a very attractive woman, and pleasant, but not as chatty as some of the Irish people I know. In many ways she kept herself to herself."

Diana was surprised at Jane's little jibes against both the Irish and Italians. "My own grandmother was Irish, you know," she said, pointedly . "She came from Dublin. We visited it twice when I was a teenager and I loved it. It's a lovely city and the people are very friendly. I'd really like to go back again sometime – it's on my list of places to visit in the next few years."

Jane's eyebrows arched. "Oh, really? I can't say I know anything about it."

There was a small silence and then Jane picked up one of the magazines and flicked through it. She paused at a page and then held it out for Diana to see.

"That's a beautiful coat, isn't it? Although I'm never sure that cream is a good colour for a winter coat. What do you think?"

They chatted about fashion for a while and then, without any preamble Jane suddenly said, "I'm very worried about Stella's weight. She's always slim and says she needs to be for her ballet . . . but she seems to have lost a lot of weight in the last few weeks."

"Is she eating properly?"

Jane shook her head. "Not at all. We have arguments trying to get her to have breakfast before school in the morning, and then in the evening we have more arguments about her leaving half of her meals. And there are times when I think she's lying about what she's eaten. She will say she had a big sandwich when she came in from school and that she's too full to eat dinner with us. I've started checking how much bread there is so

I can tell whether it's been touched or not, and most of the time I don't think it has. And then when we confront her it's another argument and she feels we're accusing her of lying. It's very difficult."

"Do you think she might be ill or anything?"

"I'm not sure." Jane closed her eyes for a few moments. "But apart from eating very little, the worst thing is . . . when she does eat . . . afterwards, I think she's making herself sick.

Chapter 14

Maria woke during the night to the sound of heavy rain and flying wind. She checked the clock to find it was only twenty past three. She lay for a while with all sorts of worries running through her mind about her father. His finances and gambling problems were top of her list, and when she started worrying about his health, she switched on her bedside lamp, picked up her favourite book, *Pride and Prejudice*, and forced herself to read.

Worrying about her father becoming ill and dying was something she had done since her mother died – but she had managed to overcome it a few years back. She knew that she was letting things overtake her when her mind started back down that dark old track again. Eventually, she became engrossed in reading about Elizabeth Bennett and Mr Darcy and she relaxed again and finally dozed off around five o'clock.

She woke for the second time when her dad tapped on her bedroom door, and realised she had fallen asleep with her lamp on and that her book had fallen onto the floor.

"It's a horrid morning," her father called from the other side of the door. "Do you want to cancel the riding lesson?"

Maria thought for a moment. *Today of all days.* She glanced at the window. It did look horrible outside – dark and wet and windy. And her stomach still felt achy and uncomfortable. And yet she didn't want to miss seeing Paul and making arrangements for their date tonight. It would look very bad if she cancelled the lesson and then phoned up to make arrangements to go out.

Just as she swung her legs out of the side of the bed, she heard the phone ring. It would be Stella, she thought, checking if she was still going. She heard her father answering the phone and speaking for a few minutes, and then – sure enough – he called upstairs for her.

"It's for you, Maria. Pick the phone up in my room."

She padded across the corridor to her father's room and lifted the receiver.

"Here she is now," her father said. "I'll hang up and let you explain."

"Hi, Stella," Maria began.

"Sorry, Maria . . . it's actually me."

"Paul!" She sucked her breath in.

"Sorry for ringing the house so early, but we have to cancel all the riding lessons this morning as there's been a problem with fallen branches in the main field and a big tree has come down in the yard."

"My God – that sounds terrible! It's lucky it happened in the middle of the night so no people or horses got hurt." Maria craned her neck to look out of her father's bedroom window, which faced into the back garden, to check for any damage. There was nothing obvious. "But I suppose it's no surprise. The wind was so loud here it woke me in the night."

"It's still pretty bad out our way, so Mum is phoning around to let everyone know we're cancelling, and I said I would ring you as I wanted to speak to you anyway."

She felt a jab of disappointment – he was going to cancel their date. She didn't mind too much not seeing him at the riding school but tonight was different. She bit her lip and waited.

"The weather forecast is for things to settle down this evening." His voice was rushed and breathless. "So I think we should be okay still for Manchester – if it still suits you?"

"Yes," she said. "I'm sure the weather will be much better

and sunnier by then . . . ." The words were only out of her mouth when she realised how silly and desperate they sounded. She closed her eyes and held the receiver to her chest for a moment trying to still her racing heart. She put it back to her ear. "Well, maybe not exactly sunny!" she said, giving a forced laugh.

"There's a fundraising dinner dance on in the Palace Hotel tonight. It's for the local cricket club and my mum and dad were supposed to go but Dad's back isn't great." He was rushing on again. "I know you're a bit young, but my mother knows the manager there and since it's a private event, she says she can have a word with him so we don't need to worry about you getting in."

She thought for a moment, remembering the way her father had been the last night she was with Paul. "I'd love to go, but I just need to check. Can you hang on for a few minutes or will I ring you back?"

"No problem," he told her. "I'll hang on."

Leo was in the process of frying onions and mushrooms for omelettes when she came rushing down. She halted at the kitchen door, her hand resting against the jamb.

"My riding class is cancelled this morning, but is it okay if I go to a dinner dance in Manchester tonight with Paul Spencer? It's for the local cricket club, and his parents were supposed to go but can't – and his mother said we can have the tickets so they're not wasted."

"Paul Spencer?" His voice was high with surprise. There was a few moments' hesitancy, then he turned towards her, smiling. "Is that why he rang?"

Maria nodded, a red tinge appearing on her face. "Well, he was letting me know about the lesson being cancelled and then he asked me." She looked over at the window. "He says the weather is going to improve this evening."

Leo gestured with his hands. "He's a nice boy with good manners, and if it's a special charity event . . . I think it sounds okay if you would like to go."

"I would," she said.

"Then I have no objections." His eyes narrowed in thought.

"It will be easier for him to go from the stables straight into Manchester rather than calling out here for you, so you can tell him I will drive you in and you can meet him there."

"Okay." She couldn't help herself from smiling. "He's still on the phone, so I'll let him know."

Maria could hear the relieved tone in Paul's voice when she told him that everything was fine for going out that night.

"Your father didn't mind?"

"Nope," she said, suddenly feeling more confident. "Everything is fine as long as I don't drink more than a glass or two of wine and get home safely."

"Of course." Paul's voice lowered. "Isn't he great allowing you to have a drink at fifteen? I've only been allowed to drink in the last year."

"I've been allowed a little wine with my meals since I was twelve."

"*Twelve?*"

She laughed at the shock in his voice. "Don't forget my father is Italian, and they think of wine as being a part of the meal. To be honest, I'm not that mad about it and usually dilute it with water, so he knows I'm not going to drink too much."

"I think it sounds like a good idea," Paul said. "It probably stops people drinking too much if they grow up with it."

Her mind flitted to her father and his recent late-night glasses of whiskey but she pushed it out of her mind. "Dad said he would drop me in to the Palace to meet you."

"Fine. I'll get someone to drop me in too and we'll get a taxi back home from Manchester and drop you on the doorstep."

"Great," she said.

She went straight into the bathroom and was pleased when she discovered that her period had arrived. Her first day or two was always light so it wasn't a problem, and it was better to be prepared when she was going out than to have it arrived unannounced. Also, the stomach ache and fuzzy headache which preceded it would have eased off by tonight and she could relax and enjoy herself. The only real nuisance was that she would have to bring a handbag big enough to conceal a couple of sanitary towels.

Later, when they were having breakfast, Leo looked across the table at her. "I'm happy you asked me about Paul – and I'm happy we can talk about such things together."

"I am too," Maria said.

Maria had just got dressed when Stella came on the phone. They chatted about the weather and then moved on to talk about their plans for the evening.

"You and Paul are going to a dance in the Palace Hotel? My God, that's amazing! He must be mad about you to take you to somewhere like that."

Maria went on to explain about his father's back and the tickets going spare. "It's a fundraising thing for his local cricket club, so he'll know a lot of people there. I'm looking forward to going out with him, but I'm a bit nervous as I won't know a lot of people."

"You'll be fine," Stella said. "Paul will look after you." She paused. "Have you told your dad?"

"Yes, and he was okay about it. He says he likes Paul."

"Lucky you! I wish my mother had the same attitude to Tony. Blooming snob!"

"She might come round."

"I'm hoping that when she sees him all dressed up in his suit at the races she will realise he is as good as anyone else. I mean, look at the Spencers who everyone loves! Paul's dad was only a jockey when they met and it didn't stop her marrying him."

"A jockey with very good prospects," Maria said.

"Who knows what Tony will do? He's so talented with horses and he's got a really good head for business. He has all these plans for owning his own stables when he's older."

Maria stifled a sigh. The conversation was back to being all about Tony again.

After a few minutes Stella suddenly noticed that Maria had hardly spoken and asked with great interest: "What will you wear to the dance?" Then, before Maria got a chance to reply she rushed on. "You should wear that nice flower print one with the bell sleeves. They will all be dressed in the height of fashion in those places."

"I think that might be a bit casual for a dinner dance. I was actually thinking of wearing the evening dress I got for the Christmas party at Leonardo's. Do you remember it?" Maria suddenly felt nervous. "Everybody said it made me look older. It was the little black sleeveless one with the bodice covered in sequins and it's trimmed with a black velvet ribbon and bow."

"I don't think I ever saw it, but it sounds fab! Is it long or short?"

"It's short, a few inches above the knee. I asked Paul to check with his mother if it had to be long evening dresses, and she said no. I thought I would wear it with my short fur coat over it and black stilettos and ten-denier black tights."

"They will go perfect with it. Is it low-cut? Does it show your bust off?"

"You can just see my cleavage," Maria said, "but not too much. It has a sort of scooped neck."

"Go for it, and try to pull it down a bit lower. That's what men go for."

"Stella!" Maria laughed. "You've suddenly become an expert on what men go for! I feel nervous enough without feeling I'm drawing attention to my bust." She thought for a few moments. "Maybe I should wear something different . . ."

"No, don't – that black dress sounds absolutely perfect. Oh, I meant to tell you!" Stella's voice suddenly dropped. She gave a low, stifled laugh. "My mother has invited a friend of hers to the races, and she's going to try to be a matchmaker for her and your dad."

"What?"

"She's going to try to pair up Diana with your dad when we're all at the races."

Maria's hand came up to cover her mouth.

"I heard her talking about it to my father last night." Stella was whispering and giggling. "My mother was saying how handsome your dad was and how he was such a charming and talented man, and that she thought they would make a great couple."

Maria's stomach turned over.

"She was singing your father's praises so much to Diana that my father was teasing her later, and saying that it sounded as though Mum fancied Leo herself. Mum said he was only jealous because your dad had lovely tan and good thick hair. Can you imagine it? Imagine going on about fancying people and being jealous at their age? Wouldn't it make you feel sick?" She paused. "Although Diana is really nice. She doesn't look as old as Mum and she wears fantastic modern clothes."

Maria closed her eyes. She felt the same now as she did when she heard Mrs Lowry telling her father that it was time he met someone else.

"Maria?" Stella said. "Are you still there?"

"Yes . . . yes." Her voice felt jagged in her throat. "I was just thinking that your mum's friend will only be wasting her time coming to the races. Dad had no interest in meeting anyone. He always says that my mother was the love of his life and that no one else could ever measure up to her."

"That was a long time ago – he might have changed his mind. Maybe he just needs to meet the right one. Diana's lovely – she would make a great stepmum. You could borrow all her fabulous clothes!"

"*Stella!*" Maria cut her off. "My father does not want another wife and I do not want a stepmother. Have you got it? Is that clear enough?"

"Okay – okay." Stella was shocked at Maria's attitude. "Keep your hair on!"

There was a tense silence.

"Sorry, Maria – I didn't mean to upset you. I was exaggerating a bit. I don't think my mum was serious about Diana and your dad. It was just a bit of a laugh."

"Well, I don't find it one bit funny."

"Maria, I know you don't joke about things like that, but some people do and they don't mean any harm. They're not doing it to upset you. Everybody is different."

Maria took a deep breath. She did feel upset, but she did her best to control it. She had just made up with Stella after the row over Tony and she didn't want to go headlong into another argument. "Okay," she said. "Let's just drop the subject."

"If I hear my mum mentioning anything about it again, I'll tell her not to be so stupid. I'll tell her that your dad isn't interested in anyone else and not to make a fool of Diana."

Maria heard the sharpness in her friend's tone. "I don't want you to upset your mother," she said. "Maybe it's best if you say nothing about it."

"Okay. I won't say anything. If that's what you want."

Maria now felt Stella was making a real point of agreeing with everything she said, which made her feel as if she was the one who was being unreasonable. "So," she said, in a lighter tone, "what are your plans with Tony for tonight?"

There was a silence then Stella whispered. "Just the party. And Tony said he'll get me a taxi home."

The conversation gradually got back onto a more normal footing as they revived the safe topic of the outfits they might wear, and offered each other advice on particular ones they liked. But underneath the chat there was a small but definite strain between them.

When the phone was back in its cradle Maria stood for a long time just staring at it. She wondered if the problem was all her fault. Was she too serious and touchy? Was she too old-fashioned and judgemental? Would the other girls at school feel as shocked about the way Stella had let Tony paw her in the cinema and would they have disapproved of her plans to go to an all-night party?

She wondered why she was so suddenly annoyed with everything Stella was doing and saying. Had her friend really changed that much? Or were the different boyfriends they had chosen now highlighting the differences between them?

Maria wished she had someone she could confide it all to. Mrs Lowry was too old and she felt she couldn't trust the other girls at school not to repeat what she said back to Stella.

She wished she had someone she could talk to about her father as well – but there was no one she could think of who would understand. She fleetingly considered Franco, but dismissed it just as quickly. Her father would be devastated if he discovered she had talked about him to his friend, and it would compromise Franco's loyalty. What did other girls do in this situation, she wondered? And then the greatest sadness suddenly wrapped itself around her. The familiar sadness that she tried so hard to forget. Of course, the other girls all had mothers they could talk to about things like that.

And if her mother were alive, then her father would not be wasting his life drinking and gambling – because Maria knew he only did those things to fill his time. To fill the void left by his beautiful wife. She knew this answer so well and so deep in her heart, as she had reasoned it out so many times before.

She allowed herself to go for a few minutes to that sad – almost holy – place in her mind. A place that was like no other. A place where she was a young child again and where she could bring back to mind the memories and pictures of her beloved mother. At times it was easy to remember and at others it was very hard. This was one of the hard times when she felt sorry for herself for having no kind female to advise her.

When she felt the silent tears dropping onto her hand she knew she had allowed herself to go too far and she quickly moved to go and get dressed. It would not be fair on her father if he came up and found her in such a state. She knew that he would easily be moved to tears himself and the sadness would cling to them both and to their house for the rest of the day.

Chapter 15

As her father's car pulled up in front of the Palace Hotel, Maria spotted Paul standing to the side of the entrance and she felt her heart quicken. She pulled her fur coat around her and hoped the dress she was wearing was okay, and that she hadn't gone too mad with her eyes. As she reached for the door handle, her father's hand moved to cover hers.

"Have a good night, my darling."

She turned towards him. The very serious look on his face made her suddenly feel sad. Made her realise that this first formal date had a bigger effect on him than she had imagined. She knew that he was thinking that this was some kind of landmark – a change in their relationship that would never allow it to go back to quite what it was.

"It's only a dance," she said. "And I promise I won't be that late."

"Go and enjoy yourself and come home safely when everyone else is coming home. Don't hang about the city centre too long as it won't be as nice as it is now. It can be dangerous for a young girl later on at night when men are drunk and maybe even fighting."

"I'll be fine."

Leo shrugged. "You never know. We even had trouble outside

the restaurant recently. Young thugs teasing poor Timothy again and threatening to beat him up."

Timothy was a slow, effeminate-mannered man who was well known in the area around the restaurant, as he did shopping for his elderly mother and his sister who was in a wheelchair. He was a cheery man, but periodically he did a tour of all the local bars, rather overindulging – and on a couple of those occasions he had become a target for local teenagers.

"Oh, no," Maria said. "What happened?" She had only met Timothy briefly on a couple of occasions, but knew from what her father had told her that he was a harmless soul.

"Oh, Franco and I had to go outside and chase them off."

Maria's hand felt for the door handle. "I promise I'll be careful."

A shadow came on the driver's window and when she looked she saw it was Paul who had obviously recognised the car. Leo rolled down the window and they shook hands.

They talked for a few minutes about the windy weather earlier in the day and the effect it had had on the riding-school grounds.

"We've been clearing up all afternoon," Paul told them. "A big old tree came down, and the place was littered with broken branches. But it's all been dealt with and my father was just happy that the worst of it happened early in the morning and that no one was injured."

"Of course, of course," Leo said. "That's the most important thing."

Maria's eyes moved from one to the other as they spoke and she felt a sense of relief as she noted Paul's easy way of responding to her father, and how he bent his head as he listened carefully and with respect to everything Leo said.

She was also pleased that it was her father who ended the conversation. He glanced at his watch and said he needed to get back to the restaurant as there was a big Golden Wedding Anniversary group due in and he wanted to be there to greet them all personally.

Maria got out of the car and, as she went towards Paul, she

saw he was wearing a lovely grey collarless suit with a perfect white shirt and a fashionably skinny maroon tie. She also noticed the expensive gold tie-pin which had a single music note with a small diamond in the centre. She guessed his mother had bought it for him.

"Have an enjoyable night." Leo looked directly at Paul as he started the car engine up again. "And I know I can trust a respectable boy like you to look after Maria and see her safely home later."

"Of course," Paul said, nodding. "I'll book a taxi for us in plenty of time before the dance finishes."

They walked towards the hotel entrance, a small awkward space between them. Maria felt the same shy way that she'd felt the night they went to the cinema. Then he moved closer to her and put his arm around her shoulders and she felt a sense of relief.

"Your father is a real gentleman," Paul said. "Everyone seems to like him, and it's obviously helped his business to be the great success it is. You must be very proud of him."

They moved slowly up the steps towards the big glass doors.

"Yes, I am proud of him. And he is a lovely man – but he's not completely perfect."

"Who is? My parents certainly aren't perfect either, but I know I'm lucky that they are better than most."

She looked up at him and something about his eyes made her suddenly think that he might be the person she was looking for – the person she could confide in about Stella and maybe even about her father. Not just now, and certainly not tonight. But maybe later.

He caught her eye and drew her to a halt. Then his gaze moved from the top of her head right down to her stiletto heels. "If you don't mind me saying – you look absolutely gorgeous tonight."

Maria looked down at herself. "Do I?"

"Absolutely!" He suddenly seemed flustered. "I'm really pleased that the weather improved. I was afraid that we would have to cancel our date."

"Were you?"

"I know we could have re-organised it for another night, but I'm glad we didn't have to."

Maria nodded and gave a self-conscious smile, and then she suddenly worried that he might think she wasn't as enthusiastic as he would like, so she said, "Yes, I'm glad too."

He took a step towards her, but moved back again when an elderly couple came towards them.

"Hello, Paul!" the woman said.

"Hello, Mrs Tordoff." He smiled and then stepped forward to shake hands with her husband.

The woman smiled warmly at Maria. "We're neighbours of the Spencers. I take it you're here for the dance?"

Paul quickly introduced Maria and then explained about his father's bad back and how he and Maria were using the tickets.

"I'm so sorry your parents won't be here, but I'm sure it will be a lovely night. The cricket crowd are great at organising things." She took her husband's arm. "We won't keep you – I know you young people will be waiting to catch up with all your young friends."

After they left, Paul turned to her. "To be honest, I'm not that friendly with anyone from the cricket club so I haven't a clue about what table we'll be sitting at or anything like that. I think my mother mentioned something about it, but I wasn't really paying attention." He gave a weak smile. "I was too busy thinking about asking you to come with me."

She could see by his face that he was not as confident as she imagined he would be, and in a way it made her feel closer to him. As if they were both in the same boat.

"It doesn't matter who we sit with," she said. "We'll still have a good time."

As they walked into the hotel, Maria thought it was the nicest, place she had ever been in. It was fairly busy, with very well-dressed people sitting on sofas and chairs chatting over drinks. A few people at different tables spoke to Paul as they went past, but he only politely acknowledged them and didn't stop to chat to anyone. Maria smiled at anyone who looked at her, and quietly took note of what the younger women were wearing. When she spotted a few other girls with similar short styles – although none in black or sequinned – she decided she was happy enough with what she was wearing and she felt herself begin to relax a little.

They found the cloakroom and Paul held her black handbag for her while she slipped off her coat and gave it to the lady to hang up. Then, as the attendant turned away, Paul moved behind Maria and kissed her on the back of the neck.

"That dress is absolutely gorgeous – you look stunning in it," he whispered. "I can see I'm going to have to keep a close eye on you with all the other men."

She laughed and slid her arm through his, and they walked back to where all the others were.

Paul indicated the long bar. "We've loads of time before we need to go into the ballroom, so I'll get us a drink first. What will you have? A wine or a sherry? Or maybe a Babycham?"

She shrugged and then leaned towards him. "Maybe a lemonade would be safer? I don't want you embarrassed if they start checking my age . . ."

"Stop worrying," he said quietly. "You look as old as any of the girls in here, and I've never had trouble being served alcohol in any pubs I've been in, so if you want a drink I'll get it."

"Okay, that would be lovely. A glass of red wine, please."

"We'll find a table first, so you can sit down." He looked around, then he spotted one over in the corner near the entrance to the ballroom. "That's in a good spot and we can see everyone coming and going." He touched her elbow and then guided her across the carpeted floor towards the long, low table which had a nice big comfortable velvet couch with a couple of high-backed matching armchairs opposite it.

The touch of his hand on her bare arm as they walked along made her catch her breath and sparked a small flame in the pit of her stomach. She recognised it as the same feeling she had a few nights ago when he kissed her. She went around the table to sit on the sofa, and, as she watched him going back towards the bar – tall, good-looking with his quietly confident way – she couldn't believe how lucky she was to be out at a dance in Manchester with Paul Spencer. There were plenty of girls at the riding school – some older than her – who would be thrilled to be asked out by him.

She could see him talking to another boy at the bar who looked around the same age, and thought it was good he had met up with someone he knew. As she watched, two dark-haired girls with quite daring, low-cut strapless dresses came over and started chatting to the boys and Maria could tell, by the way the taller one flicked her hair back and then leaned in close when she was talking to Paul, that she fancied him. She also knew, by the way the girls were acting, that they were older than her, probably around eighteen like Paul and the age difference niggled at her, because the girls that age at school in sixth year were often dismissive towards the younger ones like her.

Maria's eyes narrowed in watchfulness, and then she saw Paul moving away from the group to catch the barman's eye and when he gave his order she was pleased to see that he didn't move back to join them again. Then, at one point, she saw him looking over at her and when he caught her eye he smiled and raised his eyebrows, checking she was okay, and she smiled back and nodded her head.

As he came back towards the table carrying their drinks, she suddenly wondered what he saw in her that had made him single her out. When she was growing up, she knew from adults' comments and from her friends in school that she wasn't unattractive, but she did not feel she was as pretty as some of her other friends or as fashionable as Stella. It wasn't exactly a question she could ask any of her friends, as it would sound weird or as if she was fishing for compliments.

Paul came back to the table and told her that the boy he had been talking to was called Jim McPherson. Paul had known him from primary school but hadn't seen him in ages.

"He's a keen cricketer apparently," Paul told her, "which is quite surprising as I don't remember him being very sporty at school. But then, I don't suppose we should judge people on what they were like at eleven years old." He smiled. "God, when I think back, I was probably absolutely awful at that age."

"And who were the two girls with him?" Maria asked.

Paul shrugged. "I don't know – he didn't introduce us."

He said nothing more about them, instead commenting on how much busier it was getting and how all the seats were starting to fill up. After a while, two older couples came and asked if they could sit at their table. The two men took the chairs and brought a third chair over for one of the women. Paul moved a space or two along the sofa to let the other lady sit at the end, and then he reached for Maria's hand to help her move alongside him. He waited until she had lifted her handbag and was settled again, then put his arm around her shoulders and drew her near, so that she was leaning in towards him and their legs were close together. Maria thought it felt wonderful.

They were just finishing their drinks when the woman next to them pointed out to the others in the group that people were starting to head into the ballroom. When the older couples got up from the table, Paul and Maria followed along behind them. The queue was moving, so within a couple of minutes they were at the ballroom door. Paul handed their tickets over to a man in a tuxedo and tails and he told them to go inside and check their names on the lists that they would find on a table there.

"This is going to be interesting," he said when he found their table on the list.

"What do you mean?" Maria asked.

"I hope you're feeling all grown up and serious, because we're down as Mr and Mrs Spencer."

"*What*?" Her voice was incredulous.

He started laughing. "It's okay, you don't need to panic – they still have my parents' names on the list and probably at the places on the table."

"Oh God," she said, laughing along with him, "I know we both want to look a bit older, but being taken for a married couple is pushing it just a bit too far."

When they walked in, Maria's eyes were immediately drawn to the five sparkling chandeliers – four in the corners of the room and a larger central one – and she thought it was easily the most elegant room she had ever seen. It had dozens of big round tables, and each one was decked out with a white tablecloth that pooled onto the floor, topped with a smaller black-and-gold square cloth and fancily shaped napkins. Each table was circled by ten white linen-covered chairs, the backs of which were adorned with bows fashioned from gold material. There was an elaborate silver candelabra on each table and two tall vases filled with lilies on either side of it.

They were the first to arrive at their table and within a few minutes of sitting down a young waiter in tails came to take their drink order. This time Maria asked for a glass of lemonade, and when Paul checked she said that she would rather have that for now, and maybe have a glass of wine along with her meal.

More and more people were coming in now, looking around the room and debating as to where they were seated. Three older couples joined their table, and they all smiled and said good evening to Paul as though they knew him, and smiled at Maria.

When the group were all settled and occupied chatting amongst themselves, Paul whispered to Maria that he hoped she wasn't going to be bored sitting with another older crowd and she laughed. He then said he was embarrassed that he didn't know any of their names, as they weren't close friends of his parents, just people they knew from the group who were running the dance.

"Lots of people are bound to know your father, with him being a jockey," Maria whispered back. "As long as you smile at them, and be really friendly when they speak to you, you'll be fine. My father says that's what he does in the restaurant as all the customers like it if he remembers them."

He smiled and squeezed her arm. "That sounds like good advice – I can't argue with that."

Jim McPherson came in with a pretty blonde girl on his arm – neither of the girls who had been talking to him at the bar – who was wearing a long orange sparkly dress which drew a lot of glances. He paused at their table and Maria could feel his eyes taking in every detail about her, and she began to feel awkward and wondered if he thought she was very young-looking. Paul introduced them and then Jim introduced the girl he was with as

Dawn, which Maria thought was a much more glamorous name than her own.

When another young couple came to the table and sat in the two spare chairs beside Maria, Jim and Dawn moved away to look for their own places. Paul had never met the new couple before, so he waited until they were settled and then introduced himself and Maria, and they said they were Alison Wood and Michael Murphy. They told them they had come with a group but there had been too many for the one table, so a few of the couples had been put on other tables.

Alison was a bubbly friendly girl, and within minutes Maria felt she'd known her for ages. She loved Alison's gorgeous long cream dress with a gold bodice, and when she complimented her on it Alison confided that she had tried on loads of things and ended up borrowing the dress from her older sister.

"Michael is eighteen, but I'm only turned seventeen," Alison said, "and I was afraid I would look too young in my own things."

Maria then whispered to her that she wouldn't be sixteen until May.

"I don't believe you!" Alison's eyes were wide with surprise. "I thought you were about nineteen!"

Maria smiled and liked her even more.

After a while people started to pick up their menus and discuss whether they were going to have melon or prawn cocktail and, for the main course, coq au vin, beef bourguignon or salmon.

When the wine was being poured, Alison leaned towards Maria to say weren't the waiters very serious in their fancy uniforms, and she had to stifle a giggle when they were all addressed as 'sir' or 'madam'. Maria giggled along with her and did not say that she spent many of her evenings in a restaurant and was so used to hearing people being called 'sir' or 'madam' that she did not even notice it any more.

The chatty girl then went on to tell her that she and Michael had been going out for nearly a year and were planning to get engaged in the summer. "We haven't told anyone else yet, so you're the first to know." She then put her hand to her mouth.

"If any of our group come over to talk to us, you won't say a word, will you? It's just that Michael's sister is here and we'd be in big trouble if she thought I'd told a complete stranger that we were getting engaged before her!"

Maria assured her she wouldn't say a thing.

"And how long have you two been going out?" Alison asked.

Maria moved closer to her and said, "We've known each other a good while, but we've only actually been on one date before this."

"What?" Alison said. "I don't believe it. You'd think you'd been going out ages!"

After the meal the tables were cleared and a lively band came on, playing up-to-date music. At the beginning only a few couples braved the floor, but when they started on a string of Beatles hits and then The Twist, the floor began to get busy. When Alison and Michael got up it was evident they were great dancers, and they kept waving back to Maria and Paul – who were happily watching everyone dance and commenting on the better dancers – to come and join them. Paul seemed reluctant to and it struck Maria that he might not actually be any good at dancing, and the thought made her feel a bit wary of actually getting up. She loved dancing and she and Stella often danced around to the radio in their bedrooms. She unconsciously moved in her chair in time to the music now, thinking that she wasn't quite sure how she would feel if Paul was clumsy on the floor or uncoordinated.

She went to the ladies' and took a few minutes checking her hair and make-up. Then, as she was on her way back to the table, enjoying the band playing 'Day Tripper', her hand was suddenly grabbed by Alison, who insisted she come and join them on the floor.

"We've already hijacked Paul," she said, giggling, and pointed across the dance floor to where he was standing chatting to Michael.

"I don't know if he likes dancing," Maria said. "I don't even know if he *can* dance."

"There's only one way to find out," Alison laughed. "And if he can't, then we'll just bloody well have to teach him!"

118

As they weaved their way through the crowds, Maria told herself that she would have to remain relaxed and easy with him even if he was an awful dancer. It struck her as they passed a particularly loud group who were carrying on, laughing and switching partners, that even though she had never seen Tony on a floor, she guessed he would be a good dancer. Confident, chatty boys were nearly always good dancers, she thought, and Paul was definitely not like that, being quieter and more thoughtful in his ways.

Just as she reached him the band finished playing 'Day Tripper' and after a few seconds' break they started playing 'Unchained Melody'. He smiled at her and moved to put his arms around her waist and she leaned in towards him and put her head on his shoulder. After a few steps, she realised it was okay because, although they were moving slowly, they were actually moving in time together. Later, when the faster music came back on again, he kept in time, but Maria noticed that he repeated the same safe steps over and over again rather than varying them as she did.

At one point he said to her, "You're a terrific dancer – you've got great rhythm. I'm afraid I've not danced for ages and I'm not exactly Fred Astaire at the best of times."

"You're absolutely fine," she told him, and his slightly embarrassed admission made her warm to him even more.

As the night wore on she thought his dancing had definitely improved and, by the time the band were calling for the final dances, she was dancing in her usual way and Paul's movements were much more relaxed.

When the band finished playing the usual final number, Engelbert Humperdinck's 'The Last Waltz', they headed out to the cloakroom so they would be in plenty of time for their taxi. As they were standing in the cloakroom queue, a distinguished grey-haired man spotted Paul and came across to them. Paul introduced him as William Ashton, a friend of his father's, who owned a stud farm out in Pot Shrigley.

"The last time I was speaking to your father he asked me about good stable-management courses, and I told him I'd heard of one up in Northumberland and I'd find out the name of the college."

"It was for me, actually," Paul said. "I finish school this year and I want to get some qualifications before I start full time in the stables."

William smiled. "Lesley, my wife, said she guessed it might be for you as your mother told her you were leaving school in the summer. The women are never far wrong. It's called Ponteland Equine College – I believe it's just a few miles outside Newcastle and near the airport. From what I've heard it's one of the best."

Paul frowned. "Northumberland is a bit of a distance from here, isn't it?"

Maria felt her stomach muscles tighten as it dawned on her that Paul might in fact be planning a move away from the area – which meant he was moving away from her. He obviously didn't reckon on them being a good long-term bet – he was only filling in time with her until he found something better. She tried to smile and look as though she was interested in equine courses, but her face felt stiff and unnatural and she was relieved when the cloakroom attendant asked for her ticket and she could turn away from them before it was noticed.

William laughed. "Well, you wouldn't want to be driving there every day, but I suppose it wouldn't be too bad coming home at weekends."

Paul looked thoughtful. "How long does the course run?"

"The Horse Breeding and Training diploma is a year, but there are other advanced courses in things like Equine Business Administration you can progress on to after that if you want. The chap who went there said if you just give them a ring they'll send you a brochure and application form. I think he said you have another month before the application date closes."

"Thanks, William," Paul said. "It sounds exactly what I'm looking for. I'll definitely look into it."

They put their coats on and went outside to see if their taxi had arrived. There was a late winter frost on the ground and on the tops of the taxis waiting there, and Maria found herself shivering.

"No sign of ours yet." Paul put his arm around her and drew her close to him. "You are absolutely gorgeous." He kissed her on the nose. "My God!" he exclaimed. "Your nose is absolutely freezing!" He held her at arm's length, laughing.

She looked at his bright, animated face and started laughing too.

"Come on," he said, taking her hand and swinging their arms back and forth. "We'll go back inside and watch for the taxi through the glass door."

Inside, as they stood huddled together, he put his hand under her chin so he could look at her properly. "There's more than a fair chance I'll end up going to Northumberland in September and, if I do, do you think you could put up with us just seeing each other at weekends?"

Her eyes lit up, and when she looked back at him she could tell by the serious expression on his face that he wanted to keep seeing her – that he wasn't just filling in time. "I think so," she said, smiling. "I'm sure I'll find something to do to keep me busy during the week."

"As long as it's not other boyfriends," he said, raising his eyebrows.

"I could say the same about girlfriends . . ." She looked back at him and then smiled and raised her brows to match him.

"Are we agreed?" he said. "I meant what I said earlier on about not being interested in anyone else. I'm a little bit older than you and I've had a few girlfriends, but they were only casual. I've never got on with anyone the way I get on with you."

"I know I'm younger and have never had a serious boyfriend before, but I feel the exact same. And, if things are still going well with us, then I'll be happy to know you're doing a course that will help you with your future, but I'll be even happier to see you at weekends."

His face became solemn now and he just stared at her, until she had to ask him if there was anything wrong.

"Not a thing," he said. "I just can't believe my luck. I was so worried about going away to Northumberland and maybe losing touch with you that I was even thinking of not applying. I thought I might just do a local course. It wouldn't be as good, but at least I would be near you."

"But it's important," she said. "It's your future."

"Yes," he said. "But so, I hope, are you."

She saw the sincerity in his eyes and felt her heart quicken. "I'd like that too," she said.

They turned to look back now as a noisy group came out from the dance hall, and then Maria heard someone calling her name and Alison came rushing towards them.

"We didn't get your address and phone number!" she said, all out of breath. "Michael and I were just saying what a lovely couple you were, and we thought you might like to come to our engagement party."

"Oh, that's lovely of you," Maria said. "I think I've got a pen in my bag."

Paul dipped into his inside pocket and brought out a little black notebook.

"Hey," Alison said, laughing, "I hope that's not full of other girls' addresses!" She dug Maria in the ribs. "You know what they say about men with little black books, don't you?"

"No," Maria said, raising her eyebrows, "and I don't think I want to know."

"Better off not knowing, love," Alison said, mimicking a wise old Northern woman.

Paul shrugged, trying not to laugh. "Do you honestly think," he said, "that I would look at anyone else when I have someone as lovely as this?" Then, in full view of the others, he bent his head and kissed Maria passionately on the lips.

Alison let out a shriek of laughter and started to clap, then Michael and all the other people around joined in.

When Paul finally let her go, Maria turned her blushing face towards Alison and said, laughing along with them all, "I could kill you!"

Michael tapped his girlfriend playfully on the head. "Come on, trouble," he said, "or I'll be digging out my own little black book and looking for a replacement for myself."

Chapter 16

It had been ages since Maria had gone to eight o'clock Mass on a Sunday morning. She usually accompanied her father to the one at eleven o'clock, but after last night she was wide awake and feeling too happy to sit about the house waiting.

She had been lying in bed for an hour, going over and over the highlights of the night before, remembering when Paul had told her that his going to Northumberland would not affect them, and then reliving the best bit at the end of the night when he had kissed her in front of everyone.

She had just picked up a book from the bedside cabinet and was ready to start reading when she suddenly thought it would be a change to walk down to the church while it was still so early. It would also give her the rest of the day to herself, to chat to Stella about the dance when her father was at Mass, and to think about her and Paul.

She crept quietly along the hall into the bathroom so as not to wake her father and, after a quick bath, she got dressed in her smart red woollen coat with a black polo-neck sweater, short grey skirt and long black boots. She stopped in the hallway to put on the black hat with the red trim that matched her coat. Then she scribbled a note for her father to say where she was and went quietly out of the door.

123

It was a misty morning with the last vestiges of winter stamped all over it. As she walked along the avenue towards the main road, she noticed the hedges and trees were all hung with cobwebs like delicate white lace curtains and it made her smile. Things like the way the fir-tree branches were edged with white and the pattern the frost made on car windscreens seemed more interesting to her than normal, and she couldn't decide whether it was a particularly unusual day, or whether it was just the extraordinarily good mood she was in.

Going along the main road, it occurred to her that Sunday morning was not like any other day of the week. The weekdays were busy with everyone going to work or school, and Saturday had its own busyness with early shoppers and people walking their dogs or out for the morning papers. Eight o'clock on a Sunday, she thought, was just quieter and slower, and the few people who were around were more inclined to acknowledge you with a nod or a 'Good morning' rather than just walking past as though you were a ghost.

The traffic got a little busier nearer the church and there were more people around.

Inside the church, Maria found an almost empty pew about a third of the way up the aisle on the left. There was only one other person in the pew, sitting at the opposite end – a nicely dressed woman who Maria guessed to be somewhere in her thirties.

When she was settled in, with her gloves off and bag on the floor, Maria glanced around her to see if she knew anyone, but there were only people she knew by sight – no school friends up this early or any of their Catholic neighbours. On second glance, she thought the woman at the other end of the pew was older than she first thought – probably nearer her father's age, and he was now heading up to forty. She tried not to look too obvious, but she couldn't help but admire the woman's lovely black-and-white checked coat which had a black fur collar and matching fur muff.

At one point, the woman caught her eye and smiled and Maria gave an embarrassed smile back. The church was only half-full when Father O'Donnell came on the altar, although, as usual, a few others crept in a bit later when he had his back to the congregation. Then an elderly lady came slowly up the aisle and stopped at the empty pew in front of Maria. She hesitated for a few moments, as though not sure it was where she wanted to sit, then she eventually moved in and sat down around a little to the left of Maria.

When the priest came on the altar the congregation all stood for the opening prayers. Then, after they were finished, and everyone went to kneel, Maria noticed the old lady in front struggling to kneel down. After a few attempts, she gave up, perching uncomfortably on the edge of the hard wooden seat.

Most weeks, Maria found it difficult not to let her attention stray, and this morning she found it harder than usual. Her mind kept flitting back to the night before in the Palace Hotel with Paul. Although she had felt out of her depths at certain times, she had really enjoyed it. She was pleased that they seemed to have so much in common, and that Paul felt the same way as she did about a lot of things. It was also reassuring, she thought, that her father wasn't the only man she knew who took things to heart. And yet, like her father, Paul had a sense of humour about things. She liked the way he always caught her eye when something funny happened and just raised his eyebrows.

She was jolted back to the Mass when everyone stood up for the Creed, and it was then that she noticed the old lady in front struggling to stand. She watched her now, putting both hands on the back of the pew in front and trying to lever herself up. She managed to get to her feet at one point, but after a moment or so, she very slowly sank back down into the seat again.

Maria wondered if she should offer to help, but it was rare in church that people spoke. She didn't want to draw attention to either herself or the poor lady who might be embarrassed and perhaps not want her help. Maria could quite clearly remember an occasion a few years ago when her father went to help an old woman across the road who seemed to be struggling. When he put his hand on her arm, the old woman had shouted out loud that he should keep his hands to himself and then hit him with her stick. Even though they discovered later that the poor woman wasn't quite right in the head, and there were some funny elements to the incident, it had stayed with Maria and made her think twice before rushing to the aid of anyone else.

When Communion time came and Maria moved out into the aisle to join the queue to receive the Holy Eucharist, she noticed that the old lady didn't attempt to move from her place, and stayed sitting with her head bowed. The elegantly dressed woman at the end of the pew came out into the aisle behind Maria, and Maria could tell that she too was looking at the old woman with some concern.

When Communion was over, Maria thoughts drifted back to the night before and she was only jolted out of it when everyone stood up as the priest started saying the closing prayers. She quickly moved to her feet and joined in the responses once again. The priest had barely left the altar and Maria was just lifting her bag off the seat when the woman in the black-and-white coat came purposefully towards Maria's end of the row. Maria was just going to step into the aisle to let her out when the woman came to a standstill behind the old lady

"Mrs Flynn?" she said. "Are you all right?"

The older woman looked over her shoulder to see who was talking to her and obviously recognised the well-dressed woman. She shook her head. "Oh . . . I'm not too grand." Although her voice was quiet, the accent was unmistakably Irish. "I had a bit of a fall coming into the church, and I've not felt right since. I felt sort of dizzy so I thought I'd better not go out to Communion."

Maria felt a hand touch her arm, and when she turned around she saw their housekeeper smiling at her.

Mrs Lowry whispered, "I was sitting across the aisle and down a bit from you. I was just watching you to catch your attention, and then I saw Mrs Flynn coming in and I noticed that she didn't seem too well."

"I fell at the church gate," the old woman explained again to Mrs Lowry. "I think I must have slipped on a bit of ice."

"Where did you hurt yourself?"

"I don't rightly know . . . but it hurts when I move. I think it

126

might be my hip or something like that, and I feel a bit light-headed."

"Do you think you can stand?" the smartly dressed lady asked.

"Well," Mrs Flynn said, giving an anxious smile, "we'll soon know . . ." She made to move out of her seat, but as soon as she put her weight on her legs, a flash of pain crossed her face. "Ah no . . . no!"

Mrs Lowry moved into the pew beside the old lady now, and the younger woman followed. They each took an arm, and between them they eased her back down into the seat.

"It's got worse," Mrs Flynn said in a wavering voice. "I don't think I can walk at all now."

"You just sit there," the younger woman said kindly, "and we'll find a way to move you without hurting you." She looked at Mrs Lowry. "Would you mind staying with her for a few minutes and I'll go into the vestry and let the priest know."

"Oh, we can't go bothering the priest!" Mrs Flynn said.

"Don't worry about that, he's nice," Maria said. "He'll just be worried about you." She looked at the well-dressed woman and whispered, "Is there anything I can do to help?"

She smiled warmly at Maria and said in a low voice. "Just keep chatting to her and it might keep her mind off the pain." Then she set off towards the vestry, her heels tapping on the mosaic tiles.

The elderly woman suddenly got agitated. "What's going to happen now? "

"They might have to take you to the hospital," Mrs Lowry said. "You might need a bit of a check-over."

"But what about my dog? I can't leave her at the house on her own all day."

"Don't worry," Maria said. "If you're not well, somebody will do it for you."

"But *who*?" Mrs Flynn said. "My neighbours aren't the kind you could ask and poor Poppy will wonder where I am and she'll need feeding as well."

"You live in Heaton Chapel, don't you?" Mrs Lowry asked.

"Yes, on Range Road. It's not that far from here."

"Well, don't you worry," Mrs Lowry said. "If you do have to go to the hospital, one of us will look after your dog."

"I love dogs," Maria said. "Is she friendly?"

The old lady nodded. "She's a lovely little thing. A Shih Tzu called Poppy. She wouldn't harm a fly."

Maria smiled. "One of my friends has that breed, and they are really friendly."

"She's the best company you could have," Mrs Flynn said. "She's that clever she could nearly talk to you."

"How is your hip now?" Mrs Lowry said.

"It's all right, as long as I don't move. It's my head that's the worst. It feels like it's spinning around."

Mrs Lowry looked over the old lady's head at Maria and pulled a face as though she were worried. Then they heard voices and footsteps and they saw Father O'Donnell and the woman coming back out of the vestry.

After talking to Mrs Flynn for a while and patting her hand, Father O'Donnell told her that he had phoned for an ambulance to take her to Stockport Infirmary to get checked over.

"Oh, no!" Mrs Flynn's face crumpled at the news. "Not the hospital!"

"Don't go upsetting yourself. I'm sure everything will be just fine." He gave her a reassuring smile. "Have you any family you'd like me to phone? Maybe somebody to go in the ambulance with you?"

"My daughter is in Wythenshawe," she explained, "and she works Sunday mornings in a paper shop so she'll be busy, and my son is married with a family down in London. I have a sister here in Heaton Moor, but she's not too great herself."

"That's right," he said, remembering. "I take Communion out to her every month."

The young lady said, "A neighbour or a friend maybe?"

She shook her head. "Not on a Sunday morning. I wouldn't like to ask . . . I'll be grand on my own."

As she listened to the old lady trying so hard to be independent, it became clear to Maria that she actually had no one available to come and look after her. "I'll come in the ambulance with you," she offered.

Mrs Lowry's eyebrows shot up and before Mrs Flynn could reply she said, "No, no. It's very good of you, but you're too young, Maria. I'll go with her."

Maria felt slightly stung by the remark about her age but she said nothing. She knew the housekeeper meant no harm.

Mrs Lowry put her hand on Mrs Flynn's shoulder. "I just need to let them know back home, make a phone call. You see, I have a crowd coming for Sunday dinner later on and somebody will need to put the joint in the oven for me. I can see to the vegetables later."

"I could go," the nicely dressed lady said. "You sound busy at home and I've absolutely nothing on this morning, so it's no problem for me."

"Are you sure?" Mrs Lowry checked.

"I don't want to put anyone to any trouble," the elderly woman said.

"It's no problem, Mrs Flynn," the woman said smiling. "Honestly, I can go with you."

The priest rubbed his hands together. "Well, that's sorted that."

"What about poor Poppy?" Mrs Flynn said, her eyes filling up now. "She'll be wanting out to do her business soon."

Maria suddenly saw her chance to be helpful. "Do you want me to look after the dog?" she asked. "If you don't mind giving me your address and your key, I can see to her. In fact, I can keep her until we know you are okay. I love dogs and so does my dad, so he won't mind."

"Oh, that would be a weight off my mind if you could. She's tiny and no trouble and she loves company. She has tins of food and her lead and brushes and everything there in the kitchen on the shelf."

"I'll collect her now on my way home."

Tears came into the old woman's eyes. "Oh, thanks be to God! You're a little angel!" She looked up at the two women. "I feel much better now that I know Poppy will be looked after.

And she'll love having a young girl that has the energy to play with her."

The priest asked Maria if she had a phone number and, when she nodded, he said, "Maybe if you give Mrs Flynn your phone number, she could ring you when she gets home from the hospital and you could bring the dog back to her house?"

Maria smiled at him. "No problem."

"I have a pen and a bit of paper here," Mrs Lowry said, rummaging in her bag.

A siren sounded outside. The priest looked at the women. "I think that's the ambulance."

"Oh, no!" Mrs Flynn said, closing her eyes and shaking her head.

"I'll walk out and meet them," said the priest.

Maria quickly wrote down her address and phone number on the piece of paper and put it in the old lady's handbag.

There was a noise at the back of the church and then the ambulance men came in, carrying a stretcher between them. Within minutes, they had Mrs Flynn all settled and strapped on the bench in the ambulance. The other woman climbed in and sat opposite her. Mrs Lowry went up the steps and said a few words to her and when she came out Maria went in.

She bent down to the old lady and gently touched her hand. "You just get better and don't worry about your little dog. I'll look after her well."

"Most people haven't a kind word for youngsters these days," Mrs Flynn said, "but you're one of the good ones, and I didn't even get your name."

"It's Maria," she said.

"Well, Maria," Mrs Flynn said, "you're a credit to your mother and father, and they should be very proud of you."

"They should indeed," the other woman said. "If all the other youngsters were like you, the world would be a different place."

Maria caught her breath as she often did when people assumed she had two parents. But, she had learned by now it only embarrassed them to explain her mother was dead, so she just smiled and thanked them.

She came out of the ambulance and went to stand with Mrs Lowry while the men closed and bolted the doors. They both stood in silence until it went off, then they started walking down the road together.

"It's true," Mrs Lowry said, "what Mrs Flynn and the other one said about you being a good girl. And you made no issue of them thinking your mother was at home. A lot of girls your age would be all dramatic about it, but you've never been like that."

"Thanks," Maria said quietly.

"And although I know it's not easy for you at times, at least you know Leo has always done his best. He might take the odd drink too many, but he always makes sure you're looked after, and he does no one any harm."

For a moment, Maria wondered if she should confide in the housekeeper. Not to criticise her father, more explain she was worried about him. But something held her back. Her sense of responsibility and loyalty, and her appreciation of his love and dedication towards her, was too great.

She could not bring him down to someone else, not even their trusted housekeeper.

Chapter 17

Poppy was a sturdy little dog, with gold and white hair clipped short. She had barked ferociously when the key was put in the door of the two-up, two-down terraced house, making Maria very wary and wondering if she had made a mistake. But, when she opened the letterbox carefully and spoke softly to her, she could see the dog's tail wagging. She kept talking to her for a few minutes and, when the dog seemed to calm down, she decided to chance it and go in.

The dog jumped up and down for a few more minutes but, when Maria patted and stroked her, she eventually settled down.

Maria glanced around the small hallway and then went into the sitting room, which she thought was typical of an old lady's house, very tidy with only the necessary three-piece suite and a small coffee table and a television.

She went into the kitchen, Poppy at her heels, and saw the dog's basket on the floor with some toys in it, her food and water bowls nearby, and her food, lead and brushes on a shelf above. She found a shopping bag and put all the dog's requirements in it. The basket would have been awkward to carry so she just took the small cushion and blanket out of it and put them in the bag along with the other items.

She led Poppy outside and checked the house was safely

locked. Then she walked back home to Heaton Moor, Poppy trotting happily beside her.

Her father was upstairs in the bathroom when she got home, so she called up to him. "We have a visitor!"

When he came downstairs into the sitting room, Poppy started barking again and jumping backwards as she did so.

"Good God!" he said, looking from the barking dog to Maria. "What's all this?"

"We're looking after her," Maria said.

When the dog had quietened down and was busy sniffing at Leo's feet, she went on to explain about going to early Mass and Mrs Flynn, and all that had happened.

"And all this while I was peacefully sleeping!" he said, smiling at her. "From the way you describe Mrs Flynn, I don't think I know her . . . It was good of you to help her, Maria." He looked at the dog, which had gone over to lie by the fire. "Do you think you can manage?"

She told him that she had everything Poppy needed and she would let her out into the garden to do her business and take her for a walk when she came in from school.

"Well," he said, "in that case, I think it sounds as though we have got ourselves a little hairy friend for the moment."

Poppy took up residence with the Contis for over a month, during which time both Maria and her father got into a routine. In the mornings Leo took Poppy for a long walk and a run around the local park, and when he came back he fed her, and then Maria took her for another walk as soon as she came in from school. As the weeks went past, the weather softened and Maria began to really enjoy her daily walks with Poppy and looked forward to seeing her every evening when she came back to the house.

Then, all of a sudden spring was there, and cheery yellow-and-white daffodils and purple crocuses seemed to be everywhere. Michael Lowry was back in the garden, digging out dead bulbs and planting new seedlings, while Mrs Lowry kept reminding Maria, "Cast not a clout till May be out!", as she did every year, and saying more people caught flus and colds going into their summer things at the first sign of a spring sun.

On one of the first fine Saturdays, Leo drove Maria out to the stables to see the filly of whom he had such high hopes. Bella Maria was a beautiful, strong-looking animal, and Maria was relieved when the trainer and the other stable staff she met echoed her father's belief in the horse's wonderful abilities.

Not only had the weather changed, the pattern of Maria's weeks had also changed over the last few months. After discussions with her father, she had taken a long break from her ballet classes, explaining that she needed her evenings and weekends to study for her exams. The teacher was fine about it, and Maria said that she would probably be back in September, as fifth year was an easier one in school with no major exams. After the first few weeks of feeling strangely free on her usual ballet nights, she was surprised to find that, after all the years of attending the classes, that she didn't miss it one little bit.

Stella had complained bitterly about not having her company travelling, and leaving her on her own at the dance school. "It's awful, I've nobody to talk to at the ballet class and I'm stuck in the car with my mother coming and going. It's absolutely boring, boring, boring and awful!"

"But the other girls are very nice," Maria had pointed out. "You said you liked them, and we've often gone shopping with them and stayed at some of their houses."

"That was when we were younger – it's completely different now. I can't talk to them the way we talk about things like Tony and Paul, and they don't have the same sense of humour that you and I have."

"But you're the one with all the talent, Stella," she said. "The one who hopes to make a career out of dancing. I'm only average at it, and I don't enjoy it as much as I did when I was younger. And anyway, you should be concentrating on it – taking it seriously and not giving a damn about what I'm doing. You have to realise that we can't always do the same things. We're getting older, Stella, and the time will come when we have to find jobs and mix with other people. We'd be a bit sad if we were stuck together all the time like Tweedledum and Tweedledee!"

Stella had looked at her in annoyance, and then she had started to laugh. "You better come back to classes in September or I'll kill you!"

Her father seemed much happier and talked constantly about Bella Maria, even though she hadn't won any of her recent races, coming in second and third. He said that they were only warming-up races, and the race he really had high hopes for was the big one on Easter Monday. He went down to the training stables to watch her several afternoons a week and met up with Charlie Ford, the co-owner, for regular chats which gave Maria the impression that he wasn't spending as much time at the bookmaker's. He was also coming home earlier after work more often, which she thought indicated that he wasn't playing cards as often either.

When the phone call came to say that Mrs Flynn was back home, and now well enough to look after Poppy, both of them were reluctant to give her up, and Maria actually had tears in her eyes when she handed her over to Mrs Flynn.

"Oh, don't get upset, dear, you can come and visit Poppy anytime," the old lady said. "I'd give her to you, but I can't – she's a lifeline to me. To tell you the truth, she's the only reason I get up some mornings." She had kissed and cuddled the bundle of fur. "There are times when I think she's more human than me – she can almost talk to me. Did you find that too?"

Then, when Maria was going, she thanked her again and gave her a card in a sealed envelope, saying not to open it until she got home.

When Maria got home later, she opened the envelope and found a ten-pound gift voucher for a ladies' shop in Heaton Moor called Gladrags. It was a shop she rarely went into because it sold mainly older women's clothes and lingerie, but she had heard Stella saying that it had some nice bits and pieces in it recently. She thought the voucher was very generous, and put it safely in her dressing-table drawer to use the next time she saw something nice in the shop window.

She continued with her horse-riding lessons which she still enjoyed and travelled to with Stella, and of course it meant she saw Paul, who continued to be the main focus in her life apart from her father. They went out most Friday and Saturday nights to the pictures or to the dance halls in Stockport and occasionally Manchester, although none of the dances were ever as grand as the dinner dance in The Palace. Occasionally they went to one of the local hotels where Maria only drank lemonade, and Paul had only one or two drinks because he was driving and, as he often said, when it came to alcohol, he could take it or leave it.

Sometimes Stella and Tony joined them at the dance halls and, although Maria enjoyed Stella's company, she always felt awkward knowing that Stella's parents didn't know she was with Tony, and dreaded phone calls to the house from her mother wondering if she was with her. Tony had recently got a second-hand car – an old banger, Stella called it, when she was teasing him, but Maria thought she was actually proud of him for having it, and every chance they got they went for runs out to different places where no one would know them.

Paul was, Maria discovered, even more grown-up and sensible than she thought. He was concerned that she still hadn't decided what she wanted to do after leaving school and, every so often, brought the subject up.

Like her father, Paul had made suggestions such as working in a bank or an office, maybe book-keeping, a building society or even teaching. But nothing suggested so far had appealed to her. Just last weekend they had discussed it again when he was over at their house for Sunday lunch.

"The only problem is," Paul said, "you're going to be studying for your A-Levels after the summer and you need to know which ones to choose that will help with your career."

"I don't have to decide on my subjects until after the summer," Maria said, "because I won't have my results until August. If I fail any O-Levels I'll have to re-sit those, and then if I do hopefully pass some I'll have to decide which ones I might have a hope of passing at A-Level."

"English and Maths are always safe bets," he told her. "And a language is always a good choice."

"I hate Maths," she said. "I don't mind arithmetic, but I can't stand algebra and geometry."

"Well, stick to arithmetic," he advised. "It's the one you need for most jobs anyway." He paused, thinking, and then his eyes widened. "What about a travel agent's or something like that?"

Maria suddenly perked up. "That sounds a bit more interesting . . ." She smiled. "Yes, I think that could definitely be a possibility."

"Right," he said. "We'll find out exactly what you need for that."

A few days later Paul had turned up at their house armed with brochures and sheets of paper with notes. Then the two of them and her father, who was delighted to see Maria interested in something, spent some time going over the requirements of the job.

"'*Give advice on destinations*' – that would be easy enough," Paul said, reading from a brochure which had a section in it called 'A Day in the Life of a Travel Agent'. "'*Make arrangements for transportation, hotel accommodation, car rentals, tours, and recreation*'."

"That would be using the phone, and getting on well with people," Leo said. He laughed. "A bit like working in the restaurant."

"'*Advise on weather conditions, locations, restaurants, tourist attractions, and recreation,*'" Paul read. "I would think Geography would definitely come in there, and Maths would also be useful for things like currency exchange rates and discounts when you're dealing with international travellers."

Maria pulled a face. "I like Geography, but as I told you I'm not too keen on Maths,"

Paul smiled over at her. "Typing would also be a good skill."

"Yes," Maria said. "I was actually thinking of that for other jobs too. It would be useful for loads of things. Even though I've never done it before, one of my teachers said I could do it as an O-Level alongside my A-Levels. She said I could use any free periods to practise or even sit in with one of the other younger classes who've been doing it for a few years."

"You're keeping French on, aren't you?" Paul checked.

Maria nodded. "Yes, I'm not bad at it, and I definitely need a foreign language. I can speak a bit of Italian too, although I never took it as a subject in school. I picked it up over the years from Dad and Franco, and when I was on holiday in Italy."

"Yes, Maria," her father said, laughing, "you improve every time we visit Italy, then you forget when we come back home."

She laughed along with him. "When I'm older I'll learn it properly, I promise."

Leo was looking over Paul's shoulder and he started to report from the brochure now. "What about '*Visit hotels, resorts, and restaurants to evaluate comfort, cleanliness, and quality of food and service*'? You will have to send them to Leonardo's to sample Franco's excellent cooking, and see his lovely clean kitchen!"

They had all laughed and, as Maria watched her father clapping Paul on the back, she felt a bit emotional to see that her father and Paul got on so well.

After Leo went upstairs to the small office he had in the smaller, spare bedroom to sort out some papers, Maria sat down on the sofa beside Paul and gave him a hug. "Do you know something, Paul? I think you might be going into the wrong career yourself."

"What?" he said, a quizzical look on his face.

"You should be going into teaching."

"Teaching?" he repeated, not catching her drift.

"Well," she giggled, "I reckon I've learned far more from you this afternoon about career advice than I've ever learned from any of my teachers."

He gave her a sidelong grin and then his face became more solemn. "I love being here with you," he said. "I wish we could be like this every single day, not doing anything particularly special. Just spending every minute with each other."

She was now serious too. "So do I, Paul," she said. "So do I."

Chapter 18

Maria woke to sunshine on Easter Monday morning and to the sound of her father knocking on her bedroom door.

"Maria? I have your breakfast on a tray. Can I come in?" His voice was high and jovial.

"Just a second, Dad . . ." She stared around her, still disorientated from sleep . . . and then it hit her.

It was the day she was both excited about and dreading. Today was the day they were all going to York to watch Bella Maria's first big race – her father and all his friends including the Lowrys, herself, Paul, Stella and her parents, and Tony. And whilst Paul would be there as part of her father's group, his parents and all their friends would be there as well.

There were so many problems associated with the day out that she had lain awake until three o'clock in the morning worrying about it. What if her father drank too much and made a fool of himself? What if he laughed or even cried in front of Paul and his family? What if Stella's mother found out that Tony was going to be part of the group when Stella had been explicitly banned from seeing him again? What if Bella Maria came last and they were humiliated in front of everyone?

Just thinking about it made her breathless and made her feel that there was a metal band tightening around her head.

She sat up now, positioned her pillows behind her and then checked that her pyjama top was buttoned properly. "You can come in now!" she called.

Leo came in, well dressed as always, in a nice pin-striped suit and a red-and-navy tie, carrying a tray with two freshly made pancakes with her favourite toppings – one with maple syrup and the other with lemon and sugar. There was also a large mug of frothy coffee made with milk. The sight of the small vase on the tray with a single rosebud from the garden immediately reminded her of her mother as he had often done that for her when she was alive.

Leo placed the tray in front of her and then perched on the end of the bed. "This is going to be a wonderful day," he told her. "The sun is shining, Bella Maria is on top form, and I'm going to have my beautiful daughter on my arm as we walk into the owner's enclosure. We'll be mixing with all the top people in Manchester and drinking champagne and cheering our very own horse along as it wins the race. What more could we ask for? It's like a dream come true."

A lump formed in Maria's throat. "Dad . . . you won't get carried away and drink too much, will you?"

He shook his head and smiled. "Maria, you have nothing to worry about. Drinking champagne is like drinking water, it has no effect on me. And anyway, when have you seen me drink too much recently? Not since I got involved in the racing business. I just sip the odd whisky or glass of wine – nothing too much. I have too much responsibility now with Leonardo's and Bella Maria – and too much pride in myself to let you and all your nice friends down." His face suddenly became solemn. "I know there are times when I've had more than I should, but you know I hardly drank at all until your mother died, don't you? The grief of losing her nearly drove me mad and kept me awake night and day . . ."

Maria nodded, praying he wouldn't go into his usual long explanations as to why he had started drinking in the first place – reminding her of all the sadness and loss they had both gone through. One part of her wished now that she hadn't said anything, whilst the other part knew that if she had said nothing, he might think it was okay to drink as much as he liked.

"The only thing that helped me to sleep was a few glasses of wine but, when I realised it was overdoing it, I cut back." He took her hand, his eyes pleading now. "You know I drink very carefully now, Maria. You know I would never do anything to let you down. If you're very worried, I'll drink nothing at all today. Not even a drop of champagne when the others are all celebrating the day . . . I'll buy them as much drink as they want, but I won't touch it myself. I'm the sort of man who can take it or leave it. You only have to say the word and not a single drop of wine or any alcohol will pass my lips."

"But it's not for me to tell you what you can and cannot drink!" Having this same old pathetic conversation was agony. "And I don't want to spoil the day for you. Everyone else will be enjoying a drink and celebrating. I don't want you to feel any different from them."

Relief washed over his face and then he smiled. "Okay," he said, getting up from the bed now. "We'll agree that I have just a few drinks and leave it at that." He gestured towards her tray. "Now, eat up and drink your coffee and I'll go and run you a nice bath with bubbles."

"Thanks." Maria looked down at the pancakes he had so lovingly made, and wondered why her father couldn't be a normal, boring father like Stella's and Paul's.

Her clothes were all laid out for the occasion – a fabulous outfit her father had bought her from Kendals department store. When she was buying day-to-day stuff, she usually went with Stella, but this was so important that she and Leo made an afternoon of it, with lunch in a lovely restaurant across the road. Leo had joked and said it gave him an opportunity to check out the competition.

He had told her to take her time and had waited outside the changing room while she tried on several outfits that the assistant said she thought would look wonderful. In the end, one ensemble stood out above the rest – a lilac satin fitted dress four inches above the knee, with a matching edge-to-edge coat with one large sparkly purple button at the neck. She teamed the outfit with high purple patent T-bar shoes, a purple fascinator and a small bag covered in pink, lilac, purple and clear stones.

When she came out of the changing room wearing it, Leo had clapped his hands, saying, "This is it! You will be the best-dressed lady they've ever seen at the races." Then, he had to wipe his eyes as he felt so emotional looking at her. "*Mia bella, bella Maria*!" he had repeated in a low voice, over and over again.

On the way to York Maria sat in the back of the car with Stella and Franco's wife, Bernice, while the two men sat in the front. There was a feeling of excitement amongst the passengers with talk about the races and the sunny dry day that was forecast.

When the men drifted off into a conversation about horses that was too detailed for the females, they found much to discuss about the new clothes they had all bought for the day. Bernice, who was much more talkative and forthcoming to the girls than most women approaching forty, was also seeking reassurance that the new pageboy haircut she had got that morning wasn't too young or too short for her.

The girls, enjoying the way that Bernice treated them on an equal footing, told her she looked much younger with her new hairstyle and to never grow it long again. They also said they loved her wide-bottom navy velvet pants and the fashionable loose shirt she was wearing with a chain belt and a long black-stoned pendant. Bernice was thrilled with the compliments and Maria noticed that, in order to continue the discussion, she kept finding small details to criticise about herself which she knew the girls would vigorously argue against.

"I suppose I'm just worried," she told them, "that some other women my age who aren't very fashion-conscious might say that I'm trying to be too young." .

"Let them talk," Stella stated. "They're old fuddy-duddies who are behind the times. It's the Swinging Sixties and I think your outfit is so gorgeous that it would suit any age. I would definitely wear it and, if my mother was only modern enough, she would look nice in it too."

Bernice was quiet for a few minutes, and Maria thought Stella might have said the wrong thing when she said she would wear the same outfit, given that she was only sixteen. Bernice might well have thought that she was implying it was an outfit for teenagers, and therefore far too young for herself.

When Bernice leaned forward to talk to Franco and Leo, Stella turned to Maria and said in a low voice, "I can't wait to see Tony today. He's travelling with the Spencers, so my mother can't say a thing." She then thumbed in Bernice's direction and said in a low voice, "Pity my mother isn't as modern as her!"

Maria thought they had talked enough about Bernice and her clothes and that that it might be safer to move on to another subject. "What time are your parents setting off?" she asked.

"Soon, but they had to pick up my mum's friend, Diana, first." Stella halted, then took a deep breath. "And you don't need to worry," she whispered, making eyes in Leo's direction. "I've already warned her that you don't want any stupid matchmaking plans. She said she hadn't mentioned it to Diana so she doesn't even know anything about it."

"Good," Maria said. She folded her arms and smiled, and thought that it was one less thing to worry about today.

The racecourse car park was already busy when they arrived, so they had to park a good way back and walk in through the main gates. The two men led the way, while the girls walked behind with Bernice, watching all the other women and passing comment on the fashions. Bernice was relieved to notice that there were other women her age wearing similar outfits and some who were sporting more outrageous ensembles.

Leo and Franco went straight to the ticket office and sorted out race programmes for the day for everyone in the group. When they came back and gave Bernice and the two girls their programmes, they all turned to the page with details of Bella Maria's race and were delighted when they saw her name.

Maria could see the pride on her father's face, but she couldn't stop from saying, "We'll have a great day out whether she wins or not."

Her father held two crossed fingers up and said, "I have to go over to the stable area to meet with the trainers and Charlie, but

I'm sure you will all find something to keep you busy until the rest of our group arrive. There will be stalls selling drinks and things outside, but if it gets too cold there are plenty of places under cover. " He looked at Maria. "You have money for tea or something to eat, don't you?"

Maria assured him she had and so did Stella.

"I'll meet you later in the bar," he told them, giving a theatrical bow. "We have two tables booked in the restaurant for lunch at one o'clock for our own group, and some of our other friends will have their own tables there too. After that the betting will be open."

Franco threw his hands in the air. "And let us pray that Bella Maria is lucky today!" Then he laughed. "If she is lucky, we are all lucky!"

As they all joined in with the laughter, Maria wondered if she dared let herself think for one minute that her father's horse might win her first major race today. It just seemed to be too huge an accomplishment to expect from the horse so early on in its career, and one that had not had much luck in her recent races. She only hoped that her father wouldn't be too disappointed if the young filly came trailing in near the end.

Leo went off in one direction, disappearing into the crowds, and then Franco and Bernice told the girls they were going for a walk around to catch up with some of their friends and would see them in the bar later.

Stella put her arm through Maria's and they started to walk in the direction of the main buildings. "I'm glad the oldies have gone off and we're getting some time to ourselves." She started to giggle. "What did you think of Bernice's outfit? Do you think it's a bit young for her?"

Maria looked at Stella in surprise, after all the complimentary things she had said. "I thought she looked lovely, and you told her that she did as well."

"What else could I say?" Stella rolled her eyes. "She would look lovely if she lost a couple of stone. Didn't you notice how tight the trousers were on her thighs where her shirt didn't cover them? They are meant to be loose."

"Bernice is not *that* heavy," Maria told her, pretending to be more indignant than she really was, as she could see her friend was in one of her giggly moods when she exaggerated everything. "I think you're being really mean about her."

"Come on!" Stella laughed, squeezing her arm. "You're just being nice because she's your dad's friend's wife."

"You are just dreadful," Maria said, laughing along in spite of herself. "I thought the trousers looked fine on her, and the top comes down almost to her knees so you can't really see much of her thighs."

"She'll be okay if she keeps her coat on!"

"And you'll be okay if you keep your mouth shut!"

Then they both went into peals of laughter, falling against each other and making people look around to see who the skittish girls were.

Stella kept glancing back to the car-park area. "I just hope the Spencers' car arrives before my parents so I get a chance to see Tony for a bit."

"Will your mother mind you being with him today?" Maria asked.

"She minds me seeing him any day! But she can't really say anything if she just sees us chatting. I won't be able to act like his girlfriend – she'll go off at the deep end if she sees us holding hands or anything like that."

"You'll have to be careful then – we don't want anything to spoil the day."

"You are so lucky," Stella said. "I wish I was allowed to do all the things you get away with."

Maria raised her eyebrows and gave her a wry smile, but said nothing.

Paul and Tony arrived along with Paul's mother and father. Before Paul's parents went off with their friends, they came over to the girls to wish Bella Maria good luck.

"I'll keep an eye out for Leo," Paul's father said. "And in any case I'm sure we'll catch up with him later."

The four young people then wandered around. Tony, who was used to going to the racecourses was pleased to show them all the different function areas and the stand. Then, after a bit, they went into one of the marquees where they had soft drinks and sandwiches. They were having lunch later so Tony bought them all a lemonade, saying, "I suppose it's too early for the hard stuff," and they all laughed.

They were thinking of making a move when Maria noticed a brightly dressed figure coming towards them.

"Stella!" Jane Maxwell's voice was unmistakable.

"Oh, God, it's my mum!" Stella said. She looked over to where her mother stood at the door of the enclosure – a grim look on her face.

Maria noticed how Stella pinned a smile on her own face and waved back, obviously hoping Mrs Maxwell might just let things slide for once. That she might just go away.

"Hello, Maria, dear," Jane Maxwell said in a formal voice. She was exceptionally well-dressed for the Easter occasion, wearing a yellow woollen edge-to-edge coat with a matching pill-box hat which had a little black bow, and black shoes and gloves.

Maria smiled over. "Hello, Mrs Maxwell." Then, to make things seem more normal, she said, "Your coat and hat look lovely!"

"Thank you, dear. That's very kind of you." Jane Maxwell shifted her gaze to the boys. "Hello, Paul . . . hello, Tony."

They both said hello back in a polite and respectful manner, although Maria could see that Tony looked most uncomfortable.

Jane Maxwell turned back to her daughter. "Stella, your father and the others are outside. You were supposed to meet us at the ticket office when we arrived. We've been looking for you everywhere!"

Stella raised her eyebrows as though surprised, but didn't move. "Oh, sorry, I actually thought I was meeting you inside – I was just going to look for you now."

There was a tense silence in the group now, everyone picking up on the atmosphere.

Jane Maxwell folded her arms now, still waiting. "Can I have a private word, please?"

Stella turned to pick up her handbag from the chair behind.

"Come with me," she hissed to Maria. "She won't say as much if you're there. She won't want to show herself up."

Maria took a deep breath. "It might make it worse if I'm there." The last thing that she wanted was to be involved in an argument between Stella and her mother.

"Look! My mother is signalling to us *both*," Stella said. "Are you coming?"

"All right, oh God . . ." Maria muttered, turning back for her own bag. Then she said to Paul, "I hope I won't be long, but if we're not back soon then I'll catch you in the bar. That's where my dad said to meet him and Charlie and the others."

Tony touched Maria's arm as she passed. "Is there going to be trouble?"

"I sincerely hope not."

"I wish I was old enough to leave home," Stella said as they walked to the door.

"Don't be so dramatic," Maria told her. "It won't be that bad."

"You don't know the half of it. My mother tries to control every single thing I do – what I wear, what I eat, who I see – it's endless."

When they got outside, Stella's mother was standing, still wearing a grim look on her face. She walked on a few yards until they were in a quiet area just outside the ladies' room and away from the bars.

"Well, Stella," she said, "it would appear that your father has gone off with the other men, and I'm now going to have to trail around the racecourse looking for him. This is a bad start to a day we were all looking forward to."

"You don't have to make such a big issue of everything," Stella said.

"I am not going to pretend in front of Maria that I'm happy when I'm not. You promised your father and me that you would behave properly today, and here you are already going your own sweet way."

Stella, a steely, resigned look on her face, sighed and then folded her arms, her gaze fixed far above her mother's head. "All the other young people here are allowed to mix together. I don't know why I have to be different."

Mrs Maxwell looked over at Maria. "I'm sorry you have to witness this, but you obviously know what's going on. Stella assured her father and me that she would have nothing more to do with that fellow, Tony, and I've just walked into the room and there is Stella, mooning all over him once again."

"I wasn't *mooning* over him," Stella snapped. "I like Tony and everyone else thinks he is a very nice person. And, at nearly sixteen years old, I think I'm old enough to choose my own friends. Maria's father trusts her to make her own judgements on people, and I don't know why you and Dad can't do the same with me."

Maria kept gazing straight ahead, not wishing to be dragged into the argument.

Her mother gave a little, sarcastic laugh. "Oh, Stella, please don't act as though your father and I are complete imbeciles. It's perfectly obvious that you see Tony as . . . more than just a friend. And apart from the fact that he's totally unsuitable, it's obvious to anyone with an eye in their head that you're throwing yourself at him."

"I'm not going to stand here and listen to this!" Stella said. "Everyone else can see that Tony is a really nice boy – it's just that you're a complete snob! You think he's not good enough because he's not from a professional or moneyed background. That's all you and Dad think matters."

Maria felt her heart sink. This was the last thing she needed.

"Maria," Jane Maxwell said, "maybe Stella will listen to you. Please try and talk some sense into her. We really don't want the day spoiled with all this carry-on."

Maria looked over at her friend and then at her mother. "Maybe it would be best if you sort it out privately when you get home later on?"

"But we have to get through today," Jane said, "and it's going to be very difficult if Stella keeps on acting like this."

Stella walked off into the ladies', and Maria and Jane followed her.

A short while later, when Maria was washing her hands, a

whispered argument started up again between mother and daughter. Maria went over the mirror to reapply her lipstick, and pretend she couldn't hear them.

The tapping of stiletto heels coming along the corridor to the ladies' sounded and without a word everyone went back to washing or drying hands or checking make-up in the mirror.

"So sorry I got sidetracked, Jane," a lady's voice said. "I met an old customer."

Maria glanced in the mirror but could only see the side of the woman's face. Even though she wasn't looking forward to meeting her, at least the row between Stella and her mother was unlikely to continue now that Jane's friend had arrived.

"Oh, Maria," Jane said in a high, gushing tone, "I'd like you to meet my friend, Diana! She owns Gladrags, the lovely ladies' shop in Heaton Moor. I'm sure you must know it."

Maria sucked in her breath and then turned around, and was completely surprised when she saw who it was.

"You're the same Maria!" the woman said, equally surprised. "I don't believe it! You're the girl who looked after Mrs Flynn's little dog!"

"And you're the lady from the church! The one who went in the ambulance that morning with Mrs Flynn!"

Diana was actually beaming now. "Well, I must say I'm delighted to meet up with you – and here in York of all places! I've been thinking about you on and off for weeks and hoping I'd see you at Mass again."

"I don't normally go to that early Mass. I wondered about you, too." Then, in spite of her intentions to be cool and distant with Mrs Maxwell's friend, she found herself smiling warmly back. There was simply nothing else she could do in the company of this very nice, friendly woman

"Who would believe it?" Diana said, laughing now.

Jane Maxwell looked from one to the other. "So you two have met before?"

"Yes," Diana said, "in church, but we weren't properly introduced."

Between them both, they relayed the story about Mrs Flynn

and Poppy, and Diana then went on to ask Maria how she had managed with the dog. Maria explained how she had loved having Poppy so much that she had decided if she ever had a dog in the future it would be the same breed, a little Shih Tzu.

She then went on to ask how poor Mrs Flynn had coped when she first arrived at hospital and whether Diana knew how she was now. She explained that she had visited her once to see Poppy, but didn't want to go back because she felt the poor dog got all confused, constantly running from her to Mrs Flynn and back. And Mrs Flynn had seemed a bit put out when the dog jumped up and stayed on Maria's knee.

"I've been to see her several times. They were worried because she had broken her hip, but thankfully it was only a small fracture and some fairly bad bruises. She's recovering well – she's a great old lady."

"I felt really sorry for her," Maria said,

"Did you know about all this, Stella?" her mother said. "I don't remember you telling me anything about it."

"I told you Maria was looking after a dog for an old woman," Stella said defensively. "You don't always listen properly."

"Well, I just presumed it was a neighbour. I didn't know about all the drama in the church." She looked back at Diana. "I don't remember you mentioning it at the time, although I'm sure you would have told me."

"Didn't I?" Diana said. "I suppose it's one of those stories that you tell immediately to several people after it's happened, and then you forget about it. Amazing, isn't it though, the coincidence of me meeting Maria here?"

"I don't know if you remember me telling you about Leo, the friend who owns the racehorse? The reason we're all actually here today. Well, Maria is his daughter. She's taken her father's Italian good looks."

"Yes, I do of course remember you mentioning him a few times." Diana's face gave nothing away. She turned to Maria. "You must be really excited being here today to watch your father's horse."

Maria nodded her head. "Yes, yes . . . although I hope

nobody puts too much money on her, as we can't be sure she's going to actually win the race." Her gaze met Diana's and she lowered her eyes quickly as she suddenly felt as though Diana knew what she was thinking.

When they came outside, Maria spotted Stella and her mother walking ahead in a deep discussion, so she hung back a bit to let them talk on their own. As they went along, she naturally fell into step with Diana, who chatted away, asking her about school and her riding lessons.

Then, Maria asked Diana about her shop. "I've been in it a few times, but I don't think you ever served me."

Diana explained she wasn't there all the time and that she had two other girls who helped her.

"Actually," Maria suddenly remembered, "I have a voucher for the shop. Mrs Flynn gave me it for looking after Poppy."

"Did she?" Diana said, smiling. "Wasn't that kind of her? She must have asked someone to buy it for her, because I didn't sell it to her. I don't think she's fit enough to walk to the shop yet anyway, so maybe a neighbour or a friend got it for her."

"It was very generous," Maria said. "I must come into the shop and pick something."

"Do," Diana told her. "I'm sure you'll find something you like. I'm beginning to cater now for younger customers than before."

As they walked along, it dawned on Maria that Diana might know nothing at all about Mrs Maxwell's matchmaking plan with her father and that, if she did, she might well be as embarrassed about it as Maria was.

Diana then slowed down, and indicated Stella. "I think you and I might now find ourselves in an awkward situation."

Maria looked at her.

"Jane and Stella. They're clearly at loggerheads over this boy Tony that Stella is seeing."

There was no point in denying it, but neither did she want to be disloyal to her friend, so Maria just shrugged and nodded.

"It can't be easy for you being caught in the middle."

"I usually try to avoid it," Maria admitted. "But there are times, like today, when it gets a bit much."

"I normally wouldn't talk about Jane to anyone, but I know you know the Maxwells much longer than me. I know today should be a special day for you with your father's horse racing, and I really hope they don't make it awkward for you."

Maria looked at Diana now, and something made her feel that it was okay to confide in her. She had seen how kind and understanding she was that Sunday in the church and, after all, it was Diana who had brought the subject of Stella and her mother up.

"It is awkward," she confessed, "because I'm seeing Paul, one of the boys from the riding school – his parents actually own the stables – and Tony is one of the riding instructors. They're both here today – they came with Paul's parents."

"Oh dear, that is rather awkward for you! And do you think that Jane feels you're encouraging the romance or giving Stella an alibi or anything like that?" She quickly added, "Not that Jane has suggested anything like that – I'm just trying to work it out."

"I hope she doesn't blame me for anything," Maria said, "because I don't really know Tony that well, and Paul is only friendly with him through work. But I do know that Stella likes the four of us going around together because she thinks her parents won't mind as much."

"I know her mother thinks you're a good influence on her." Diana smiled. "And I think from the short time we've spent together that I agree."

Maria's face brightened up at the compliment. "Well, that's very nice of you to say . . ."

"Confidentially," Diana said, touching her elbow, "I think Jane and Stella are very similar, both strong-minded, and that's why they clash so much." She paused. "Do you think her father is as set against Tony?"

Maria shrugged. "I really don't know. I think he will probably agree with Stella's mother."

Eventually Stella and her mother, both wearing grim faces, came back to join them and they all walked over to the bar area where they thought the men might have gathered by now.

Chapter 19

It was decided by Stella's mother that the ladies should sit together for lunch at one table, while the men would sit at the other. When it was announced, Diana caught Maria's eye and she raised her eyebrows. Maria presumed that she thought the same as herself – that Jane Maxwell had decided on the separate tables to ensure that Stella and Tony did not get the chance to sit together.

Maria was very grateful to have Bernice and Diana and Charlie Ford's wife, Helen, seated with her, as the tension between Stella and her mother continued all through the meal. Stella, she noticed, ate very little, instead pushing her Chicken Supreme and vegetables around her plate with her fork and every now and again taking the odd tiny mouthful.

At one point Maria overheard her mother saying, "Is there actually something wrong with your meal? Is it not hot enough? Do you want me to call one of the waiters to bring you something else?"

Stella had just shrugged and said, "I ate too much at breakfast and I'm not hungry."

"Well," her mother said, "you're going to be on your feet most of the afternoon and we don't want you getting weak and fainting again."

"That was because of my period," Stella said in a low, tense voice. "Now, can you leave me alone and stop going on at me in a public place, please?"

Maria was surprised on hearing about the fainting, as Stella had not mentioned anything about it to her.

Afterwards, when they moved into the Premier Enclosure, the men and the women all started to mingle together and Paul and Tony came to join them. At first Stella was very subdued and kept close to Maria but, after Leo came over to discuss the racing programme with them and to make sure the girls understood the betting, she perked up a little. Then, when Charlie Ford came over to chat and bought them all a glass of white wine, which Stella downed in two mouthfuls, she seemed to regain some of her usual bounce.

Bella Maria would be in the sixth race, the second-last race of the day. Maria wasn't sure if it was better or worse waiting through all the other races until theirs came up. She supposed that if the filly was in an early race and lost badly, then it would cast a cloud over the rest of the day. On the other hand, if she had been in one of the early races and won, or was even placed in the first three runners, it would lift things and let her relax and enjoy the remainder of the races.

Paul helped take her mind off the impending race by getting her to watch all that was going on around them and, to her surprise, so did Diana Freeman.

When they first went into the bar Maria was chatting to Diana when her father came in and she introduced them. He shook Diana's hand and was about to walk away when Maria told him that Diana was the lovely lady who had looked after Mrs Flynn in church that day. Then, although he was distracted with all the racing things going on around him, he had stayed for twenty minutes chatting to her.

"He's a very nice man," Diana said after he left, smiling at Maria.

"He is," Maria said, "and he's a fantastic father as well." She said nothing more, but it came into her mind several times afterwards that her father and Diana Freeman would make a very nice, good-looking couple.

Paul and Tony decided on their bets and helped the girls choose theirs for the first race and they all walked down the few grassy yards from the enclosure to stand at the fence to get a close view.

The races were surprisingly short – some only a couple of minutes – but Maria was surprised at how exciting they were. Stella kept shrieking and jumping up and down and grabbing people's arms any time a horse she had bet on overtook another one. Her mother came back and forward to them a few times, during which visits Tony diplomatically kept his distance from her. After a while, Jane Maxwell just stayed with the older group and Maria sensed that she had given up her policing of Stella either because she'd had enough of it and decided to enjoy her own day, or because her husband had told her to stop making a show of herself and Stella.

There was an air of tension mixed with excitement when the sixth race was due. Instructions were being relayed over the Tannoy about the five-furlong flat race, and people were rushing over to the counters to place last-minute bets, while others were distributing betting slips to other members of their groups.

Maria went over to her father and Charlie Ford and wished them both good luck, and she could hear a breathlessness in her father's voice and see that his movements had quickened and got more jerky, which she knew indicated that he was anxious. Her heart went out to him and she said numerous silent prayers that he would be able to cope without embarrassing them both, if and more likely *when* his filly trailed in after the winners.

A short while later the fillies were under starter's orders. A hush came over the place and people got their binoculars out, checking they were on the right setting. Then, there was a collective gasp of excitement and the horses were off, and the place was filled with noise and chatter again. Groups of people once again set off through the glass doors to cross the grass down to the fence to get a better view.

Maria stood outside, clutching Paul's arm, both of them listening as the commentators gave the numbers and jersey colours of each filly. Bella Maria's jockey, Frankie Kelly, was in blue-and-yellow stripes and yellow cap and carried the number 3. After a minute or so, Stella came rushing up asking if anyone knew what was happening and if they could see the horses in the distance.

Then, Charlie Ford let a roar out of him and shouted that Bella Maria was in fourth place and moving up, and Maria did not know if that was good or bad at that stage. Seconds later the horses went thundering towards the finishing line.

"She's moved into second now!" Tony suddenly shouted, and started jumping up and down.

Her father and Charlie and the other men were in rapt, silent concentration as they watched through their binoculars and then the race ended and the noise fell again as they waited on the commentator's verdict. The muffled announcement came and there was a moment before any reaction then suddenly the greatest roar went up from their group.

Maria turned to look at her father and her stomach somersaulted when she saw him standing with his hands over his eyes and she knew he was crying, and then she looked at Paul who was just standing there as though in shock. She closed her eyes. She could not bear it.

Please God, she prayed, *please God, let it not be a total disaster! Please let her at least get placed!*

"What happened?" she shouted over the noise, grabbing Paul's arm again. "What place did she come in?"

He turned to look at her with stunned eyes. "First!" he exclaimed. "Bella Maria came in first! She won the race!"

Maria opened her mouth to speak but was so shocked that nothing came out. She then moved towards her father just as he started moving towards her, both with tears running down their faces.

"She won, Maria! She won!" He threw his arms around her, lifted her up in the air, and twirled her round and round.

Maria hugged him tightly, unable to remember feeling so happy, and so very relieved, in a long, long time.

After the group had finished hugging and congratulating, they all followed an elated Leo and Charlie down to the winner's enclosure to congratulate the jockey and the trainer. Then the champagne bottles and the glasses were brought out and Bella Maria and the jockey were toasted. Then Leo and Charlie were toasted. Maria drank one glass and then it was refilled and when she looked again it was empty and she was hardly aware of having drunk it.

Everyone was heading back to the bar when Leo came over to Maria and Paul, and after excusing himself to Paul, he took his daughter's hand in his and led her away.

"Come with me, Maria," he said. "This is the happiest day we've had in years and I want you beside me because we're going to celebrate in style. This is the start of big things in our life – bigger things and better things!"

"Where are we going?" Maria asked.

"We are going into the racecourse office to use their phone," he told her. "To make all the necessary arrangements."

"Arrangements for what?"

He squeezed her hand so tightly it hurt and made her wonder how much he had drunk when she wasn't with him. "For a little party back at the restaurant. This is our great moment. This is our chance to show thanks that a poor Italian man from a simple family has done as well as I have. I want to share my good luck with all the kind friends who came with us today, and who would have been there to console us if Bella Maria had not won. This is the kind of moment I have waited for all my life." He gestured back towards the racecourse where Stella and Paul and all the others were still drinking and chatting and celebrating their wins.

When they reached the racecourse office Leo told Maria to wait for a few minutes, while he went in and had a quick word with the man and woman inside. While she was waiting, her mind went back to the conversation she'd had with Diana.

He then beckoned her to join him and she went in silently while he phoned the restaurant to check that Vincent and Johnny could stay on after the last customers had left, and to ask them to prepare some finger food for his guests.

"There will be about thirty people," he told Vincent, "and I would be very happy if you could have some plates of cold meats and some bread – and maybe some slices of pizza and focaccia bread and bruschetta." He winked at Maria. "And also, if you could have a table with nicely polished champagne glasses. And Vincent – tell Johnny I will pay you both double time for the extra hours and I'll pay for a taxi back home." Johnny must have said something funny then because Leo laughed and said, "I don't care what you do tomorrow, as long as everything is okay tonight!"

He came off the phone and whirled Maria around in a little waltz. "We are winning!" he told her. "At last – we are winning!"

As they danced around, Maria suddenly felt the same elation as she did when she'd heard their horse had been first across the finishing line. And, as she looked into her father's shining brown eyes, she realised she believed in him. She believed in him all over again. He had proved that Bella Maria was a winner – which meant that her father was a winner again too!

When they went back to the enclosure Leo told their group that there would be a party back at Leonardo's to celebrate Bella Maria's first big winning race and everyone cheered. Once again, Maria's heart soared as she watched her father receiving claps on the back from Franco and Stella's father and, even more importantly, Mr and Mrs Spencer. There was much discussion as the various groups got together to organise lifts back to the restaurant. Maria was delighted when Paul came over and put his arm around her and asked her to travel back in the car with him and his parents.

"It's great going back to the restaurant for a party and I'm really looking forward to being with you."

"Is Tony coming too?"

Paul shrugged. "He's chatting to some lads he knows from another stable, and I heard them asking him if he wanted to go for a drink with them."

When she checked with her father about travelling with the Spencers, he waved her away, nodding and smiling. He was happy and she knew that he and Franco and their friends would be discussing the race and analysing every move Bella Maria had made.

Stella came over to Maria and whispered in her ear. "Can we go into the ladies'? I need to talk to you in private."

Maria's heart sank a little. This couldn't be good. "What's wrong?"

"Two things," Stella said, propelling her across the room, "and I'll tell you when we get there."

When they closed the door of the ladies' behind them, Maria turned towards her friend. "What is it? What's going on?"

"Can you ask Paul to ask his parents to give Tony a lift back to the restaurant?" Stella joined her hands together as though praying. "I really, really want him to come, and if the Spencers bring him then my mum won't be able to say a thing."

Her friend looked so desperate that Maria had no option. "Okay. I can't promise you that they'll do it, but I'll ask Paul."

Stella hugged her. "Oh, thanks, thanks!"

"What's the other thing?"

"I don't want you to be annoyed with me after what you said last week."

"What do you mean?"

"Diana. My mum has asked her to come back to the restaurant and –"

Maria cut her off. "It's okay, I don't mind if she comes."

Stella's eyebrows shot up.

"She's a very nice woman. I liked her the minute I met her in the church weeks back and then, when I was speaking to her earlier on, I still liked her. In fact, I wouldn't have a problem if my dad did go out on a date with her."

"Well . . ." Stella said, looking really taken aback, "that's surely a big change."

Maria shrugged. "It's funny how it turned out, and it made me think. It's not fair for me to make decisions about my father's life. If he wants to be friends with someone then that's up to him."

"I'm glad to hear you say that, because he's been really great about you and Paul." Stella's eyes suddenly filled up. "Your dad has always been great. You are so lucky. I wish my parents were as understanding . . . at times it's hell in our house."

Maria felt sorry for her friend and went over and put her arms around her. "Give them time. When they see you are both really serious and grown-up about it all, then they might change their minds."

Stella shook her head. "Not my mother. I didn't get a chance to tell you yet – in fact, I couldn't face talking about it. When she asked if Tony was going to the races and I told her that he was, she said she wasn't going and there was a big row between her and my father. To keep the peace between them she eventually agreed to go, but later she came up to my bedroom and said I was the cause of all the trouble in the house. She said I was spoiled and that if I kept going the way I was I'd come to a bad end. Can you believe that? Imagine a mother saying that to her daughter."

Maria squeezed her arm. "I'm sure she didn't mean it. She was probably just annoyed."

"Oh, she meant it all right. She said she wished she had sent me to boarding school so that I would have learned the difference between the right kind of people and the wrong kind. Thank God she likes you and doesn't want to upset your dad, or I'm sure she would stop me going to riding lessons because of Tony." She rolled her eyes and made a snuffling sort of noise. "She said she wished I had half your brains and had got myself a nice boy from a decent family like Paul Spencer." She started to laugh then. "And don't ask – yes, she did say James Granger as well!"

Maria didn't know whether it was a good thing that Mrs Maxwell liked her. She was grateful for being accepted – but it made her feel responsible for Stella in a way. The door opened now and two women came in, so the girls moved back out into the main area.

"Are you okay?" Maria checked.

"Yes, but will you go now and ask Paul about giving Tony a lift now before it's too late?"

"Okay . . . but maybe it's pushing things with your mum. Maybe it would be better if Tony went home."

"I want him to come. I want my mother to see how he and

160

Paul are such good friends and I want her to see how well Tony gets on with the Spencers too."

Stella obviously had no idea that Paul only thought of Tony as a workmate, and Maria knew that she couldn't tell her that. As they walked back to meet the others, she thought how complicated things were becoming.

It was almost ten o'clock when all the cars arrived outside Leonardo's and, as the groups walked up the cobbled street towards the restaurant, Maria felt a sense of pride when she heard those who hadn't been in it before saying how lovely and cosy and welcoming it looked. As she reached the door she smiled when she heard Grieg's 'Morning', one of her favourite pieces of music, playing. When they arrived inside, the tables had been relaid after the customers had gone, with fresh red-and-white tablecloths and flowers and new candles, and everything looked perfect.

It struck her it was early for people to be gone, but she guessed that her father had not taken any late bookings that night on purpose since Franco had the bank holiday off for the races, and the customers usually asked if he was on when they made their table reservations. She also thought that he might well have been hoping that they would all be coming back for a private celebration, and it would be easier to organise if the restaurant was empty.

As soon as people's coats were off and they were all sitting at tables or standing around chatting, Franco and Johnny and Vincent appeared with bottles of sparkling wine and once again Leo's win at the races was toasted. The Spencers arrived with Paul and Tony and came to stand with Maria and Stella. The Maxwells were over at a corner table with Diana and another couple, but Maria kept her gaze away from them, while Stella stood with her back to them.

The platters of food were brought out to much discussion and, after the trip back from York, most people were happily filling their plates.

"It's an amazing place," Mrs Spencer said, "and the food is

wonderful." She smiled at her husband. "I think Leo's personality just shines through in this place."

People moved around and when Maria was talking to her father on her own again, she said. "Isn't that a lovely woman with Stella's parents? The one I met that day in the church."

"Yes," he said, looking across at Diana. "She is very nice."

"She's very attractive, don't you think? And her hair is such a lovely reddish colour."

Her father looked thoughtful. "Yes, she is a lovely woman and beautifully dressed."

"And she is so easy to talk to, and seems very intelligent. She has her own businesses, you know. She owns Gladrags on Heaton Moor Road – the one Mrs Flynn gave me the voucher for – and another shop in Didsbury."

"Really?" he said. "She certainly sounds like a clever woman."

"I know she came with Stella's mum, but she's not like her. They just met because Mrs Maxwell goes into the shop." She stopped for a moment, and then she looked him in the eye. "She's single too, never been married. Do you know, Dad, I think you and Diana would have a lot in common."

He looked astounded. He took her by the arm over to a quieter space. "Maria . . . what are you saying?"

"I'm saying that I think that if you like her, you should maybe ask her out."

"But you know . . ." he shrugged, "you know that I haven't really been involved with any women since your mother died."

"Well," Maria said, "that was a long time ago, and I was just thinking recently that it might be nice if you did." She smiled. "And I must confess, I started to think it when I met Diana."

He suddenly smiled. "You know something? Maybe I might just go over and talk to her now. Nothing too serious – just see how we get on."

She went back to join Paul, Stella and Tony.

"What do you think of this one?" Tony said, gesturing with his wineglass towards Stella.

Maria was puzzled.

"She hasn't touched a bite since we came in!" he said.

"Everyone else is tucking into the fantastic food and Stella says she's not hungry." He shook his head. "Don't you think she could do with a bit of meat on her bones?"

Stella pulled a face at him. "Be quiet, you!" she said, "I get enough nagging from my mother about food without you adding to it."

Tony started to laugh just a little too loudly and it suddenly occurred to Maria, when she really looked at him, that he had drunk a bit too much wine.

It was during a lull in the music – as Johnny was changing one record on the player for another – when Maria heard the first shouts outside the restaurant. At first she thought it was teenagers carrying on, but then she heard a louder scream which stopped her in her tracks. She looked at Paul and saw him frowning and she knew he had heard it too.

A sense of responsibility about something bad happening outside her father's restaurant washed over her, and she told Paul she was just going to have a word with her father. He and Franco were in a circle of Italian men who were listening as Paul's father was regaling them with one of his famous horseracing stories. As she moved towards him she heard the shouts again.

She tipped Leo on the elbow. "I think there's something going on in the street outside. There's been a lot of shouting and screaming."

"Is there?" His face looked very serious. "Okay, we'll go out and check it now." Leo stepped close to Franco and said something into his ear, and then both men moved quickly towards the door.

Maria went back to the others and joined in with the chat. She noticed that Stella's gaze kept darting across the restaurant to where her parents were sitting to see if her mother was still keeping an eye on her. Her own gaze moved over to Mrs Maxwell's friend and, when Diana caught her eye and gave her a big cheery smile, Maria wondered if her father had spoken to her as he had said he would.

A few minutes went by and, when Paul went to the gents', Maria said she was just going to have a word with her father and would be back in a minute. She went out the front door and into the cobbled street. Thankfully, the noise had all died down. She walked a few yards and then she could see her father and Franco further down the street talking to Timothy. Even from a distance, and although he was talking quietly, she could tell by his gestures that the tall, bulky man was upset.

"Is everything okay?" she called.

Her father waved a hand at her. "It's all sorted! You go back to the restaurant and we will be in with you soon!"

Timothy moved out to see who it was. He smiled when he saw her and raised his arm. "Hello, Maria! I haven't seen you for a while. Are you keeping well?"

Maria smiled back at him. "I'm very well, thanks."

"Good, good." He held his shopping bag up for her to see. "I was just out at the chip shop for our supper. My mother's not eating too well at the minute, so I thought a bit of fish and a few chips might perk her up."

"Good idea," Maria said. She gestured back towards the restaurant. "I'll leave you all to it and head back inside."

Maria went back to join her friends and then a few minutes later Leo came in on his own.

She went over to him. "Is everything okay? Where's Franco?"

He was smiling but she could tell by his eyes that something was wrong. "Everything is under control," he said in a low voice. "And Franco is fine – he came in by the back door."

Maria nodded. "What was it all about?"

He shrugged. "It was some stupid teenagers thinking it was funny to tease poor Timothy and steal his fish and chips from him. Franco and I had to chase them away and threaten to call the police. We then had to check that he was okay walking back home."

Maria shook her head. "That's awful."

Paul's father came towards them now, and they stopped talking.

"Tell me, Leo," he said, beaming at them both, "when does Bella Maria run next? It's one race I don't want to miss. She's the freshest little filly I've seen in a long time."

"Ah, thank you," Leo said, taking his hand and shaking it. "Praise from such a man as yourself is praise indeed!"

Maria left them chatting and was just going back to join Paul and Tony and Stella when she noticed Franco hadn't returned to join the party. She went towards the swing door at the back of the bar which led into the kitchen. As she did so, Johnny, came out.

"It's okay," he said quietly. "We have sorted him out in the back."

"Is something wrong?"

He nodded. "He has a bad graze on his hand, so Vincent and I got the First Aid box out and cleaned his hand and bandaged it up for him."

"How did that happen?"

Johnny's eyes moved around to check that no one could hear them. "One of the thugs pushed him up against the wall and Franco hit him back, and then there was a bit of a fight."

Maria's stomach churned. "Oh God! I had no idea it was so serious. Dad said that it had all been sorted and I thought it was just silliness. Is Franco okay?"

"Oh, yeah," Johnny said. "It's bad-looking but it's only surface stuff. Franco said your dad sorted it all out in the end. Two of them tried to take Leo on, but he squared up to them and soon sent them running."

"My dad?" Maria said. "But I was talking to him a few minutes ago and he didn't say it was as serious as that." She turned to look back and could see her father laughing and chatting with Mr and Mrs Spencer, the Maxwells and Diana. It then occurred to her that her father would do exactly that, even if something serious had happened, so as not to spoil the night for anyone else. He had often talked about how your staff must put their best foot forward when it came to serving the public. And that if even if the kitchen was on fire the staff must always act calmly, as though everything was perfectly okay.

Chapter 20

Diana towel-dried her hair and then pulled on her dressing-gown and went downstairs to make coffee and toast. She got a plate and knife from the cupboard and then went to the fridge for butter, thinking how markedly her life had changed in the last few months. And for the better. How different her mornings were, knowing she had Leo to look forward to at some point in the day – whether it was a phone call, or a night out at the cinema, or him just calling round to the house for a chat and a glass of wine in front of the fire. Ordinary things were now events and something worth looking forward to and talking about later.

And, by some small miracle, the handsome, kind, interesting Leo Conti seemed to feel exactly the same way about her. He told her that he looked forward to things unfolding every day, instead of planning to fill all the little empty gaps between work and Maria by joining friends for drinks or late-night card games . . . Maria, who he candidly admitted needed her father less and less.

"She has school, friends, horse-riding, and now a real boyfriend to take up most of her time," he had confided in Diana when they sat chatting for hours in her place after their first date together. "And of course that is the way it should be. I am not complaining, it is the natural order of things. I left Italy and my parents when I wasn't much older than Maria. I have been a father and a mother to her since she was a young girl, and Mrs Lowry became her second mother and the restaurant became her second home. Between all those things, we tried to fill the big empty gap that Anna left. Of course we all knew that it couldn't really happen, but we did our best and Maria is as good as any girl her age."

"Oh, she certainly is," Diana said earnestly. "She is not only as good as but much better than any girls I know."

"Thank you, but I have to realise that she now does not need me so much. I must be there for her and look after her for another few years until she is fully independent, but I must help her learn to live her own life."

Since then, they had spent any evenings that Leo had off together. If Maria was out, they went to the cinema or theatre, or he came to her place for a drink or something to eat. And, if Maria was in, sometimes Diana came up to sit with her for an hour in the evenings, maybe watching television or discussing magazines, music or fashion. Maria often popped into Gladrags on Saturday mornings for a browse and a chat. Mrs Flynn's voucher had been spent a while back, but it had introduced her to the rails of dresses and tops that Diana had sourced for her younger customers. On a couple of occasions when he was not working, Leo had made supper for the three of them, and, when it was Maria's birthday, Leo treated the three of them, plus Paul, to a show in Manchester. And, recently, he asked Diana to come and join him mid-week for a late supper at the restaurant. All so very, very different from the routines they had before meeting each other.

And each time they met up, they had confided more and more in each other. Diana had listened carefully when Leo confessed about his late-night drinking and the card games after work. And, although it had concerned her, she told him that altering his routine and finding different things to do at that time was the only answer.

She had not been coy, and had said, "I'm very happy to spend as much of that time with you as you want, Leo." Then, she had looked him straight in the eye. "But, if it doesn't work out between us over the long term, I would advise you to find someone else to spend your time with, otherwise the drinking and the gambling will become the replacement for a real life."

"I know, I know," he had said. Then he had reached for her hand. "These past few weeks I have been doing a lot of thinking, and I realise that I have been travelling down the wrong path since Anna died – and a lot of the time I have been travelling alone. And I cannot blame anyone else, because I had good friends who told me this and I would not listen." He shook his head. "Even poor Maria. I feel very guilty about her because she has worried so much about me, although I think she knows deep down that I meant no harm. She knows I would give my life for her."

"Oh, Leo," Diana said, "Maria worships the ground you walk on, and she is happy as long as you are okay."

"And I am determined now to be okay," Leo had said. "For Maria . . . and for you."

Diana now brought her tea and toast over to the small kitchen table, to have it while checking her latest stock orders which she hoped would be delivered today or tomorrow. She had ordered from her usual places in Manchester which supplied the popular safe women's lines in dresses, skirts and blouses, plus underwear and nightwear. She was particularly excited about a completely new line of clothing she had ordered as she hoped it would broaden her range of buyers. She had discovered it when she was visiting her cousin, Nigel, in Newcastle, when she and his wife Clarissa had gone shopping together.

The visits to her cousin served several purposes. First, they filled otherwise empty weekends and, secondly, one of her favourite department stores – Fenwicks – was in Newcastle. On her last visit, just after she had started seeing Leo, she and Clarissa had taken a walk around the city since it was sunny, and they had discovered a fabulous new boutique called Love. Diana thought it was an amazing place, and before she had looked at any of the clothes, she had taken time to just walk around and appreciate the bohemian furnishings. She loved the fabulous chandeliers and the gilt-framed mirrors, the deep-buttoned, green-leather sofas, velvet chaises-longues and the tall oriental vases filled with peacock feathers. It looked so exotic and decadent – and deeply feminine – that it made her want to rush home and throw out all her modern straight-edged furniture and buy replicas of every item in the shop.

Eventually, when she and Clarissa had finished mooning over the shop décor, she turned her attention to the rails of bright, ultra-modern dresses, skirts, tops and trousers.

And it had been one of her lucky Saturdays because the owner of the shop – a beautiful Irish girl called Sarah Love – was actually working in the shop on that day. Diana had discovered this fortuitous news quite by accident when she asked the assistant who they got their stock from and found out she was talking to the both the owner of Love and the designer of all the clothes. Sarah had been more than happy to discuss her business, and when she heard that Diana had shops around Manchester and Stockport, she told her that she supplied a couple of boutiques in Manchester City Centre. Within half an hour Diana had bought herself three outfits, a bag and several belts, scarves and necklaces. She had then ordered a considerable amount from Sarah Love's current stock for her own shops back in Manchester.

It was only at dinner with Nigel and Clarissa that evening, when all the excitement over everything she had bought died down, that it dawned on her that she was going to have to find space to display all the new stock in La Femme and Gladrags. Reorganising the shops had taken the last few weeks and, after a lot of juggling around, she now had the perfect areas for her new lines.

As she finished her tea, she also jotted down ideas for the window display for Gladrags. She told Elaine and the other girls that they really had to get the windows just right, as she was determined to bring in younger customers and trendy older ones, who she knew would love this new range.

When she had finished breakfast, she tidied the kitchen and then went along the hallway on her way upstairs to finish drying her hair and get ready for work. It was then that she noticed the mail – a few brown and white envelopes – scattered on the mat at the front door. One of the white envelopes caught her eye, and her heart sank as she recognised the handwriting. It was Brian, trying out another tactic to get her to listen to him, since she refused to talk to him on the phone.

She checked the other items – bills and adverts – and tucked the letter in her dressing-gown pocket. She had got halfway up the stairs when the door knocker sounded and, with a sigh, she turned and came back down. It was her next-door neighbour, Mr Singleton, explaining that he and his wife were going away to their caravan in the Lake District in a few days, and wondering if Diana would be so good as to feed Minnie their Persian cat as usual. Diana took the spare key he offered her, and reassured him that she would feed Minnie at her regular time and leave milk out in the evenings until they returned. Then, she ran back upstairs to get ready so that she wasn't late for work.

She spent the morning in the Didsbury shop, La Femme, helping Elaine and the girls out serving when needed, and when it was quiet going over ideas for the window displays and discussing better ways to organise the new smaller items like belts and scarves. In the afternoon she drove back over to Heaton Moor and went through the same process. During the break the girls all chatted about what they had been up to the previous night and, although Diana chipped in with comments about herself and Leo, she found she wasn't inclined to give too much away. It was almost as though she might put a jinx on things by talking too much about the relationship.

Around three o'clock Leo rang the shop and asked her if she'd like to come into the restaurant about eight thirty as they had a table due to a cancellation and by then he would be free to join her. She immediately said yes, and that she would be happy if he surprised her with something from the Italian part of the menu, which Leo was delighted to hear.

She knew there was a feeling amongst women that it was best to play things cool and not agree to everything, as men like to feel they were doing the chasing but, at her age, Diana felt there was absolutely no point in pretending.

Jane Freeman called into the shop later in the afternoon, interested in any news about Diana and Leo, but more anxious to talk about Stella. She was delighted to hear that all was going well with her friend's romance, and had an air of being instrumental in bringing them together, although Diana did subtly point out that it was in fact Maria who had been the link.

"Talking of Maria," Jane said, lowering her voice so the other shop assistants couldn't hear, "we were surprised to hear she has completely given up on her ballet lessons. We knew she had taken a term off to have more time for studying for her O-levels, but we presumed she would go back after the summer. Stella was quite upset about it as they've been going together for years."

"Well," Diana said, "I suppose when girls reach a certain age they decide it's for them or not. I gave my ballet classes up when I was fourteen." She paused. "From what Maria has said to me, she has been thinking of dropping out for a while. When she had the break from it, she realised she has outgrown it. She said she was really only mediocre in any case and openly admits that Stella is much more talented and could make a career out of it."

Jane's eyes widened. "Oh, yes," she said in a weary tone, "it's the one thing she certainly seems to be talented in and has always enjoyed, but recently she's lost interest in talking about it and if you suggest that she needs to practise more it's all-out war in our house. And now that Maria won't be going to classes with her, goodness knows how it will affect Stella's interest in it."

"She'll be fine," Diana said, "and I'm sure Maria will encourage her to keep up her practice. She said the teachers are always praising Stella, and have said she has a great future in ballet."

"I'm glad to hear all that, especially with all the money we spent converting a spare bedroom into a mini-studio for her." Jane sighed. "And of course I do know that Maria would only have Stella's best interests at heart. It's Stella herself who is the problem. She's her own worst enemy. At least she's eating a bit better at the moment since we threatened to take her to the doctor." She paused. "It's that damned Tony is to blame for everything. He's like a black shadow hanging over her life. She

171

has never been the same since she became involved with that boy."

"Have you ever thought," Diana ventured, "that if you allowed Stella to see him openly, maybe it would all fizzle out? You often hear of that happening."

"We've discussed it from every angle, but both Richard and I think she would just become more attached to him if she were to see him regularly and, if it didn't fizzle out, we would find it hard to stop it then." She sighed. "We've even thought of sending her abroad for a year – to one of those finishing schools in France or even Switzerland."

"Finishing school?" Diana said. "Good Lord – do they still have them? I thought they had died out."

"Well, it was only a thought. We don't really want to send her away."

"And it's probably not a good idea when you're so worried about her eating problems. You don't know how she would be away from all her family and friends."

The conversation halted as a customer came in and came over to the desk.

"Oh, if only life were simpler!" Jane said quietly. "If only Stella were simpler."

When at last the shop door closed behind Jane Maxwell, Diana and the girls set to unpacking the boxes with the psychedelic Love label, so they would be ready for sale the following morning. Each item of clothing was unwrapped with much anticipation, then every inch of it examined and admired before it was hung carefully on the rack. By the time the shop was closed, all three assistants left with a bag each of items from the new collection, bought with a good staff discount. Diana had quickly tried on a short chiffon dress, with panels in pink and black and with long sheer black sleeves. She was slightly unsure about the length as it was shorter than she usually wore – a good four inches above her knee – but she got such an overwhelmingly positive reaction from the girls that she decided to wear it to the restaurant that night.

When she got home, she took half an hour to put her feet up and watch the evening news, then she went upstairs and ran a bath. She pinned her long red hair up to keep it dry, since she had already washed it that morning, then had a long leisurely soak. When she got out she dried herself and then spent a few minutes rubbing body lotion all over her skin, finishing off with a few drops of Chanel No 5 applied behind her ears, on her wrists and between her breasts.

As her hands moved over the different parts of her body, her mind automatically moved to Leo and she wondered if and when there would be any physical intimacy between them. She was not a naïve young girl and, although both she and Leo were Catholics, there had been a definite change in general attitudes towards sex and freedom in the last few years. Many people their age were now making their own decisions about relationships outside of marriage regardless of what the Church and other people thought. There was also a growing belief among some couples that it made more sense to find out if they were compatible physically before committing themselves to marriage. And even though she would not have previously subscribed to that sort of thinking, there were certain events in recent years that had now made Diana reconsider those values.

Diana was also very aware that Leo had been married for a number of years and had obviously been used to having regular sexual relations during that time. And, as far as she had been led to believe by Jane Maxwell, even though he had been the object of several women's desires he had spent the years since his young wife died on his own.

Her own physical experiences were quite different, in that they were more or less non-existent. Before Brian there had been one or two close encounters – one notable one when she had stayed the weekend with friends in a country house in Cheshire – but something had always held her back. She supposed it was the old-fashioned value of waiting for the right one. She had been almost sure that Brian was that person but, as time went on their relationship just never really developed either physically or emotionally, and they were almost like a distant brother and sister. By the end, she discovered that she hardly knew him at all.

She put some hand-cream on, then went over to the hanger

on the door for her dressing-gown. As she put it on she suddenly remembered the letter she had put in her pocket that morning. She took it out, then went into her bedroom and sat on the dressing-table stool to read it.

There was nothing new. All the same things he had been saying on the phone for weeks and weeks. That he still loved her, that he had learned the biggest lesson of his life being apart from her, that he wanted to marry her and have a family with her. She read on and on – it was just more and more repeats of everything he had already said. She had told him when he last phoned that she had met someone else, and had hoped that might deter him. The tone of the letter told her that it had just panicked him and made him more determined to convince her that they were right for each other. And, although she had never made it explicit, he had referred to her feeling that perhaps he had not shown his feelings for her physically enough. And of course he hadn't.

She crumpled the letter and threw it in the wastepaper bin by her dressing-table. The thought of him making love to her now seemed ludicrous. That was something that would never ever happen whether her romance with Leo lasted or not . . . because they would never have any kind of relationship ever again.

She pushed all thoughts of her ex-fiancé out of her mind and went over to the wardrobe where her new pink-and-black dress hung. Then, as she got dressed and made-up, the more she thought of the night ahead the more excited and full of anticipation she felt about seeing Leo and sitting in his lovely restaurant listening to him tell her about his day and all his customers.

Diana parked the car just down the street from the restaurant and then carefully picked her steps over the damp cobblestones towards the door. As she got closer, she could see people sitting at the tables by the window. For a few moments she felt self-conscious walking in on her own, but she made herself lift her shoulders and take a deep breath as she pushed the door open.

Leo, standing by the cash desk, looked over to the door just as she came in. He smiled at her as though surprised to see her and came towards her to kiss her on the cheek. He helped her off with her coat and gave it to one of the waiters. He then indicated the table in the corner where they were to sit, and as she wended her way through the tables towards it, Diana had to stop herself from grinning because she knew that Leo had positioned himself purposely near the door, watching and waiting for her.

Diana sat back in the chair and smoothed the hem of her new dress down as far as it would go. Then she glanced at the perfectly set table, and smiled to herself. It wasn't different as such from the others – the customary vase with small red roses, the tall crystal candlestick, but she knew he had picked the corner table for privacy, and had chosen the opened bottle of Chianti because she told him the last night she was in the restaurant that she liked the pretty, traditional Italian basket that it came in.

Leo came back to join her, immediately complimenting her on her dress and her hair, and then he told her that she smelled lovely. They chatted about what they had been doing during the day and he said he had called out to the stable in the morning to have a meeting with Bella Maria's trainer, then he had called back home in the afternoon to bring his other Maria a dish of lasagne. They talked then about the advantage of owning your own business, and how you could choose how to spend your time.

"I suppose really that we mix home and work all the time," Diana mused. "I often stay late if I'm working on something, and bring books home or go into the shops on a Sunday if I want to change things around."

Leo had agreed, and said that the restaurant had been his saving grace after Maria's mother died, and how he had been able to bring his daughter to work with him if necessary. He then went on to tell her that Maria was much happier since finally telling her ballet teacher that she was giving up her classes for good. Diana listened carefully and said Maria had mentioned it to her as well, and that, in her own opinion, Maria was doing the right thing. She decided not to venture Jane Maxwell's views on it as it wasn't going to add anything helpful to the conversation and she did not want to give Leo the impression she was a gossip. She was also being careful not to seem too interested in what Maria was doing in case it looked like she was already considering herself a part of their little family.

Things between herself and Leo – and herself and Maria – were going so much better than she could ever have hoped for, and she did not want to jeopardise that. Fate may well have intervened when she and Maria were introduced in the church, but she knew that it was common sense to tread carefully with the close relationship between father and daughter.

They had a plain melon dish to start and afterwards the waitress came with the main course.

"I hope you like the dish that Franco has cooked for us," Leo said, smiling.

"I'm sure I will."

"This is Pasta Carbonara with chicken and bacon," Leo told her. "It's a traditional dish from Rome, although there is some argument as to how old it is. Some say it goes back as far as Ancient Rome and others say it's as recent as World War Two." He shrugged and smiled. "Who cares how old it is as long as it tastes good?"

"It looks and smells fantastic," Diana said, enjoying the way he gave her the history of Italian food and his obvious pride in it.

After the meal Franco himself, still dressed in his chef's apron and hat, brought them out a dish of tiramisu, and when Diana asked what was in it he gave a brief rundown.

"So it has cream and sponge in it?" she checked. "Apart from the coffee it sounds just like a –" Franco held his hand up to stop her, laughed and said, "The worst thing you can say to an Italian is that it is like an English trifle."

"But what if the person likes English trifle?" Diana said, laughing along with him, "and means it as a genuine compliment?"

He paused for a moment. "I would have to think about that," he said, heading back into the kitchen.

When they finished and the waitress had cleared the dishes away, Franco, without his uniform now, came back to the table with another bottle of Chianti. Then, as the last meals had been cooked and served, he pulled out a chair and joined them in a glass of wine.

Again, Diana thought how wonderfully easy it was to slip into even the working side of Leo Conti's life. Meeting Franco and his wife at the races, and Charlie Ford and some of Leo's other friends, meant that there had been no awkward introductions to be made. It also helped when they discovered that they were both Catholics, and attended the same church on Sundays. Although, so far, since she usually went to the early Mass while Leo preferred the later one, they had not gone together.

Now, listening to the two men talking about Italian food and wines, and about the different regions they came from, the thought crept into Diana's mind that, if things worked out, perhaps she and Leo might go there for a visit. By the following summer, it would not be outside the realms of possibility that they might go together with Maria and Paul. The thought warmed her immensely, as there were so many places like Rome and Florence she always wanted to see, and she could think of no better companion and tour guide to take her around than Leo. So far, everything that she did with Leo she enjoyed more than she had ever done with anyone else or by herself. In fact, she thought, she even liked *herself* more when she was with Leo.

Later, as she laughed along with some funny joke Franco had told, she thought that no matter what happened she was grateful to be in this lovely restaurant and part of this lively, colourful group.

Leo lifted the wine bottle but as he went to pour Diana another glass she stopped him.

"I have the car," she reminded him, "and I've already had two glasses so I'd better not."

Franco immediately got to his feet. "Would you like coffee instead?"

When Maria said she would love a coffee, Leo said he would have one as well, and suggested that they could perhaps drive their own cars back to her place, and finish the wine off there. She felt her face flush as she nodded and said that it was a great idea.

They were just finishing their coffee when they heard noises in the street outside. Franco went out to check and after a few moments he stuck his head back and gestured to Leo to follow him.

Leo was on his feet quickly. "I won't be a minute," he told her, squeezing her arm as he passed her.

Diana, glowing from his touch, lifted her bag. "If I'm not here when you come back," she said, "I'm only in the ladies' room!"

A short while later, after checking her hair and touching up her make-up, Diana came back into the restaurant. The two waitresses were putting fresh tablecloths and napkins out and resetting the dining places, but there was no sign of the two men. She sat down at the table, and picked up her cup of lukewarm coffee and took a sip for something to do. Her mind was full of what might happen later. She was quite sure that nothing really physical would happen that night or even the next night they were on their own together. But she could with some certainty feel deep inside her that in the not too distant future it would all happen. In the meantime, she would enjoy every minute of all the other pleasures he had brought to her, until the right time came.

When the waitresses went through the swing doors to the kitchen carrying bundles of linen, Diana glanced towards the door to see Leo and Franco standing outside. Something about the way Franco had both his hands on either side of Leo's head, and looked to be talking very seriously, made her suddenly anxious. Were they having some sort of row, she wondered? It seemed unlikely, given that only a few minutes ago they were laughing and chatting. And neither of them had drunk that much – little more than she had. She glanced at the second bottle of wine and it was still two-thirds full. She looked back to the door and this time Leo had turned around and Franco seemed to be examining the back of his head. The gesture was enough to make her move quickly from the table and towards the door.

"Is there anything wrong?" she said, looking at Franco.

"Ah, stupid, stupid boys teasing Timothy again."

Diana didn't know who Timothy was, and didn't feel it was the right time to ask about such inconsequential details. She came around the side to look at Leo. "Are you okay?"

"I'm fine," he said.

"He's not fine," Franco said, looking at her with worried eyes. "He got a bang on the back of the head. There was a fight and Leo moved backwards and lost his balance – and hit his head on the postbox outside. He hit it badly. I heard it – it was a big thud. He needs to see a doctor."

"I'm okay," Leo said.

Something about his eyes worried Diana. "I agree," she said. "I think we should get you into casualty. Stockport Infirmary should be fine, and it's only five minutes from home."

"I'm sure it's all right."

She smiled at him. "I'm sure it is, but Franco is right – it's best to get it checked out."

Chapter 21

As she settled down to watch *Top of the Pops* with a glass of lemonade and a packet of crisps, Maria felt relaxed and unusually happy. For once, everything seemed to have fallen into place in exactly the way she wanted it. Paul and she were getting on better and better, and things were wonderful with her father since he had started seeing Diana. He was always good-natured, but these last few months he seemed different, more relaxed and, in a funny way that Maria couldn't describe, he seemed more confident. And he certainly wasn't drinking as much or staying out late playing cards.

Today she was particularly relieved that telling her ballet teacher that she was dropping out of classes had gone much better than she had expected. The teacher had just shrugged and said she wasn't surprised and that a lot of girls left at around fifteen and sixteen due to exam pressure and lack of time to practise. Only the most dedicated stayed on, and that's exactly how the ballet school preferred it.

Apart from the slight inference that Maria wasn't the material they required, she was delighted to be let off so lightly. Of course Stella hadn't been at all happy about it, but Maria wasn't too worried about that, as recently her friend seemed to find something to moan about every single day. If it wasn't her mother forcing her to do things and practise her ballet when she didn't feel like it, it was her father or her younger brothers annoying her.

Stella would just have to get over her leaving the ballet class and it might even help her to concentrate more if she didn't have someone to gossip and giggle with during the breaks. And, they always had their horse-riding class – that's if Stella didn't muck it all up by going against her parents over Tony.

She curled up on the sofa, her feet tucked under her, her shoulders moving now and again in time with Union Gap singing one of her big favourites 'Young Girl'. Love Affair came on afterwards singing 'Rainbow Valley' and they were just near the end when the phone rang.

She hesitated for a minute before going across to the table to pick it up. Unless it was something really, really important, none of her friends or Paul would ring her when *Top of the Pops* was on. The phone often rang directly *after* the programme, as Stella loved to discuss in great detail which groups or singers were on, whether she liked their new song and what they were wearing. As she lifted the receiver, she had decided it had to be her dad on to remind her to do something or other.

"Hello, Maria?"

"Yes?" Maria thought she recognised the voice – an older woman's – but she couldn't be sure.

"It's Denise Spencer here, Paul's mother."

Maria's heart quickened. "Oh, hello, Mrs Spencer."

"Sorry for disturbing you, dear, but I had to wait until Paul was busy watching the television so he wouldn't hear me."

Maria caught her lip between her teeth and waited, with no idea what to expect.

"I was just wondering if your father is home tonight?"

"No, I'm sorry," Maria told her, "he's in the restaurant. You can always phone him there if it's important."

"No, no." There was a pause. "It's actually to do with you, Maria. I wondered if you have anything planned for the weekend of September the tenth? It's about a month away."

Maria quickly thought. "I don't think so . . . but I'm not sure."

"I thought I would ring to give you plenty of time. You see, it's Paul's eighteenth birthday, and we're thinking of going down to London for a show, and Paul's dad and I wondered if you would like to come? That's if your father has no objections, of course."

Maria caught her breath. *London!* She could hardly believe it. Not only did she definitely want to go to London – she *definitely* wanted to go with Paul and his family. "Oh, that sounds great!" she said, "I'd love to go!"

"Well, I'm sure Paul would love you to go too. I think he would enjoy it much more if you were there."

Maria felt a thrill run through her. "I'll check it with my father when he comes home tonight," she had to take a deep breath to calm her voice as she felt so excited, "but I'm sure it will be okay."

"Make sure you explain that you will both be very well chaperoned. We'll be staying for two nights at my sister's house in a nice part of London called Hampstead Heath. It's very central and we'll have time to see a show and go round the sights."

"I'll tell him all that when he comes in tonight," Maria promised.

"Now, we're keeping it a surprise until it's all organised. We've discussed it and think we should tell Paul maybe a week before we go, so he can look forward to it, and so the two of you can chat and decide where you would like to visit, because we may need to book tickets in advance. Is that all okay, dear? I'll ring Leo tomorrow or he can ring me – whatever suits – and check that everything is okay."

"Thank you, Mrs Spencer, I'll really look forward to that."

"Good," she said, giving a small laugh. "That's what we want to hear."

Then, after she put the phone in the receiver, Maria hugged herself and jumped about the room with sheer excitement. *London – London – London! And with Paul for two days and nights! And his mother saying that he would enjoy it much more if I was there. How absolutely fantastic!* She had to phone Stella. This was much too big to keep to herself.

She went back to the phone and dialled Stella's number. Mr Maxwell answered and said he would get her.

Stella's voice came on the line. "This better be good news," she said. "I can't believe you're phoning me in the middle of *Top of the Pops!* I'm missing The Equals singing 'Baby Come Back' and I love it!"

Maria started to laugh. "It's not just *good* news," she said. "It's absolutely fantastic!"

Chapter 22

Maria's evening flew by between phone calls and TV and homework. And she was pleased with herself for spending twenty minutes talking to Paul without letting anything slip about the planned trip to London. She knew of course that it was easy not to mention it while it seemed so far away – the difficulty would be when it got closer to the time.

She went upstairs and got her English and Maths homework and then came back down to do it in front of the fire. She found concentrating on schoolwork difficult at the best of times – especially since she had started going out with Paul – but tonight it was absolutely impossible.

Her attention wandered between the television and the radio, her homework and magazines and going into the kitchen for drinks and biscuits. She was glad her father or Mrs Lowry wasn't there to ask her what on earth she was doing, flitting around like a bee in a flowerbed.

It was after ten when the phone rang again, and Maria had actually become so engrossed in her English Comprehension questions that she didn't take time to wonder who was calling at that time before picking up the receiver. If she had, in all probability she would have guessed that it was her father.

"Maria? It's Diana here. I'm really sorry to ring you so late at night. I just wondered if it would be okay if I call at the house in five minutes?"

"Yes," Maria said, alarmed. "Is there anything the matter?" It suddenly reminded her of the morning in the church with Mrs Flynn.

"Nothing very serious, but I've just been at Stockport Infirmary with your dad tonight, as he got a bit of a bang on the head. He's absolutely fine, but he has to wait to have an X-ray, and I thought you might want to be with him. I've just driven back to pick you up. I'm at my house now as I needed a warmer coat and I thought I'd give you a ring so I didn't give you a shock."

Maria felt a prickly feeling over her back and neck. "What happened?"

"Well, I was at the restaurant with your dad tonight, and there were some teenagers outside in the street teasing a man called Timothy and your dad and Franco went to sort them out."

"Oh, my God! Did he get badly hurt?"

"No, he said he didn't. He and Franco chased them off, but he said there was a bit of a scuffle and apparently he hit his head off a postbox."

Maria's hand came up to cover her mouth.

"He's insisting he's okay and he's talking fine and everything, but Franco said he got a bit of a bang and he does have a headache, so we thought it was best to get him checked out."

"He's never sick," Maria said in a low voice. "I can't imagine him in hospital."

"Don't worry – it is only the X-ray department. I'm leaving the house now, and I'll be with you in a couple of minutes."

When they got to the hospital and she saw her father sitting in the X-ray waiting room, Maria was immediately reassured. He was smiling and shrugging and telling her he was fine and it was only a little headache and a fuss about nothing.

"But I don't want you to think I am complaining about Diana and Franco insisting that I come to the hospital – quite the opposite. They were very good and just concerned for me."

"It won't take long to have an X-ray done and then we can

go home," Maria said, giving him a hug. "And this was all over poor Timothy again?"

Leo shrugged and nodded, and Maria saw him wince as he moved his head.

"Have you a pain?"

"A little one," he said, "and I'm just slightly dizzy . . ."

"Will I get someone?" Diana asked.

"No, no, I'm fine." He looked at Maria. "I hope Franco called the police. We can't have this happening with Timothy again. They're only boys, but they're frightening him and causing noise around the restaurant. I don't want to be selfish but, apart from upsetting Timothy, they might drive our customers away."

"Did they attack you and Franco?"

Leo raised his hands. "Ah, it was nothing but a scuffle. More dancing around than fighting. Nothing to worry us, but it might be best if the police speak to them and to their parents. That will probably be enough to frighten them off – to put a stop to them annoying poor Timothy." He shrugged and looked over at Diana. "He's a harmless man, he wouldn't harm a fly. He spends his life looking after his mother and sister, and the only outings he gets are to the shops or the occasional night in the pub at the bottom of the road. They taunt him because he is different and call him a nancy-boy and a queer and awful words like that."

Diana throat tightened as she imagined the scene. And then her heart warmed even more to Leo, thinking how kind and selfless he was defending someone like that. "And you say this has happened before?"

Maria nodded. "It happened that night after we were at the racecourse. The night Franco had the cut on his hand."

"I didn't realise there was a problem that night," Diana said, sounding surprised. "It was my first time in Leonardo's and everything seemed lovely."

"It was only a scratch, a graze," her father said. "Franco forgot it very quickly."

Diana knew he was playing the incident down so as not to worry them.

"But it's terrible," Maria said. "And we can't let it happen again. If Franco has not gone to the police already then I'm going to tell him that he absolutely should go tomorrow."

"Okay, okay," Leo said. He looked over at Diana and smiled. "I'm so sorry your evening was spoiled."

She smiled back at him. "It doesn't matter, we can do it again."

"That's what I was hoping."

A woman came into the waiting room with a little boy with his arm in a sling, and then a man came in supporting a limping teenage boy who was wearing a football strip. The man started chatting to Leo, telling him how his son had been viciously tackled by one of the opposition team and had gone over on his ankle.

While he was occupied, Diana turned to Maria. "He definitely seems better now," she said. "But I think it's still worth checking it out. He could have mild concussion or something like that."

"I agree," Maria said.

She turned then as she heard footsteps coming along the corridor and then a nurse came around the corner and called her father's name.

He got to his feet, slightly unsteadily, and Diana and Maria rose, ready to help him if necessary.

"We'll be about twenty minutes," the nurse said.

"Sorry, girls," Leo said, giving a weak smile. "I know it's not the most exciting way to spend your evening."

"You even made me miss finishing my homework," Maria joked, "but I suppose I'll have to forgive you since you have a reasonably good excuse."

They all laughed and then the nurse and Leo went walking down the corridor in the direction of the X-ray department.

"He's never sick," Maria said. "It feels strange being in a hospital with him." Her eyes narrowed in thought. "I think the last time I was in a hospital with him was the night that my mother died."

Diana put her arm around her. "It must be hard for you being here and remembering that," she said softly. "But you don't need to worry – this is just a routine check that they do on everyone. Your father will be okay."

Maria thought how nice and kind Diana was. As soon as she mentioned her mother, she felt that it might have made Diana feel awkward, but she could not detect even the slightest feeling of that being the case, and it made her warm to her even more.

The door opened, causing a sudden draught, and a porter came in to talk to the receptionist. Maria gave a small shiver.

"You're cold," Diana said, rubbing her shoulder. "There's a small café across in the main block. We might as well go and have a cup of tea while we're waiting."

As they walked along Maria wondered if Paul had rung the house while she was out. They were supposed to be going to the cinema the following night, and hopefully the date would still be on as long as they didn't keep her father in the hospital for a couple of days or anything like that. She then caught herself, realising how selfish she would sound if she said that to anyone.

The café at this hour was quiet. Only a few tables had customers and Maria could see that most of them were nurses on their breaks. Over in a corner there was a table with five young men in white coats – one with a telltale stethoscope around his neck – who had to be doctors who had finished their evening rounds.

While Diana went to get them hot chocolates, Maria went over the evening in her mind, wondering how things could change so quickly because of one phone call. She had been almost delirious with happiness after Paul's mother had rung and now, a few hours later, she felt the opposite. She knew of course that her father would be fine. He was a fit healthy man, and a small knock on the head wouldn't do him any great harm, but the incident itself had shaken her and made her wonder at the way things happened.

She looked over at the counter where Diana was standing, and thought about the changes their chance meeting had brought into their lives. How different her father was since meeting this lovely woman, and how silly she had been when Stella had first lightly mentioned that it might be a good thing if her father met someone. She realised now that since her mother had died there had been a real gap in her father's life – a much bigger gap than she could ever have imagined. And that her stubbornness and selfishness had almost lost him the chance of the happiness she could see he now had with Diana. If it hadn't been for Mrs Flynn taking ill in the church, Maria knew in her heart she would probably not have even looked at Diana at the races that day, and would certainly not have got into conversation with her for fear it might have encouraged things.

And as she watched the attractive, friendly woman now putting the mugs on a tray for them, she thought how much less her own life would be without her in it. Without being intrusive or over-involved, Diana had been a great support to her, someone who had her best interests at heart. And, Maria thought, it was very separate and different from her friendships with Stella and the girls at school and did not intrude in any way. And the link between Stella's mother and Diana actually helped things, as she could share her ups and downs with Stella and the situation with Tony without feeling judged. And Maria was grateful that Diana only ever mentioned Paul if Maria herself brought the subject up.

She was of course desperate to tell her about the proposed trip to London, as talking about it would make it more real. But she felt that the hospital café, when they were waiting on news of her father, was not the place to discuss something so frivolous. As soon as her father got the okay, they would all head home, and it might be something nice to cheer them all up on the journey back.

Diana put the tray on the table now. She put Maria's hot chocolate in front of her along with a cellophane-wrapped packet of two chocolate biscuits. "I thought these might help keep you going in case you're feeling a bit tired."

Maria thanked her, then Diana looked at her watch.

"It's after eleven now," she said.

"Is it?" Maria hadn't given the time a thought. They sat in silence for a few minutes, sipping the hot drinks, then she looked up at Diana. "He will be okay, won't he?"

Diana touched her hand. "I'm sure he will. It's just routine."

Ten minutes later they walked back to the X-ray department, and were both relieved to see Leo sitting there chatting to a nurse.

"I'm just out," he told them, "and I think everything is fine."

Maria's heart lifted and she realised she had been more worried than she thought.

"I was just talking to your dad," the nurse said, "and we think it might be best to keep him here overnight for observation. The X-ray wasn't clear, so we don't have any accurate results yet."

Leo looked at them and smiled. "I'm really fine. I don't need to stay."

"It's your own decision," the nurse said, "but we'd feel happier if the headache was settled."

"Maybe you should think about staying overnight, Leo," Diana suggested. "Just to make sure."

"I'd rather be home . . ." He stood up, and then he suddenly swayed. He put his hand out to the wall to steady himself.

Maria's heart lurched. "Dad!!"

The nurse, Maria and Diana all rushed to catch him and help him back into the chair.

"That's it, Dad," Maria said. "You need to stay in. You're still not a hundred per cent."

"It's just the dizziness," Leo said. "It just came back when I stood up."

"You're okay, Leo," the nurse said. "It might be a touch of concussion, and it's best if we keep an eye on you."

"Okay, Dad?" Maria said, placing her hand gently on his shoulder. "You'll be fine."

Leo nodded and then he slowly leaned forward in the chair, closed his eyes and vomited all over the floor in front of him.

"Oh, Dad!" Maria exclaimed. "Are you all right?

"Just hold him there," the nurse said, rushing over to the desk to the phone.

Maria's heart was racing. This wasn't right. "Don't move now, Dad," she told him. She went to stroke his head and then she remembered and stopped. "Just wait until the nurse comes back. I think they will probably be happier if they get you in bed for a while to let it all settle down." She remembered an accident in school where one of the girls banged her head during a gym class, after falling awkwardly off the vaulting horse. As soon as she got sick, the teachers rang for an emergency ambulance. It was, as the nurse had said might be the case with her father, concussion. Thankfully the girl was fine and back in school in a day or two.

Diana moved to sit at the other side of him. "Maria's right," she said, "it wouldn't do you any good to travel home tonight. You'll feel much better in the morning."

"I apologise for being sick," Leo said. "I'm very, very sorry."

"We've all been sick, Leo, one time or another," Diana said, kissing him on the forehead. "But it's nice you're such a gentleman."

The nurse finished on the phone then she came back over to them carrying paper towels, an ordinary towel and a theatre gown.

She threw the paper towels over the puddle of sick and put the gown around Leo's shoulders, then she held the towel to his mouth. "You'll be okay," she told him. "It's quite common after a head injury."

"I'm sorry . . ." Leo tried to lift his head but couldn't.

The doors from the main waiting-room suddenly flew open and a trolley was pushed in, and within minutes Leo was up on it and being wheeled out, back to the treatment room.

The next couple of hours passed in a haze as Maria and Diana waited for news. Then they were brought through to the casualty ward to see Leo settled in bed. He looked paler than before and was very tired.

"I'm sorry to be such a nuisance," he said, "but I think the bang was a little more severe than I imagined." He smiled. "I hope I didn't do the postbox too much damage, but I have a feeling I came off a little worse."

"You should sleep now, Leo," Diana said. "It will do you good."

"I do feel like sleeping but the doctor has told me to wait a little longer as they are waiting on some results of tests."

Diana's throat tightened. "Well, you must do exactly as the doctors tell you."

Then he put his hand out and took Diana's and squeezed it. He then held his other hand out to Maria. "Two lovely ladies," he said, "who have both been looking after me so well."

Maria lifted his hand up to her cheek. "You always look after me."

"Tonight I will have to stay here," he said, "but I would feel happier if I knew that you were both together, looking after each other."

"Maria can stay with me tonight," Diana said. "The spare room bed is all made up."

Then, a nurse came in and said it might be best if they let him rest. Diana and Maria kissed him and said they would see him soon.

Leo smiled and raised his hand as they walked away.

Chapter 23

It was five in the morning when the house phone rang.

On hearing it, Maria's heart started pounding. She sat bolt upright in bed then she checked the time on the clock on the bedside cabinet. She listened as Diana's footsteps went quickly down the stairs, but she could only hear the murmur of her voice as she spoke and nothing of the conversation. Then, all the dreadful possibilities racing through her mind, she climbed out of bed – wearing the green satin pyjamas that Diana had lent her last night – and went to the top of the stairs.

Diana was coming up towards her, her face white and expressionless. "It was the hospital . . . they want us to go in."

Maria felt the same strange calm descending on her that sometimes came when she was worrying about her father late at night. The calm that helped her through her worst times.

She turned back towards the bedroom. "I'll get ready."

"The roads will be empty at this time of the morning," Diana said. "So we can go quickly."

Maria did not answer. She went back into the bedroom to pull on the same clothes she had worn last night.

They hardly spoke on the drive in. When they arrived at the hospital public car park there were only two other cars.

As they went towards the main door, Diana said, "The nurse

I spoke to said to go straight to Reception and they will take us up to the ward."

Maria slowed to a halt. Now they were so close she needed to prepare herself. "What did they tell you?"

Diana looked straight ahead. "That he is in a . . . a deep sleep . . . and they are concerned."

"But that could be a good thing. He might feel a lot better when he wakes up."

"Yes," Diana was nodding her head slowly. "Hopefully he might feel better."

There was a nurse waiting for them in Reception and Maria saw Diana's face tighten when she asked them to follow her into a consultation room where the doctor would speak to them. As they walked along, Diana reached back and took her hand in hers and held it tightly. They went down a corridor and when the nurse showed them into the room, there were two doctors already sitting at a table waiting to see them.

The doctors stood up and shook Diana's hand and then Maria's, and it crossed her mind that they probably thought Diana was her mother. They all sat down and there was a silence for a few moments and then Maria heard one of the doctors saying he was very sorry, but that they had done everything they could.

Diana gasped and said in a whisper. "What exactly are you saying?"

Maria felt a rushing in her head and ears and couldn't quite make out what anyone in the room was saying. She shook her head to make herself concentrate and then she heard one of the doctors explain there had been a problem with bleeding immediately after banging his head. That was when she realised they had made a mistake and weren't talking about her father at all.

"But he wasn't bleeding," she said, looking from one to the other. She noticed that both doctors looked away when their eyes met her. "We checked, and there was no sign of any bleeding."

"I'm so sorry," the doctor said, "but it was internal bleeding between the skull and the covering of the brain . . . by the time he was checked it was too late. He went into a coma, and I'm afraid he passed away just before you came in."

Diana gripped her arm tightly and Maria heard her say in a strangled voice, "Oh, no!"

As Diana dissolved into devastated sobs, Maria felt the strange calm coming over her again. And she suddenly remembered feeling exactly the same way when her mother died – as though she had a shell around her that she carried everywhere she went. Back then, she at least had her father, who she knew would love and look after her. As he had done in all the years since. But that love and care, she now knew and understood, would be no more.

Chapter 24

From the moment they had left the hospital, Maria became Diana's main priority. She knew she had to put her own feelings aside and do everything that was necessary. After her initial devastated reaction, she had kept herself resolutely on autopilot as the doctors and nurses took charge, taking them down to the side-room where Leo would be kept until the post-mortem procedure. They explained what would happen next and took details such as Leo's religion, and then advised Diana and Maria who to contact regarding funeral arrangements.

They left the hospital and drove back to the Contis' house and, while Maria was in the bathroom, Diana phoned Franco to tell him the tragic news and then spent five minutes crying on the phone with him and trying to comfort him. Mrs Lowry was next on the list, and Diana found herself crying on the phone along with the housekeeper too. In between the tears, she had arranged that Mrs Lowry would come down to the house and stay there all day with Maria, as Diana said that she thought the girl needed to sleep.

When she came off the phone from Mrs Lowry, Diana went up and tapped on the bathroom door to check that Maria was okay. When Maria confirmed that she was, she asked her if it was okay if she rang Jane Maxwell to let them know, or if she would prefer to ring Stella herself.

After a few moments Maria said she would be grateful if she rang for her.

Jane was in shock with the news, as was Stella when her mother called her downstairs. Diana had been glad that Maria hadn't phoned her friend as she could hear her crying hysterically in the background. She had forgotten how highly strung Stella was and, having recently got used to Maria's quiet ways, she somehow thought all teenagers were as calm and sensible as her.

In the midst of her shock, Jane would still have liked a full, blow-by-blow account of the evening and the night in hospital leading up to Leo's death, but Diana told her in a stiff voice that she was not up to going over it all again. She said she would know more details about the funeral when they had spoken to the priest, then she got off the phone as quickly as she could.

She went back up to the bathroom and knocked on the door again and called to Maria to tell her who she had rung. When there was no answer, she asked her to please come out as soon as she was ready because she was worrying her.

Things, Diana thought at that point, were just as bad as they could be, and Maria withdrawing into herself would not make the situation any better, and might well make it intolerable. But of course, she could not say that, and she had to be patient and handle things as well as she possibly could. She walked back downstairs and sat on the sofa, staring out of the window into the small cul-de-sac, just waiting, and not allowing herself for one minute to consider her own loss.

Eventually, she heard the lock on the bathroom opening and she jumped to her feet and went out into the hallway and stood at the bottom of the stairs. "Maria?" she called.

When there was no answer Diana made her way up the stairs and found Maria in a crumpled heap on the landing, her body trembling with silent sobs. Diana gathered the girl in her arms and held her tightly and they cried together, their sadness echoing throughout the house.

Eventually, Maria put words to her misery. "Why," she asked, "did we not stay with him? Why did he have to die alone?"

Diana struggled to find answers to the questions that she had been rattling around in her own head. "He wasn't alone," she said softly. "The doctors and nurses were with him. And from what the doctor said, he fell asleep quite quickly after we left the hospital and never really woke up."

"But I should have been there! He should have known that someone who knew him and loved him was there!"

Diana stroked her hair. "Just remember the last time we saw him. Your father was happy and smiling. Do you remember what he said?"

Maria said nothing for a few moments then she nodded her head.

"He told us to look after each other, "Diana had said. "And we said we would, and knowing that made him happy."

"Yes," Maria said, wiping the back of her hand over her face, "I do remember that. Thank God I have that to remember. It makes me feel a tiny bit better knowing that he was happy." Then she halted again. "Will you help me, Diana?"

Diana looked at her, not quite sure what she meant. "Of course, I'll help you any way I can."

"I mean, will you help me with the . . ." She couldn't say the word 'funeral'. "Will you help me with all the arrangements? I know Dad has lots of other friends and we've only known you a few months, but because you were here a lot with Dad I feel you understand me better in ways."

Diana felt a lump forming in her throat. "Maria, I'll help you with anything I can." Then, afraid that she was going to break down again, she loosened her arms from around the girl. "Let me get a towel for you."

She got to her feet and went into the bathroom to the shelf where there was a tidy pile of half a dozen hand towels. She lifted two from the pile and wiped her own face with one and then went back to the hallway where Maria was now sitting upright with her back against the wall. She took the proffered towel and held it to her face, and for a moment Diana thought she was going to start sobbing all over again. Instead, she rubbed the soft material over her red, puffy face and then took a deep breath and sat back again.

198

"So this is it?" she said, shrugging. "This is it now. I'll never see my father again. I'll never see his face or hear his voice, ever, ever again."

"Don't think like that," Diana had said, although the words had struck her to the bone.

"But it's true. It's going to be exactly the same as it was when my mother died. It will be as if he never existed at all – just a huge empty space." She struggled now to get to her feet, straightening her clothes as she did so. "It's true what people say – death is final. There's nothing of that person – apart from photographs or clothes or music – ever again."

"You have all the wonderful memories of your father," Diana said. "And I know in the coming weeks and months that he will help you to cope through those memories."

Then, a car drew up at the gate and a minute or two later a knock came on the door and Diana had to go downstairs and let a distraught Mrs Lowry in.

Eventually, after Franco and Bernice arrived, there came a point where there were enough people in the house to care for Maria without Diana feeling she was deserting her if she left for a while. Somehow, after only a few months of knowing this lovely young girl, she seemed to have found herself responsible for her.

Chapter 25

It was midday before Diana arrived back home, closed the door, and allowed herself to think about all that she herself had lost.

With caring for Maria and dealing with the immediate practical details following Leo's death, there had not been the space or the time to think exactly how losing him was going to impact on her life. And there had been the feeling at the back of her mind that, after knowing him for such a short time, she did not have the entitlement to be as upset as those who had known him longer. And even the list of names that Bernice had mentioned who would need to be notified – customers, business acquaintances and the Manchester Italian community – it was obvious that there had been many other people who had liked and loved Leo Conti.

The house, though ordered, felt cold and cheerless so she went into the kitchen and switched on the central heating to warm it up and then she headed for the stairs to go and have a shower. It was only when she caught sight of herself in the gilt hall mirror that she suddenly stopped in her tracks. Overnight, her face seemed to have aged by years. She continued to stare at her reflection for a few minutes until her eyes glazed over and she could hardly see herself, then she continued upstairs to her bedroom.

And it was when she looked at the bed she had made up the previous evening with the new navy and cream Habitat bed cover that her own loss of Leo finally hit her. The bed signifying the stage that she and Leo had carefully reached in their relationship, and where, she knew, they would soon have lain together.

She thought back to the dreams and plans she had built around their relationship – the dreams she had not allowed herself to have with any other man for years. And now, it had all fallen apart. It was never to be.

The tears that overwhelmed her were a mixture of sadness and anger. The sadness was for Leo – a fine man cut down at a time in life when he should have been enjoying himself and reaping the rewards of all the hard work in the restaurant. And there was great sadness for Maria who was now left without either parent, and at that delicate, confusing time when she was neither a child nor yet a woman. And Diana could already feel the heartfelt sadness from all the friends and people who had known and loved Leo for his kindness and generosity.

But underneath it all, Diana was struggling even harder with the bitterness and anger she felt against life – against fate.

Once again, her hopes and dreams had been shattered, but this time it was much worse than it had been with Brian. Her romance with Leo had been following an easy and natural course, and there had been nothing to suggest it would not continue. They had talked easily and both had been open with each other about their pasts. Leo had told her that meeting her was the best thing to happen him since his wife had died, and that he had never imagined himself in a relationship again where he would feel so relaxed and able to talk about things. And he had confided in her about his gambling and drinking, explaining that he could now see he had been using them to fill a huge gap in his life – a gap that Diana had slipped so easily and naturally into.

Diana had not been naïve about the situation – she knew that Leo had a lot of work to do to sort out his finances and to break the habit of late-night drinking and card games, but she had somehow known deep inside her that all that would have been be resolved now that he had found other things to replace them. Now they had found each other.

She felt that his difficulties and his trusting of her had made their relationship more real – more human – and it was because of those reasons that she was finally able to open up to him about Brian. She was able to tell him the truth about their long-standing – but going-nowhere – relationship, and the truth about their break-up – something she had never imagined sharing with anyone – friend or lover.

The relief she had felt after sharing that particular burden was more than she could ever have envisaged. And that, coupled with all his other attributes, had led her to imagine that she could build a future with Leo Conti.

But it was not going to happen because he had been kind and stood up for a man who many people ostracised because he was effeminate and different. Leo had not been sure whether Timothy had even been a practising homosexual, but he chose not to judge him whatever the case. And he had stood up for Timothy on not one but several occasions, because he believed in right and wrong and had the courage to live out his convictions.

Brian, Diana knew to her cost, had done the complete opposite. He had lived a lie and had sucked her into his world for too many years. And yet he was still willing to lead a life built on hypocrisy. The recent letter she had received only yesterday from him contained numerous declarations of love and another marriage proposal. He described a big, rambling house he had seen in Wilmslow that would suit them if she would agree to a wedding, and the landscaped garden that was perfect for the two or three children they could easily have before it was too late. It was all down to her, he wrote. The ball was in her court. She only had to say the word and he would put the plans in action.

She noted that there was not a single mention of the reason they had split up. Nothing about the young man who had rung his apartment to ask for directions to the hotel they were meeting in that night. Nothing about the horrendous, sexually explicit male magazines she had found when she searched his desk for clues. And after she had confronted him with all the evidence about his homosexuality, and after he had admitted that he had been leading a double life, he still expected her to trust him again and even marry him and have his children.

How ridiculous, she thought, when Brian had obviously not felt any inclination or desire for her during all the years they were together. If he felt that he now could change and feel physical attraction for her after all this time, then that was most unfortunate, because she certainly did not feel the same about him.

If she had the slightest regard left for him, she might have asked out of curiosity if she was the only female he had ever had any interest in. Something told her that she should not flatter herself and that Brian would always have looked for a 'normal' relationship to cover up the truth. But, she may well have been one of the few women that he had been able to fool for all those years.

It had crossed her mind on more than one occasion that Brian would never be honest about his sexual inclinations because he himself could not face what he was – and he probably knew his family and friends could not support it. In a different situation, she might have had sympathy for someone in his position, knowing how difficult it must be to be open and honest when facing a wall of prejudice. And even though it had been legalised recently, it was a long way off from being socially acceptable. But even taking all these things into account, she could never forgive him for making her part of his deception.

She felt utterly exhausted. A couple of hours' sleep was necessary if she was to continue to function and be a support for Maria. She sat on the bed for a few minutes, deciding whether to shower now or go to bed for a couple of hours and have it later. Then she wondered at herself thinking such an ordinary thought, as though she had not just lost the man who had made her whole life complete. How was she to cope with this? How was she supposed to go back and live again as a thirty-odd-year-old spinster?

How was she to act as though Leo Conti had never existed?

Chapter 26

For Maria, the house was becoming less and less familiar by the hour. The space and the quiet she was used to were gone, the daily routine she was used to was gone, and most of all – her father was gone. A strange house she hardly recognised was left in place of the warm home she had been used to.

The only spaces that remained more or less the same were her bedroom that no-one else came into, and her father's bedroom. So far, she had only pushed the door open to look in. It was spotlessly tidy as always. Leo was an organised man who had automatically hung things up in the wardrobe after he wore them, put his shoes on the rack and put laundry in the basket for Mrs Lowry. Stepping over the threshold and walking around her father's room and seeing his alarm clock and his rosary beads, and the polished wooden box where he kept his cufflinks and tiepins, was not something that she was ready for yet.

Everything in her life was upside down and her moods veered from being in an almost trance-like calm – which even she herself knew was not normal – to the periods of total clarity when she realised exactly what had happened. During the clearer periods she was apt to suddenly break down into hysterical sobbing.

It was after one such emotional episode that Father O'Donnell and the elderly Father Quinn arrived at the house.

Mrs Lowry showed them into the dining room as it was more private than the sitting room where some of the immediate neighbours were. Maria, now more composed, came downstairs with Bernice to speak to them.

Father O'Donnell stood up and, coming forward with outstretched hands, took both of hers.

"Ah, Maria," he said, "this is a sad time for us all. Leo has gone to meet his maker much much sooner than we would have thought or would have liked."

Father Quinn stayed sitting, but he nodded his head in agreement. As Maria looked at him, she suddenly thought he looked very old – surely beyond retirement age – and the vague look on his face made Maria wonder if he even knew who she was.

"Leo was a good and decent man," Father O'Donnell used the same formal voice he used on the pulpit on Sundays, only softer, "and we have no doubt but that he is already enjoying the treasures stored up for him in heaven." He then stepped back, his hands held behind his back.

There was silence for a few moments, then Maria realised he was waiting for her to say something, so she murmured, "Thank you, Father."

Maria did not look directly at him because she knew he was uncomfortable but trying to cover it up. She felt almost sorry for the priest. She thought it must be an awful depressing sort of job where you have to go around to people's houses on a regular basis, to talk to them about the person who had died and then about the funerals. The parish was big with lots of elderly people, so she imagined he might have to do this every other week.

"Now, my dear . . . I hope you are feeling well enough," Father O'Donnell said, not looking directly at her, "because I am afraid we will soon have to think about the funeral details."

Maria's stomach churned. She was still thinking of her father as being in hospital. "When will that be?"

When Father O'Donnell raised his eyebrows, and held his head to the side, she realised she had spoken in a whisper. She repeated it again in a louder and clearer tone. "When will it be?"

"Well, that depends on when he is released from hospital . . .

and whether we will have to wait for any relatives coming from abroad."

Maria looked at the floor. "I don't know anything about that yet."

"Someone will need to call the undertaker's. There are two particular firms that the Italian community tend to use. They have their own traditions about these things."

Bernice moved forward to put her arm around Maria. "Don't worry," she said. "Franco and some of your father's friends will help with all of this. He will know what's to be done."

"You will have to give them any paperwork," the priest advised. "Insurance policies and documents of that nature. Does your father have a filing cabinet or anything like that?"

"Yes," Maria said, "he has one in the spare room where all his work things are." She shrugged. "But I don't know anything about them."

"Franco will sort it all out," Bernice said.

Maria looked at her and said, "Thank you."

Bernice turned to the priests now. "We have tea and coffee and sandwiches, if you would like to come into the room across the hallway."

When Maria followed her into the sitting room, she was a little overwhelmed by the number of people there, and thought it did not seem like her own home any more. Since the news of Leo's death began to spread, downstairs had been constantly occupied, which felt strange since she had become used to spending most evenings there on her own when her father was working.

The sofa, armchairs and dining-chairs were lined up in a regimental fashion around the perimeter of the room to allow more people to be seated, and the teak kitchen table had been carried through into the sitting room and placed against the back wall to accommodate food and drink for visiting mourners.

Maria had been relieved when Diana and Franco's wife, Bernice, said they would stay in the house to be with her at all times, sleeping in the spare bedroom which had twin beds. They kept busy, and seemed to be constantly moving between the kitchen and sitting room. Mrs Lowry stayed for most of the day, only going home to feed her family. Franco was also a fixture in the house but would go home that night to be with his three children, who were being looked after by good, dependable neighbours. Still in shock, he was uncharacteristically quiet – a ghost of himself.

Maria did not know how to react when Franco told her he had closed Leonardo's, and had put a sign up to let customers know about the tragedy.

"When will it open again?" she asked.

Franco stared at her for a few minutes and then he shrugged. "I don't know . . . it is something that needs to be talked about."

She stared at him now. "Who will talk about it?" she asked. "You're the only one who knows everything about the restaurant and how it's run. Who else is there?"

He turned his head to the side, now avoiding her eyes. "I don't know, Maria. I can't think about it now. I can't imagine being in it without Leo. There are a lot of things to think about the restaurant . . . but not now." He shrugged. "There are too many other things for me and you to think about."

"Will you help with the funeral arrangements?" she said. "I don't know anything about that either."

He turned back to her now, a sad smile on his face. "Of course. It will be a privilege. I loved Leo – he was like my brother."

Tears welled up in her eyes. "How can we manage, Franco? How can we do things without my father?"

He answered her honestly. "I don't know, Maria . . . I don't know."

She had never seen Franco look and sound helpless before – he had always been laughing and joking with everyone. A cold fear gripped her now as it dawned on her that Franco had depended on her father almost in the same way that she had. He had been in total control of everything – both at home and in Leonardo's. But he had handled things in such a light and easy way that it seemed as though everyone else had shared in the responsibility, and making the decisions too.

What, she wondered now, was going to become of the

restaurant and the house without her father. What was going to become of her?

Diana arrived back at the St Aiden's Avenue to find the house full of people. She joined Bernice and Mrs Lowry in the kitchen and they passed their time making tea and sandwiches, washing and drying cups and saucers, and brushing and mopping the kitchen floor. Although they chatted in quiet voices amongst themselves, they seemed to be listening all the time and automatically moved the minute they heard a car coming up the street or if anyone knocked on the door.

Maria found their presence reassuring, but every so often she found herself watching Diana who was quietly talking to people and doing all she could to help, but who Maria thought was not quite herself. But then, she reasoned, how could she be? Nobody was really themselves after what had happened.

Mrs Lowry was certainly distraught when she first learned about Leo but, after she had got over her initial shock and had cried for a while, she had just said, "When you get to my age, Maria, you learn to accept that life is going to knock you. And it's usually when things have been going well for a while and you become complacent that it catches you unawares." Then she had patted Maria's hand. "It's an old saying, but it's the truth – time is a great healer. You're a young girl, Maria, and a strong girl and you'll survive this. Better things will come your way."

"But I don't want anything different," Maria said, tears beginning to choke her. She had another cry and so did Mrs Lowry.

Then, the housekeeper took her in her arms. "You'll be all right, Maria. Your father had good friends, and we'll all make sure that you are well looked after until you're old enough to do for yourself."

Her words, meant to comfort Maria, instead left her anxious and wondering what the future held. Lots of questions rattled around in her head – could she still live in the house on her own? What was going to happen to the restaurant? What about Bella Maria? What about her and Paul? How would she get to her riding lessons without her father?

Her father was the one person who would have had answers to everything.

After their chat, Mrs Lowry went off to the kitchen to find cleaning materials for the downstairs toilet as she wanted to give it a quick going-over and, after that, she told Maria, if anyone was looking for her, she would be upstairs tidying up the bathroom.

"Poor Mrs Lowry," Bernice said. "She's heartbroken, but she's the old sort who copes by keeping busy."

At one point in the late afternoon the phone rang and Maria asked Bernice to answer it. Bernice listened for a while and spoke only a few times. When she came off, she went into the kitchen and spoke to Diana, and then the two women asked Maria if she would come up to her bedroom with them where they could talk in private. As she followed them up the stairs she felt as though there was a heavy weight in her chest because she knew she would hear something she did not want to hear.

"We've had a call from the hospital, Maria," Diana said, "and they asked us to tell you that they have been doing some tests on Leo today and will let us know when they are able to release him. It could be sometime this evening. He'll be taken to the undertaker's first of course"

Maria swallowed hard and tried not to imagine what that meant. All day she had been afraid that someone would tell her that the hearse was at the gate, and that she would have to face seeing him lying in a coffin. And yet, another part felt she desperately needed to know that he was back in their house, because something at the back of her mind told her that it would make life more familiar again.

"Is that normal?" she asked quietly. "Does that happen to everyone?"

Diana lowered her eyes. "Yes," she said, "I would think that it's very common."

Maria looked from one to the other. "What will happen tonight then?"

"I think it will be just the same as today," Bernice said, "with people coming and going and paying their respects to you."

Maria pictured how the rest of the afternoon would be and then the evening stretching ahead. Having to speak to more and more people she did not know, and sense the awkward, self-conscious way certain ones felt when they had to offer her their condolences. The worst part was listening to them all saying how they could not believe what had happened, and then overhearing them talking in low voices to Mrs Lowry or Bernice about the accident and pressing them for the exact details.

"How long will it be until . . ." She could not finish. She could not say the words *until the funeral*.

A flicker of alarm crossed Diana's face, as though she had been trying not to think of it herself, and she turned to Bernice.

"We don't know exactly when," Bernice said. "Franco is trying to contact your father's relatives in Italy. They will have to organise flights if they are coming over."

"But my grandparents are very old," Maria said. "They won't be able to come. They wouldn't be fit enough for the journey." She paused to think. "My Aunt Sophia stays at home looking after my grandparents, and my uncles – his two brothers – are in America. I don't think they have been there that long, so they probably wouldn't be able to come either."

Bernice nodded. "I'll speak to Franco."

Footsteps sounded on the stairs and they all stopped talking.

Bernice went to the bedroom door and looked out to see who was there. "Here he is now."

He told them he had come looking for some addresses and some documents. Bernice explained to him what Maria had told them about her grandparents and relatives in Italy.

He listened carefully and then he looked at Maria. "I understand what you're saying, but I think we must let all your father's family know, because someone will probably want to come – maybe a cousin or an uncle or someone like that. I know that some of his family came to Manchester before. Not recently, a few years ago."

Maria thought of all the people she saw when she went to Italy each year and could not imagine any of them travelling over to Manchester.

"If anyone does come," Bernice said, "you don't need to worry about them staying here. They can stay at our house or with some of your father's Italian friends."

"I have to ask you something else," Franco said.

His face was so grave Maria thought she hardly recognised him.

"I know you and your father have not seen your Irish relatives for a long time . . . but maybe we should contact them too."

Maria shook her head. This was the last thing she expected him to say. "No, no. I don't want them here. They wouldn't come anyway. They hated my father!" Her voice was becoming higher now, almost hysterical. "No one from Ireland has been here since my mother died and I don't want them coming here now that he's died too!"

"I don't want to argue with you, Maria," Franco said, "but your father told me that when you were older he wanted you to get to know some of your Irish family. He said –"

"If they didn't want to see him, then I don't want to see them!"

"That's okay," Diana said. "That's okay. You don't have to see anyone you don't want to."

Maria started to cry and put her hands up over her face, repeating, "I don't want them here – I don't want them here!" Then she went across the room, threw herself down on the bed and broke down into great heaving sobs that she could not control.

Seeing her so upset was the last straw for Franco and he had to leave the bedroom and go out into the hall, his shoulders heaving and huge silent tears running down his face. When Bernice followed her husband, Diana went over to the bed to try to console Maria or at least to check that she was not becoming so distraught that she was going to make herself sick. She sat quietly on the side of the bed, stroking Maria's hair, while she just kept crying and crying until she started to cough and choke.

"Bernice!" Diana called. "Would you bring Maria some water, please?" Then she turned back to Maria. "Don't let it overwhelm you – your father wouldn't want you to make yourself ill. He loved and adored you, and he would be so upset to see you like this."

Maria made a little muffled noise as though she was trying to speak but Diana could not make out what she was saying.

"We're all so sad, Maria," Diana said, trying not to break down herself, "and you're entitled to be sadder than anyone, because you were the most important person to him in the whole world. You were all that really mattered to him."

Maria suddenly went still and then the sobbing began to subside. Eventually she moved out of Diana's arms, wiped the back of her hands over her eyes and sat up. Then she looked up at Diana with her red and swollen eyes and said, "But you made him happy too. He never showed any interest in any woman after my mother died until he met you. I've never seen him as relaxed and happy in years."

Diana looked back at her and her chest felt so tight that she had to take a deep breath. "Thank you, Maria," she said. "Thank you. That means an awful lot to me."

"Don't thank me." Maria was shaking her head. "I don't deserve it. I feel so terrible – I feel so guilty."

"But you have nothing to feel guilty about."

"I have." Her voice was now a whisper. "When Stella told me that her mother was going to matchmake you and my dad at the races that day, I was really angry with her and I planned to do everything I could to keep you away from him. Everything she told me about you made me really want to hate you."

Diana looked astounded. How could Jane Maxwell have talked about her in such a way to her daughter? How could she have made her sound like such a pathetic, desperate case?

"If I hadn't met you in the church that morning," Maria said, "and discovered what a really nice, kind person you were, then you and my dad wouldn't have had all those lovely months together." Maria bowed her head now. "I wish he'd met you years ago because he wouldn't have been so lonely that he sometimes drank too much or gambled away his money. I wish he'd met you because he would have been so much happier than he was."

Diana pulled her back into her arms. "You have to stop thinking like that," she said. "It won't do you any good. And from what your father told me, he wasn't ready or interested in meeting anyone else up until now. Sometimes it's just the way life works out." She stroked Maria's hair again. "And maybe it's the way it was designed to be, because it was a million to one chance that you and I met in that church and then met up again at the races. The more I think about it, it's as if was as if it was all meant to happen."

Maria's head suddenly jerked up, as though something had just struck her. "Do you think that it was all in God's plan to bring us together?"

Diana's hand came up to her throat. "Who knows?"

Maria was silent for a moment. "Well, all I can say is that I think God is very, very cruel. Why did he bring us all together and let us be happy for such a short time – and then do such a terrible thing to my dad?"

Diana closed her eyes and Maria knew that she had no answers, and that she had probably been asking herself the very same thing since they got the call to go to the hospital.

The word continued to spread about Leo's death through neighbours, the church congregation, talk in the local shop and phone calls. Most of the people who called at the house to pay their respects were neighbours and local people who knew Leo from the church and the newsagent's and the other nearby shops. Then there were the others who knew him from the restaurant, the local pub he had frequented, the bookie's shop he placed his bets in, and the trainers and staff from the stables who looked after Bella Maria.

And there was a constant flow of Italian people who knew Leo from when he was a young boy first landed in Ancoats from Lake Garda. They arrived, several of them openly crying, carrying Italian bread and cakes, and some of the men brought bottles of Italian wine and liqueurs. They were quiet at first when they were drinking tea or coffee, but became more talkative afterwards when the ladies in the kitchen brought them glasses of whiskey or wine or sherry. When one or two of the Italian women were uncertain as to what to drink, Diana went into the kitchen and a few minutes later returned with a tray with small glasses filled with the Italian liqueurs which they found much more acceptable.

When any of the Italians came to speak to her, they all made it clear to Maria that she only had to ask for anything if she needed it and they would be there, and they all embraced her and told her what a fine man her father had been. She found their offers of help very touching, but struggled when some of the more emotional mourners started crying and going over all that had happened to Leo again.

Quite a few people were intrigued about Timothy, the man her father had defended, and wanted to know whether he knew what had happened to Leo. Maria heard two of the men asking Franco if Timothy had had the decency to call to the house to offer his sympathies, and she found she could not listen to it as it upset her too much and made her relive the night again.

Each time a group of people left, Mrs Lowry and Bernice said how surprised they were at the number of people who knew Leo, but not one bit surprised that they all spoke so highly of him.

Diana found that each person who came in with a story of Leo's kindness or his great sense of humour left her feeling sadder that she hadn't known him as long as some of these acquaintances. And, on a number of occasions, she overheard people asking Bernice or Mrs Lowry who she was, and why Maria was sitting with her most of the time. Whilst she was gratified to hear them both describe her as Leo's girlfriend, the fact that they didn't know she existed and seemed surprised underlined just how new their romance had been.

Maria's friends also appeared at the house in small groups for moral support, or with their parents. Stella arrived with both her parents, and when she saw Maria in the sitting room she ran over to her and they stood hugging and crying until they were separated when Mrs Lowry took Maria gently by the shoulders and Stella's mother did the same with her.

When the girls went upstairs to Maria's bedroom, Jane

Maxwell went to speak to Diana and said that Leo's death was the biggest shock she'd had in a long time, and that she still could not believe that such a fit-looking man in the prime of his life was gone. She had then thrown her arms around Diana, crying and saying how sorry she was because she knew that Leo had been the love of her life, and how awful it was for her to lose him so soon.

Diana, her heart sore with grief, silently and politely took herself off into the kitchen. She knew she could not trust herself to speak without telling Jane exactly how she felt about her. Bad enough that she had been talking all the nonsense about her matchmaking schemes, without adding to it by making a huge emotional drama out of her and Leo's relationship. But she knew it was not the time or place to let fly with her anger now, and so had to bottle it up along with all her other feelings.

More people arrived and gave their commiserations to Maria and Diana and Franco – who some people mistook for Leo's brother. Bernice and Mrs Lowry kept putting teacups and saucers on the table, and milk and sugar, and frequently did the rounds with an extra big teapot borrowed from Leonardo's. When plates of sandwiches and sliced fruit cake and biscuits were passed around, the sombre mood in the room eased a little and people began talking about the weather and things they had heard on the news.

At one point Diana and Bernice brought Maria to a quiet corner to explain that it was customary to make a small altar-like area, using a table and candlesticks and maybe a holy statue. It was too late to buy flowers today for it, but they would order enough flowers first thing in the morning to put on a small side table as well. Maria had asked what she was going to do about paying for the flowers and other things like the food, and Bernice told her that at some point she would be entitled to an insurance pay-out which would cover all these costs. Until then, she and Franco had discussed it and would pay any bills and the money could all be sorted out later.

Then, another car pulled up at Contis' gate and Diana saw two young men get out. She turned towards Maria and said, "I think you have some friends arriving."

Maria looked towards the window and saw Paul and Tony coming up the path. She felt an unexpected thrill at seeing Paul which was quickly followed by an enormous wave of guilt. She took a deep breath and went to open the door herself. She greeted them both quietly and then she guided them into the empty dining room and closed the door behind them.

"How are you?" Paul asked when she turned to face them.

She looked up into his concerned eyes and thought how grown up he suddenly seemed, with the same responsible air she felt around Diana. It made her feel a little safer in the midst of the nightmare situation she was in, and she wished that that Tony wasn't there so she could talk to him properly and he could reassure her that things were not as wholly awful as they seemed.

"I'm okay . . ." Her voice was faltering, and she was trying not to break down. "I still can't believe it . . . I just can't believe he's gone."

He moved towards her now and put his arms around her and held her close to him. She leaned against his chest and closed her eyes. She would have loved to have just stayed in his arms, but knew that it would make Tony feel awkward.

As she drew away, Paul held her shoulders gently and kissed her on the forehead.

"I don't want to ask you to go over it all again," he said, "but if what we heard is true – it shows what a brave and Christian man he was."

"It is true," she said, her eyes filling up. "He died because he went to help Timothy – a vulnerable sort of man – who was being bullied."

Paul nodded his head. "I remember your dad talking about him the night we were at the Palace Hotel and, when I heard, I guessed it was the same man."

Maria took her hanky out and rubbed it under her eyes. "It had been happening for a while – they're a bunch of lads who go around looking for trouble."

"I know what I'd like to do to them," Tony said, clenching his fists. "I'd like to give them some real trouble. Bloody morons!"

Maria looked sad. "Well, there's no point in us thinking like that. Both my father and Franco said it was an unfortunate accident and that they were just stupid boys showing off. They shouldn't have bullied Timothy, but they didn't deliberately set out to do something that serious."

"Have the police been involved?" Paul asked.

"I don't honestly know. I don't even want to think about it. If they are involved, then Franco will probably deal with it since he was there." She went to open the door to take them to the sitting room when she suddenly thought of Stella and her parents. "Oh, Tony," she said in a low voice, "I'm sorry, but Mr and Mrs Maxwell are in the sitting room with Stella. I don't want things to be awkward for you – would you rather stay in here until they are gone?"

He shrugged as if he didn't care, but she could see he looked uneasy. "I don't think they will say anything to me today. It's not the time or the place."

They went into the sitting room and when Maria saw Mr and Mrs Maxwell sitting on a sofa near the kitchen door, she led the boys over to chairs in the corner at the opposite side of the room. When they were seated, Maria – trying to think of something to talk about that would not be too sad or awkward – asked about a big race that was coming up the following weekend. It was a race she had heard her father and Franco discussing the last time she was in the restaurant and that she knew the boys would have a great interest in. It seemed bizarre to be thinking of anything else but her father, but she knew she needed to focus her mind on something ordinary for a while, and the three of them needed a topic that would also help distract Tony from thinking about Stella's parents.

She was listening to the boys quietly talking about the horse that was the favourite when Stella appeared at Maria's side to say hello and check if they wanted tea or coffee. She naturally spoke in a more serious tone than normal, but when Maria glanced at her she could see that her whole attention was focussed on Tony as if there was no one else in the room. For a moment Maria felt angry with her, as if Stella felt that even a sad occasion like this was worthwhile if she could be with him. But then she remembered how she had felt when Paul arrived and how she had wished they could be on their own, and she thought that maybe she was being hard on her friend.

When the boys said they would both have tea, Stella went back towards the kitchen. As she passed the sofa, Maria saw her mother reach over and catch the cuff of her jacket, pulling her to a halt.

Although they were quiet, and Stella kept her head bent low, it was plain to Maria that her mother was saying something very serious, and at one point she seemed to be appealing to her husband to become involved in the hushed discussion too. Stella appeared to be saying little, but Maria knew her well enough to know by the set of her jaw that she was not happy, and this was confirmed when she saw her friend jerk her arm out of her mother's grip and walk into the kitchen. She reckoned that Mrs Maxwell had been telling Stella off for being with Tony, and thought that if the romance continued there was going to be a big showdown over it, one way or the other. Over the weeks she had seen Stella getting more and more upset and annoyed with her mother about Tony and, from what Maria could see now, her mother was not budging one inch to meet her on this issue.

Paul and Tony went back to discussing the race, Tony talking quickly and dominating the conversation, but Maria thought there was an uncertainty in his voice and she was sorry for him because she knew it was all a cover-up because he felt uncomfortable with the situation. She remembered the anxious way she felt when she first started seeing Paul, in case the Spencers might not think she was good enough for him.

She now felt Paul discreetly reaching for her hand and giving it a little squeeze and when she looked up at him he leaned down and asked her in a low voice if she was okay. She looked up into his eyes and nodded, wondering whether, if they were alone, she could somehow explain that there were times when she felt she was her normal self – which she knew wasn't right – but there were other times when she felt that the people there and all the other things going on around her were like a strange, foggy sort of dream. And she would also have to explain that there were even times when she felt that this was not her house and that her father was not really dead.

She was listening to Tony saying something about one of the horses at the stables having problems with its front hoof when, out of the corner of her eye, she saw Stella coming out of the kitchen. This time she did not go too close to where her parents were sitting, and acted as if they weren't in the room at all. As she approached, carrying two china cups of tea with saucers, Maria noticed that the dark checked slacks Stella was wearing had slipped down lower on her hips, revealing what looked like her younger brother's snake belt. Maria had been with her in Stockport the day she bought the trousers about a month ago. They had been the smallest size in the shop and had just fitted her. She had obviously lost more weight since and they now looked almost baggy on her, and Maria wondered if maybe something was wrong with Stella that was making her continuously lose weight.

As Stella passed the teas over, Maria saw Diana come out behind her carrying a huge platter of sandwiches. She watched the elegant, attractive woman quietly going from group to group of the mourners, pausing to have a few polite words with each one, and she realised that things would be very different today if her father had not met her.

Diana was just coming towards Maria and the boys when the phone rang in the hall.

Bernice came out of the kitchen, looked over towards Maria and mouthed, "Shall I get it?"

Maria nodded.

A few minutes later Bernice came back into the sitting room and went over to speak to Diana, who placed the sandwiches on a table and went back out into the hall with her. When the door opened again, Maria looked over at them with anxious eyes and they beckoned to her to join them.

Beatrice took both her hands in hers. "Maria," she said, "that was the hospital. They said they've released your father and he's now on his way to the funeral director's." She was talking quickly as though she wanted it all over, as though she did not want Maria to think of him in the black hearse. "They said that someone needs to go to collect his belongings and – and collect the certificate. If it's okay with you, Franco and another friend of your father's will go for it."

"What certificate?" Maria asked.

Bernice looked down at the floor. "The death certificate."

Maria closed her eyes as the reality of the situation hit her once again, making her stomach feel as though it were doing somersaults. Then, just as she thought hysteria was going to descend on her, the strange foggy feeling came in its place.

"After that," Bernice said, "they will need to go through his things and get his birth and marriage certificate and some other documents so they can register it all."

"I told Franco that everything will be in the filing cabinet in the spare room that he used as an office."

"I'll tell him to get them now," Bernice said, "and if there's anything else we need he'll come and ask you."

Diana touched her shoulder. "Are you okay?"

Maria nodded.

"It's nice that your friends have come – it must be a help to you."

"It is nice." Her voice was flat. She looked from Diana to Bernice. "Is there anything else I should do?"

"We'll come to you if we need anything else," said Diana.

Maria turned to go back into the sitting room and, when she entered the room, she stood for a few moments with the door not quite closed, trying to compose herself before joining Paul and Stella and Tony across the room.

Then, she heard Bernice's voice from the hallway saying, "My heart goes out to that poor, poor girl, and it's awful having to ask her things about the funeral, but we can't just go ahead and choose things without her opinion. She shouldn't have to deal with all this at her age – there should be some relatives to do it for her."

"Is there really no one?" Diana asked.

"It doesn't look like it, but Franco is doing his best to contact some of them, although he's devastated himself about Leo. What I'm concerned about are the difficult things we still need to ask her."

"What's do you mean?"

"The coffin has to be chosen and it has to be decided what Leo is to be dressed in . . ."

"Oh, God . . ." Diana said.

Maria stood now as rigid as a statue, images of what now lay ahead for her father crystal clear in her mind. She suddenly felt that she needed to get out of the house, but she could not go to the front door and have to face Diana and Bernice after what she had heard Bernice say. She looked over towards the kitchen where she knew Mrs Lowry was, and wondered if she could go out into the garden without having to stop and explain herself to anyone.

She was just about to move when she heard Tony call out: "Stella!" Then she heard a loud thud which cut through all her previous thoughts. She turned to look over to where Tony and Stella were standing and her eyes widened in shock when she saw Stella collapsed on the floor, Tony and Paul kneeling beside her.

Then she saw Stella's mother rush across the floor and push Tony to the side. "Get your hands off her! Don't touch her!" She lifted her skirt a few inches to allow herself to kneel down at her daughter's side.

"I was only trying to help," Tony said as he got to his feet. "I didn't do anything wrong. She just suddenly fainted."

"*Get away!*" Jane Maxwell hissed, patting both sides of Stella's face in an attempt to rouse her. "It has nothing whatsoever to do with you. *She* has nothing to do with you! Her father and I will look after her."

Maria, somehow unable to move, felt sorry as she saw Tony's face flush with discomfort and embarrassment. He took a few steps back and, for something to do, stuck both hands deep into his jacket pockets. He then stood watching, shifting anxiously from one foot to another as though ready for a quick getaway.

Paul moved closer to Mrs Maxwell. "She was fine one minute – chatting away – and the next minute she just seemed to go into a dead faint."

"Thank you, Paul," she said graciously. "I'm sure it's just a little faint. Lots of girls get them. I'm quite sure she will be fine."

Maria watched as Stella's father appeared now with a glass of water. "Stella?" he said quietly, crouching down beside his wife. "Sit up now like a good girl and have a sip of water and you'll feel better."

Stella stirred a little as though she had heard him but moved no further.

"Come on now, Stella," her mother said. "You need to move. It's time for us to go home."

The door opened behind Maria and she had to move to the side to allow it to open fully. Diana and Bernice came in, followed by Jennifer Cox from next door and her mother and father.

Diana looked over to where a small group were gathered around the Maxwells then she looked at Maria. "What's happened?"

"Stella fainted," Maria said in a low voice, surprised to feel fairly normal again. "She seemed fine one minute and the next she fell to the floor."

"Oh, my goodness," Diana said. "I hope she's okay."

Jennifer Cox looked back at her mother and said, "I think we've come at a bad time. It might be best if we come back tomorrow."

Maria looked over and could see Stella sitting up now. "It's okay," she said. "I think my friend is recovering. Come in and have a cup of tea." The Coxes then in turn shook Maria's hand and had a few quiet words of sympathy with her, while she stood pale-faced and quiet.

A short while later Stella was helped up into a chair and then she drank some water, looking as if she was gradually coming back to herself. While her father was checking if she was fit to stand, Jane Maxwell came over to Maria. The Coxes excused themselves politely and left them to talk.

"I'm terribly sorry about what happened, Maria," Jane said, her face strained and pinched. "I know that things are hard enough for you without this happening. I think we need to get Stella straight home and into bed."

"I hope she's okay," Maria said quietly. She looked over and could see that Stella was on her feet now, and her father had his arm around her protectively.

"We must get her to a doctor and get her checked out. As you probably know, she has had a few fainting episodes over the years when her periods are due."

"That's probably what it is." Maria hesitated. "She's also lost a lot of weight recently . . ."

"Yes, a lot of people have noticed that. I hope it's not the ballet taking too much out of her. She's been doing more practice lately than usual – she's never out of the studio." She raised her eyebrows. "It's a change – a few months ago she was the opposite – we couldn't get her to do anything. But that's Stella all over; you can't tell her to do anything." She gave a loud sigh. "Oh, hopefully we'll get it all sorted."

Maria looked over to the corner where the two boys were and could see Paul talking to Tony, who was still moving from side to side and looking more uncomfortable than ever.

Jane followed her gaze and then pursed her lips and shook her head. "Dear God! She'd be an awful lot better if she kept away from that boy. I don't know what she's doing with him, and I hope she didn't arrange to meet him here."

"Tony being here had nothing to do with Stella," Maria said. "He came with Paul. He knows me and my father from the stables, and he's always been nice to us, and I think it was kind of him to come."

Jane looked back at Maria, her eyes filled with doubt. "Well . . . I'm so sorry it happened today. You have enough on your mind without this. We're so sorry about your father." Then, her eyes started to fill up. "Dear, dear Leo . . . How very unfair life can be."

Chapter 27

Maria found it strange when she woke up the following morning and realised she had slept through the whole night. She lay for a while just staring across the room at the window, getting herself prepared to face another of the endless days she would have to learn to live without her father. This day, she knew, would be harder than yesterday because her father was coming back to their house and, when he returned this time, she would no longer be able to believe that something miraculous might still happen that would change things back to the way they were.

At certain times – the foggy, weird times – the idea of Leo being dead was still like a dream to her. But, on wakening this morning, something at the back of her mind helped her prepare for what was coming. Today, she knew, the undeniable truth would be in this house along with her.

Nothing was going to change that now. No tears, no prayers, no hysterical breakdowns – not one single thing she could do was going to change what had happened.

Today, she realised, was the day when she would have to become a full adult.

The morning went by quicker than the previous day as a routine had begun to establish itself.

After discussions with Maria the previous night, it had been decided that this morning Franco and two of her father's Italian cousins who had travelled over would go to the funeral director's to register the death, and then they would choose the coffin. Although she was given the choice, the thought of looking at row upon row of polished wooden boxes that held the dead only served to terrify and upset her again.

But, after she had recovered enough, Maria took time to think about how Leo should look when he was in his final repose, and she decided that he should be buried in his black tuxedo. She knew he had been very proud of the handmade tailored suit and he had always looked at his best when he wore it on special occasions.

Diana ordered flowers from the local shop to be delivered to the house and two tall brass candlesticks, and one of the Italian men brought a full-size Italian flag which would stand in the corner until the day of the funeral and then it would be draped around the coffin.

Around lunchtime Maria phoned Stella's house to see how she was and her mother told her that she wasn't very well and was still in bed.

"I do apologise, Maria, for Stella fainting last night," she said "but I'm afraid her constitution seems to be very low at the moment. She has little or no appetite, and her father and I think that she was also probably overwhelmed by the sad occasion, as indeed we all were. Stella was very, very fond of your father, you know, dear, and she has no experience of that kind of thing at all."

Maria did not know what to say to that, so she said nothing for a few moments, then she said, "I hope Stella feels better soon."

"Oh, you're very kind, Maria, thinking of her at a time like this. I think bed is the best place for her until she's fully recovered, so she won't be going to school or ballet classes this week. I've made an appointment for Stella with our doctor so hopefully we'll get to the bottom of it and she'll be soon sorted out. She won't be over to you today and probably not tomorrow, but we are thinking of you, dear."

Maria was not surprised that no mention had been made of Tony or the way Mrs Maxwell had treated him last night.

Paul phoned during his lunch break to check how she was, and ask if he could do anything to help. He said his mother had suggested that maybe a run out in the car somewhere quiet might help, and that the car was there for him any evening to come over to the house. Maria thanked him but said she didn't feel she was very good company, and that she would ring him if she felt better.

People came and went to the house as before, and then the time moved on to mid-afternoon when the shiny black hearse turned off Heaton Moor Road and came slowly up the avenue to stop at the house.

Diana had kept herself busy with phone calls to the florist's and to La Femme, and then she had taken the time to cut and prune the white lilies and the roses and the gypsophila and then display them in the two tall crystal vases that Maria had found for her. She had taken another call in the privacy of the hallway from the shop about a dress a lady had ordered for her daughter's wedding and was worried might not arrive in time. She told Pippa to reassure the lady that the dress would arrive at least a week before the wedding, and then asked her for the number of the supplier and said she would straight away double-check. Five minutes later she rang the shop back and told her manageress that it was due to arrive the following day. While her own life was in disarray and she felt she would never care about a trivial issue like having a dress on time again, she knew other peoples' lives and routines still had to carry on.

She had just heaved a small sigh of relief that the shop issue was sorted when she turned around and saw the large dark shadow on the glass in the door. When she came into the sitting room to join the others to watch the hearse slow to a halt outside, she realised she was not at all prepared to see it or to see Leo's coffin. A tightness clutched at her throat and chest and her first instincts were to run upstairs and bury her face in a pillow somewhere and cry her heart out, but when she saw the pale frozen look on Maria's face she knew that she did not have that option.

A silence descended on the house and then Bernice went to open the door while Mrs Lowry shepherded Maria and Diana into the kitchen to wait until the funeral directors had the coffin settled in its place. Mrs Lowry took to her refuge of washing up the few cups and saucers that had gathered and Diana automatically picked up a tea towel and started to dry.

Then, when she heard Maria quietly crying, the housekeeper dried her hands and then went over and put her arms around her. "I've been to many funerals and lost a lot of people I loved. And I've learned that when we get over this part, Maria – the coming home – things will get a small bit easier. I don't know why, but I think we all find it harder without the person there. You'll feel better when you know he is here beside us all."

Maria closed her eyes and leaned her head on Mrs Lowry's shoulder.

"Do you think," Diana said in a low voice, "that I should go out there to help? I wouldn't like Bernice to think we're leaving her on her own."

"No, there is nothing we need to do," Mrs Lowry said. "Bernice is good doing the things we find hard. She is able to be out there with the men because she didn't have the same close feelings for Leo that we all have as she didn't know him so well. It's Franco who feels it much harder because he was with him in the restaurant every single day. She'll come for us when it's time to go in."

There was the sound of footsteps moving around and low talking, and then at one point there was the sound of metal falling against something.

There was a silence as they wondered what it was, then Mrs Lowry said, "It's the flag, it's only the flag."

A few minutes later Bernice quietly opened the door. "It's all sorted," she said. "You can come in as soon as you're ready."

The three figures in the kitchen froze and then, after straightening her back and clasping her hands in prayer, Mrs Lowry, who had faced this same challenge when she lost her own daughter, was the first to go in. Diana felt her heart beating so fast that she could hardly breathe. She glanced at Maria and thought perhaps she should go ahead and leave her to follow, but then thought better of it and she forced herself to put her arm around the still and shocked girl's waist and guide her step by step until they were at the side of the dark mahogany casket.

And there they all stood, each locked in her own individual loss, staring down at the dark-haired handsome Leo, as he lay in the deepest, most peaceful sleep amongst the delicate folds of cream satin and lace.

Chapter 28

About six o'clock that evening, Diana took some time off to go back to her own place to check on things and make a few phone calls. She only had an hour and a half or so, as Father O'Donnell was due back down to say the Rosary and prayers. The weather had kept dry and she was grateful to be out of the Conti house and in the fresh air for a while, and not have to think and constantly talk to people. As she walked along, it dawned on her just how bone-weary she felt, and she wondered how she could keep this up for the rest of the week.

After a few minutes the worst of the tension in her body eased off and her mind drifted back to the incident with Stella and her mother. She wondered whether there was actually anything wrong with the girl or whether it was all emotional upset due to her mother's disapproval over the boy she was seeing. Diana thought that Tony had looked and dressed appropriately for the occasion, and he had been every bit as polite and respectful as any of the other mourners. But, without even talking to him, she could tell that it was small things like his modern hairstyle and way of moving that stamped him as an ordinary working-class boy in the Maxwells' eyes and therefore not good enough for Stella.

Diana thought that if anyone had been inappropriate it had been Jane Maxwell when she snapped at Tony in front of everyone else when he tried to help. And even though her husband had obviously been trying to calm things down after Stella had fainted, Jane had still been quietly arguing with Stella about saying goodbye to Tony as they left the house.

Diana also felt sorry for Maria, caught in the middle of all this – being pulled between Stella and her mother was the last thing she needed at the moment. She worried now what was going to become of Maria when the funeral was over. She wasn't old enough to live on her own and, from what Diana understood of Leo's financial situation, the house might well have to be sold. He had explained that he had extended the mortgage on the house to pay for the restaurant and, from what he told her, she suspected that he owed money from some of his old gambling debts. After any insurance was sorted out and everything owed was cleared, it might not leave enough to hang onto the big house. It was something that Franco might be able to help sort out with Leo's solicitor.

She unlocked the door and saw several envelopes lying on the floor. She picked them up, then kicked off her shoes and went into the sitting room. She sat with her stocking-feet up on the sofa and opened the mail, quickly checking through it, glancing at bills and a letter from her solicitor about a legal issue some of the shop-owners in Didsbury had about the commercial rates. There was nothing of any importance. She threw the envelopes across to the coffee-table, some landed on top of it and some fluttered down to the floor where she left them. She wondered if she would ever find anything important again after all this with Leo was over.

She remembered feeling like this after her parents died within two years of each other. Her father had died suddenly of a heart attack, and Diana and her older brother, David, had to take turns at living with their mother week about, as she couldn't bear to be in the house on her own. David, a divorced vet living in Liverpool, did his best, but there were times when work demands got in the way and he rang Diana at the last minute to cover for him.

Then, exactly a year later, her mother had been diagnosed

with an unusual and aggressive form of liver cancer. She had received various treatments, but it became clear that none of it was working and her mother refused to have any more. She went downhill quite quickly and, just a month off her father's second anniversary, they were back in the church for her mother's burial.

Although she had got on very well with both her parents, her mother's death seemed to hit her much harder. Later, when she had to go to her doctor because she couldn't sleep and was constantly exhausted, he told her that she was probably suffering from delayed grieving over her father because she had been so involved with caring for her mother after he died. It was common, he said, and she needed to look after herself and give herself time to get over it all. He had given her a prescription for some sleeping tablets for a month, as he said getting back into a proper sleep routine would make the biggest difference.

After a few weeks she had begun to feel better and within a month she had been almost back to her old self. She realised then that she had run herself down with looking after her mother and not giving any real time to herself. She had a holiday with her sister that year and then later met Brian and everything suddenly changed.

Diana wondered now how she was going to put her life back together after losing Leo. After losing the person she believed she had been destined to meet all her life. She'd had enough experience to know that she would have to do it somehow, but at this very moment she just couldn't see how she was supposed to do it. As she felt tears coming into her eyes, she made herself move to her feet.

She went upstairs and turned on the bath and while it was running she made quick phone calls to the two women in charge of her shops. They both reassured her that all was fine and to take as much time as she needed. They gave her quick updates on sales and any deliveries and then told her to forget about work and look after herself.

She felt a little better after her bath and then, wearing her dressing-gown and with a towel wrapped around her hair, she phoned her cousin Nigel and his wife Clarissa in Newcastle and allowed herself to cry as she told them all that had happened.

"Diana," Clarissa said, "your life changed in a matter of days when you met Leo. You were ticking along thinking you would never meet anyone and then he turned up. I'm sure this will happen again. Just give yourself time to get over things and you never know what is around the corner. And you know that Nigel and I will do whatever we can to help you in the meantime. You only have to ask."

"Thank you," Diana said. "But I just cannot see beyond what's happening now."

"And Diana, please look after yourself and don't wear yourself out. It sounds as though you've taken on a huge burden helping out with the funeral arrangements. Don't forget you've only known Leo and his daughter a few months. Surely there must be other people there – family members – who can help?"

Diana suddenly felt stung at Clarissa's words. "It's complicated," she said, trying not to sound as hurt as she felt. "But thanks, I appreciate your concern."

When she hung up she quickly did her hair and then put on a plain navy dress and pearls and headed back to Leo's house about half past seven. As she walked along the quiet streets she mulled over the conversation with Clarissa. The suggestion that she had taken on far too much and had become over-involved in Leo's funeral made her feel naïve and almost foolish. But she couldn't be too angry with Clarissa because she was one of the kindest people herself, and obviously had her best interests at heart. But Diana had to admit that the comment had struck a raw nerve with her.

As she turned the corner into St Aiden's Avenue, it began to dawn on her that several other people had made similar comments about how good she was helping out at the house and looking after Maria. She suddenly wondered if Bernice and Mrs Lowry thought that she was pushy and too involved in things? They had seemed to welcome her help and had asked her advice on a number of occasions. Surely, she thought, they did not think her foolish as well? Did people think her own life was so sad and empty that she was filling the gaps in her own life with Maria even though Leo was no longer there?

No, she reasoned with herself, she could not allow herself to think like this. Given that she was so closely involved with Leo over the last number of months and had got close to Maria as well, it would seem strange if she deserted the girl now when she desperately needed support. People who had known about her relationship with Leo, like Mrs Lowry and Franco and his wife, had all seen them coming and going together and had all told her individually that they had been delighted for her and Leo.

Even the girls in La Femme and Gladrags had been delighted when she brought Leo to the shop and when Maria had started calling in. Even this evening they were telling her not to rush back to work, and to give herself time to recover from her loss. It was only people who didn't socialise with either of them on a regular basis or people like Nigel and Clarissa who hadn't been used to seeing them as a couple who took that attitude. As she came in sight of the house, she determined that she would stay as long as she was needed and then see what happened.

There were already about twenty people gathered for the prayers, so she had a few words with anyone she knew and then went into the kitchen. Bernice was there at the sink on her own, washing a pile of cups and saucers and glasses. She was pleasant as usual but looking tired which made Diana feel guilty for having deserted her. She told Diana that Maria had gone upstairs for a rest and that Mrs Lowry's son had collected her to sort the evening meal at home, but she would be back any time now as she wouldn't want to miss the Rosary.

"Is there anything I can do?" Diana asked. She picked up a tea towel. "I'll dry these for you."

"Would you mind checking first if anyone else would like tea or a drink or anything?" Bernice said.

"No problem."

When she checked and came in for two cups of tea, Bernice turned to her and said, "I'm glad you're back, Diana. You're such a great help here, because half the time I don't know what to say to people. I'm not so good with strangers, and you have a really easy way with them."

Diana paused as she poured the tea and looked at her. "I was worried earlier that people might wonder what I was even doing here. I've only known Leo such a short time – only a matter of months."

"But what does that matter?" Bernice said. "And anyway, it seems much longer because you've fitted in so well." She glanced at the door. "And Maria's taken so well to you. You've been such a help to that poor girl."

Diana felt her eyes fill up. "Thank you. You don't know how much better you've made me feel saying that."

"Oh, don't go getting upset again," Bernice said, half-laughing, "or you'll only start me off."

Diana blinked back the tears and smiled. "I'm fine, I'm fine." She started pouring again. "Let me take this tea through and I'll give you a hand to dry the cups and tidy up."

She came back a few minutes later.

"Everybody is fine in there – they're just chatting quietly," she said.

"Thank God." Bernice rolled her eyes. "Let's hope we don't have any more dramas like we did with Maria's friend. Wasn't that unbelievable? The poor girl faints and then the mother has a go at her boyfriend who was only trying to help!"

"I think there's a bit more to it than that," Diana said. "But hopefully they'll get Stella sorted out at the doctor's and then her mother will be a bit calmer. Jane Maxwell is one of my regular customers, and to be fair she's usually a nice enough woman, but she's been worried about Stella for a while, and I think the shock of what happened to Leo made her more highly strung than normal."

"You could be right there. I suppose people react in different ways." She halted. "The girl, Stella, is very, very thin, isn't she? Has she been ill?"

"Not as far as I know." Diana was choosing her words carefully now, not wishing to break any confidences between her and Jane.

"Well, at least Stella has her mother and father and they will see that she's all right. What's going to happen to poor Maria? Of course Franco and I could take her in, but we're not family. Mrs Lowry and me and Franco were talking this afternoon and we think we need to get in touch with the family in Ireland. I know her mother and Leo didn't have anything to do with them, but they are her flesh and blood."

"It's the last thing she wants," Diana said, "if you remember how she reacted before."

"Franco is going to have a word with Father O'Donnell, so we'll see what he has to say."

Diana glanced up at the kitchen clock. "I'll go and see if Maria's ready to come down." Then she looked back up at the clock again and gave a sad sigh. "This time two nights ago I was just heading into the restaurant to meet Leo. I would give anything I could to be able to turn all the clocks back those forty-eight hours."

Chapter 29

The evening passed with tears and talk and sympathy, and ended for those who loved him with yet more tears. And in the midst of the sorrow and the pain there was always the practical that had still to be dealt with. Mrs Lowry and the other women kept the domestic side of things running, letting the normality of the chores carry her and those with her along.

A devastated but dignified Franco consulted Maria on all the appropriate issues, and plans were put in place for the church service. Father O'Donnell guided them in the Catholic burial traditions whilst incorporating all the Italian traditional customs that were suggested by Franco and the other Italians.

One such custom was that of keeping an all-night vigil by the coffin. So it was arranged that Franco and Marcello Biagi, an older man who had known Leo from his early Ancoats days, would stay the night.

Mrs Lowry left straight after the Rosary and Bernice had also gone home to spend a night with her children, so Diana and Maria sorted Franco and Marcello with food and drink for the night ahead.

At one point Franco drew Diana aside and asked her to stay downstairs for a few minutes after Maria had gone to bed as he needed her advice on something. She said she would after she had made sure Maria was settled for the night.

Diana gave Maria time to get washed and into her pyjamas and then went up to check she was okay.

"I wish I still thought it was all a dream," Maria said as she climbed into bed, "because now I know this is the way it's always going to be about my dad, and I don't know what I'm going to do without him."

"You will manage – somehow," Diana told her. "It's best to just take it one day at a time and don't think too far ahead. Just try to get a good night's sleep and that will help."

As she tucked the bedcovers around Maria and kissed her on the forehead, it suddenly dawned on her for the first time that she was probably old enough to be Maria's mother. And, as she closed Maria's door and tiptoed back down the corridor towards the stairs, that thought set her mind to wonder what Anna Conti had actually been like. She knew from the photographs Leo and Maria had shown her that she was a striking woman with thick tawny-coloured hair and vivid green eyes.

When she came back downstairs, Franco beckoned her into the dining room, and when she went in he closed the door behind her. He sat down at the table and then he indicated a small pile of documents.

"I have some papers I want to show you which are about Maria," he said. "When I was looking for the birth and marriage certificates I found papers which were left by Leo should anything happen to him. There is one letter addressed to me and inside it there was one for Maria that I haven't opened." He rubbed his chin. "It was a shock to me when I read the letter, and I am just not sure what I should do about it."

She shrugged. "What does it say?"

"Read it, please . . ."

Franco lifted a long white envelope from the top of the pile and, when he handed it to her and she saw his name written in Leo's neat, distinctive handwriting, her heart lurched. She slid the two pages out and began to read.

January 1st 1968

My Dearest Franco,

I am so sorry you are reading this because it is something that I prayed would never happen. It means that I am gone and Maria is alone in the world. So now, I have to ask you, as my oldest friend and Maria's godfather, to do certain things for me.

I have decided to write this in English in case you choose to show this letter to Maria at some stage.

Since Maria is not yet eighteen, she will not be of a legal age to live independently, and it is my wish that she spend the time until she reaches that age with her mother's family in Ireland.

I know this will sound strange to you because, as you know, Anna had no contact with her family for years and it seemed they wanted nothing to do with her because she married a foreigner. Of course some old-fashioned Italian people can have similar ideas, so I did not take this personally and I encouraged her to go back home to visit them many times, especially after Maria was born. But, if you remember, Anna did not like travelling even in cars. She had a terrible journey when she first came on the boat to England and she told me that she could not face it again. I offered to pay for the aeroplane flight back to Ireland, but she said that was worse.

I did of course wonder why her family did not visit her, but she became upset each time I mentioned it, saying it was because of my being Italian and because she had chosen to stay in England, and there was nothing we could do. She seemed happy enough so I did not wish to upset her, but it did trouble me that Maria and I visited my family in Italy every year and my brothers came to stay before they left for America, and yet Maria never knew her mother's side of the family.

Some time after Anna passed away, I was sorting out her private possessions (just as you are sadly now doing with mine) and I discovered from reading a few pages of her diaries that there were reasons that she did not tell me for her leaving Ireland and never going back. She had secrets she did not want me to know, and because of this she cut her family off and would have nothing to do with them. The secrets were not important and I did not read everything as I felt it was not my business. I do not blame her now as she was a young girl when it all happened, and I am only sad she could not tell me and thought I would not have married her because of it.

I am also sad because I could tell at her funeral that her father and mother were broken-hearted and had missed her very much. But I think Anna maybe had told them that I didn't want to have anything to do with them and they seemed very awkward. Another complication, if you remember, was that Anna's mother had another child just after Maria was born and he had serious health problems so that Anna's mother could not leave him. I'm not sure whether he died soon afterwards or not. I wrote to them afterwards but they never replied.

So all these years have quickly passed and I was so busy with Maria and the restaurant, and using any time off I had to visit my old parents in Italy that I never thought of Ireland again. If I am truthful, Franco, I didn't want to go there and find out things about Anna that would make me think differently about her. But it has bothered me recently and, when I came to sort my will, I thought that maybe if I wasn't there Maria might spend some time with them before it's too late for her grandparents and uncle to get to know the lovely girl she is. I know they have room for her, as they have a large old house with land, and it would be good for her to spend some time in the country. You know how much I missed the Italian countryside myself and looked forward to seeing it every year.

Now, Franco, I know you – and I know you will be laughing at this, because you always told me that Lake Garda could not hold a candle to all the beautiful old buildings and statues in Florence, but who needs old buildings? That is something we will always disagree on.

You are my dearest friend, Franco – more like a brother to me – so I am asking you, if anything happens to me, to help to sort this out. I always hoped that when Maria was older she would want to visit Ireland, but she may not even think of this, so I am asking that it will be done for her now. After she reaches eighteen, if it hasn't worked out for Maria in Ireland, then I know that you and Bernice and Mrs Lowry will all help her to make a good life for herself in Manchester.

She has had a better education than you or me and we did okay, so hopefully she will find something to do that she loves.

I suppose if I had been a sensible man, I might have remarried and Maria would have a new mother and maybe brothers and sisters to look after her, but so far I have never met any woman who could replace Anna, and Maria always preferred that it was just the two of us.

You will notice the date on this letter, I have written one every year since Anna died and I update it on the first of every year. As you know, my finances have not always been steady, but this year things seemed to be improving – so hopefully, if the worst happens, there is money to clear everything I owe.

I am of course leaving everything I own to Maria, but I have not forgotten you either, Franco, my dear brother, and have left you something in my will to remind you of me.

If we do not get time to talk before you read this, you know how much your friendship meant to me as a young boy coming to England from Lake Garda, and how much I enjoyed working with you, and I thank you for all the happy years we spent together in Leonardo's.

I hope you remember me as well,

With much love to you, Bernice and your beautiful family,

Addio amico mio,
Leo

When Diana finished reading the letter, she did not look up at Franco because she knew how he must have felt on seeing those words – how devastated he still was at losing his dear, dear friend. Instead, she moved the pages around, reading sections of it over again. Apart from the sadness she felt for Franco, her heart was rent with the words that Leo had written before she had become a part of his life. How – up until this year – he had not imagined meeting anyone else because Anna, his wife, had still been the great love of his life.

Of course she had not expected him to announce that she had replaced his wife, given that they had only known each other a short time, but something deep inside her knew that if they had been together a bit longer, then that might well have been the case. Not only had Leo told her on a number of occasions that she had totally changed his life, but also how unbelievable it was that Maria had more or less found her for him. For a moment she stopped to wonder and even let herself imagine that she and Leo would have married and then had children – those brothers and sisters he talked about in the letter.

And of course, she could tell by the things that he had written – *anyone* could tell by the things that he had written – that all had not been as perfect in the marriage as it seemed. Anna Conti had not turned out to be the musically talented saint that Leo and Maria and everyone else had imagined her to be. She had obviously done something fairly bad for her to leave her home and family in Ireland never to return, and then she had compounded things by lying to her husband and others about it.

Then, as further thoughts and resentments began to form in her head, Diana, with the common-sense compassionate side of her, forced them away knowing that it was unkind and demeaning of her to think like that. Who, above all people, was she to judge anyone? She who had hidden dark secrets of her own?

She finally looked up. "I don't know what to say, Franco . . . I am shocked that Leo thinks Maria should go to Ireland and I don't think she will want to go."

Franco nodded. "I agree. But what is the alternative? I know the first person she will think of is Mrs Lowry, because she came to the house regularly to look after her and Leo, and things would remain the same if she kept coming. But Mrs Lowry is an elderly woman with children and grandchildren, and she isn't really fit enough to take over the full running of a house. Leo told me last year that she was finding it harder and was hoping to give up work."

"What else could be done?"

Franco leaned his elbows on the table now. "Maria can of course come to live with us but we have only a small three bed-roomed terrace house with two children in each room. Maria is used to all this!" He waved his hand expansively around the room. "She is used to so many things we would not be able to give her."

"Could she not stay on here? Maybe we could find someone suitable to come to live with her?" Diana wanted to rush in and suggest she herself might be able to do it, but she held back. If it was the right thing then she would be included and asked if she could help out.

"Who?" Franco asked. Tears then came into his eyes. "Who can give up their own home and move in with Maria?"

There was a silence during which she waited to be asked if she could be that person. She waited for a sign that her relationship with Leo meant something, and that the genuine feelings she had for Maria had been recognised.

"And if Bernice and I decided to move in here to look after her, would she want six more people in here? Younger children running up and down the stairs? I don't think so."

Diana knew now that Clarissa had been right. She had presumed too much on the relationship with Leo and his daughter. It was acceptable for her to be in this house helping during this sad, difficult time but, after that, it would seem that no one would expect her to have a place in Maria's life.

He joined his hands. "I don't want to sound as though I am saying anything bad about Maria – she is a beautiful girl both inside her heart and outside. But, she has always got on better with adults. Her mother was a quiet person – they read books a lot and listened to music and that kind of thing, and it's the way that she was brought up. And then, of course, afterwards she spent many of her evenings in the restaurant – it was her second home."

"But she loved it," Diana said. "She talked about it all the time."

"Yes, she did love coming to Leonardo's for a few hours, but Leo always told me she liked peace and quiet at home. I am afraid she would not get it with my family." He took a deep breath then he lifted up the pile of papers. "There is another problem about her staying in the house. There are complications here, legal and financial, which might make that difficult . . ."

"Do you mean there might be a problem about the house?"

"Yes," Franco said. "There might be big financial problems with the house and the restaurant. And then there is Leo's racehorse." He shrugged. "Who knows what might be left when it is all sorted? It was different when Leo was here and money was coming in. Like everyone else he would have eventually paid things off, but something tells me that the house will have to be sold. Who knows – even the restaurant might have to go. After that, the money left is Maria's but whether or not it will be enough for her to buy a home I can't say – and who would give a schoolgirl a mortgage?"

"I didn't realise things were so bad."

"They may not be bad," Franco said. "I just don't know until we speak to the lawyers and the bank. But it may take a long time and bills would have to be met on the house. If she were in Ireland with her family then she wouldn't have to worry about anything immediately. By the time it's all sorted and she's old enough to find work and live on her own that will be fine. It won't be long until she's eighteen."

"But Ireland!" Diana shook her head. "It's a lovely, friendly place – but she doesn't know anyone there. If she has to go away, wouldn't she be better going to Leo's family in Italy?"

"No, no. His parents are very old and feeble and, as soon as they are gone, his sister who looks after them is to join her brothers out in America. After that, there are only cousins there who she only saw once a year. Besides, they don't speak English and Maria only knows a little Italian. That would be much worse for her."

"It's very difficult." There was so much she wanted to say – to suggest – but she felt it wasn't her place to say anything.

"It is difficult, but Ireland is not that far away, less than an hour on the plane." He looked up at her. "I haven't told her yet, but Maria's grandfather and uncle are arriving tomorrow from Ireland to be here for the funeral. Father O'Donnell was in touch with the Parish Priest where they live and her uncle phoned him back at the presbytery before the Rosary this evening. He said he sounded very nice and was grateful someone had got in touch."

"It's just that they are strangers to her . . ."

"But they are her blood," Franco said, his voice matter-of-fact. "And that is very important. You read what Leo thought – it is a chance for them to get to know each other – for Maria to have some real family."

Chapter 30

Mrs Lowry put the lid back on the newly washed teapot. "I think a few hours down at your friend's house would do you the world of good, Maria. It's a lovely sunny afternoon and you need to get a bit of fresh air. I'm going to go home myself in an hour when either Diana or Bernice comes back. As long as there's one of us in the kitchen, the other women who arrive will give a hand with the teas and things."

Maria looked at her. "But what if I meet people? What if they ask me . . . I wouldn't be able to talk to them."

The elderly Irish lady put the teapot down on the worktop and came over to stand beside Maria and slip her arm through hers. "You won't meet anyone, love. Mrs Maxwell is coming to collect you at the gate." She squeezed her arm gently with her own. "I honestly think it would do you good. You need a little break out of the house, and your friend needs a bit of company with her not being too well. A bit of a chat will help you both."

Maria glanced back into the sitting room where Vincent and Johnny from the restaurant were sitting opposite the coffin, talking quietly to some customers from the restaurant that she didn't know. They had all had tea and sandwiches and were now sipping on whiskies and water or Italian liqueurs. Johnny had clearly been affected by her father's death and seemed totally

245

different to the boy she knew from the restaurant. His eyes were red-rimmed and not once had he tried to lift them to meet hers, instead just shaking her hand and muttering his condolences in a low, respectful voice.

It occurred to her that both the men and the women from the restaurant, who had not been working since Leo died, must be wondering what would happen when her father was completely gone from them. At some point she knew she would have to start wondering about the future herself. But for now she would just continue to take things hour by hour, minute by minute.

"All right," Maria said now. "I might go down to Stella's for a while."

Ten minutes after Maria rang her friend, Mrs Maxwell pulled up at the door.

As they drove along Stella's mother told her that Stella's younger brothers, Thomas and George, were at a special horse-riding summer school that week.

"Is it at our riding school?" Maria asked.

"No, it's a different one out in Prestbury. I thought it would be a bit of a change from the Spencers' stables, as we've been going there for years with Stella. It's probably about time she gave that up anyway with her A-levels coming up in the next few years."

Maria said nothing as she could tell by the tone in Jane Maxwell's voice that Spencers' stables was not her favourite place at the moment. Jane then went on to ask her how she was bearing up, and told Maria she had been praying for her to keep strong during this sad and difficult time. She said she had every confidence in her as she was a mature, sensible girl. When Maria said she was doing okay, she then repeated the apology for Stella's fainting and said that she was a bit better now, although she still wasn't eating all that she should. She talked about how concerned they were about Stella generally, and then gradually came around to the subject of Tony, which Maria guessed had been uppermost in her mind.

"I've no wish to be a snob or any of the things that Stella calls me but, tell me honestly, Maria, do you really think that boy and she make a suitable match?"

There was a small silence during which Maria desperately tried to think of a reply that would not betray her friend or make her mother feel snubbed. "I haven't really thought about it," she hedged.

"No, no, I suppose you wouldn't. But before all this – before this week – do you know how often Stella saw him? Do you know how close they actually were?"

"I don't know," Maria said. "Stella doesn't tell me everything and I don't ask her."

Jane slowed up as she came to the turn-off for their road. "I suppose what I'm trying to ascertain is – do you think Stella regards this Tony as her boyfriend?"

Maria shrugged. "I don't know how she regards him." She knew it was a lie which would normally have bothered her, but somehow at this moment it seemed of little consequence. Prior to her life being so horrendously changed, she would have felt like a rabbit trapped in Mrs Maxwell's headlamps, but today she did not feel compelled to say or do anything she did not want to.

They pulled up outside the Maxwells' house.

"Well, I just hope that it stops, one way or another, because he's not suitable for her at all." Jane made a grimace. "He's nothing but a Cockney wide-boy. It would be different if he was like Paul Spencer. He's a lovely boy. Now, why couldn't Stella go meet someone like him or that nice boy at ballet – James Granger?"

For the first time since her father died, Maria actually had the urge to laugh. It was such an automatically funny subject between her and Stella. How, she wondered, could Stella's mum not know how ridiculous Stella thought poor James was? Had she never really listened to Stella going on about him during practically every car journey back from ballet? She could see now that James's father being a hospital consultant meant more than whether Stella actually liked him or not.

As she walked down the Victorian-style hallway with the imposing mahogany staircase and the ornately tiled floor, Maria thought how absolutely perfect Maxwells' house always seemed to be. The lady who came in to help here, Gloria, was not relaxed and friendly like Mrs Lowry, who was always stopping for cups of tea and a chat. Gloria did everything with military-like procedure which delighted Jane Maxwell, but made Stella feel as harassed by the housekeeper to keep things tidy as she was by her mother.

When Maria went into the sitting room she found Stella sitting pale-faced in the high-backed chintz-covered armchair, by the fire. She was still wearing her pyjamas and a thick fluffy blue dressing-gown, and her fancy blue velvet slippers. When she saw Maria, she rushed over to hug her and then laid her head on her friend's shoulder and began to cry.

"Don't . . ." Maria said, moving back. "I can't cry any more. I keep getting terrible headaches after it."

"Oh, I'm really sorry!" Stella said. She went to sit back in the armchair with her feet tucked under her and her arms around her body as though she was hugging herself for comfort. She looked over to Maria, now seated in the armchair opposite. "Are you okay?"

Maria nodded. "As long as I don't think about it all too much." She noticed the dark circles around Stella's eyes. "How are you? Do you feel better?"

Stella shrugged. There was a noise in the hallway and they both turned towards the door.

Jane Maxwell stuck her head in. "Stella, I'm just popping out to the shop for some milk. If your dad rings from the office you can tell him I'll be back in ten minutes." She looked at Maria and realised she was still wearing her coat. "Sorry, dear," she said coming across the floor, smiling. "You must be wondering what sort of hostess I am? I didn't even offer to take your coat." She waited until Maria took it off and handed it to her, and then, as she was walking towards the door to hang it up in the hallway, she stopped dead. "Stella – how many times have I told you about putting your feet up on the chairs?"

Stella tutted and sighed under her breath and then shifted her feet onto the floor.

When the front door closed Stella said, "Thank God she's gone," and drew her feet up and tucked them back under her again. She looked over at her friend. "Maria, I need to talk to you . . . but is it okay to talk to you now while you're still so upset?"

"Well, you and me talking isn't exactly going to change anything, is it? And I suppose we can't sit here in silence."

"I wouldn't normally be so selfish wanting to talk about myself at a time like this . . . but it's really important . . . something I can't tell anyone else."

"What is it?"

Stella got to her feet now and came to stand in front of Maria. "Promise me . . ." Then her voice faltered and she dissolved into floods of tears.

Maria stood up now, realising this was serious and nothing to do with upset about the funeral. She put her hand on her friend's shoulder. "Stella, what's wrong?"

"Promise me you won't hate me! Promise me you won't hate me when I tell you what it is!"

"Of course I won't hate you. Don't be stupid!"

"Maria, I think . . ." she could hardly get the words out. "I'm almost sure that I'm pregnant."

"You're pregnant?" Maria repeated, her mind going back, trying to think when Stella would have had the opportunity to become pregnant. She couldn't remember any occasions when she and Tony had been away overnight or anything like that. "Are you sure?"

"I haven't had a period for nearly two months!" The tears were streaming down her face now. "I could be ten or eleven weeks by now."

"Oh my God . . ." Maria bit her lip. "I don't know what to say. Have you told anybody else?"

Stella shook her head. "Nobody . . . not a soul but you."

In the small silence that followed Maria couldn't stop herself imagining her friend in the physical intimacy that would have led to this happening, and found herself shocked, but she knew that Stella did not need to hear that, especially from her. There would be plenty of other people only too willing to voice that same shock along with disapproval and condemnation. And for all that Maria did not approve of what she had done, Stella was her best friend. They might have their ups and downs – and Stella might drive her mad at times – but she was truly fond of her. She loved the laughs they had together, and the way that Stella always seemed to bounce back whether it was from an argument at home or from when she was in trouble at school.

Maria suddenly thought. "What about Tony?"

Stella closed her eyes and shook her head. "He hasn't spoken to me since the other night in your house." She shrugged. "He hasn't a phone in the house where he lives, and any time I phone the stables they say he's out in the fields or that he can't leave the horses. I've left loads of messages for him to phone at certain times when I know Mum's out but he hasn't got back."

"Maybe he's really busy," Maria ventured. "Or maybe he's afraid to phone the house."

"Usually he gets one of the girls to call, and when I come on the phone they hand it over to him."

Maria caught her breath at all the deception that Stella used so easily to get around things. Stella had always done everything to get her own way, but it had usually been about harmless, trivial stuff. "And are you going to tell him about this?"

"I don't know . . . I keep thinking I should wait until it's definite."

"Your mum said that you're going to the doctor tomorrow."

Stella nodded. "The problem is she's taking me there. I know if I go on my own that I can tell the doctor in confidence, but I can't say anything if she's there." She looked at the clock. "I wonder if I could phone the doctor and ask him to call me in on my own for a while." She bit the side of her thumb. "Do you think he would do that?"

"I don't know . . . it depends what he's like. Do you know him well?"

Stella moved her thumb from her mouth. "He's the youngest one in the practice and more modern than the others."

"He might be okay."

"I'm going to ring now," she said, jumping to her feet. "I need to find out, and I can't talk to him when my mother is there." She went quickly out into the hall.

Maria's eyes followed her as she went, and she once again noticed how very thin and fragile her friend was.

Stella came back a few minutes later, looking relieved. "Thank God, he was really nice! I just told him my mother was bringing me down to the surgery because I had fainted, but that I needed to talk to him in private without her hearing. He said he'll bring her in at the beginning to ask her a few questions, then he'll ask her to leave as he wants to do an examination or something like that."

"That's great." She waited until Stella sat down. "Do you feel sick or has your stomach got bigger, or do you have any other symptom that might make you think you are expecting a baby?"

"It's the fact I've not had my last two periods that's worrying me, and that I've fainted a couple of times." Stella thought for a few moments. "I don't really know . . ." She opened her dressing-gown and pulled her pyjama top up a few inches and looked down at her stomach. "I suppose it's a bit early to tell. Oh, God, I hope I'm not!"

"I don't know anything about having babies," Maria said, "but I think you look thinner rather than heavier."

Stella gathered her dressing-gown around her and tied the belt. "You can't do ballet and be fat, Maria, you know that." She gave an odd little laugh. "And you definitely can't be pregnant and do ballet."

"What are you going to do if you are?"

Stella closed her eyes and then covered her mouth with her hand. "I don't know what I'm going to do. I've been praying since the other night. My mother will kill me and so will my father. They'd kill me if I was expecting a baby with Prince Charles, so God knows what they'll do when they find out that it was Tony."

"When could this have happened? I thought you didn't have many opportunities of being on your own? Was it the time of the all-night party? I thought you left early?"

Stella looked at her. "Who told you I stayed?"

"Nobody," Maria said. "I'm just asking because you can't have had many opportunities of being on your own."

There was a little silence during which Stella did not deny

staying late at the party and Maria did not push the point. Things were too serious, she decided, to argue about a lie told months ago.

Stella looked down at her nails. "Well, it was mainly in the car . . ."

Maria caught her breath at her friend's casual attitude about them having sex. If it was more than once, there was a fair chance that Stella was pregnant.

Stella looked up now as though sensing disapproval. Her face was still pale but there was a jut of determination in her jaw. "I'm not ashamed, you know. I love Tony, and when you're with the right person making love is the most special thing."

"Oh, Stella!" Maria said. "You're only sixteen. How can you be so sure?

"Well, I can't imagine feeling like this about anyone else, and I just feel we're going to be together forever. What about you?" she asked. "I'm sure you love Paul, don't you?"

"I certainly like him a lot, but I wouldn't . . ." She stopped herself from saying that she was not ready to think of going the whole way with him yet. She wasn't up to an argument about something that couldn't be changed and neither was Stella. "I don't know what the future holds for us –" She suddenly stopped. "I don't even know what *tomorrow* holds for me, Stella. When I start to think about it my brain just sort of closes over . . ." She could feel her eyes filling with tears.

Stella stared at her friend, her eyes wide and anxious. "I'm so sorry, Maria – I didn't meant to upset you. I shouldn't have told you all this – I know it's the completely wrong time. I'm so selfish. It's just that I didn't know where else to turn. I still don't know what I'm going to do if the doctor tells me for definite."

Maria wiped the tears away with the back of her hand. "It's okay, Stella," she said. "Nobody can change what's happened to my dad, and I understand you have your own problems to worry about and I'm glad you felt you could tell me."

Stella swallowed hard. "I'm scared, Maria." She closed her eyes. "All that stuff I said about thinking it was fine what me and Tony did – it's just to cover up how really scared I am. I know I've been stupid and I don't know why I did it. It's just at times I get really fed up with my mother and father always treating me like a child, and it makes me want to go and do whatever I feel like when I get the chance. But I know I've done something really wrong this time, and I just wish I could turn the clock back so that none of this had happened."

Maria tried to think of something to say that might console her. "Other people have had babies at sixteen," she said. "You won't be the first. Look at that girl in the year above us who left school last Christmas. Everybody knew she was pregnant."

Stella's face sort of crumpled. "But everyone thought she was a complete tramp, Maria!" Her voice sounded cracked. "All the other girls said it."

"I didn't mean you were like her – of course I didn't. I just meant that it happens to other people all the time."

The front door opened and Stella's mother called out to say she was back and Stella moved quickly to sit properly in the chair. A few minutes later she stuck her head in the door.

"Tea or coffee, girls? Or would you prefer some lemonade?"

Maria said she would have a cup of coffee and Stella said she would have the same.

"Did you have a nice chat while I was out?" She smiled brightly at the girls. "I'm sure you did, and I hope you both feel a bit better now."

Chapter 31

While Maria was out, Franco and Diana went up to the presbytery to discuss how they were going to tackle introducing Maria to her relatives. It was a sunny, dry afternoon, so they decided to enjoy a breath of fresh air and leave the car. As they walked along, Diana thought what a decent, solid man Franco was. She felt she had got to know him and Bernice well these last few days, and that he had all the fine points that Leo had described before she met him – he was a good worker and a real family man.

"I was worried that Mrs Lowry might go against things," Franco said, as they went along, "but when I showed her Leo's letter this morning I thought she seemed to come round."

"I thought the same," Diana said, "because she told me she had met Anna's parents briefly at their daughter's funeral, and couldn't understand why they didn't make things up with Leo then."

"We'll never know the true story," Franco said. "Leo obviously did not want to tell anyone what he had found out."

"Well, I suppose it shows you what a loyal person he was."

Father O'Donnell was very positive about it all. "They sound like decent, caring people," he said, "and after we got talking, the first thing her uncle suggested was that she go back with them until she's old enough to live independently. He said his mother and father would be delighted to have her back in Ireland, and had always hoped she'd come to them at some point. They said they'll have someone in taking care of the farm while they are over, and they also have not booked their flights back yet. They will stay up in the Elizabethan Hotel until she decides whether she is going back with them or not. They also said not to worry about money for Maria's flight back with them, that it will all be taken care of."

Franco threw his hands up. "Well, that's all very good news," he said. "And I have the letter her father wrote to her, so we just have to decide now whether we give her the letter before they come, or let them come and introduce her to them first before she knows what Leo intended for her."

"I've been thinking about it constantly since last night," Diana told them, "and I think it would be better to let her meet them first and spend a day or two with them before giving her the letter. It's going to be a big enough shock when she reads it and knows her father had been so worried about leaving her that he had to plan all this in advance. Also, if she knows that she might be going to Ireland, she might refuse to meet them at all."

"She's not that kind of girl," Franco said. "She has always taken heed of her father."

"But she's not herself at the moment – you saw how she reacted when it was suggested they even come for the funeral. She's still distraught at having lost her father and she's not thinking straight."

"Do you think she will be upset when she sees them?" Father O'Donnell said. "Could it make her go hysterical or anything like that?"

Diana looked at Franco then back to the priest. "I have no answer for that. The problem is she thinks they wanted nothing to do with her father all those years because he was Italian, but it turns out that her mother had other reasons for not going back to Ireland."

Father O'Donnell nodded his head. "I know. Anna talked to me about it when she was marrying Leo. Some of it was during Confession, so you both understand that I can't discuss anything that she said in the confessional box, but she talked to me here at the presbytery about other things related to it, which is quite different." He cupped his chin in his hand. "I think a way round it might be if I see Maria before they arrive this evening, and explain to her that the family had absolutely nothing against Leo, and that her mother had her own reasons for not wanting to go back to Ireland. She has to realise that it was her mother's decision to drop contact with the family and not theirs."

"And do you think that she will agree to see them after hearing this?" Diana asked.

"I think so," the priest replied. "Then hopefully she will get on well with them and after the funeral we can show her the letter when all the other people are gone and everything has quietened down."

"I think also, Father," Franco said, "that if she understands that there are financial difficulties to be sorted out and the house and the restaurant may have to be sold, she might see things differently."

Father O'Donnell sat back in his chair. "It's an awful lot for a young girl to take on when her life has been so shattered by her father's death. But we have looked at all the options and it would seem that this is the best one she has."

Diana could not stop herself. "Have all the options been examined? Is there nowhere here she could live and continue with the life she is used to? I am just so worried about her going to a strange place where she knows no one. She has good friends here."

Father O'Donnell looked doubtful. "But we have to remember her age. It's important at this delicate, impressionable stage in her life that she is with relatives who will guide her in the proper ways that her father would have wanted. And it appears that the Italian side is not an option as Leo's parents are very elderly and there's the language problem and all of that."

Franco nodded in agreement. "Plus we have to remember it's what her father wanted," he stressed. "It's what Leo has instructed should happen. If I had not found that letter, then it would all be very different. Bernice and I would have assumed that we should take responsibility for her because she's my godchild and we both love her very much – though we're not blood family and our way of living is not what she has been used to on her own with Leo."

"I feel that we have to abide by her father's wishes," the priest said. "It was all laid out in the letter."

Diana looked from one to the other, thinking that her relationship with Leo and Maria counted for nothing because it had been so short, and yet she knew deep down that he had cared deeply for her. She was sure that if they had only had a few more months together – if they had only reached the first of January when he was updating his letter – then he might have mentioned her as a possible guardian for Maria.

She kept quiet throughout the rest of the discussion as the men planned how Father O'Donnell would come down to the house and he and Franco would explain to Maria about why they had informed her grandparents about the funeral, and why they felt it was important that she should be receptive to them.

After the meeting, she walked back to the house with Franco and she could see and hear the relief in him, while she herself felt flat and apprehensive.

"I think I will make a special macaroni dish for tomorrow," he told her. "Just for ourselves, the people who are doing all the work. Maria loves it, and it will be a change from the quick food we have been eating."

Back at the house Diana helped the ladies with the usual domestic chores and looking after the mourners and then she set out for home just before five o'clock to freshen up for the evening. She was able to leave a little earlier since Maria was at the Maxwells' and probably wouldn't be back until just before the Rosary at eight. Two of the waitresses from the shop had volunteered to stay in the house with Franco, so Bernice had gone home as well and so had Mrs Lowry – they were anxious to be back to make sure everything was as it should be for Maria's Irish grandfather and uncle arriving.

When she arrived at her own place, Diana got the impression that her next-door neighbour, Mr Singleton, had been watching for her, because the minute her hand touched the latch on her gate, he appeared at their door. He wanted to know if she would, in the circumstances, still be able to feed Minnie for them, as they would really like to make the trip to the Lake District since the weather was so nice.

"How are things at your friend's house?" he asked. "Mavis and I are still shocked to think that lovely man is dead and gone."

She turned to check she had put the latch properly on the gate. "I can still hardly believe it myself," she said. "But that's life. You just have to get on with things."

"And the young girl? How is she coping?"

"Up and down," she sighed. "Up and down."

"When is the funeral?"

"The day after tomorrow."

He held a finger up. "I've just remembered. We have a sympathy card for you. Mavis told me to watch out for you and give it to you. I've got a head like a sieve these days. " He went back into the house for a few moments and through the open door she could see him pick up the card from the hall table.

"You're very kind," she said, when he gave her the card.

"Is it very busy down at the house?"

"Yes," she said, "there are people constantly coming and going."

"When it's as busy as that, it's nice to get a bit of a break on your own from it." His face became sad. "I had a younger brother who died last year and it was non-stop from morning until night. That's what you get with big families, isn't it? It was mainly his wife's relatives – she had ten brothers and sisters."

After receiving the usual instructions about the feeding times of Minnie the cat, Diana went in and made her phone calls to the shop before they closed and checked all was well. Then she went upstairs and had her shower. Choosing her clothes didn't take long as she had a limited wardrobe of dark or black things. The warm weather made it more difficult as her summer clothes were all colourful, but she settled for a black knee-length fitted skirt and a black short-sleeved chiffon blouse with a bow which tied to the side.

As she was putting her mascara on in front of the small bathroom mirror, she noticed how pale her face looked against the black and her dark auburn hair. She wondered also how she would introduce herself to Leo's in-laws. A family friend? A friend of Leo's? All the other mourners could be described in the exact same way. 'Girlfriend', she felt sounded too flighty somehow – but she supposed that's all she had been.

The phone rang as she was leaving and when she picked it up it was Clarissa.

"Diana," she said, "I've been thinking about you and hoping you're doing okay?"

"It's been hard," Diana admitted, "but I suppose it's sunk in now and it's just getting through until the funeral is over the day after tomorrow."

"I know it's been hard on you," Clarissa said. "And I don't want you to think I don't understand what you've been going through and the effect it's had on you. I was worried after our last chat when I said you hadn't been seeing Leo very long, that I might have given that impression. When you meet the right person it doesn't matter how long you've known each other." She halted. "I just wanted to say that to you."

"Thanks, Clarissa," Diana said. "I appreciate that."

"I also wondered if a nice break might do you good after this long week. You haven't had a decent holiday these last two years, and it doesn't look as though we're going to get away until after Christmas as Nigel is really busy at the moment at work. It just occurred to me that there's no reason why you and I couldn't have a trip away by ourselves. I have about a month's annual leave I could use, and if you could sort the staff out at the shop it would be lovely to head away somewhere nice."

"Oh, I'm not sure . . . I haven't thought about holidays or anything like that."

"Well, as I've said, it might just do you good – why don't you think about it?"

Diana looked at her watch. "I'm afraid I've got to rush now, but when it's all over I promise I will think about it."

For the first time it was quiet back at the house. Instead of seeing small crowds of people over by the corner where the flowers and the candles and the holy pictures were, Diana caught her breath when she saw the coffin on its own, with no one standing or kneeling or praying beside it. The door to the kitchen was closed, and she could hear Bernice talking to the Italian women. She stood for a moment looking over at it then she slowly went across the room.

He looked the same as the first time she had seen him in the coffin, but there was a waxy pallor to his tanned, handsome face that she had not noticed before. She closed her eyes and remembered the first time she saw him at the races and how, apart from his good looks, she had been captivated by his energy and enthusiasm and interest in everything around him. Poor Leo, she thought – far, far too young to die. And he'd had such a love of life and people – and so much to live for.

Within half an hour the house was busy once again, and Diana was again serving refreshments when Jane Maxwell dropped Maria off, and came to the door to have a few words with Diana. She told her that she thought the few hours together had done both girls the world of good. She then talked about Stella's doctor's appointment the following day and said, what with Stella still not being well and fainting on her last visit, she hoped nobody minded if they didn't see them again until the day of the funeral.

Diana walked out to the car with her. "Is there no improvement at all with Stella?"

"I honestly don't know," Jane said. "All I do know is that there is something wrong with her and we need to find out what it is. I'm trying not to think about it tonight. We'll face whatever it is when we find out tomorrow." She closed her eyes. "I'm just hoping and praying we haven't got another Astrid on our hands. If it is, God knows what will happen."

Diana looked at her for a moment, her brow knitted in confusion.

"The old school friend I told you about. Who ran away from home to marry a lower-class boy."

"Oh, yes," Diana said quickly. "I remember now. I'm sure it won't be that. Stella's a sensible girl."

"I am glad you think so, but I'm afraid I know different. All this getting sick, fainting . . ." Jane shook her head. "My heart is in my mouth all the time." She paused. "Just at the end there when Maria was in the bathroom, Stella said Maria had got upset. It was something about her not knowing what's going to happen to her after the funeral. I know she's not old enough to be here on her own, but we presumed she would go to live with her dad's friend from the restaurant. Is that not the case?"

Diana hesitated. "It may not be as straightforward as that," she hedged. "I think there are a few options."

Just at that point a car came up the avenue and they both turned to look. When Diana recognised Father O'Donnell's car her heart started to race, knowing that any minute she was going to come face to face with Leo's father-in-law and brother-in-law. She wasn't sure whether to walk quickly back into the house now or stay and greet them. When they saw the priest trying to manoeuvre his car into a tight space at the corner, Jane said she'd better move the car to give them more room, and that she would see Diana at the funeral.

By that time, Diana felt it would look rude if she just walked in, so she waved Jane off then stood just at the gate. She watched as the back door of the car opened and a tall, sandy-haired young man, who she estimated to be around thirty, with a strong nose in a dark suit, got out and went to open the passenger door. A few moments later a slightly shorter, stockier grey-haired man in his mid-sixties emerged, and then the priest, dressed in his dark soutane and carrying his prayer book.

It struck Diana that Maria did not look at all like her Irish relatives, apart perhaps from her eyes , which although dark, were not quite as dark as Leo's were.

"Ah, Diana!" Father O'Donnell said, coming towards her. "This is Mr Patrick Donovan and his son, Jude. Diana was a close friend of Leo and Maria."

The two men came forward, the younger man first. "Very nice to meet you, Diana," Jude Donovan said, coming to shake her hand. His father did the same and she noticed he was limping slightly. When they both smiled at her, she could see a strong resemblance between them, and thought they were both surprisingly good-looking men. She saw no reaction other than friendliness on their faces.

The priest gathered them together, and then said in a quiet tone. "I've explained the situation to Patrick and Jude, and they agree that it's best if we tackle things one step at a time. We want her to get to know them a little better before broaching the subject of her going to Ireland. I think it best if I go in ahead and speak to Maria in the dining room and get her prepared to meet them." He turned to Diana. "If you wait outside here for a couple of minutes until I have her safely in the dining room, then you might bring her grandfather and Jude into the kitchen for a cup of tea."

"Thank you, Father," Patrick Donovan said. "We appreciate the help you're giving us."

Father O'Donnell clapped him on the shoulder. "She's a good girl, and we need to do the best we can for her."

They watched as the priest went into the house and then Jude Donovan looked at Diana and said, "It's a lovely street, isn't it?"

"It is," she said.

He glanced at his father then he said, "Do you know Maria well?"

"Yes, I think so. I only got to know her and Leo this year, but we all got on very well."

"It's a terrible situation," Patrick Donovan said, "terrible altogether. The last thing you expect to hear about a fit and healthy young man."

Diana swallowed hard and nodded.

"According to Father O'Donnell he was helping some poor harmless *créatúr* when it happened."

"Yes," she said. "That's what happened. He died because of a bang to the head." She was surprised she could say it so easily when a few days ago she could hardly bear to think of what had happened.

"Shocking, shocking . . ."

"Leo was obviously a very decent man," Jude said, "and

Father O'Donnell said he was held in high regard by everybody who met him."

"Yes," she said. She suddenly felt she had to give the very best account she could of Leo. She had to make sure they understood the kind, generous man he was, because she had no idea how his wife had painted him to her family. "Hundreds of people have called to the house to pay their respects. People from when he first came to England when he was a young man, people from the places he worked in, members of the local Catholic Church where Father O'Donnell works, customers from the restaurant and of course all the Italian community."

"That tells you the measure of the man." Jude looked over at his father. "We're just very sorry we never got to know him."

Patrick Donovan nodded his head. "What can we say? It's not the way we wanted it . . . it's just the way things have turned out." He looked at Diana now. "How has Maria taken it?"

"I think it's gradually sinking in." She looked now and saw Father O'Donnell at the door, gesturing to them to come into the house. He pointed at his chest then the dining room, then he pointed to Diana and then at the sitting room. Diana looked at Maria's grandfather and said, "I think it's safe for us to go into the house now."

Diana brought them into the crowded sitting room. They seemed oblivious to the other mourners as they went straight to the corner where the coffin was. They bowed their heads in prayer, Patrick taking his black rosary beads from his pocket and threading them through his fingers. She waited a few minutes by the door to the kitchen until they had said their prayers and then they came over to her.

"He looks well," Jude Donovan said in a quiet and respectful voice. "He's hardly changed since I last saw him all those years ago."

Diana saw a look of wretchedness cross Patrick Donovan's face, but he just bent his head and said nothing, and Diana knew that for a moment he was reliving his own daughter's funeral. She then brought them into the kitchen and introduced them to Bernice, Franco and Mrs Lowry. Whether any of them had been introduced on that previous occasion by Leo, she could not tell, for no one said anything, and she supposed it would be difficult for the Donovans to remember after all that time. After shaking hands with them, Diana noticed that Mrs Lowry said nothing, instead turning to the teapot and cups to sort drinks. It occurred to her that the housekeeper of course knew Anna Donovan well and, even though she had read Leo's letter, she probably still had mixed feelings about meeting the family after all those years.

Bernice offered them food but both men thanked her and said tea alone would be fine. Diana moved to the sink to help Mrs Lowry with washing up while Franco talked quietly to the men as they drank their tea. From the small snatches of conversation she overheard and the way both Irishmen reacted to him, Diana could detect no awkwardness about his nationality or anything that he said. When she went over to offer them refills and they thanked her warmly, she again could only detect a pleasant friendliness about them that seemed genuine.

Twenty minutes had passed since they came into the house and there was no sign of Father O'Donnell. Diana felt the knot of anxiety in her stomach tighten, and she could see the others glancing at the clock.

"What time did you say the Rosary would be?" Patrick Donovan asked.

"Eight o'clock," Franco said.

Everyone then looked up at the clock to see that it was just after half past seven.

Father O'Donnell, looking very serious, came into the kitchen and closed the door behind him.

"I think I've made a little bit of headway," he said, "although it wasn't easy at first. But, after a good discussion with her, I'm delighted to say that Maria is willing to meet Patrick and Jude." He joined his hands together and closed his eyes for a few moments as though in prayer.

"How is she, Father?" Jude asked, his forehead furrowed.

"Given all that girl has gone through," the priest said, "she is better than could be expected." He looked over at Diana. "Maybe you and Franco would come into the dining room with us?"

Diana's heart was pounding as they all made their way through the mourners in the sitting room out into the hallway and across to the dining room. Maria was sitting at the far end of the table, with her elbows leaning on it and her hands clasped together over her face.

As soon as the door was closed everyone sat down – the Donovans at the opposite end of the table from Maria – and Father O'Donnell started off. "I don't know if you remember your grandfather, Maria, but this is him – Patrick Donovan – and this is your Uncle Jude."

Maria lifted her head and looked over at them and Diana saw the red rims under her eyes.

"They understand it's very difficult for you meeting them like this," the priest continued, "and they just want you to know that they have come here tonight with the utmost respect for you and your father."

Jude Donovan's eyes flickered anxiously from the priest to Maria. "The last thing we want, Maria," he said quietly, "is to make you feel in any way uncomfortable. We're very grateful that Father O'Donnell was good enough to contact us and tell us about . . . tell us what had happened and, if you feel okay about it, we would like to stay for the Rosary tonight and come back for the funeral."

Maria's head drooped and her hair came down to cover her face, and instinctively Diana moved from her place to put her arm around her. She wanted to tell her that it would be all right and that her grandfather and uncle seemed like very nice people, but instead she kept quiet for fear of it looking as though Maria had no say in the matter.

"Maria . . ." her grandfather drew a weary-sounding breath, "we know that it's very hard for you, but there have been misunderstandings about the past, and if you'll give us the chance we would like to make up for that. What's past is past, but you're our family and this might be the time for us to get to know each other in the way we should have a long time ago."

Maria suddenly sat up straight in her chair, her body stiff. "Where is my grandmother? Why didn't she come with you?"

Jude leaned forward now. "She's back at home with my

younger brother, Ambrose. He's not in the best of health . . . and she doesn't like us all to be gone from him at the same time."

There was a strained silence, then Father O'Donnell looked at his watch. "I think maybe now if we all go inside for the Rosary, and you can chat between yourselves later."

Everyone rose apart from Maria.

Jude spoke quietly to his father and then leaned over to Diana and said, "If it's okay, I'd like a quiet word with Maria on my own."

Chapter 32

The sun glinting through the curtains woke Maria early the following morning and her first thoughts were of her father lying in the room below and then, one by one, all the events of the previous day fell back into place. She wondered if Stella had slept at all knowing she had her doctor's appointment this morning, and she wondered what would happen to her after that.

She then thought of Paul and his exam results. After hearing Stella's mother say that the A-level results had come out a few days ago, she had asked if he had received his when he rang her the night before. He then told her he had got the results the day he and Tony had come out to the house but he hadn't wanted to start talking about something like that when he knew there were much more serious things going on. He then said he had got three A-levels which he was astounded by – two B's in English and History and a C in Maths. She said it was fantastic news and congratulated him, and asked if it the grades were enough for the college in Northumberland he had applied to.

He told her that it was, and he was sure he had a place on a year-long course in Horse Breeding and Training which would help in his proposed stable-management career. The course, he said, started mid-September, so he had a few weeks to sort out all the things he needed and maybe go up for a visit beforehand to see the college accommodation where he would be living.

"I thought," he said, "that if you feel up to it, I could get the car one day after the funeral, and maybe we could take a drive up to Northumberland for the day. I thought it might do you good to get away – a run out in the country to get a bit of fresh air?"

Maria thanked him and said she would see how she felt and this morning, as she lay there, she still could not think that far ahead or imagine enjoying a day out. Apart from gearing herself up for the funeral tomorrow, she had the complication of her uncle and grandfather to think about.

During the years since her mother had gone, she had built up a picture of a cold, heartless family who had rejected both her mother and her father, and had made little effort with her. But the two men who had sat with her in the dining room had not fitted into that picture at all. And the brief talk she'd had with her uncle had forced her to rethink everything she had believed. He said that hopefully one day they would get the chance to sit and talk properly about all that had happened between his parents and his sister and Leo.

She had looked at him, her face white with tension. "Why couldn't you have said this when my dad was alive? Why couldn't it all have been sorted out years ago?"

Jude Donovan had looked back at her with sorrow in his eyes. "I have no answer to that. I cannot answer for those involved but, for what it's worth, I agree wholeheartedly with you. I was only young when it all happened and didn't understand anything about it. But what I do believe is that no family should have been shattered the way ours was. And it should have been fixed up long ago. Time just added to all the damage."

"It's too late to do anything about it now," she said. "What's done is done."

"I fully understood how you feel," Jude replied. "But I think for the people that are left it would never be too late to get to know you." He went on to tell her that he and his father would be up in the Elizabethan Hotel all day the following day and they hoped she might come up and join them for lunch or a sandwich or whatever she felt like.

When her grandfather and uncle had gone, Maria had sat on her own trying to make sense of this latest bombshell that had dropped amongst the debris that used to be her life. She was also disconcerted by the striking resemblance that Jude Donovan bore to her mother, not just by the shape of his face but in his accent, mannerisms and even in the way he held his head to the side when he was listening. Although he was a number of years younger, and had that stronger but not unattractive nose, there was no denying that they were brother and sister.

He had immediately presented as a pleasant and polite man and she had instantly sensed he had that same warmth and innate decency and consideration for other people as her father had, and he had also shown himself to be a good listener. She also thought that something about the way his eyes crinkled so easily as he talked indicated that, under less serious circumstances, his face was a smiling one and he would have a good sense of humour.

She had not yet formed an opinion of her grandfather. He was a much quieter and, she felt, a shyer sort of man. But he had been equally nice to her, and his face and eyes had been very sad-looking when he said how sorry he was about her father and the long estrangement between them and how he wished with all his heart it hadn't happened.

Now, as she thought about it her eyes filled up, thinking of the terrible waste of time during all those years when they maybe could have been like a normal family, going on holidays to Ireland in the summer in the same way as she did to Italy. She manoeuvred her spare pillow into her arms and held it in a tight hug, wishing she had someone there to put their arms around her and tell her that everything was all right, even though she knew that nothing would ever be right again. She wished Paul was there to hug and hold her or even Diana, who she could hear downstairs already. And then she almost smiled to herself when she wished she had a little dog like old Mrs Flynn's Poppy, who she could cuddle like a baby.

She eventually moved from her bed and was just slipping on her dressing-gown to go to the bathroom when she heard hushed voices outside the bedroom. She carefully opened the door just a crack and listened for a few moments, and then she realised it was Franco and Bernice.

"I warned you, Franco," she heard Bernice say in an angry whisper, "I warned you not to let that woman anywhere near us again."

Maria shrank back from the door, her hand over her mouth. In all the years she'd known them, she'd never heard them argue before. She'd thought they were one of the happiest couple she knew.

"Ah, Bernice, you can't keep going on like this about her," she heard Franco saying. "You've being going on about it since last night. You have to understand that I had nothing to do with her being here – it was Vincent who brought her in the car with the other waitresses. I haven't seen her since she left the restaurant last year. I have nothing whatsoever to do with that woman. Who comes to the house to pay their respects to Leo has nothing to do with me."

"You should have warned Vincent not to bring her – he knew about the row I had with her after that Christmas party. And Leo wasn't keen on her anyway – he wouldn't have had someone like her in his house."

"Shh…. you'll waken Maria!"

Maria moved over to the bed and climbed back in, so she could pretend to be asleep just in case Bernice came in to wake her. The sound of them arguing shocked her and made her feel very uncomfortable.

"To think I let that woman baby-sit our children," Bernice said, "and all the time she had her eye on my husband!"

"Nothing happened," Franco said. "She was drunk and acting stupid – I told you that and Leo told you that."

"It didn't look like nothing when she was all over you, and when I tackled her she didn't deny it. She acted as though any man would fall for her, the bloody trollop!"

"Bernice!" Franco's voice rose an octave above the heated

270

whisper. "You should know I am not interested in any other women. Why would I be when I have you? You are the love of my life and I wouldn't do anything to hurt you."

There was a pause during which Maria felt a wave of relief wash over her.

"You say that, Franco," Bernice said now, "but you did kiss her that night. I caught you both when I came to drive you home. You can't deny it."

"It was only a stupid Christmas party kiss," Franco said, "under the mistletoe. Everyone was kissing."

"She better not turn up at the funeral," Bernice said.

"But Bernice, the church is a public place – you can't stop people coming into the church."

"Well, she better not turn up at the restaurant afterwards, that's all I'm saying."

"Okay," he said. "Okay. I would not want her there either. I'll make sure that Vincent and the others know that the meal afterwards in Leonardo's is by invitation only."

"Good," Bernice said. "I should think so. And let's hope we don't need to discuss the trollop ever again, Franco. I'll ignore her if I see her in the church, but if I find out she ever comes near you again, then I won't be responsible for my actions."

Maria waited until she heard them go downstairs and then she got out of bed again and went to the bathroom. As she washed and brushed her teeth she mulled over the argument she had overheard, and she realised that the decision she had been putting off making had now been made for her. She had thought that the best option – until she was eighteen – was to ask Franco and his family to come and live in their bigger house. Alternatively, she could close the house up and, in the interim, go live in her godfather's house. She had worried that it would be a squeeze and guessed that she would have to share a room with the two girls, but some friends she knew at school shared bedrooms with their sisters, and she would just have to learn to do that.

But now, having heard how things could be, living with a couple in close proximity, she thought her other option was a better one. Although she had hated hearing them argue, it hadn't changed her feelings for Franco and his wife. It had, however, reminded her how upset Stella got with all the rows in Maxwells' house and it had made Maria now presume that uncomfortable disagreements were perhaps part of many families' lives. She supposed now she had been lucky in a way, being an only child who had been so well looked after by two loving parents, and then latterly by a single father who would have moved heaven and earth for her if he could. And while she knew that the experience of losing her father now would now mark and scar her for the rest of her life, she did have consolations. She knew without a shred of a doubt, that – in spite of his weakness with gambling and occasional drinking bouts – her father loved her and always had her best interests at heart.

At some point today, Maria decided, she would speak to Diana and ask her if she would move into the house in St Aiden's Avenue. They got on great, and she was now sure that if her father hadn't died they would have married and Diana would have been her stepmother. That was as close as having a real family, and they would both have shared memories of her beloved father.

For the first time since her father died, she felt something close to being in control of her future. She would ask Diana to come and stay here until she reached eighteen and was old enough to live on her own.

Chapter 33

Maria sat with a slice of toast and a cup of coffee in the kitchen under the watchful eye of Mrs Lowry. She still had no great appetite, but the housekeeper and the other women were making sure that she did not slip into lengthy periods of not eating.

Mrs Lowry asked her if there was anything she needed washing or ironing for the funeral, and had she given any thought to what she might want the priest to say about her father from the altar. Maria told her she had not thought about either, but promised she would soon and would come back to her about it.

Later, as she was sorting through her clothes she found a plain black jersey dress she thought she could wear along with her mother's two-strand crystal necklace. Then she thought of something that she would like at the funeral and in Leonardo's afterwards. She went downstairs and found Franco standing by the coffin, with folded arms, just staring down at her father.

She wondered if he was thinking of this time tomorrow when the coffin would be closed and her father would be buried deep in the ground in Stockport Cemetery beside her mother. She found the burial thing so terrifying that she tried to think of everything she could to distract herself from those thoughts.

She took a deep breath. "Franco," she said, "I wonder if you could help me with something?"

"Of course." He did not turn around, and instead took his hanky from his pocket and quickly wiped his eyes. "Tell me and I'll do whatever I can."

He turned towards her now – smiling, she knew, to make her feel better.

"I'd like for my father's last night in our house," Maria said, "to play some of the music that he loved. Could you bring the small tape recorder down from my father's bedroom . . ." She halted. They both knew she still had to cross the threshold to Leo's room. "Could you bring the tape recorder and the box with all the tapes? There are special ones in it that he and my mother listened to, and there is a tape that he loved of my mother playing classical music on the violin." She looked down at her hands. "And I love it too."

Franco nodded. "I know the ones you mean. I will go up to his room later and sort them out."

"Thank you. I think it would be nice to have the music playing, very low, in the house here tonight and maybe in the morning before he leaves the house." She looked at him again. "And maybe tomorrow, when we are having the meal in the restaurant, we could play the tapes he kept there."

There was a silence. "Are you sure, Maria?" Franco's voice was choked. "Are you sure it won't be too much for you to be in the restaurant and hearing the music playing without him?"

"It will be much harder if we are in the restaurant and we don't hear it," she said. "If it is all quiet then it will be as if he has completely gone and I don't want to feel that. My father played that music after my mother died because he said it made him feel that she was still around us."

"I think then that it sounds like an excellent idea."

Then, as she turned away, Franco said, "Actually, Maria, there is something I want to ask you about . . . and something I have to give you." He went towards the kitchen door. "Diana, could you give me a few moments of your time in the dining room please? I just need to go upstairs for something."

While they were waiting for him, Diana discussed the readings at the church for the funeral with Maria and said that, if it was okay with her, Franco would do one reading and one of his friends from the Italian society would do another. She also said that there was an Italian woman who was a beautiful singer who would do hymns accompanied by a pianist.

Maria said whatever they thought was best would be fine by her.

Franco came in carrying a long white envelope and, when he sat down, Maria noticed he had a little nerve jumping in his cheek. Then, when he placed the envelope on the table, she noticed it had her name on it in her father's handwriting and her face creased with distress. Then she clenched her fists and closed her eyes.

There was an uneasy silence then Franco said, "Maria, we have something serious to discuss about your future this morning. Your father left letters for me and for you." He slid the envelope across the table. "I think it's the time for you to read this."

She steeled herself for a few more moments and then she lifted the envelope and gently peeled it open. She slid a letter out and sat quietly reading it.

When she had finished it, she said, "I don't believe this." Then she handed it to Diana.

Diana looked at her. "Are you sure?" When Maria nodded she picked it up, and, after noticing with some surprise that it was much shorter than Franco's letter, she started to read.

My Dearest, Darling Maria,

How very, very sorry I am that I have left you all alone. It was the last thing I wanted to think might happen but, in case it does, I am writing to tell you above all that I love you with all my heart.

You, my precious, darling daughter, have been the sun, the moon and the stars in my life since your mother left us. I am not going to make this letter long or sad. I just wanted to write and say to you that my plans for your future are not what you would have imagined.

It was something I could not have talked to you about before, as I did not want to think about being away from you. Also, I hoped that I would be around until you were at least eighteen, and you would be with me until you were an adult, but I am so sorry that has not happened.

Franco will explain to you where you should go and why I am asking this of you. I know you will be shocked and not be happy with my wishes to begin with, but please do this for me and for your mother.

You were fifteen when I wrote this letter and the oldest you will be when you receive it is sixteen because I update these every year. That means you have only around two years to spend with your new family. Believe me, the time will go very quickly and you will know more about yourself after it.

When you are older and have your own family, you will look back and be glad you know who you are and where you came from.

With regards your career, all I have to say is that I wish you to find something you love that will make you happy – and maybe earn you some money!

Do not grieve for me too long. Life is to be lived and enjoyed. Think of me when you hear the music we loved and remember all the happy times we had as a family, and please, my darling, remember your mother kindly whatever may come up in the future.

And always remember the happy times you and I had on our own and those lovely evenings in Leonardo's.

With all the love it is possible for a father to give to his daughter,

Dadxx

"What does it mean?" Maria said. "Does he want me to go to Italy until I am eighteen?"

"No . . ." Franco's voice was uncertain, "he wants you to go to Ireland with your grandfather and your uncle."

Maria looked at him in shock. "What are you saying? Ireland?"

"Yes."

"That's not possible."

She waited for them to respond but they said nothing.

"In any case, can I not stay on here in the house I grew up in?" She sat still, although inside her heart was pounding and her stomach was clenched. She looked at Franco and then at Diana.

Diana reached for her hand, but she was too agitated and pulled it away.

"It is complicated," Franco said. "There are legal matters . . . financial problems . . ." He was fumbling for words now, not wanting to say the things that made him feel he was like Judas betraying his dearest friend. "We don't know for sure, but it's possible that the house and the restaurant might have to be sold."

"Because my father was in debt?" Her voice was small now and her gaze fixed on the table.

"It was business debt," Franco said. "But it was linked to the house. The house has to go to pay your father's suppliers and various loans. Things like the horse . . ."

Maria's heart was pounding so hard she could hear it in her ears. "I knew it . . . that damned horse is the cause of all the trouble. I bet it started him back gambling again."

Diana couldn't stop herself. "No, Maria, it didn't. I know he wasn't gambling – he talked to me about it and it was only Bella Maria's racing he was involved in. He stopped all the other betting and the card games."

"Well, that's at least something. So now all I have to worry about is going to a strange family in Ireland who hated my father and mother. Fantastic!" Maria's tone was uncharacteristically sarcastic. She held her hands up. "Is there really no one else here who wants me?"

"Of course we want you," Franco said. "But this is all about what your father wanted for you. He wrote it to me in another, much longer letter. He explained it all and . . ." he fumbled for the right words, "and things are not the way he understood it between your mother and her family."

Maria suddenly became still and calm and a cold, detached look came on her face. "Can I see it, please?"

Diana caught her breath. Her eyes darted over to Franco. "This might not be the right time . . ."

He looked back at her, then he said, "I am so sorry, Maria – but there is no right time. I have hardly slept since I got the letter as I have worried so much giving it to you. But I thought if we leave it until after the funeral it would be very difficult for you and your relatives. It's best if we can sort things out now."

Franco went upstairs and came back down with the letter.

Maria read it all and then she looked at them both. "I don't understand any of this. Does my father mean that they never rejected her, that it was my mother's decision to cut off from her family? And it was all because of something she did before she met my father?"

"Yes," Franco said. "I think that's what it says."

"So it had nothing to do with him being an Italian?"

"It doesn't seem so."

Maria hugged her arms across her chest. "I don't understand," she repeated. "Why would she do that? Why would she not tell him the truth? It can't have been anything that bad that he wouldn't have forgiven her."

Franco looked at her worried face. "People see things differently. What troubles one person might not trouble another."

Diana got out of her chair now and went to put her arms around her. "You have the chance to find some answers," she said, "if you go up to the hotel to meet your grandfather and Jude."

Maria went quiet for a few moments. "I don't care what they say – I won't go to Ireland! If I can't stay in our own house then I'll go and get a job and find somewhere else to live." Her voice became almost hysterical and she tried to struggle out of Diana's embrace. "I'll ask Stella's parents if I can stay there for a while . . . or I can ask Mrs Lowry if you two don't want me."

"Of course we want you, and we'll do whatever we can to help." Diana's arms tightened around her and she held her until she became still again. "But I think you should go and at least talk to Patrick and Jude. You should try to get to know them while they are here."

Franco picked the letter up now and put it back in its envelope. "They seem like very nice people, I am surprised how nice," he said, "and it's what your father would want."

"My father," Maria sobbed, "is *dead – dead!* And dead people can't make decisions for the people they left behind."

Then she pulled out of Diana's arms and rushed upstairs to her bedroom.

Chapter 34

It was one o'clock when Diana came tapping on the bedroom door. "It's the phone for you, Maria," she said. "It's Stella."

Maria lifted her face from the damp pillow, and then she closed her eyes again when she felt the tight band that always wound around her head after she had been crying. She didn't know if she was fit to talk, and was just about to shout back to Diana to leave her alone, when she thought that Stella might have stolen a few minutes on her own to make the call. Things could not be worse for herself, but she knew that her friend was in deep trouble. She dragged herself off the bed and went downstairs to the hall to take it.

After checking that the hall door was closed and that no one could hear her, she lifted the receiver which Diana had left on the table. "Hi," she said.

"Maria?" Stella's voice sounded quiet and a bit muffled.

"How are you?" Maria asked in an urgent whisper. "What's happened?" She put her hand up to her forehead to ease the throbbing.

"The doctor doesn't think I'm pregnant."

Maria thought Stella didn't sound as ecstatic as she would have expected. "Well, that's great news. And was the doctor okay about seeing you on your own?"

"Yes . . . but he examined me. It was terrible . . . it was an internal. It was painful and I was mortally embarrassed."

"Doctors are used to doing things like that all the time," Maria said. "Don't let it worry you."

"But the thing is, he thinks I'm sick. He thinks that there's something wrong with me that's stopped my periods."

"Really? I thought that only happened when . . ." She didn't want to say 'pregnant' out loud in case anyone heard her. "Well, hopefully they'll sort it soon."

"He kept going on about my weight, and then when he brought my mother in, he made me get weighed in front of her. I had to take off my cardigan and dress and shoes and get weighed in my petticoat."

Maria sucked her breath in. She knew that Stella's weight was a problem. "What did you weigh?"

"I've no idea. I was so embarrassed at being half-naked I didn't look."

Maria heard the defensive note in her voice and knew she was lying.

"I've got to go to a special clinic in London." Stella's voice was dull now. "My mother has phoned and they told her they have a place for me on Friday. I don't want to go, but the doctor said I've got to go and get checked out immediately."

"Stella, as long as it's not something serious, then it's better news than the other option."

"I know," she said, "but the doctor also told me I've to stay in bed until then, and rest as I'm very weak and he thinks I'm anaemic too. I'm really sorry, Maria, but I'm not allowed out, so I won't make it to the funeral." She started to cry. "I would never have missed your dad's funeral . . ."

"Don't worry," Maria said. "It's more important that you get well." Then she suddenly thought. "Have you heard from Tony?"

"No," Stella said, her voice all quivery. "I've still heard nothing from him since that day in your house. Have you heard from Paul?"

"He rang last night. He did very well, three A-levels." The girls' O-level results would be out later in the month, but they meant nothing to her now.

"So, he'll be going to college up in Northumberland."

"Yes, I suppose he will be."

She could hear Stella taking a deep breath. "I'm sorry to say it, Maria, but romances never last when people go away to college – so it looks like we're both being dumped."

"Does it?" Maria stopped to think, and then she said in a flat, distant voice, "I wouldn't be at all surprised if you're right. The way things are going in my life at the moment, it would be more surprising if Paul *didn't* dump me when he goes away."

After another hour lying on her bed, Maria sat up. Her head had eased but, more importantly, it had cleared. Everything seemed clearer now.

She brushed her hair and put some light powder on her face and a touch of mascara and lipstick. Then she went downstairs and into the sitting room. There were a dozen or so people in the room, and she said hello to those she knew and acknowledged anyone who looked at her. Then she went over to the coffin and stood looking down at her father. She closed her eyes and silently said, *I'm sorry, Dad. I'm sorry for the horrible things I said about you to Franco and Diana.*

She realised now she had got things very wrong. How could she have been so stupid? Her father was the one person who had never let her down in her life. He might have gambled and drank too much, but that was a weakness within himself. And, she knew he had been working hard to get out of any financial problems that he had caused. She was also sorry knowing now that he had been deceived by her mother, and had kept quiet about it so as not to tarnish her mother's memory for her. Everything he had done, he had always done with her best interests at heart.

How many other people had come forward to help her? From what she could see there were none. Nobody was standing up and insisting that they would take her in until she was old enough to look after herself.

No, her father wasn't the reason for the situation she was now in. It was because she had trusted other people.

When she walked into the hotel lounge she could see her grandfather and her uncle sitting at a table by the window, reading papers. They each had a pint of beer in front of them. Jude looked up when she came towards them, and when he saw her his face lit up.

He tapped his father's newspaper. "It's Maria," he told him.

Jude pulled out a chair for her and then they both folded their newspapers up and put them down.

"Will you have a lemonade or a shandy or anything?" Jude asked.

"No thanks," she said. "I'm okay."

"We're delighted you came," her grandfather said. "We've been waiting here on and off since breakfast this morning."

She looked at them both, then her hand came up to hold on to the crystal necklace. "I don't know if you know anything about it, but my father left some letters."

Jude's hand came over to cover hers now. "We do know," he said. "You don't have to explain it all again – Franco came to the hotel to see us."

She looked from one to the other, unable to find the words she needed.

Her grandfather moved forward in his seat and she noticed that his eyes were shining with tears. "We were afraid to ask you," he said. "But that's why we came over, Maria. We came to pay our respects to your father, and then we hoped that we might persuade you to come back to Ireland with us."

Jude's hand tightened on hers. "It needn't be forever," he said. "You can come back here for holidays and go to your father's family in Italy and all that sort of thing. We were talking about it before we left Ireland and we have a good friend who says she thinks she can sort out a year or two at a nice girls' school for you, or there are colleges we can look at for next year." He looked at her face now, trying to read her thoughts. "You don't even have to go to school – there's plenty to do around the house and the farm. That's if you want to."

"We don't need to do anything quick," her grandfather said. "You can take your time and find your own way."

She closed her eyes. A picture of her father came into her mind. She opened them again. "I'll come," she said. "I'll come back to Ireland with you."

Chapter 35

The airport in Manchester was surprisingly busy for an eight o'clock morning flight as the three of them made their way to the check-in desk, Jude carrying Maria's large black case for her, the one she used to take to Italy every summer, and her grandfather carrying Leo's old brown leather case.

Her grandfather had warned her that the house in Ireland was big and old and she would need warm jumpers and cardigans as they didn't have central heating. She had packed both cases with a mixture of light and heavier clothes, and had dressed in jeans and a blouse with a mohair cardigan which she could take off if it got too warm on the plane. She also brought a heavy gabardine raincoat to wear just in case.

The weather had taken a complete change, the sky now dark and grey instead of the sunshine they'd had over the last few weeks, and the early part of the flight was far from pleasant. The plane hit patches of turbulence and each time it did, she heard some of the other passengers beside her gasping, and she noticed one elderly lady kissing her rosary beads every time the plane dipped. It reminded Maria of her mother's fear of travelling and, although she did not feel anxious herself, a little part of her could understand someone feeling like that. Then, she put it out of her mind as she knew she would be travelling by plane or boat a lot more in the future.

Eventually the turbulence eased off, and, even though it was a lot shorter than the journey to Italy, they were served a full meal with a dessert. As she picked at the food, her mind went back to the funeral, which now seemed like a distant haze of people dressed in black, flowers and music. Franco and Diana had dealt with all the difficult things for her and had made sure that everything she wanted was included – from her father's favourite music being played in the house and restaurant, to the flowers that were thrown by selected people on top of the coffin when it was lowered into the grave beside her mother's.

Her mind then moved from the sad funereal images to the previous night when she had said her goodbyes to both Paul and Stella. They had been shocked at her news about moving to Ireland, and even more so at her speedy departure. Their own lives were due to change too, but not in the quick, tragic way that hers had.

Paul had tried to be as positive as possible. "It will only be for a year – eighteen months at most," he said. "And I'll be in Northumberland for most of it. When you come back we'll pick up where we left off."

Maria had nodded and said they would see what happened.

"We'll write every week," Paul told her. "And you will, of course, come home for Christmas, won't you?"

"Hopefully," Maria said. She didn't tell him that she might never come back home again because she had nowhere to live, and she had no idea what money would be left when all the bills her father owed were paid.

Stella had been distraught. She had missed the funeral because she wasn't well and had not been allowed outside the house. She had another week of this then she was going to London, to spend time in a special clinic that dealt with girls who had problems eating. Stella had been sketchy about the details but, when she went upstairs to the toilet, her mother had come in and told Maria the very stark truth.

"I know you will keep this to yourself," Mrs Maxwell said,

"but Stella is seriously ill. When the doctor made her stand on the scales, we discovered she was barely five stones in weight." She had closed her eyes to stop the tears. "And when we came back home her father told her that he had found empty boxes of laxatives hidden in her room, so that she got rid of anything she ate by making herself sick or going to the toilet." She lifted her eyes to the ceiling. "She's probably up there now making herself sick because I made her eat a bowl of cereal."

"I've never heard of anything like this before," Maria said quietly. "Will the clinic help?"

Her mother shrugged. "We have to try. It's a new modern place run by a specialist from New York who has been studying eating disorders in young girls for a few years. Thank God she's not the only one in the world like this, so someone might be able to help her before she starves herself to death." She had looked at Maria. "The doctor told her that's where she's heading if she doesn't get help."

Maria stared out of the plane window now, and then she closed her eyes and said a silent prayer for Stella and then she said another one for herself. The waitress came around and cleared the trays away. A short while later they brought drinks around, and her grandfather and Jude had a whiskey each and she had a lemonade. By the time the air hostesses had cleared the glasses away, it was almost time for the plane to land.

Maria's grandmother, Eileen Donovan, had driven up to Dublin from where they lived in the country near Tullamore in County Offaly, and was sitting waiting for them in Arrivals. Maria's first impression was that she looked thinner and older than she remembered she had at her mother's funeral, and now had grey streaked in the hair she had swept up in a bun. But, Maria thought, she was still a good-looking woman, and reminded her of the old-fashioned film stars with her three-quarter-length blue duster coat, white gloves and shoes, and a navy leather bag. She smiled when they came out, shook Maria's hand, and said, "Welcome to Ireland, Maria," but there was a wariness in her eyes that made Maria feel anxious.

Her grandfather drove on the way back, her grandmother in

the front beside him, while Jude sat beside her in the back, pointing out various places they passed as they drove out through Dublin city and then later down through the country roads of Meath and then Offaly.

Eventually, just as they were heading towards Tullamore, dark clouds moved across the sky and by the time they reached the rambling old farmhouse, drops of rain had started to fall.

When they got to the door her grandfather ushered her in after her grandmother so she didn't get too wet, and Maria found herself stepping into one of the biggest kitchens she had ever seen, with flag-stoned floors and painted cream cupboards and two big old pine dressers full of blue-and-white china. There was an open fire in a big old stone fireplace with what looked like a small settle bed to the side of it, and a big green, turf-burning range to the other side which looked as if it was used for cooking. Maria thought it was strange when she noticed there was also a smaller white electric cooker in the corner. When her gaze moved around, she noticed that there was a wooden staircase at the back of the kitchen, and she wondered if it led to the bedrooms.

In its own old-fashioned farmhouse way, Maria thought the kitchen was nice and bright, and it was spotlessly clean, but it was a world away from their nice, neat kitchen back in Manchester.

Maria's grandmother took her coat off and then took Maria's and hung them both on the rack behind a door at the end of the kitchen.

"I'm sorry now if the fires are a bit low," Eileen Donovan said, "but we'll soon have them going."

Her grandfather brought his and Jude's bags in, then Jude came in carrying Maria's cases and took them upstairs for her.

A short while later, while the two men were busy with the fires and bringing in turf, Maria followed her grandmother up the creaking wooden stairs, which, like the stone flags below, had not a thread of carpet to dull the sound of their footsteps.

As if reading her thoughts, Eileen Donovan said, "It's a big old house with plenty of noise in it, but you'll get used to it. We hardly notice it."

At the top they turned right and her eyes fell on the long narrow rug that ran the whole length of the corridor. It had cream fringes at either end that looked as though they had been combed into place, and the main part was worked in faded blues, cream and wine.

For some reason, the runner gave her a moment's glimmer of comfort, and then she realised it was because Mrs Lowry had a similar one on her stairs back in Heaton Moor. Back in what was her old life – her real life.

They passed three small windows hung with lace curtains and she saw that each sill had a white jug filled with blue forget-me-nots, and she wondered if her grandmother kept them like that all the time or whether she had put the jugs there because of her arrival. They continued their path along the dimly lit corridor to the bedroom at the end.

Eileen Donovan halted, her hand on the painted doorknob. "This was your mother's bedroom," she said quietly, without turning to look at Maria. "And now it will be yours."

Maria felt something tighten in her chest. It only lasted a moment or two and then the blanket of numbness descended on her again. All the years when she had wondered what her mother's family would look like, what her home would look like, and what the bedroom she had grown up in would look like, faded into a grey mist. The pain and loss she had felt all those years when she thought of her mother, now felt ludicrously small compared to the gaping hole in her heart that losing her father had left.

Her grandmother opened the door and she followed her into the room. She immediately felt the chill in the old house, and she realised they did not have the modern central heating that the houses in England had. Then it registered at the back of her mind that it would feel much colder when she was only wearing her pyjamas. The pyjamas that she had bought on a shopping trip with Stella into Marks and Spencers in Manchester. The day that Stella had teased her, saying she should buy one of the sexy baby-doll nighties for Paul Spencer.

She pushed her old world out of her mind and looked down at another floral rug not quite big enough to cover the varnished wooden floorboards. Then she looked at the yellow rose wallpaper and the silver crucifix above the high double brass bed made up with starched white linen sheets and lace-edged pillowcases. There was a folded pink satin quilt on top. Like the kitchen downstairs, the bed linen and everything else in the room was spotlessly clean but, apart from a bookcase filled with books, it was empty of anything personal.

She looked around at the other three yellow walls and found the holy pictures on each one depressing. Then she looked down at the carpet, and wondered if it had been there when her mother slept in this room.

"Jude is going to collect Ambrose. He stayed down at a neighbour's house while I came to pick you all up at the airport." She turned directly to look at Maria now, and there was a sadness in her eyes. "I might as well warn you about Ambrose now. He's your youngest uncle, not much older than yourself. I had him late. What they call a change-of-life baby." Her eyes shifted towards the door. "He did that all right . . . he certainly changed my life forever."

"My grandfather and Jude told me a little about him," Maria said. "I'm looking forward to seeing him."

"He's not like other boys his age," her grandmother continued. "And I wouldn't like you staring at him or anything like that."

"That wouldn't be my way," Maria answered. "I'm not the sort to stare at people because they are different. My father brought me up better than that."

"That's good to hear, because poor Ambrose is just himself. He has his own little ways. There are times when I wish the others in the family had been more like him. For all his health difficulties and his inclination to say things he doesn't understand, he has caused us the least trouble." She narrowed her eyes. "We've had more than our share of life's knocks – and I sincerely hope you're not going to cause us any more." She held her hand up. "I don't mean to sound critical before you've even settled in. I just want you to know that I wouldn't be able for trouble."

"There was no trouble in our home," Maria said. "My father and I got on very well."

"I'm sure you did."

Maria recognised a terse note in the old woman's tone which she had heard Jane Maxwell use on occasions when speaking to Stella.

"And I don't ever remember my mother having to tell me off very often."

Eileen Donovan's face stiffened. "And was she very modern and lax with you? I suppose she brought you up the way the English do things?"

"I don't know the difference between the English or the Italian or the Irish ways," Maria said quietly, "but I know I've been taught good manners and to always respect my elders."

Her grandmother regarded her for a few moments and then gave a deep sigh.

As she turned away, Maria stared after her, wondering why she seemed so much less welcoming than the two men. From the first moment she met her grandfather and Jude, they had done and said everything to make her feel welcome into their family, and they had been very understanding and kind both during and after the funeral. Her grandfather had told her not to worry about money, that he would pay her flights and make sure she got anything she needed back in Ireland. When she said she couldn't take money off them, Patrick Donovan told her that if they had been able to see her over all the years, they would have spent a good bit of money on her between Christmas and birthday presents and holidays, and they were delighted to get the chance to make up for it all now.

She suddenly remembered the day the two horrible men had come round to the house checking everything out, and she wondered if her father had actually owed them money and, if so, whether he had managed to pay them off. He had never mentioned them again, but he had sounded so determined to get to the bottom of it that she was sure he had sorted it out straight away. Franco said her father's solicitor and his accountant would take care of all the legal and financial things and they would sort out things with the bank and the insurances.

"You will have some money," Franco had reassured her. "But

the solicitor said it will take a bit of time." He told her that if it was confirmed that the house was to be sold, they would leave the furniture in the house until after the sale. Then, all the furniture and her father's personal effects would be put safely into storage for her, as she might want them if she decided to return to England full time when she was of an age to look after herself.

Diana also said that when Maria came back for a holiday, she might feel more in the mood to go through them and decide what she wanted to keep. The mention of holidays and coming back home made Maria feel less like she was being deported from the country for good, and gave her a little comfort. Franco also told her that they would keep in weekly touch with her, and let her know as soon as they heard official word whether they could save Leonardo's or not.

"What's going to happen to the restaurant, until you hear from the solicitors?" she had asked.

Franco had shrugged and looked sad. "We can't re-open it until we know how things are. We would have to pay the suppliers and all that sort of thing, and we don't know if the money is there to do it yet. If I had the money myself I would do it, but I'm only a worker – I was never the businessman your father was."

Maria had thought that when he looked at her there was shame in his eyes that he had not been able to do anything to save Leonardo's, just as he had not been able to save her father.

She and her grandmother were on their way back downstairs when she heard the front door open and recognised Jude's voice calling a greeting. And, as she heard her grandfather calling back and then a younger voice she presumed was Ambrose's, she was surprised and relieved to feel there was some life in the old house for the first time.

By the time they arrived downstairs, Jude was heading out of the front door again. He stopped and smiled at Maria and said, "Are you getting settled in all right?" When she nodded he looked at his mother. "I'm just going back down to Sister Theresa's to get the rest of Ambrose's things. I put his wheelchair in the parlour."

"Did she say if he was okay while we were away?"

"Grand. She said he had a bit of a coughing fit, but that he came out of it quickly."

Eileen Donovan's shoulders heaved and she gave a sigh but said nothing.

Jude reached out and patted her arm as though trying to comfort her. "I won't be long."

Jude left and Maria followed her grandmother, expecting to see a young man of her own age who wasn't quite right. There was a special school down near the church back home, and she often saw the pupils being dropped off in coaches or cars, and some being pushed along in wheelchairs. There was a range of conditions, and she presumed her uncle would look like some of those pupils.

"Here she is now," Patrick said when Maria and her grandmother appeared.

Eileen Donovan went over to the half-settle bed by the side of the fire, her frame obscuring the small figure ensconced there.

"Ambrose," her voice was suddenly softer and lighter, "this is Maria, the niece we told you about from England." She then stood back to allow uncle and niece to view each other. "I'll leave you to have a chat while I get the frying pan on, as we're all hungry."

Maria found herself staring into the most intense pair of blue eyes she had ever seen. So intense she was almost startled, and then she realised that the face that was looking back at her – scrutinising her – seemed not young at all, but more the face of a wise old man topped by thick fair curls. He was nothing at all like she had expected. While her grandmother had been correct in describing him as not like other boys, she couldn't have prepared Maria for the fragile little figure she was now looking at, which was reclining on the little bed she had noticed, in a colourful nest of cushions. Even though he was wearing woollen trousers and had on a shirt and sweater – it could not disguise the fact that he had the body and arms and legs of a scrawny twelve-year-old.

"Hello, Maria." He used one thin arm to support him on the side of the bed as he held out the other towards her. "Welcome to Offaly."

Patrick Donovan rattled the poker loudly on the iron grate under the pile of burning wood and turf, and Maria knew the noise was to cover up any resulting silence or awkwardness on her part. She moved towards Ambrose with an outstretched hand and, when she saw the welcome in his eyes and felt the frail but warm hand in hers, her face broke into the first spontaneous smile in a week. And for a few moments as she looked at him the heavy sadness she carried seemed a small bit lighter.

"Hello, Ambrose," she said, "I'm very pleased to meet you."

He patted the bottom of the settle bed. "Sit down," he said, "and take the weight off your feet. You must be tired after all that travelling. I never was on a plane myself. How did you find the journey over? Was it a smooth flight or was it rough?"

His curious manner almost amused her. "It was a little rough at the beginning," she told him, "but thankfully it settled."

Ambrose patted the end of the settle bed again.

Maria's eyes flickered over towards her grandmother who was standing at the electric cooker melting a lump of lard in the huge frying pan. Maria could tell she was watching them and listening to every word that was being said. She could not work out whether it was the right or wrong thing to sit on the bed, but she decided she would take the risk and sat down.

He studied her face again with his old man's eyes, then reached for her hand and held it in his. "I know you had a sad journey. You must be feeling very lost. "Your father was an Italian, wasn't he?"

"Ambrose," his mother said, "you'll only tire yourself out talking so much. Maria's had a long journey and she mightn't feel up to chatting."

"Leo Conti – I like the name," Ambrose continued as though no one had spoken. "I'm sorry I didn't get to meet him – and I'm even sorrier I never got to know your mother. She was my sister, you know. I pray for her every night. Losing one parent is sad enough, but it must be very sad for you having lost both your parents. Very sad indeed."

"It is," she agreed, feeling somehow comforted by both his words and his direct manner.

He lifted a thin little arm now and waved it in his mother's direction. "Isn't it strange to think that I have my older parents – your grandparents – still alive, while yours are gone?"

Eileen Donovan tutted loudly several times in a row, as she cut a string of sausages and let them fall into the pan. Then when Ambrose started off again, she whirled around towards her husband. "Patrick! Will you say something to him – please?"

Patrick Donovan gave another loud metallic rattle of the poker as he put it back on the brass stand and then he looked over at his son. "Ambrose," he said, "that'll do now. You heard your mother – don't be talking so much about personal things. Maria has her case to unpack and things to sort out while your mother cooks us a bite to eat." Her grandfather's voice was kind but matter-of-fact, as though he were used to telling his son this kind of thing on a regular basis.

The small face looked up at him and shook his head. "Am I to say nothing? Am I just to pretend to people?"

"Now, now," Patrick said, "there's no need for talk like that." He looked over to Maria and smiled and rolled his eyes.

Maria now knew what her grandmother had meant when she said Ambrose said things he didn't understand. But in the few minutes she had spent with him, she wasn't sure she agreed. From what he had said, Maria thought Ambrose knew and understood exactly what he was saying. She thought he was fearless and it made her like him even more. Not wishing to cause any further friction between them, she squeezed Ambrose's hand and stood up.

"We'll talk again later," she said.

"Oh, we will," he said. "Nothing surer."

"Oh, Ambrose," his father suddenly remembered, "I have a few things in my bag for you. Some comics and a new jigsaw puzzle."

Ambrose's face lit up. "Good man, Patrick!" he said laughing. "What's the picture of? And did you get the *Superman* comics?"

"Hold your horses!" Patrick winked over at him and smiled. "You'll just have to wait and see."

As they walked up the stairs her grandfather said, "Don't mind Ambrose, now, if he says things straight out that might upset you. He means no harm."

"I don't mind," Maria said. "And I know he doesn't mean to upset me at all. He's only speaking his mind. I can tell he's a very good person, and I like him a lot."

"Begod!" her grandfather said, laughing now. "I think you have the measure of him, and if you can get along with Ambrose, then we'll be the finest."

When she was up in her mother's bedroom on her own, Maria went to stand by the small iron fireplace. As she looked down into the empty grate a picture from home flashed into her mind – a snapshot of Leonardo's restaurant as though captured by someone walking through the front door. She closed her eyes and let it run behind her lids like a movie screen. Then, she watched as the rosily lit restaurant came to life with people at every table and Franco and the waitresses rushing back and forth from kitchen to table with menus or fluttering order slips or bottles of Italian wine. Then, the film slowed down and from the swinging doors emerged the handsome, perfectly groomed figure of her father. She froze the picture of him and let it fill her mind. She held the image of him as long as she could, until she felt strange and dizzy and was unable to hold it any longer.

She let it go with a loud shuddering gasp, and only then realised that she had been holding her breath for all that length of time. Then, the horrendous reality of what had happened in one single week and the life she had lost swamped her again and again. Pictures flashed again in her mind of the house in St Aiden's Avenue, of groups of her school friends and then Stella and Paul. She wished with every tiny vessel in her body that she could go back to the ballet classes she had considered giving up, that she could go back and sit in exam rooms in the school she had dreaded, that she could even go and live in the empty house on her own.

But the decision had been made and her old life – like her father – was officially dead and gone. And there was nobody who loved and cared for her here in this bleak, overwhelmingly strange place. There was nobody here who even knew her. Not one single person who knew the kind of girl she was or knew the kind of life she had lived.

The realisation of her situation hit her once again and washed over her like a monstrous dark wave that was determined to sweep her off her feet and carry her away into the blackness. She moved slowly across the shadowy room again to sink down on the old bed with her head in her hands. She tumbled down somewhere deep inside her mind towards a place she was terrified of, until some basic survival instinct drew her back, warning her that if she went that far there might be no saving her, and she might never return to any normal kind of life again.

She choked back the sobs that had gathered in her chest and throat, and dragged herself over to the window, in the hope that even the smallest sliver of natural daylight just might comfort her.

And as she looked out over the flat green fields she prayed now to the mother who had lived in this house, slept in this bed, to help her. She asked her help to find the strength to survive and live through the coming days and months until the time came when she could make her way back to places that were familiar and what was left of her old life.

She stood for a while staring at nothing and eventually the storm inside her began to subside. Her gaze moved up towards the sky and the white and grey clouds slowly moving across it. Then her attention came back to where she was and she became aware of noises and cooking smells in the house. She could hear her Uncle Jude's voice again and then she thought of Ambrose and his piercing, inquisitive eyes and his refusal to be silenced on the subject that everyone else in the house didn't want to acknowledge.

She thought back to the small scene where she had seen a lighter side to her grandfather, when he had spoken to Ambrose about the jigsaw and winked at him, and she hoped that she would eventually see this same difference with her grandmother, who was so much more serious.

She turned to look at her cases which stood at the end of the brass bed and then went over to unzip the larger black one. She lifted the lid and looked at the piles of clothes she and Mrs Lowry had packed into it. Her hand moved amongst the sweaters and blouses and skirts and slacks, then cellophane bags with her underwear and more delicate garments. As she looked at each item she could recall where she had bought them and who she had been with. She could remember wearing certain outfits on certain days.

But those days were gone now. She was in this house in Ireland now, and would have to remain so until the time came when she could make her own decisions. Until then, she would have to do her best to live this new life with the people in the house. She could make it easier for herself or make it even harder by fighting against them all.

She had to make the choice. She knew that her father would want her to make as best a life for herself as possible. She would have to choose to do it now or do it eventually.

Heavy, quick footsteps sounded on the wooden stairs and then they carried on more softly on the runner as they made their way towards her room to knock on the door.

"Maria?" Jude called. "Are you all right there?"

"Yes," she said, "I'm just sorting out a few things."

"Grand," he said, "my mother said to tell you that there's food out on the table for you."

She swallowed hard and then called back to him that she would be down in a minute. She didn't feel like going downstairs and talking to him. She didn't feel like talking to any of them.

Maria looked again at the unpacked case and suddenly felt a huge weariness descend on her. She wished she could just climb into bed and pull the covers over her head. But, like everything else here, it wasn't her bed and what she really wanted was her familiar comfortable bed from home. It didn't even matter to her that this had been her mother's room and maybe even the bed she had slept it. She could feel no evidence of her mother's presence anywhere in this room or even in this house.

She realised that all her memories of her mother were wrapped up in the house in St Aiden's Avenue, and she wanted to go back there. Back to her real home.

The house she was in now and the people she was with had nothing to do with her.

Another ten minutes passed and then Jude came back up and tapped on her bedroom door. "Are you sure you're okay?"

"I'm coming," she called back. "I'll follow you down."

Then, she rose from the bed and went over to the chair where she had left her handbag and took her powder compact out. She went over to the mottled mirror which hung over the fireplace and checked her pale reflection and the dark circles under her eyes. Then, she rubbed the powder puff over her face, hoping that it would make her look more like herself.

They were all seated around the table waiting for her. There was a radio on now playing some sort of American country music she vaguely recognised. And as she walked self-consciously across the floor she saw that Ambrose was sitting at the table too, and wondered if they had carried him over or whether he had managed to walk.

"Come in and sit beside me," he said, indicating an empty chair between him and Jude. He tried to pull it out for her, but when he found it difficult, Jude just caught the back of the chair with one hand and moved it to let her in.

Maria sat down and then her throat closed over when she saw the big white plate in front of her with sausages, bacon, an egg, a slice of fried soda bread and two small circles of black and white pudding.

"I wasn't sure what you liked," her grandmother said, her head bent over her own plate, "so I gave you a bit of everything."

"Thank you. It looks very nice ... but I'm not really hungry."

Her grandfather looked over at her. "You'll feel better if you eat something. You ate very little when we were travelling over. We don't want you to think we're getting on to you – but we don't want you to go making yourself sick or anything." He turned back to his wife. "Isn't that right, Eileen?"

"It is indeed," she said.

"She'll be grand when she settles in," Jude said, cutting a rasher of bacon. "Won't you, Maria?"

Ambrose touched her arm. "It's not easy making yourself eat when you're not hungry or feeling as upset as you must be. I'm often not hungry myself, but my mother's soda bread is the freshest and finest in Ireland, and it's even better the day after it's been baked if you fry it. When I'm not at my best, I can usually manage a piece of fried bread dipped into the soft egg." He nodded towards her plate. "You know eggs build you up, don't you?"

Maria nodded.

"Well, you wouldn't know it to look at me, but they've been giving me them for years to try to build me up. But then, I'm a lost cause."

She looked at him, not knowing what to reply.

"Ambrose, for goodness sake," his mother said. "Don't be talking such rubbish."

"On the other hand," Ambrose continued, as if there were only him and his niece in the room, "I might be long gone if I hadn't had the eggs. But they will probably work well for you."

Jude laughed. "Good man, Ambrose! We're only back from one feckin' funeral and you want to depress us all with talk like that!"

"Enough now!" Eileen Donovan whirled around to her handsome, fit son. "And you can mind your language while you're in this house."

She suddenly reminded Maria of Mrs Lowry when she was on her high horse.

Jude was silent for a moment, then he looked up at his mother and said, "Sorry."

Her grandmother, Maria decided, had finally found somewhere to vent her anguish at the conversation as she obviously thought Jude was well able to withstand the sharp edge of her tongue.

Again, as though no one else had spoken, Ambrose smiled over at Maria and pointed a finger at her plate. "You should try a little bit with salt."

"I will," she told him.

She took her knife in one hand and pierced the centre of the soft yellow yolk, then she reached for the salt cellar and shook a few grains on top. She cut off a small slice of the crispy fried bread, dipped it into the runny golden liquid, then took a bite. When she tasted it, she thought he was right. It was lovely. As she finished the last bit, she turned towards him and saw the concern in his eyes and she smiled.

"Good girl," he said, as though she had achieved something wonderful, and Maria felt ashamed that a person like him should be worried about her.

When everyone rose to leave the table, Eileen Donovan looked over at Maria and, seeing only a small amount left on the plate, remarked, "You'll feel a bit better now you've something in your stomach."

"It was very nice, thank you," Maria said. She stood up and pushed back her chair, and then she picked up her own plate, Jude's and Ambrose's. "Can I help you with the washing-up?"

There was a momentary softening in the look her grand-mother gave her. "Another time. You need to have a few hours' sleep to make up for your journey. Ambrose has a sleep at this time most days and, after us all being up so early this morning, I think we might all need a bit of a rest."

Maria went over to the worktop beside the sink and put the plates down, then she lifted the top one, which was her own, and scraped the remainder of her breakfast into the bin that stood below.

"Sure, I'm not tired, I'm grand," Jude told his mother. He went over to the hooks on the back of the door and lifted his coat. "I'm heading down to Mick Carney's for an hour."

Eileen Donovan's head jerked up. "Don't be going near any of the pubs in town now," she warned. "Don't get into any talk about what's happened . . ." She glanced over to where Maria was still standing by the sink. "I have to go into town to the bank and the chemist's this afternoon, and I'm not ready for any interrogations. It will be time enough in a few days."

Maria wondered what she meant by 'interrogations' and guessed it might be to do with her arrival.

Jude looked at Maria. "I'll see you later."

The door closed after him, and then Patrick Donovan came over to the table beside Ambrose, holding two small sticks. "Now, Master Ambrose, do you need a hand?"

"I think I can manage," Ambrose said. He put his two hands flat on the table and then levered his slight body up into a standing position.

Maria noticed that both his tiny arms were trembling with the effort, and her heart speeded up as she watched him painstakingly get his balance, and then turn to take one stick from his father and then the other. After a few faltering steps he had to stop to readjust one of the sticks in his hand and catch his breath. It was then that Maria noticed that both his mother and father were watching him with great apprehension, as though they were measuring each step that he took. When her gaze moved to her grandmother's face and then her grandfather's, she instantly knew that they were afraid of something.

Not knowing what to do or say, she just stood with her back pressed against the old stone sink and waited the necessary minutes while the frail figure of Ambrose made its way across the flagged kitchen floor until he came to rest in his bed by the fire.

Patrick Donovan went over to take the sticks off him, and lift Ambrose's legs up onto the bed. "Well done," he told his son. "You're getting stronger every day."

Ambrose did not answer his father and instead, once in a sitting position, said to Maria. "Are you going for a lie-down now, too? You surely must be tired."

She suddenly realised that she was tired. She had slept little in the past week. "Yes," she told him, "I will go upstairs in a minute and have a rest."

She checked once more with her grandmother as to whether she could help with washing the dishes, and again she was told it was fine.

"Maybe," Ambrose said, "when you're rested, we could make a start on the jigsaw that my father brought me from England? Did you see it yet? It's a fine one."

Maria told him that, no, she hadn't seen it.

"She can see it later," Eileen Donovan said gently, "Now, it's bed for us all for a few hours, or otherwise we'll be fit for nothing tonight."

As Maria went up the stairs she heard Ambrose say, "Maria is such a lovely girl, isn't she?" She paused on the step she was on and listened.

"Yes," her grandmother said, "but it's early days. We'll have to wait and see."

"Well, I have my own opinion," Ambrose informed her. "And I think she's very nice."

"And so do I," his father agreed.

There was a silence then her grandmother said. "Well, nice or not – it's hard getting used to that English accent, but hopefully it will grow on me."

Maria quietly tiptoed the rest of the way up to the bedroom and, once inside, she closed the door.

Chapter 36

Darkness was falling outside when she woke, and for a few careless, happy moments, she thought it was morning and she was back in St Aiden's Avenue in Heaton Moor. She thought her father was downstairs making her pancakes for breakfast and that she would be seeing Stella at school and seeing Paul at the stables later on. And then, she remembered where she was, and the enormity of her loss and the change in her life all hit her again and again until she went tumbling down to the hopeless place inside herself.

She lay there for some time, until her thoughts became more rational and logical and she again came to the same realisation that there was no alternative for her. This strange in-between life that had been thrust on her by her father's death, and by his last wishes, would have to be endured until she was old enough to make her own choices.

This damp corner of Ireland, where her mother had grown up, felt more foreign to her than the wide lakes and mountains in Italy where everyone spoke a language she hardly understood. And she had to keep telling herself that even if she were free to somehow find her way to Dublin and board a plane back to where she knew as home – she would not be returning to their old place in Heaton Moor. The house where she had lived with her father might already have a 'For Sale' sign on it. And, as she had been told last week so many times, and by so many different people, she was neither old enough nor independent enough to find a place of her own.

But, as sure as night would follow day, as Mrs Lowry often said to her, the time would eventually come when she would make her own decisions. And that thought alone would sustain her. She could not bear to work out exactly how long that might be. The thought of knowing the exact number of days, weeks, months, and maybe even years, terrified and depressed her.

Then, as tears of hopelessness trickled down her cheeks, she felt a spark of something deep inside her that told her she would somehow survive until that day came. It might well be in the far-off, dark and distant future – but it was out there and she would count off every single day until the one she was waiting for came.

In the meantime she had to survive. She would have to go back downstairs and re-join all those strangers who were her family, knowing that her grandmother found her voice and probably other things about her annoying.

She came into the kitchen, where the tall sash windows had trickles of condensation running down them, and two large steaming pans – one filled with soup and the other with a large lump of ham – were simmering on the stove.

There was no one else around except Ambrose, who was propped up in his child's settle bed by the open fire, surrounded by all the colourful cushions. He had a tray on his lap which held a bowl of soup and two slices of thickly buttered soda bread. On the stone-flagged floor just within his reach was a small pile of American comics.

"You're awake!" he said. "I hope the sleep did you good?"

The unmistakeably sincere and warm greeting lifted Maria's heart. In the midst of her misery, she had almost forgotten about her uncle. "Yes," she said. "Although I'm not sure I've quite wakened up yet. I can't believe I've slept so long – practically all day."

"It's the best thing for you, so I'm often told." He held his spoon out in the direction of the cooker. "My mother said to tell you to help yourself to the chicken soup and bread. She has a piece of bacon on boiling and we're having that later. It's probably cooked now, if you want to cut a slice off it."

Her father had rarely cooked bacon, although she clearly remembered her mother doing it on occasions. She still did not feel that hungry. "The soup will be fine," she said, going over to the cooker. "It looks and smells lovely."

"Our neighbour, Mary Hynes, made the soup and handed it in, because she knew Mammy was away early this morning and she said it would be handy to have when you all arrived."

"That was very kind of your neighbour."

"People around here are very kind," he said. "But then, Mammy would do the same for them."

"Where are . . .?" she halted, not sure what to refer to her grandparents as. "Where are your parents and Jude?"

"They're all out," he said. "My mother is down visiting Sister Theresa – you know, the woman I was with this morning when you were all away, and my father and Jude are out at the sheep."

"I thought it was cattle they had on the farm."

"They have both, but my father has a good few sheep so he's always out doing something with them." He craned his neck to see what Maria was doing. "Can you manage? Can you see where everything you need is?"

"I'm just looking for a soup bowl . . ."

"You don't use the china that's out on display on the dresser unless you want to give my mother a heart attack." He started to laugh. "That's just for show – we use the plainer delph in the cupboard to the side of the cooker. It's all a bit of a mixture as some of the sets have got broken over the years. I suppose you might be used to grander stuff back in England?"

"No," Maria said, opening the cupboard he directed her to and taking out a white bowl with a blue rim. "We had a glass display cabinet for all the fancy stuff, and we used ordinary plates too. I think most homes are like that." She started to ladle the soup into her bowl, filling it only halfway in case she couldn't finish it. Then, she cut a small slice from the large round soda loaf, as she didn't want to feel her grandmother's disapproval again if she left her food.

Ambrose gestured towards an old leather button-backed chair by the fire. "Put your dish on a tray and bring it over here to the fire, where it's grand and warm."

"The whole kitchen is lovely and warm."

"You'd need it. The summer is nearly over. Do you feel the cold, Maria? I feel it something dreadful, right in my bones. I'd swear that's what makes them so sore at times."

"I do feel cold sometimes."

"My mother knits me heavy woollen sweaters, and makes me wear these thermal vests and everything, but there are times when nothing will warm me." He sighed and shook his head and then lifted his spoon up and dipped it back in his bowl.

When they had finished, Maria took Ambrose's tray and he sank back down into his colourful cushions as though the effort of eating had worn him out. The thought made Maria catch her lip between her teeth and then she felt his eyes on her.

"I was just thinking how lovely and bright those cushions are," she said.

"Sister Theresa and some people from the church make them for me. I think they must feel sorry for me being laid up so much or something like that." He suddenly smiled, and Maria noticed a little devilish glint in his eye. "Although it's not all bad . . . from the summer on now they let me sleep down here by the fire. It saves me all the walking back and forward in the cold to the bedroom. It's bad enough I have to do the walk along the corridor to the bathroom." He beckoned her closer then said in a low voice as though they might be overheard, "Between you and me, it suits me fine down here where I'm up later and can watch the telly and listen to the radio and hear all that's going on around me. I'm fit enough for the bedroom, but who would leave this nice little perch if they didn't have to?"

Maria shook her head and laughed. "There's no flies on you, Ambrose," she said.

"None at all," he said, winking and laughing along with her. He lifted a patchwork cushion to the side of him. "Now, this is a rare one. My mother actually made it, although she prefers knitting to sewing. She cut out squares from the dresses that your mother used to wear when she was young. She just appeared with a bag of them one day and started to cut and sew them. She must have kept them all those years."

Maria stared at the cushion, worked in squares of pastel satins, light floral cotton, checks and stripes. She thought of her mother wearing dresses in those fabrics as a child, and then she thought of her sombre-faced grandmother who had kept those dresses all those years.

She took both trays back to the sink and, after running the water from the old copper tap to check that it was hot, then asking Ambrose where the washing-up liquid was, she set about washing the dishes. She had just started drying them when the door opened and her grandmother came in followed by a small, slim woman with wonderfully thick brown-and-grey-streaked hair, tied back with a strip of maroon velvet, who Maria presumed was Sister Theresa She was wearing a long strange-looking green waxed coat, the sort a man might wear. Maria had assumed Sister Theresa was a nun, but she did not look like any nun she had ever seen. Perhaps, she thought, she was from a very modern order that did not require them to wear habits.

"So this is Maria?" the woman said, her eyes bright and friendly.

"Yes," her grandmother said, taking her raincoat off, "this is Maria." She turned to Maria. "This is our friend and neighbour, Sister Theresa Callaghan."

Maria thought the woman's voice sounded younger than she looked and, if she wasn't mistaken, she spoke with an American accent. Then, she caught the frown on her grandmother's face and she suddenly felt self-conscious, as though she had been caught doing something wrong. She wondered if she shouldn't have made herself so free in the kitchen, and put the plate and the dishtowel down on the worktop.

Sister Theresa came over to shake hands. "Welcome to Tullamore!" Her grip was warm and she shook Maria's hand firmly. Then, as Maria went to let go, the woman put her other hand on top of Maria's and held it tightly. "I'm so sorry for your sad loss . . . I know it's not a happy reason for coming to Ireland, but I'm sure that something good will come out of it. Some things are meant to happen in life, and this might be for a reason."

Maria couldn't think of a reply. She couldn't think of any reason that could justify her father having died in such tragic circumstances, but she knew the nun did not mean that literally. Then, when she met her eyes, she saw the innate kindness in them and she smiled.

"Pity about the weather," Sister Theresa said. "We've had a dreadful summer here. But I suppose it's not a lot better in Manchester? The weather tends to be fairly similar any time I've been over there."

"You're perfectly correct," Ambrose chipped in, struggling into a sitting-position. "It would be more or less the same weather because we're nearly in a straight line on the map." He held his arm up and drew a line with his finger. "You go from Tullamore to Dublin, then you go across the Irish Sea, and then to Wales and straight across to Manchester."

"Good man, Ambrose," the nun said. "Your geography has come on in leaps and bounds."

He shrugged. "Sure, when you have an interest in something or somewhere, it makes you more inclined to find things out. Over the years, I was always wondering how far Maria and her father was away from us so every now and again I'd get the atlas out and check it up."

Maria felt a sudden jolt at what her uncle had just said, and how he had spoken so matter-of-factly about thinking of her and her father. Because of the distant way her mother had been about her family back in Ireland, she had thought that they too would have been as distant and remote about her. She never imagined that someone would have cared about the distance they were from them or what kind of weather they were having.

"Maria," her grandmother said, "thanks for tidying around the sink."

"I hoped you wouldn't mind."

"Not at all." She almost smiled. "It's a change to have another female helping around the place."

"Sister Theresa," Ambrose said, "my father brought me back

a great jigsaw puzzle of *Classic Scenes of London,* and myself and Maria were going to make a start on it now. Would you like to give us a hand?"

"Oh, Ambrose," his mother said, "Sister Theresa has been good enough to have you this morning while we were away – we can't take advantage of her any more."

But the nun was already shrugging her coat off, saying, "What else do I have to do on a wet evening? There's nothing on at the church this evening and, if I'm not imposing on anyone, I'll be happy to join you."

"You don't have to be told," Eileen Donovan said. "You know that there is always a welcome waiting here for you."

"Well, that's kind," the nun said. "Very kind."

Maria came over to help Ambrose pull the jigsaw out from the side of his bed, and when Sister Theresa came towards her she noticed that she was not wearing anything that would indicate she was a nun, apart from a plain silver cross on a long chain. She had a tiny slim figure under the shapeless coat, and was wearing a modern, short smock-style dress in a floral pattern.

Maria wondered if she had bought them in America, because she had heard enough of her accent to be convinced that she was from there. She also thought that if it hadn't been for the greying hair from the back the dainty nun could easily be mistaken for a young girl.

Maria asked Ambrose if he would like her to take the cellophane wrapping off the jigsaw and get all the pieces out, but he said he would prefer it they did it together.

"I think the card table would be the best," Eileen Donovan stated, then went over to the pantry and came out with a small wooden folding table.

"I hope it's not as big as the dinosaur jigsaw," Ambrose said, holding the box out to check the picture. "Do you remember the dinosaur one, Mammy?"

"Oh, I do," she said, her voice momentarily lighter. "How could we forget it?" She placed the card table in front of her son's bed and pulled her husband's well-worn armchair next to it.

"Wasn't it gas?" he said, his voice bubbling with laughter.

"And one of the best nights I ever remember with a jigsaw." He then explained to Maria how he and his father and Jude had started this great jigsaw puzzle on the card table only to find the puzzle was exactly half an inch too wide. His father thought they should move it over to the kitchen table, but Jude insisted it would as good as fit. "And then," Ambrose said, starting to laugh again, "we were just putting the last few bits on when Daddy pressed down a bit too hard on a piece in the middle and the whole thing shot up in the air and then fell asunder. There was bits of the poor dinosaur scattered everywhere!"

"Don't remind me!" his mother said. "We were finding bits for weeks afterwards."

Maria watched as Ambrose laughed heartily at the memory, laughing so hard that his mirth became contagious and Sister Theresa started to laugh along with him. And, as tears ran down Ambrose's face, Maria suddenly found herself laughing along with them. As she did so, she wondered at how her pitiful-looking uncle had inspired her to smile within minutes of meeting him, and on that same day was now making her laugh when she thought she would never laugh again.

Sister Theresa sat down in the leather armchair next to Ambrose and then Eileen Donovan brought a kitchen chair over for Maria so the three were close together. When Maria glanced at her she could tell that, although her grandmother was not joining in with the laughter, she was not unhappy with the lighter atmosphere in the house. The jigsaw was duly unpacked and piled up on the table, then all three set about sorting out the pieces under Ambrose's military-style direction.

"Now," he said, his face most serious and his hands gesturing towards the table and the puzzle, "first we have to look at the picture carefully, and then we have to find the four corner pieces, and then we have to find the straight-edged pieces that make up the border and start with those."

There was silence as everyone studied the picture of six classic scenes from the city of London, featuring the Houses of Parliament, Tower Bridge, Nelson's Column, Tower of London, Piccadilly Circus and Buckingham Palace. Then, hands moved to scatter the pieces and all three started sifting through to find the required straight-edged ones.

Every now and again, Maria became conscious of her grandmother's quiet presence as she moved about in the background, switching on the radio to a programme with low music, sweeping the stone floor, lifting the lid on the bacon to check it wasn't over-cooked and falling to bits, and then slicing up freshly baked bread and covering it with a clean tea towel. At one point when she had finished the chore she was doing, she came over to silently place a wooden tray with three glasses of red lemonade on the stone ledge of the fireplace. On a couple of other occasions she stopped to just watch Ambrose and his helpers as they built up the border and then started on the individual pictures.

When she slipped on her raincoat and wellingtons and went into the yard, Ambrose paused and looked at Maria and then said in the direct way she was now becoming accustomed to, "Sister Theresa probably wants to explain to you that she's not really a nun. I'm saying this now when my mother is out, because she doesn't like me talking about things like this. Myself, I prefer things to be above board and more open, and I know my good friend Theresa is exactly the same."

Maria looked over at Theresa, not quite sure how to react to this piece of news.

"Well," Theresa said, smiling over at her, "I suppose Ambrose is right, as you will no doubt find out from other people eventually. The reason I'm referred to as Sister Theresa is because I was away in a convent in New York for a number of years training, and I did go through postulancy and the novitiate and took my temporary vows."

New York confirmed Maria's thoughts about the American accent.

"But you never took your final solemn vows," Ambrose chipped in. "Isn't that right?"

Maria felt a smile coming to her lips and pursed them tightly together to stop it.

"Indeed it is," Theresa said, reaching over to add another piece to the Buckingham Palace picture.

"I had my doubts for a while about whether I could live such a restricted life and when it came to taking my final vows I decided that I wanted to be a part of the bigger world outside of the convent. I went into teaching for a number of years in schools in New York and Boston and then, when my mother was ill, I decided five years ago to return to Ireland permanently to help look after her. In truth, I wasn't too well myself at that point, so it suited me too."

"That must have been a big change for you," Maria said.

"Oh, believe me, it was," Theresa laughed. "It was an awful shock altogether coming from a multiracial, very modern society like New York back to a small town in the middle of Ireland." She raised her eyebrows. "Not to mention the weather."

Maria felt a tight feeling in her chest. "Did you find it hard to settle?"

"Yes, at first I did," she admitted, "but as time passes, you realise that people are people the world over. It's just a case of adapting and getting used to their different ways. It was a nine-day wonder when I came back, as people wanted to know why I had left the convent and that sort of thing, because most of them thought I was a fully committed nun. It's understandable as they had seen me wearing my habit and had been calling me Sister Theresa on the few visits I had made back home over the years."

"But they still call you that," Ambrose said.

"Well, I'd prefer it if they just called me Theresa, but it doesn't really matter. Most people treat me very nicely and that's the most important thing."

"I'll call you Theresa from now on," Maria said.

"And I," Theresa said, "will do everything I can to help you to settle here until you are able to look after yourself and live wherever you want."

"Do you think that, after a while, I might be able to go back home?"

"Of course you will."

"Nobody can stop you when you're eighteen," Ambrose said. "You'll be a full adult then. You can do what you like. It's not as if you're like me, a weak individual who will always be dependent on others."

Her heart gave a little twist at her uncle's words, but she couldn't help but take some reassurance from them. And, for the first time since leaving England, she sensed that a tiny light had been switched on somewhere at the end of the nightmarish tunnel she felt she was now living in. The relief that it brought made her bow her head as she felt the tears welling up inside her again. Then, she felt Theresa's hand on hers.

"There are good things and good people here too, Maria. It's not going to be as bad as you think. And I, who have had to move and settle, only to move again, know exactly how you feel."

"And I," Ambrose said, "who have been nowhere worth talking about, am happy that you have come to live here, be it long or short."

Maria's eyes swam again, and she knew if any more kind things were said to her she would start crying and not be able to stop. She pushed her chair back. "I must go upstairs for a few minutes . . ." Then, without looking at either of her companions, she quickly went out of the room.

Chapter 37

The following morning, the beginning of Maria's first full day in Ireland, she got up out of bed and went quietly across the floor to her cases. She had taken a few things out of them, but they still remained largely unpacked. Although she knew she would eventually have to take things out and hang them up in the big old wardrobe or put them in the chest of drawers by the window, she was not ready or willing to do it yet. The fear still remained that if she were to lift her dresses and blouses and skirts and hang them in the dark depths of the Victorian wardrobe that she might somehow disappear inside with them and never be seen again. And although she knew it was impossible, while the case remained on the old chest, there was a chance that someone might come and tell her that things had changed and she was going back to live in Stockport after all.

She suddenly remembered a writing set that Diana had given her before she left and she unzipped the compartment in the lid of the case and took it out and laid it on the bed. Going to the hook on the back of the door, she got her dressing-gown and put it on, then climbed back into the warmth of the bed and started to write the first of the three letters she intended to post today. Although writing was the last thing she really felt like, she forced herself to start because she had promised everyone important to her that she would. She also reasoned that she could not expect to receive any letters from home if she did not first write to them.

She started off with Paul but, after writing only the barest introduction, she put the pen down trying to think of something to say that was neither sad or depressing. After a few minutes she picked it up again and started writing a short diary of all the major events that had happened to her in the two days since she last saw him. She started off telling him about the airport and then the plane journey, and after that she gave her first impressions of Dublin. She wrote down only practical details, omitting any references to her feelings about leaving England and all her friends behind.

She went on to describe the big old house and her room and the view she had from her window. Since Paul had already met her grandfather and Jude, she mentioned little about them but, when she went on to introduce Ambrose and Theresa, she found herself smiling.

But it was when she came to ask Paul in the letter if he had any news, and mentioned Stella and Tony and some of the other people from the stables that she found herself becoming sad again, and she wondered if this would always happen every time she thought of Manchester and her old life. Apart from missing Stella, she was worried about her. It was hard to imagine that she was so ill and so thin because she actually chose not to eat. Maria could understand someone being upset when something awful happens, and not feeling like eating – as she herself still did now – but she could not imagine anyone not wanting to eat for months and months with no good reason. There was obviously something seriously wrong with Stella.

When the smell of bacon and sausages permeated through the upstairs, she knew that it was time to go down and join her new, strange family again. In only one day she had already learned that the atmosphere in the house was lighter when the men were in. It wasn't that her grandmother was much cheerier in herself, more that her grandfather and Jude lifted things when they joked with Ambrose or talked about general things that were happening in the news or locally.

Maria glanced down at the few pages she had written so far

and decided, instead of rushing the ending of Paul's now, that she would wait until after breakfast. The other two letters she knew would only take half the time as she would merely copy out parts of Paul's letter, giving the same details of her journey and arrival in Ireland. She put her writing set carefully on the bedside cabinet and then moved out of bed to get ready for this first long day.

As they sat at the breakfast table, a big dish of sausages and bacon and eggs in the middle, Jude looked over at Maria. "Have you any plans for the day?"

"Not really," she said. "None that I know of."

She saw her grandfather look at her grandmother and raise his eyebrows in question. Her grandmother finished the piece of bacon she was eating and then dabbed her mouth with her napkin. "Sister Theresa said you might go down to her cottage later this morning – she wants to chat to you about school and that sort of thing."

Maria put her knife and fork down and then her hand came to rest at her throat. She hoped no one was going to try to persuade her to go to a school here in Ireland. She had already made that plain to her grandfather and Jude when they were in the hotel, and then later again the day of the funeral when Franco and Diana were there too. She was sixteen years old and, as far as she was concerned, school was finished. Hopefully she had gained enough O-Levels so that, when the time came, she would be able to get a job doing something reasonable.

Ambrose sat forward in his chair. "Will I go with her? Maria can push me down in the chair." He looked at Maria. "Is it okay if I come?"

"Of course," she said. "I'd like your company."

"As long as you don't talk too much and don't interfere," his mother said. "They have important things to discuss."

"I'll bring my comics down and sit quietly reading."

Jude smiled over at her. "Well, it sounds as though you have an outing today whether you like it or not." He leaned forward to the dish and speared an egg with his fork. "There's a dance on in Tullamore on Friday night if you fancy it."

There was a sharp intake of breath, then Eileen Donovan swung round to her older son. "Jude, for God's sake! If you can't make a sensible suggestion then don't make any."

"What have I said now?" Jude asked, his eyes wide.

Ambrose looked across at him and made eyes and then shrugged.

"You know well," his mother said. "The poor girl has only just arrived and the last thing she needs is to be paraded around the dance halls for everyone to gawk at."

"Sure there are girls her age at the dances, and I'd be there to keep an eye on her. What harm would it do?"

"Wouldn't it look good now if she was seen around Tullamore for the first time at a dance and her father only cold . . ." She halted and then lowered her eyes. "At times I wonder . . ."

Maria did not move or look at anyone.

Her grandmother turned towards her. "I'm sorry now," she said, although her voice sounded more strained than apologetic, "but Jude wasn't thinking, and I didn't mean to go upsetting you by mentioning . . . anything like that."

Maria took a deep breath. She knew that her grandmother wanted her to say that it was all right and she was okay, but she did not like the harsh way she had spoken to Jude and she was not going to make her feel better.

"You'll like Sister Theresa's cottage," Ambrose suddenly said. "That will cheer you up. It always cheers me up when I go down there."

"Sister Theresa is a great woman," his mother said, and then she started gathering up the plates.

Patrick Donovan sighed and then he looked around the table at Ambrose, Jude and finally at Maria. Then he said, "Things will change again. They always do. I've seen it all before. This time will pass and there will be better days ahead."

"Let's hope there will be better days," Jude said, "for all of us."

Maria thought he was making it clear that he was not happy with his mother's attack on him.

Then Jude looked over at her and smiled. "We might leave the dance this time and maybe have a night out at the pictures instead. What do you think?"

"Now you're talking," his father said, his voice a touch too jovial to be genuine. "The pictures would be ideal, don't you think, Eileen?"

"Whatever they like now," she said.

"I think I saw in the local paper that there was an Elvis film on," Jude said. "Do you like Elvis?"

Maria lifted her eyes. "Yes, I do."

He winked at her. "I'll check it out later this evening, so."

The last thing Maria would have thought of was going to an Elvis film, but, with the way her grandmother was, it was better than staying a long night in at home. It was, she thought, any port in a storm.

Chapter 38

A decidedly cool breeze hit Maria when she stepped outside the house, and she wondered had she been so numb to everything when she first arrived in Ireland that she had not felt the change in the weather. Her grandfather and Jude lifted the wheelchair out with Ambrose well wrapped up in an anorak with fur around the hood, a thick sweater and fleece-lined boots. Maria thought her poor uncle looked like someone dressed for an Arctic expedition as opposed to a short walk down a lane in the middle of autumn. Her grandmother stood by the door watching quietly as Patrick hooked the two small walking-sticks over the handles of the chair.

"Begod, it's got nippy enough out here!" Patrick said. "It's the coldest I've felt it recently – you'd think we were in the middle of winter. Maybe you'd be wiser staying at home, Ambrose. We don't want you catching the flu again or anything like that."

"I'm grand," Ambrose said, only the tip of his nose visible from the hood. "Sure, we'll only be five minutes out in the air and then we'll be back inside again. I'm hardly likely to catch anything in that short time."

His mother came out into the yard to look in at him. "Keep yourself well covered now," she told him.

"I'm grand, I'm grand," he repeated, a stubborn note in his

319

voice. "Sure, ye will have Maria thinking I'm a complete invalid the way ye are all going on."

Eileen looked over at Maria. "Are you sure you're warm enough now?" We don't want you catching anything either."

"I'm fine, thanks," Maria said. She needed to get out of the house for a while. "I'll warm up when I start walking. She moved the rainbow-coloured scarf higher around her neck.

"We need to get moving now," Ambrose said. "Sister Theresa said she would do an American dish for us, and I don't want it getting spoiled."

"You surely can't be ready to eat much after that big breakfast you shifted?" Jude said. "That would nearly keep a grown man going for the rest of the week."

"Go away, you!" Ambrose laughed. "I'll eat what I like."

Jude looked at Maria now. "Do you want me to push Ambrose up as far as the cottage?" he checked. "You've not been up there before and there's a good few bumps and potholes."

"Maria's well able to do it," Ambrose said, "and I'll give her the directions so she avoids the worst bits." He waved his gloved hand. "Ye can all go in and enjoy the peace and quiet without us. We'll be grand."

They went out onto the main road and walked a few minutes along before turning down the small, hedge-lined laneway up to Sister Theresa's. Maria thought it looked like a country farm track rather than a lane with grass growing at the sides and in between where the wheels went. The lanes she was used to around the stables were well-kept and had smooth tarmacadam on them, and any small holes were quickly filled by the grounds-men. This one was narrow and bumpy and every time the wheelchair hit a stone or pothole, Maria checked that Ambrose was okay, and each time he assured her that he was.

Just as Maria began to feel they were walking along an endless lane, she spotted a gap between two high hedges and as they got closer she saw a red-painted gate. Ambrose directed her to go through it and, when she manoeuvred the wheelchair around a bit and straightened up, she found she was looking straight at a small, ivy and clematis-covered thatched cottage, with a red door and windows, that was reminiscent of an old-fashioned cover of a chocolate box. After a day and a half of Donovan's comfortable but fairly bare house, Maria found the colourful cottage gave her heart a lift.

"Isn't it a picture? She must be the finest gardener in Offaly," Ambrose said, proud on Sister Theresa's behalf. "Now, go around the side of the cottage to the right, as it's easier to get in through the kitchen. We can leave the chair outside as it doesn't look like it will rain."

"We'll keep an eye on the weather," Maria said, "and I can always come back and get the chair if necessary."

As she slowed to a halt, her eyes took in the small orchard to the back of the cottage with eight or maybe ten apple trees, and the well-laid out vegetable garden. A wooden-handled fork stuck in one of the freshly-turned drills told her that the ex-nun had been out working in it very recently, as did the mounds of gold and brown leaves at the side of the cottage and in the orchard. She heard some funny sounds coming from the corner of the garden and, when she craned her neck, she could see a shed with a fenced-off area and then she saw a mixture of brown and white chickens.

She had just put the brake on the wheelchair when the cottage door opened and Theresa came out, wearing a blue knitted sweater over jeans and sheepskin boots, her abundant brown hair tied up in a colourful Indian scarf. Music was playing in the background and Maria was surprised when she realised it was The Rolling Stones' 'Paint It Black'. She had presumed, if music was played in the home of someone who had been in a convent, that it would be monastic or at least classical.

"Welcome, welcome!" Theresa rushed forward to give Ambrose a hug and then she turned and took Maria in her arms.

Maria instinctively stiffened and went to pull back but then, as Theresa's grip loosened, Maria found herself moving towards her and they both stood with their arms wrapped around each other, saying nothing.

"I'm sorry, I didn't mean to be rude . . ." Maria eventually whispered. "I don't know what's wrong with me."

"It's okay," Theresa said. "And there's nothing wrong with you –how you feel is only natural after all you've gone through."

Without warning, tears welled up in her eyes and Maria suddenly knew that things could now go one way or another. She could feel hugely relieved that she had someone who seemed to understand everything she was feeling. She knew that she could either accept that support and keep going or she could just keep it all to herself and gradually crumble into little pieces.

"She's grand," Ambrose said. "She's a good strong girl and, from what she's told me, her father would want her to make the best of things here . . ."

She felt his hand touch hers and she knew that there was no real choice but to blink the tears back.

They manoeuvred the wheelchair into the small hallway. Then they helped Ambrose out of the chair and, taking an arm each, assisted him into the kitchen and got him settled into the armchair at the side of the range. After he caught his breath, Ambrose took his coat off and unwound the scarf from around his neck, and then Theresa took them to hang up in the hot press so they would be warm for him going home.

It was then that Maria could take the time to view her surroundings and, like the pop music, the bright little kitchen was not what she had imagined to find down that narrow laneway. The walls were painted in a pale yellow with a blue-stencilled border of flowers and birds running across the top, and a row of small violet-coloured hearts along the middle. Maria guessed that Theresa had spent days and nights hand-painting these herself.

An old-fashioned dresser, painted duck-egg blue, held a collection of floral cups and saucers and plates in different designs. On each wall there hung a myriad of photographs and paintings alongside white-painted functional shelves holding jars of herbs and spices. Her gaze moved along to decorative shelves on another wall which held small holy statues of Our Lady and St Francis of Assisi, carved animals, glass paperweights, and vases and bottles filled with tiny intricate flowers which looked good enough to be real but were, in fact, artificial.

Besides the comfortable blue velvet armchair that Ambrose sat in surrounded by patchwork cushions, there was a white-painted rocking chair which had the same little hearts stencilled on it.

"Right!" Theresa said, coming back into the kitchen and rubbing her hands together. "First, is the music okay or is it annoying? I'm just checking because not everyone here appreciates some of the more modern stuff I like."

"I love it," Ambrose stated. "Every chance I get, I switch our radio at home onto the pop channels. All that country music and traditional stuff my mother plays drives me mad."

Maria laughed. "I like all sorts of music, and especially The Rolling Stones and The Beatles."

"Good! Then we're all sorted," Theresa said. "The next question is, are you ready to eat lunch now? If it's too early for you, we can have it later."

A big smile spread on Ambrose's face. "What are we having?"

"Chicken and . . ." There was a pause.

"Peanut butter sauce and rice!" cried Ambrose.

"How did you guess?"

"Because," Ambrose said, grinning at them both, "I asked you last week to make it when Maria came over."

"Well, lucky I had all the ingredients in," Theresa laughed. "I would have hated to disappoint you." She looked over at Maria. "Do you like rice?"

"Yes," Maria said, "and I like peanuts although I've never tried peanut sauce."

"I left some of the chicken plain just in case you didn't like it."

"It sounds lovely and very unusual."

"American," Ambrose mused. "You wouldn't normally get that kind of food around here. My mother has a bad turn every time I tell her that I've tried something new down at Theresa's. She and my father would be very plain eaters. Now, Jude would be a bit like myself and have a go at anything. I had a great time last week when I stayed down here for the few days – we had devilled eggs one of the evenings and another one we had meat loaf with barbeque sauce."

Maria felt a small pang. "We used to have meat loaf at home . . ." she said, her voice faltering a little. "Although I think it was a bit different from yours – it was an old Italian recipe that my Italian grandmother made with a tomato sauce."

"If you would like to sit in the rocking-chair, I'll bring a small table over and we can eat in here as it's warmer," said Theresa. "The fire in the sitting room hasn't really got going yet, but it should be fine by the time we finish lunch." She smiled at Maria. "You and I can go and chat in there, while Ambrose has his afternoon nap."

"The best part of the day!" Ambrose said, stretching to put his folded arms up behind his neck. "When you're all full up and have a nice little doze for yourself."

Sister Theresa brought the table over and then, when she went to the hot press to get a cloth for it Ambrose leaned forward, a solemn look on his face. "I'm sorry now, Maria, but I could see by your face you were a bit sad when I mentioned the meat loaf."

Maria nodded. "You don't need to apologise," she said. "Nearly everything reminds me. It's there all the time." How intuitive he was, she thought. At times he gave the impression that most things went over his head, and yet, when you least expected it, he showed he missed very little.

"Last week Theresa and me were thinking of things that might help you to forget, but I suppose it's far too soon."

Maria realised then that the invitation to lunch today by Theresa hadn't been a spontaneous one and that her arrival must have been fully discussed by them the previous week. Whether it was a suggestion by Ambrose alone that she come down to Theresa's or whether her grandparents had been involved because of the school issue she didn't know. She thought it was strange, really, to be discussing such personal things with someone she barely knew. But, did it really matter, she wondered, how long you knew someone, if you got on as well as she felt she did with this particular woman? The important thing was she had been lucky enough to meet someone who seemed to have an understanding of her situation, as soon as she arrived in Ireland.

It struck her that she had found the same with Diana Freeman, who had just appeared in the church, and then later had slid so easily into her life and then into her father's. And how perfect it had all been for those precious months they had been together, to have another female around the house, to have someone to talk about feminine things. When she looked back their chats had not been about anything very exciting and, to friends like Stella with mothers and sisters, it might even have seemed ordinary and often boring. But Maria, who had been used to only Mrs Lowry's regular company, had enjoyed those afternoons and evenings so much. And it seemed that fate now had placed another two very unlikely companions into the centre of her life, and she wondered how that was now going to work out.

In a way she felt guilty for thinking it, but she hoped that they were not going to be the main figures in her life for long because she desperately hoped that Ireland was not going to the main place in her life for too long either.

Theresa sorted the table and a stool for herself and then she went over to put the food on the plates, and Maria helped carry them over to the table.

"Your kitchen is beautiful," Maria said, looking around her. "I really like the colours and the interesting things you have on the walls and shelves."

When they were all settled and eating, Maria complimented Theresa's cooking and said she would love the recipe for the peanut sauce.

"That would be great," Ambrose said, and smiled. "You could cook it for me every week."

"Of course, you must be used to all sorts of different food with your father having owned a restaurant," Theresa said. "What was it like?"

When she started off talking about Leonardo's, Maria was afraid she might cry but she managed to steer herself away from mentioning too much about her father and went into more details about the menu and the décor in the restaurant. Ambrose asked a few questions about pasta, which he had never heard of, and then, when it was explained, he said the only pasta he had eaten was tinned macaroni. Maria wasn't sure if the local shops in Ireland would have dried pasta, but, she told him, if she found somewhere that sold it, she would cook it for him some time. The conversation then moved on to American restaurants and all the different foods that Theresa had learned to cook when she was out there.

Maria helped with the washing-up and, when she was busily drying, Theresa nudged her and pointed over to Ambrose, who was dozing in the chair. They quietly finished and then tiptoed past him into the sitting room. It was every bit as vibrant as Maria expected after seeing the kitchen, with billowing green silk curtains tied back with plaited ribbons and four Van Gogh prints – which Maria recognised from her art classes – not framed, but stuck on wooden boards and varnished over.

Maria leaned back into the velvet and brocade tasselled cushions that gave a decadent look to the rather battered old claret-coloured sofa and surveyed the rest of room. Across from her, Theresa sat in an armchair that could only be described as a work of art as it was covered by scraps and squares of material in all sorts of patterns and textures.

"My Auntie Biddy's old chair," Theresa explained, "that I couldn't bear to throw out when I inherited her cottage. It was decrepit, with tears all over that the stuffing was poking through, so she used to cover it with shawls and blankets and God knows what else. She was quite an eccentric and didn't really care what people thought of her."

Maria smiled and wondered if her niece had perhaps inherited the same tendencies.

"She was a great seamstress, made all her own clothes and curtains and things, so I went through all her boxes of fabric and picked out a few bright bits that I thought complimented each other and cheered the place up." She narrowed her eyes in thought. "Auntie Biddy – my father's sister – was so different from my mother, who was more . . . oh, I suppose, rigid and conscious of her position. She had two brothers who were priests, you know. They went off to different parts of America. I think that hearing about them over the years is what gave me the idea to go out there." She suddenly looked at Maria. "Good Lord, I'm yakking away here, probably boring the pants off you!"

"No," Maria said, smiling at her turn of phrase, "I'm enjoying listening to you very much."

When Maria complimented Theresa on the room she told her to have a wander round and have a good look. "Ambrose does it all the time. Beautiful things are meant to be shared and appreciated and not hidden away."

Maria went over to the main centrepiece of the room – an ebony Victorian antique display-cabinet filled with ornaments and statues. A surprising addition was a shelf filled with dozens of snowglobes which Theresa told her she had been collecting since she was a child. When Theresa saw that Maria was fascinated by the globes, she opened the cabinet and encouraged her to lift out and examine any that caught her eye. She went on to tell her that the older globes came from Ireland, several antiques from an aunt in London, and some of the more unusual ones came from America and flea markets in France. Maria was particularly fascinated by a delicate one containing a carousel horse, which was painted in pale, pastel colours and was decorated with little flowers at the base. Theresa showed her that if you wound it up at the bottom it rotated on a central column like a real carousel and also played a tune. Maria immediately recognised the tune as one her mother had listened to, but could not remember the name and Theresa told her it was 'Für Elise' by Beethoven.

Maria finally moved from the cabinet to look at the tall bookcases on either side which were filled in a rather higgledy-piggeldy fashion which amused and pleased her, as it made Theresa seem less like a nun or a teacher and more like an ordinary person. The walls were hung with paintings and shelves that held ornaments and sculptures that looked as though they were handed down through several Irish generations, while others looked as though they came from far corners of the world. Although she had little experience in interior design, Maria knew that Theresa had a certain eye for putting things together. And, while many people back home and in Ireland might think it was outlandish and weird, there were other people who would think the cottage was a work of art in itself.

When Maria had finished looking at everything she sat back down and, without any preamble Theresa said, "You know that Ambrose is not very well, don't you?"

"Yes," Maria said, "but he's been that way since he was born, hasn't he?"

She then sat and quietly listened as Theresa outlined the heart and lung problems and the complications that her uncle had. She explained that he had only attended school for a few years until his condition had advanced to the extent that he didn't have the stamina to be out of the house and away from his bed for more than a few hours.

"So you can understand why your grandmother is not the most light-hearted person, can't you?"

Maria looked at her without saying anything. She couldn't trust herself to speak as she might tell the truth and say that she found her grandmother at times an almost sour and overly serious woman.

"I know she seems a very . . ." Theresa paused, searching for the right word, "a very *stern* sort of woman but I know her heart is sore worrying about Ambrose. I think you can see that she loves him very much – even in the short time you have been here, you must have seen the way she is about him." She reached out to touch Maria's hand. "I know your heart is broken over your own tragic loss, but your grandmother's has been broken too. She's a better woman than you think she is – if you can just give her the time to show it."

Theresa then went on to tell her how she had come to work with Ambrose. Her family's farm, which was half a mile away, had land which bordered onto Donovans' farm, so the two families had known each other a long time. She looked at Maria and could see the question in her eyes.

"I did, of course, know your lovely mother and the rest of the family. She was quite a bit younger than me, but that's something I'll talk about another day when Ambrose isn't around. Is that okay?"

"Yes," Maria said. "I'd really like to hear about her." She looked down at her hands. "I had a picture of what she was like in my mind for years and then, when my father died, I discovered there was a completely different side to her."

Theresa reached over and gently touched her hand. "I promise we'll talk about that soon."

She then told Maria that it was shortly after she had come home to Ireland that she started working with Ambrose. After visiting the Donovans, she could see that he needed one-to-one attention and, since she had done some teaching in one of her many jobs in America and she had spare time on her hands, she offered to help out with his education. Thus, depending on the weather and his energy, Ambrose came down to the cottage several mornings a week. Alternatively, if he wasn't up to leaving he house, Theresa went up to Donovan's where they did reading, writing, basic maths and current affairs.

"It's a very informal arrangement," Theresa explained. "I don't accept money for it, but Patrick helps me out with turf for the fire, potatoes and vegetables, and Eileen often bakes me bread and cakes." She motioned with her hand around the room. "Really, my needs are quite basic – I have everything here I could want. I enjoyed all the modern furniture and quick pace of life in America, but I like having time to myself and having all these old things around me that hold memories. I am also lucky in that I have a small income from some land that I own that is rented out, and of course I grow things myself." She smiled. "Including some of the more unusual vegetables and herbs I was used to in America and that I find hard to buy here."

"Do you miss anything about living there?" Maria asked her.

"Oh, yes, big time!" Theresa laughed. "When I think back to all the wonderful places I've been and the things I've done and the people I've met – it's like I'm thinking about somebody else. It's just not at all comparable to here and it never will be. But you see, when I went to America at first I found that very different and I was very homesick, and then, after years of getting used to New York, when I came back home to Ireland, I found that I'd left a bit of myself back there. I had no idea that I would miss the people and the places so much." She raised her eyebrows and sighed. "So I know the feeling you have all too well. It's a horrible lost kind of thing, quite hard to describe. And that's exactly why I want to help make things easier for you. I had to learn ways to help myself, and they worked. And I now want to help you adapt and settle here, and make the best of the experience."

Maria looked up at her. "But, the problem is I don't want to settle here . . . I just want to go home."

"It will only be for a year or two," Theresa said softly. "It will go by quickly."

Maria closed her eyes and took a deep breath. "A year or two sounds forever and it frightens me. I just cannot imagine being here all that time. To think of it makes me feel I'll go completely mad."

"Now, now," Theresa said. "That's not going to happen."

Maria's eyes filled up. "I don't mean to be ungrateful to you or to my grandparents or Ambrose. You have all done your best in your own different ways to help me to settle, but this place has nothing to do with me, and I have nothing to do with it."

"Oh, but you have – much more than you think – and I know I can help you change your feelings about it."

"I don't want to change my feelings, Theresa. I don't want to give in. I want to keep feeling like this, because it means I will keep working to find ways to get back to my proper home. Back to where there are people who really know me."

"I do understand what you're saying, and I will do my best to help you make sure that happens but, in the meantime, I want you to let me help you function here and make the best of it. You must see, surely, Maria, that it can't be good for you to have your mind elsewhere all the time. While it is good to plan for the future, you must still learn to live in the present."

"I'm not sure I know what you mean . . ."

Theresa thought for a few moments, then she held her finger up and smiled. "The jigsaw," she said, "is a good example of focussing all your thoughts on what you are doing right now, as you study the picture and then concentrate on looking at the pieces without thinking of anything else."

"But don't we do that all the time?" Maria said. "Like when

we're walking and talking and doing things like watching television or . . ." she shrugged, "just ordinary things."

"No, no – so many of the things we do are automatic, and because we don't concentrate well enough, our thoughts start wandering back onto things we're worried or anxious about."

There was a pause then Maria said, "Did you hear something?"

They listened for a bit, then heard Ambrose calling for Theresa. They went quickly out into the kitchen.

"I wondered where the pair of you were," Ambrose said. "I had a lovely sleep but I'm wide awake now and I wondered if we could maybe have a game of chess."

"A very good idea," Theresa said, "but we'll have to teach Maria."

"Now you're talking!" Ambrose clapped his hands and then rubbed them together gleefully.

Theresa looked over at Maria, and smiled. "But she'll have to really concentrate on it to become as good as you."

Three hours later, as she pushed Ambrose's chair back along the bumpy laneway towards Donovans' farmhouse, Maria realised she had learned something more than the basic rudiments of chess this afternoon.

She had learned that in certain circumstances her opinion mattered, and that certain adults listened as carefully to younger people as they did with anyone older. Theresa Callaghan, she had discovered, was one of those people. She had listened carefully to what Maria had said about not going back school, and then to the idea of her eventually finding work in a travel agent's.

Theresa had said it was definitely an interesting and worthwhile occupation, and that she was sure her grandparents would agree as well. They drew up a list of the qualifications Maria already had that would count towards gaining a position in such a place, and then they drew up another list of the skills she was lacking in or needed to improve in. Theresa then quickly set about making a plan for her to learn the skills over the coming months.

"The first thing you need to learn to do is type," Theresa said, "and I think if we move immediately, we might get you into the evening classes that are just starting this month. I think they do an office studies course which focuses on shorthand and typing but it also covers a bit of bookkeeping, which is also useful. And I'm sure your grandparents will be only too happy to sort you out with a typewriter to use at home." She had looked at Maria and smiled. "Your friends back in Manchester will be surprised and delighted to receive a typed letter from you, and the evening classes and the typing practice will give you something to do during the long winter evenings at home."

Maria's face lit up and she said that, yes, that sounded like an excellent idea.

"Geography," Theresa went on, "I can help you with here, and of course we'll make sure we keep your English and Maths and French up to date."

"But how can I pay you for teaching me?" Maria said. "And I know you have an arrangement for Ambrose, and surely it would be too much for you to teach me as well?"

"But it won't take any more of my time," Theresa said. "I'll set Ambrose off on his projects first each day and, while he is reading and writing, I'll work with you. Really, you'll be teaching yourself a lot of it from the books – I'll only be making sure you keep on the right track, explaining anything you're not sure about."

"I'll agree on one condition," Maria said. "As long as you let me pay you something when my father's money is all sorted out."

Theresa had smiled. "Well, if that happens, then we can discuss it. If not, then we won't mention it again." She had looked back at the things they had written down. "I'll be in Tullamore tomorrow morning, and I'll drop into the library or one of the schools and find out the name and phone number of the person who is running the office skills course."

"You make it all sound easy," Maria said, "and much more interesting than I had thought."

"It will all work out," Theresa said. "You just have to believe that things can be done – and most importantly – believe in yourself."

Chapter 39

When they arrived back at the farmhouse, Eileen was alone, sitting in the armchair knitting a plum-coloured sweater for Ambrose. She listened quietly while Maria told her all that Theresa had suggested, and said they would talk about it with Maria's grandfather later on. She then got up and brought Maria and Ambrose tea and slices of a fruit cake she had baked earlier in the afternoon. She moved about so quietly that it made Maria feel uncomfortable at times, and she was always grateful that her chatty uncle and the radio filled the silent gaps.

When she had drunk her tea, Maria said she was going back upstairs to finish writing her letters, but as she made to go, Ambrose said, "I was just wondering, Maria, do you play any music? Like, can you play any instruments at all?"

"Ambrose," his mother's voice had a warning tone in it, "don't be talking so much. Let Maria go and write her letters now."

While Maria did feel she needed some quiet on her own, she felt that if she turned away without answering his question it would reinforce her grandmother's comment about his chatter being too much. How, she wondered, would she cope here today, and all the days that lay ahead, if it wasn't for his cheery chatter?

She turned back and sat down again on one of the pine kitchen chairs. "No, Ambrose, I can't really play any instruments. I

333

did piano lessons when I was young, in primary school, but I started up horse-riding and that took up all my spare time along with ballet. I think you have to concentrate on one thing and keep practising to be any good, so I had to choose."

Her grandmother went over to straighten Ambrose's cushions behind his back. "I think you're right," she said quietly. "What's the saying? A jack of all trades is master of none." She ran an affectionate hand over Ambrose's hair, and smiled at him.

Maria thought that was the most tender thing she had seen Eileen Donovan do since she had arrived in the house.

Ambrose laughed and said, "Sure Maria would be called a mistress of all trades, not a master, wouldn't she?"

Her grandmother laughed and shook her head. She looked over at Maria. "What would you do with this fellow? Wouldn't he break your heart with his questions and his contradictions?"

Maria smiled back, and thought how much younger her grandmother looked when her face was not so stern, and she felt relieved that she could see signs of her beginning to thaw out.

"There's a riding school a few miles from here, you know," Ambrose said to Maria. "It's called Matthews' Equestrian Centre. Jude is friendly with one of the sons, isn't he, Mammy?"

"Yes," her grandmother said. "He went to school with Harry Matthews."

"You could go for riding lessons there," Ambrose suggested. "They might bring me down in the car, and I could watch you riding around and leaping over the fences."

Maria smiled at him. "Maybe next summer when the weather is better. It's a bit miserable coming into the winter."

Ambrose looked thoughtful. "I'd loved to have played an instrument," he mused, "but my arms don't have the strength for it. Would you believe that I can hardly hold the tin whistle for more than a few minutes? I always knew the fiddle and the accordion were too much for me, but you'd think that even a child in infant school could hold a tin whistle, wouldn't you? It's dreadful to be so weak in your arms and body."

Maria noticed the pained look that crossed her grandmother's face and she knew his words were going straight to her heart.

"I asked the doctor once what he thought was wrong that I couldn't hold things," Ambrose went on. "He wasn't just an ordinary doctor – he was the specialist up in Dublin – the one that deals with my chest. Anyway, he just said that some people were born to make music, and some people were born to listen to it. I didn't think it really answered the question about my arms, but I thought it was a good statement. What do you make of it?"

Eileen Donovan said nothing, she just quietly moved across the room to check if the stove needed more wood or turf.

Maria felt tears prick at her eyes as she pictured the scene in the hospital, and could only imagine how sad it was for her grandparents having to constantly listen to Ambrose questioning the doctors about his serious condition so openly. "I think the doctor might be right," she said. Then, she forced a smile on her face. "That means I'm the same as you, Ambrose, because I'm no great musician, but I'm one of the people who love listening to it."

He moved around in his bed now, to look to where his mother was standing by the stove. "My mother is lucky – she was born to play music. You should hear her on the piano. She's marvellous at playing."

When Maria looked over at her grandmother now, her face looked white and stricken.

"Will you play a few tunes for Maria sometime, Mammy?"

"You know I don't play any more, Ambrose. I haven't played for years."

"Well, maybe now is the time to get back to it," he said. "It might do you good because you're always working so hard. It might even cheer you up a bit."

There was a silence then she said in a choked voice. "The radio is enough music for me these days."

"But it's not the same as playing it, when you can do it as well as you."

"Ambrose!" she snapped. "We've had more than enough music in this house. Please don't ask me that again."

Maria watched now as tears started to spill down her

grandmother's well-defined cheekbones and something about the way she looked reminded Maria of her mother.

"Okay, okay," Ambrose said. "I didn't mean to annoy you." He picked up a comic and started to read as though the conversation had never taken place.

Eileen Donovan went over to the sink now, and after a few minutes Maria noticed her wiping her face with the towel. Something about her sadness and vulnerability made her take a chance on being rebuffed. She moved across the room and put her arm around her grandmother and was hugely relieved when she did not pull away.

"Thank you," her grandmother said quietly. She patted Maria's hand and then moved away. "I'll be fine in a minute." She rubbed her face again with the towel and then went over and put it into the basket where she kept the things for washing.

She came back to the range to where Maria was still standing. "I'm sorry now for getting so worked up, but sometimes I just can't help it. I think it's my age or something."

"As long as you're okay," Maria said. She paused for a few moments. "I'll go upstairs now and finish my letter off."

Then, as Maria went to turn away, her grandmother reached out and took her hand in hers. Maria noticed also that, for the first time since she arrived, her grandmother looked her properly in the eye.

"As soon as I'm able to, I promise I'll explain all of this to you," Eileen said. She glanced over to where Ambrose was by the fire, now nodding off to sleep. "It's not just me – it's your grandfather too who finds it all very hard to talk about. Thank God Jude was too young to fully understand what happened." She closed her eyes. "You've no idea what we went through . . . I know you must think I'm odd about things like not playing the piano this afternoon. But it was actually the music that started it all off. All the problems stemmed from there."

"What do you mean?" Maria was completely baffled.

"If it hadn't been for the piano playing," Eileen Donovan said, "your mother would never have had to leave Ireland, the way she did."

Chapter 40

When Maria was playing chess with Ambrose at the fireside the following Saturday night, she overheard her grandparents discussing going to Mass the following morning. Her grandmother had said it might be easier to drive into the church in Tullamore as it was bigger and not as many would know them. Her grandfather had quietly replied that it was as well to go to the small local church they always went to and get any issues over and done with there.

"It will be easier to just acknowledge people as we do every Sunday, and then go on our way as usual," he said. "Easier than meet them for the first time in a shop or when you're walking around the town and not prepared for it."

Whether it had been further discussed later, Maria did not know, but when she was getting ready for bed around half past ten her grandmother said they would call her around ten o'clock to be ready for quarter past eleven mass.

"There's no point in calling you earlier," her grandmother said, "because you can't have breakfast before Communion and it makes it all the harder not eating if you're just sitting around waiting." She gave a half-hearted smile. "Well, I don't know what you're like, but it makes it all the harder on the likes of Jude who's always ready to eat the minute he gets up."

"I think it's a load of nonsense," Ambrose suddenly piped up from his corner.

"What's nonsense?" his mother asked.

"About not eating before Communion. Who decided that? There's nothing about not eating our breakfast it in the Bible."

"Now, Ambrose," his father said, glancing over the top of his *Irish Independent*, "that'll do. It's not for you to be commenting on the Church rules. And anyway, you're one of the few that's allowed to eat because of your medication."

"Well," Ambrose said, "I'd refuse to stick to the rules if I wasn't allowed. It's a load of rubbish, and even Sister Theresa agrees with me."

"Don't be bringing Sister Theresa into your arguments," his mother said.

"I have my own views."

"Pay no heed to that fellow," Patrick said, shaking his head and rolling his eyes. "He loves to carry on like that when he has an audience."

A huge smile broke out on Ambrose's face now, indicating how pleased he was with the controversy he had stirred up. "Don't you think, Maria, that the world would be a better place if everyone told the truth?"

Maria looked over at him and smiled. "It might be, Ambrose," she said, smiling back at him, "but there's an awful lot of people who might get into trouble for saying what they think."

"Well said, Maria." Her grandmother was smiling now too. "Sometimes it's wiser to say nothing at all."

After she had brushed her teeth and washed, Maria came back down to the kitchen in her pyjamas and dressing-gown. "Do we dress up for Mass?" she asked her grandmother.

"Some do. I usually wear a hat and coat."

"That's fine," Maria said. "I'll wear a hat and coat too."

"Here you are, Maria," her grandmother said now, handing her a hot water bottle. "I was just going to bring this up to you."

As she walked up the stairs, hugging the rubber bottle to her chest, Maria pondered how easily she had settled into a routine in the house, and how quickly each evening now seemed to pass.

She had been down to Theresa's several evenings in her first week and she had been to the cinema in Tullamore with Jude, who had also brought two friends with him – Owen and Cathy. They were Jude's age, so a good bit older than her. Cathy was a nurse in the local hospital and Owen worked in the bank. They had seemed nice enough, although she hadn't spoken that much to them apart from at the intermission when Cathy had chatted to her when the men went down to the shop to buy packets of crisps and lemonade. Cathy, Maria thought, was easy to talk to and very attractive with short blonde hair. Jude had obviously been talking to his friends about her, because they mentioned Manchester a few times and referred to the Donovans as her granny and granddad.

It was raining when they came out, so they had said a quick goodbye and then run to their cars.

"It would be easier if you don't mention Cathy being there," Jude had said to Maria when they were on the way home. "My mother isn't keen on her. Although my mother is the best in the world, sometimes the less she knows the less she has to complain about."

He had asked her then how things were going and if she was getting used to living with Ambrose and everyone else in the house. She told him she liked Ambrose very much, and thought she was settling in okay, although she missed her father and old home very much.

"Give yourself time," he said, smiling warmly at her. "But I can tell you one thing – we are all enjoying having you. You've brought a whole new life to the house."

When they'd arrived back home, Maria was relieved when her grandmother just asked if she had a nice time. She then asked Jude if they had met anyone and he said they hadn't apart from Owen. Maria couldn't imagine what the problem was with Owen's girlfriend, Cathy, but she decided it was none of her business.

She had gone into Tullamore on Tuesday with Theresa to register for evening classes, and then her grandfather had dropped her in for her first typing class on Thursday night and picked her up at the end. She had enjoyed it very much and had come back with a list of the books she needed to buy for the following week.

On the Friday her grandfather drove her over to Mullingar to a shop he had been recommended, and he bought her a brand new Olivetti typewriter. He did it quietly and easily, and made it plain to her that it was her choice and she was to pick whichever one suited her and the course best.

When they got back home, they had dinner and then her grandfather brought her a small desk from one of the spare bedrooms for her typewriter, and a short while later when she was arranging her books on the bookshelf, he came back upstairs carrying a red Dansette record-player.

"That will keep you company when you're up here studying," he told her. "I don't know if you're the same, but Jude always said that it helped him to concentrate."

Each night when she went up to her bedroom she went over the day in her head, and then she allowed herself to think of her father for a while and some nights cry quietly again as she remembered all that had happened. She went over all the lovely memories she had of Paul and the time they had spent together, and wondered when she would hear from him again. She knew it could be a while before she heard from Stella, but she hoped that if Diana wrote back to her, that she might have some news of her friend.

It was at church the following Sunday that Maria realised her grandmother had been right about the great interest amongst the local people that her appearance would cause.

When they got out of black Ford car outside of the church, Patrick and Jude went to the boot of the car and lifted out Ambrose's wheelchair. Then they lifted him out of the back of the car and settled him in the chair. Then they set out for the church.

Maria had worn her red wool coat with the matching black hat trimmed in red, and had been pleased when her grandfather and Jude said how lovely she looked and her grandmother had said that it was obviously a well-made, expensive coat.

"You look like a model out of one of the magazines,"

Ambrose had said. "You obviously take your good looks from the Donovans."

They had all laughed when her grandfather had tipped her elbow and said, "I don't think anyone would believe us if we claim the nice Italian tanned skin and the lovely black hair, but we'll happily claim all the other bits about you."

Every single person said good morning as they passed, which Maria found surprising. Back in her own church in Heaton Moor, only people who knew you well spoke to you. The odd person you didn't really know might smile and say the occasional word, but most kept a polite distance.

It was when they were approaching the church door that Maria noticed that some people coming through a side gate were looking over and obviously talking about them. Then, inside the church, she felt she was being carefully studied as the family went into a row at the back to accommodate Ambrose and his wheelchair.

When the Mass started she found the priest's unusual Irish accent hard to catch, and even though she had her Sunday Missal open at the correct pages with the Latin words he was reading, she still could not follow him well enough to keep her place.

After a while she gave up trying and her thoughts automatically drifted back to Manchester and her father and Paul. When Communion time came she stood to join the queue to head towards the altar. Her grandfather stayed at the back with Ambrose and the priest came up at the end of Mass to give him and another lady in a wheelchair Communion, because the chairs hadn't enough space at the altar to turn easily. It was when she was walking slowly along between her grandmother and Jude that she noticed the slight stir in some of the rows. Then, on the way back down the aisle, she bent her head when she suddenly became self-conscious when she saw so many faces openly turned in her direction.

By the time she got back down to her seat her heart was thudding and her face was burning. And, by the time that the priest had moved on from the prayers after Communion to the closing prayers, she knew her grandmother's instincts had been correct about how people would react.

Maria realised she had little experience of small-village communities and the way they worked, but something told her that the stir she had caused in church was not just because she was a new face and not just because she looked different with her Italian colouring. And neither was it because her clothes were slightly different, being more modern and colourful than those of the other females. She somehow knew that those inquisitive eyes were looking at her because she was Anna Donovan's daughter. Anna Donovan who had left the village almost twenty years before and never come back. And something told her that these same people knew something that she did not. They all knew the reason why her mother had gone in the first place.

As soon as the priest gave his final bow on the altar, her grandfather indicated to her that they would move quickly to get Ambrose and his chair out of the church, so as not to have people squeezing past the chair. Other people in the last pews and those standing at the back all moved along with them, and as they moved in single file out of the small church doors, Maria once again could feel she was the object of discussion.

She was so quiet going home in the car that Jude and Ambrose asked her several times if she was okay, And, as she stared out of the window at the passing fields and the trees, and the houses and cottages dotted amongst them, she wondered if every person in those houses knew something about her mother that she did not.

After a while she felt her grandmother's hand reaching for hers, and she held her hand until the car pulled into Donovans' driveway. As Maria walked behind her uncle going into the house, she knew that whether her grandmother was ready or not, she was soon going to tell her grandparents that she needed to know what had happened to her mother. She wasn't going to do it tonight but it would be soon. She was going to choose her time carefully and then she would tell them what she wanted.

She would tell them that she needed to know the whole, unvarnished truth.

Chapter 41

Diana drew the Mini to a halt outside Contis' house, and sat for a few moments surveying the Estate Agents' 'For Sale' sign. Then, she breathed deeply and got out of the car. It was lunch break at Gladrags, and so she was in her working outfit of a blue bouclé dress, short co-ordinating jacket and white court shoes.

Franco was already in the house waiting for her, and when she greeted him she could see that some of the weight of Leo's death had been lifted off him. The sadness that he had worn like a heavy cloak from the minute his friend had died all through the week of the funeral had started to ease a little from his shoulders and his face. She could see that it had not entirely gone, but, like herself, normal everyday life had started to creep in. It had begun the process of carrying them both forward into a life that was less without the vibrant, kind man they both, in their different ways, had loved.

"You saw the 'For Sale' sign?" Franco asked.

She nodded. "When did it go up?"

"Last Friday," he said. "And they have had six enquiries already, and two of them are viewing the house tomorrow. The Estate Agent thinks it may well be gone by Christmas."

Diana looked around Leo's sitting room, across to the corner where his coffin had stood, and was now replaced by the usual armchair and cabinet that had always been there. The grate which had always held a blazing, comforting fire was now cold and grey and empty. Soon, she thought, there would be no trace of him or Maria in this house. All their belongings would be packed and stored and new people would be living here as if the Contis had never existed.

She went and perched on the edge of one of the armchairs by the cheerless fireplace, and Franco sat in the one opposite.

"Is there any news from the bank?" she asked.

"They think they have all the final documents now, and should soon be able to give us an exact figure as to what Leo owes."

"What about the horse?"

"Charlie has paid the rest of Leo's loan off, and he's happy to just take complete ownership of Bella Maria."

"That's good," Diana said. "That, at least, is another problem less for Maria. And when the house is sold then it's just Leonardo's . . . Any idea how that is financially shaping up?"

"I have the bills and invoices laid out on the table in the dining room, if you want to have a look at them."

Diana looked at him for a few moments and then she said, "No, Franco, I don't think I do want to look at them. I've been thinking recently that maybe I've been involved in Leo's business as much as I should."

He shrugged and held his hands out, palms open. "What do you mean?"

"I mean that what happens now is not my business. You are the one in charge here now, the one who is acting on Maria's behalf. You are the one who knows everything about the restaurant business." She shrugged. "I am not Leo's wife or even his fiancée – I'm just a girlfriend who happened to meet him a few months before he died. I don't think I have the right to be involved in the sale of his house or what should happen to his money or what should happen to Leonardo's."

"But you were more than just a girlfriend," Franco said. "Leo told me that. He said that he planned to propose to you at Christmas."

344

Diana looked at him, her breath taken away. "Really? He said that?"

Franco nodded. "He told me that one of the nights he brought you to the restaurant. He said he would have asked you sooner, but he was afraid to rush you or Maria. He told me he wouldn't wait any longer than Christmas."

"Why didn't you tell me before now? Why didn't you say something before Maria went to Ireland?"

Franco looked awkward, unsure what to say. "I didn't think about it," he told her. "I was so shocked about Leo and then with the funeral and everything. Things like that didn't seem to matter any more."

"But it would have mattered to me," she said quietly. "It would have made me feel I had more of a place in things, instead of worrying about whether I was being too pushy or presuming that I meant more to Leo than I did. It would have mattered to me because if I thought that Leo was going to marry me, then maybe I would have felt it was all right to offer Maria should come to live with me instead of going to Ireland. I could have explained that I would have been her stepmother quite soon."

Franco paused, his brow creased deeply, as though giving great thought to her words. "But what about Leo's letters?" he asked. "Leo wanted her to go to her mother's family."

"We could have given her a choice. Leo had written that letter before he met me, before he knew he had someone else to look after her. He knew you and Bernice had a busy house with your own children, and he knew Mrs Lowry was getting too old to look after a teenager. The way it happened, poor Maria was presented with no alternative to Ireland."

"I am so sorry," Franco said. "I thought we were all doing the right thing. The thing that was best for her. The thing that Leo wanted."

Diana looked at the chef now and suddenly felt sorry for him – that she had been too hard on him. "Maybe it doesn't matter . . . and maybe it was the right thing, because Maria seems to be settling over in Ireland. I had a letter from her yesterday, and she told me she was hoping to start evening classes to learn to type and that her grandparents have arranged for her to have classes in her other subjects with a teacher who lives nearby."

Franco looked relieved. "Good," he said, "that's very good to hear. I told her I was no good to write letters, but that I will phone her sometime. Her grandfather gave me their phone number. I just wanted to wait until I had some news about the house or the restaurant and, at the moment, I have nothing to say about it."

"I think she still plans to come back here in a year or two when she is old enough. She said she is doing things to fill the time until she is eighteen."

He held his hand in his chin, thinking. "She might settle there and not want to come back."

"Yes," Diana said. "She might settle there but, in the meantime, I'm going to invite her to stay with me for Christmas."

Franco's eyes lit up. "That would be wonderful," he said. "Bernice and I were saying how sad it would be not to see her this Christmas."

"If her grandparents agree, then I don't see why she shouldn't come – if that's what she wants. She might be settling with her family in Ireland, but still might like to come back here because she said that she misses her friends and even us older people."

"Good, good! And maybe by then, we might have news about the house and about Leonardo's. Maybe we might even open Leonardo's for Christmas Day." He looked sadly at Diana now. "You know we always had dinner in the restaurant, don't you? Leo and Maria, me and Bernice and the children. It gave them room to move around and play with their presents from Father Christmas. The boys would take their bicycles and scooters out into the lane to ride up and down ..."

His face suddenly fell, and Diana knew that once more he was reliving the accident in that same lane that put an end to Leo's life. The accident that changed every one of their lives.

Chapter 42

It was a quiet weekday afternoon in mid-November when the dinner dishes had been washed, the men were fed and back out working in one of the fields, and Ambrose was having his customary rest. Under the watchful eye of her grandmother, Maria sifted flour, bicarbonate of soda and a few pinches of salt together, then she made a well in the centre of the dry mix and poured a jug of buttermilk into the middle of it.

"Now, make your hand as wide as you can," her grandmother instructed, "and draw all the dry mixture into the milk. Do it lightly and get as much air into it as you can."

Maria worked on it for a few minutes, giving it her fullest concentration as Theresa had advised. *Living in the moment*, as the kind neighbour called it. She was getting better at blocking out the endless thoughts and memories that would haunt every waking moment if she wasn't vigilant. Forcing her full attention on even the smallest activity would hopefully keep her too occupied during the day to revisit the raw wounds within.

Ambrose, of course, helped her greatly to do that without realising. When he had the energy he spent hours reading to her or playing cards or doing a jigsaw or playing chess. Sometimes they just sat with the rest of the family watching television or listening to the radio. Other times, Ambrose just talked for seemingly endless hours about things like the geography he or Maria were studying, or perhaps about interesting snippets he had heard on the World News.

Maria loved their chats but there were times when he said things – usually unexpected – that put her heart crosswise in her chest. Just the other day when they were sitting by the fire, and his mother was washing towels in the sink in her usual quiet way, he had said how lucky she was to have travelled to Italy.

"I would love to go there," he said, "to see all the old statues in Florence and I'd love to see The Leaning Tower of Pisa. I would also love to go to New York and see all the places that Sister Theresa has lived in."

"Maybe you will one day," she had said, smiling at him.

"I doubt it," he said quietly. "Sometimes I cod myself that I will, but I know really that a sick individual like myself would never be fit for the journey over to Europe."

Maria's throat had almost closed over and she struggled to say, "You never know when you are older, Ambrose. You might improve."

He had lifted his thin arm up and put his hand on hers as though to comfort her. "Unfortunately, Maria," he said softly, "there will be no great improvement for me. With what's wrong with my chest and heart, I'm doing well to be as good as I am."

As his hand made the smallest squeezing gesture, she gripped his frail hand in hers as though by doing so some of her own strength might transfer to him.

He looked over to the sink. "Isn't that right, Mammy? Isn't that the truth?" When there was no reply he looked at Maria and winked and then said loudly, "But I'm grand really. I have a good life here and I'm grateful to be able to do as much as I do."

Maria glanced over at her grandmother and she could see by the look on her face that she was not able to speak. Maria had observed that look on her face so often now – almost a tragic look – that she had become afraid of adding to the burden the older woman already carried.

She had thought on several occasions that it was the right time to ask about her mother's past only for Ambrose to say or do something, and she would postpone the conversation she both needed, and yet dreaded, once again. Things had got easier in the house generally, and her grandfather and Jude now talked openly about when her mother was young and some of the funny things that they remembered about her. On one occasion her grandfather had given her some schoolbooks belonging to her mother and on another, her grandmother had given her a lovely floral chiffon scarf that had belonged to her too. Jude on a different occasion gave Maria an LP record of an Irish ballad singer that her mother had listened to, but he told her to keep it in her wardrobe and asked her not to play it when his mother was in the house.

She had also got used to being the object of the local people's curiosity and had noticed on recent visits to church and the shops in Tullamore that people had got used to her. If they had anything to say about her, they didn't do it when she was there or within earshot.

Her studies with Sister Theresa filled several mornings and afternoons and between her night classes and practising on her Olivetti typewriter in her bedroom, she had become proficient enough to slowly type out three neat letters this week to Paul and Diana and one to Mrs Lowry.

She had become more interested in her studies back in September when she received encouraging news in a large brown envelope that Franco had re-addressed to her. Seven O-level passes, four A's and two B's! She had almost forgotten about them and the excellent grades had convinced her that it was worth continuing her work with Theresa.

Over the last couple of months she had received letters from Paul at least twice a week and had received two from Stella who was still down in the clinic in London, but was now allowed home at weekends. She didn't say much about what she did there, but she said her weight had gone up a bit and that the doctors were happy with her.

Both Paul and Stella had written in their letters to say that Tony had suddenly left Spencers' stables. He had come in one Friday and said he had been offered a job in Birmingham and that he had to leave that very weekend. He hadn't given Paul any real information, but said if he was ever up in Manchester again he might look him up.

Stella wrote to tell her that she had never heard from Tony again after the day she had fainted. He had, she said, never returned even one of her calls. She said she had been heartbroken to start with but, after she had had time to think about it, maybe they hadn't really been that suited. She had spent time chatting to a special nurse in the unit about it and she thought now that maybe she had been attracted to Tony because it was a way of getting back at her mother for trying to control her life. Whichever way, she told Maria, her mother had definitely had a fright. After her parents had a few meetings with the doctors and the nurses in the unit, her mother seemed to be much more understanding and willing to listen than she had ever been.

Paul had kept her up to date about his equestrian course, and told her in every single letter how much he missed her and how much he was looking forward to seeing her at Christmas. Every time she thought of it, her heart soared. On several occasions when she had one of Jude's Beatles albums on and she thought of her trip back home, she found herself dancing happily around the room, feeling so, so grateful to Diana for inviting her to stay with her and for not forgetting her.

Her grandparents had been quiet when she told them about her letter and said she wanted to spend Christmas and New Year in Manchester.

"It's your choice," her grandmother said. She had looked as though she was going to say something else, but had remained silent.

"We'll have to let Ambrose know soon," her grandfather said. "Because he's already been talking about some of the things he wanted you to do with him over the Christmas."

Maria had immediately felt guilty but said, "We can still do those things. I know he wants me to go to the cinema with him to see *The Jungle Book*, but I think it comes to Tullamore a couple of weeks before Christmas, so we can see it before I go."

"That's grand," Patrick had said, "but the main thing is that you need to look after your own business, and get to see all those people who have been so good to you."

Maria now felt she not only had something to look forward to but each day had a real purpose as it not only brought her closer to going home, but was making her more proficient in all the subjects she was studying, both with Sister Theresa and at her evening classes. She had also become friendly with a girl from Tullamore who now kept her a seat in the class and chatted to her during the break when the students had a cup of tea. All in all, she had to admit that she was settling into life in Ireland, and as long as she didn't keep comparing people with the ones she had left back home, she found she was coping and at certain times even enjoying herself.

She looked down at the lump of dough now, then feeling that it was still too wet and sticky she used her dry hand and lifted another handful of flour to mix in. A short while later when she felt the dough was of the correct consistency, she turned it out onto the well-floured wooden table top.

Eileen Donovan carefully inspected it and said, "That looks grand."

Marie felt a small glow of satisfaction at the praise as she patted the dough into a tidy circular shape, then patted it again on top until it was the required level of thickness.

That was placed in the old oven, and then Maria looked at her grandmother. "Will I try something else, a cake maybe? Didn't you say Sister Teresa was calling up this evening?"

The older woman thought for a few moments. "We might do a few fruit scones. I think we have enough self-raising flour left and there is a full packet of sultanas." She went over to the pantry and came back with the necessary ingredients.

A short while later Maria slid a tray with perfectly circles of flat dough of just over an inch thick into the oven to join the soda bread.

A small cough came from the nest by the fire. "Isn't she very handy, Mammy?" Ambrose suddenly commented. "For a young girl who was only used to gas cookers, she's got the hang of the solid fuel. She had no problem lighting the stove today and getting it up to the right temperature for cooking."

Maria smiled over at him.

Eileen Donovan considered his words. "She's only doing what every woman should do if she's going to be able to run a house in the future."

"But isn't it great if Maria can lend a hand by doing a bit of cooking and baking now and again? It would let you go into town – or even up to Dublin – and have a bit of a break for yourself."

"Ah now, Dublin indeed," his mother said, gathering up the bowls to be washed in the sink. "Don't be getting carried away. Baking a bit of bread and a few scones doesn't mean someone's fit to run a house."

But Ambrose was not to be swayed from his topic. He shifted in his bed to look over at his niece. "My mother works too hard," he said. "She always has done –"

"Sure, that's nothing new," his mother said, running the tap to fill the basin. "When you're the woman of the house, it's the case of the oul' dog for the hard road."

Ambrose laughed and chimed in with, "And the pup for the path!" He looked at Maria now. "You probably think we're talking double-Dutch with the oul' Irish sayings?"

Maria shrugged and smiled. "I remember my mother telling me some of the Irish sayings, and my father used to tell me the Italian ones."

"I'd love to hear the Italian sayings. Can you remember any?"

Maria glanced over at her grandmother and saw the sad look on her face. "Another time," she told him. "I've some washing I need to do now."

Chapter 43

As December approached, the days grew shorter and much, much colder. Maria felt that the days were flying by and then they all began to merge together, all heading in the direction of Christmas. Theresa called a few days before Maria was due to fly back to Manchester to take her into Tullamore for some Christmas shopping. Her grandfather had given her some money, which she felt bad taking, but she did so with the proviso that if any money came through after all the legal business at home was sorted, that she would repay him.

"You're welcome to it with a heart and a half," he told her. "Just enjoy it as much as we're enjoying having you here."

They set off into town in Theresa's green Morris Minor, Theresa clad in her wax coat and hat, and Maria in her jeans and boots and a warm duffle coat and bright striped scarf that her grandmother had helped her to knit. There were lights strung outside a few of the shops, and Maria thought how scant and disappointing they looked compared to the lights in Manchester and Stockport, and the thought of seeing them all when she got home made her feel really excited now.

She bought Ambrose a Lego kit and a guide book of Italy that she had ordered in the local bookshop and a jigsaw of the map of France. She bought Jude a record token from the music shop, and she bought her grandmother a matching necklace and earrings. It was from the jeweller's, although not from their very expensive ranges, and of the same dark crystal stones that were in the necklace that had belonged to her mother that she often wore.

They were just passing a local hotel, when Theresa suggested that they go in for a hot drink to warm them up and maybe a mince pie.

Maria was very impressed with the inside of the hotel when she saw the lovely Christmas tree and decorations and the big fires that were on in all the rooms.

There were a few young men sitting at one of the tables in the bar area, dressed in suits and shirts and ties, and as they passed by one of them kept staring at Maria. He was of average height with short brown hair and a light moustache.

"Ignore him," Theresa said. "He looks as though he's had a few drinks too many. We'll sit in the room opposite so he doesn't annoy you."

When they had put their bags down and taken their coats off and sorted their hair, then given their order of coffee and mince pies to the waitress, Theresa smiled at Maria and said, "You're a very striking girl, and I suppose you will have to get used to attention from young men."

Maria had rolled her eyes and laughed. "I'm not interested in anyone," she said. "I have a nice boy who writes to me from back in England, and I'm happy enough with that."

They had just finished eating when the young man who had been staring at Maria stuck his head in the door, and said, "Would I be correct in thinking that there is a Miss Donovan here?"

Both Theresa and Maria looked at him.

"No," Theresa said, "that's not either of our names."

He walked over to the table, a slight sway in his gait betraying the amount he had drunk. "Would I be correct then in saying that there's a connection of the Donovans here? Maybe a daughter of Anna Donovan?"

Something about the look on his face and the slight sneer that on his lips when he said her mother's name made Maria's heart freeze.

Theresa remained calm and kept an easy tone in her voice. "Why do you ask?"

He pulled a chair out at the table beside them. "Because," he said, "I know her mother hadn't the neck to show her face in this town again after what she did to our family, and I'm surprised that her daughter must think we all have short memories."

As Maria looked at him now, she suddenly knew that this young man had the key to all the questions she had been unable to ask. Before Theresa had a chance to say anything else she looked him square in the eye and said, "If it's any of your business, my mother is dead."

"It's well I know that," he said, "and it is my business, because if your mother had had her way, our family would have been left with neither a mother nor a father."

Theresa stood up now. "Go away!" she said, making shooing gestures with her hands. "You've no business to be talking like that to a young girl."

The young man stood up now and placed his hands flat on the table. Ignoring Theresa, he stared at Maria.

"My name is Michael Casey," he said, "and your mother ruined our family. She played my father like a good oul' fiddle . . . and then the pair of them ran off to England together and were never seen again."

Maria's hand flew to her mouth.

"Go!" Theresa ordered. "Go now or I'll call the manager to remove you."

But Michael Casey stood his ground. "You didn't know, did you?" he said to Maria. "I can see you're shocked. I suppose the oul' Donovan one thought she would just bury her head in the sand and hope that no one opened their mouth? That no one would tell you what your mother was and how she ruined our family."

Theresa moved towards him now, her hands on her hips. "I won't tell you again," she said in an ominous voice. "If you don't move I'll move you myself."

Michael Casey looked at her and started to laugh. A small bitter laugh. "You're well met up, the pair of you – an oul' failed nun and the daughter of a whore and an I-ti!"

Maria looked at him now, hardly able to breathe, then, as Theresa went to grab his arm to make him move, she slipped between them – a sudden, unexpected spark of courage propelling her on. "My father was the most decent man you could ever meet," she said, looking him straight in the eyes, "and his Italian nationality is one I am very proud of." She stepped away from him now. "I'm sorry for whatever has happened between my mother and your family ... but it was a long time ago. It has nothing whatsoever to do with me."

He looked back at her now and she saw a change in his face. "They should have told you," he said, his voice quieter. "Because there's still bad blood between the families and it's not something that will ever be forgotten."

"You've said what you wanted to say," Maria said quietly. "Please go and leave us alone."

Chapter 44

When they left the hotel, there was a sudden icy chill that had not been there earlier, and as they walked along, flakes of snow began to fall. Normally, Maria would have had a childish delight in seeing the first snow of the winter, but now she barely registered it. When they got to the car, Theresa told Maria to get inside and try to keep warm, while she took a scraper out to clear the windscreen.

As they drove out through Tullamore towards the farmhouse, the snow still falling, Theresa kept constantly checking that Maria was okay and apologising for not telling her all this before. Maria just quietly repeated that it was not her fault and that her grandparents or Jude should have told her.

"It's hard for them," Theresa said. "They've lived with it for years without talking much about it, and they obviously thought, or hoped, that the Casey family had done the same and would continue to do so."

"I think there's more he didn't tell me," Maria said, "but before the night is over, I'll know everything I need to know, or I will be getting on a plane tomorrow and going back to Manchester. I don't care where I go or where I stay – someone will have me. I can't stay here unless I know the truth."

Theresa had shifted her gaze from the white road for a few

357

seconds to look at her and said, "It won't come to that. Please, God it won't."

As soon as they entered the house, it was obvious to Maria's grandparents that something serious had happened. Theresa took her grandmother out into the hall while Maria put her shopping upstairs and when she came back down a few minutes later, her grandmother was sitting at the kitchen table, ashen-faced.

"Ambrose," Eileen Donovan said, "we're going down to the parlour to have a chat with Maria and Sister Theresa. If Jude comes in from the Vet's Suppliers, tell him to have a cup of tea and some brown bread, and that we'll have the dinner later when we're finished. "

Ambrose sat up in his bed and, as he went to say something, he suddenly went into a fit of coughing. His father rushed to the tap to get him a glass of water, which he slowly sipped, and gradually the coughing subsided. Sister Theresa went to her bag and brought out a comic which she had bought for him in Tullamore.

"You can go and have your chat now," he told them, a wheeze still in his voice. "I'll be glad of the peace to read my new *Rover*."

As soon as the parlour door was closed, her grandmother started to cry and Patrick had to give her his white hanky.

Maria shivered as she walked over to a chair, as the room was cold with no fire on.

"This is not the way I wanted this done," Patrick said, "and it's our fault for having let it happen like this."

"Why didn't you tell me?" Maria asked quietly. "Why did you wait until a total stranger – an angry stranger told me, to sit down and speak to me?"

Her grandfather's hand came up to cover his eyes and Maria realised, with some alarm, that tears were running down his face.

Sister Theresa said, "I think it might be best if everyone sat down, and maybe, if one of you feels able for it, you might just run through the main events of what happened when her mother left this house."

"I can't sit down . . ." Eileen Donovan said, her voice cracked and faraway-sounding. She moved over to the window.

"Okay," Patrick said, brushing the back of his hand now to his damp eyes. "The truth of it all is that Anna . . ." he looked at Maria, "your mother . . . from when she was thirteen or fourteen, used to go into town for piano lessons to John Casey. He was a man ten years older than her, with four or five children."

"Five," Eileen Donovan said. "They had five young children."

"Anna was very gifted musically . . . she played the fiddle too . . . Anyway, as she got older – maybe around sixteen or so – and better on the piano, John Casey used to enter her for all sorts of exams and competitions. He often used to call out here to tell her about them, and take her up to Dublin for the day." He waved his hand over to the ebony piano. "And when we got Anna the piano, he was in and out of here all the time, supposedly tuning it and bringing her new music books. Then one night Mrs Casey appeared at the door here in a terrible state. The next thing we knew all hell had broken loose when she went for your mother, accusing her of carrying on with her husband, calling her names and pulling her around by the hair . . ." His hand came up to his eyes again and he had to stop to compose himself. "It was that bad we nearly had to call for the Guards. Poor Jude was only a little fellow and if you'd heard the screams of him when he saw them fighting! He got such a fright."

Maria sat in stunned silence, unable to imagine her lovely, quiet mother being involved in all of this secrecy and scandal.

Eileen Donovan looked over at her husband and then she came over to stand by the side of his chair, and put her hand on his shoulder. "Your mother and Casey denied it all," she said now in a quiet, thin voice, "and naturally enough we took her side . . ."

"It was her age and the fact she was a quiet girl," Patrick said. "She had never given us a minute's trouble before she met him."

Eileen gave a great sigh now. "We said we would find a new piano teacher. Then, a couple of weeks later, we woke up one morning to find that Anna was gone and a note on her bed to say she was in love with him and they had run away to England."

There was a silence and then Patrick said. "Tell her it all. Tell her the rest of the story . . ."

Maria glanced up at her grandmother and was shocked when she saw how white her face was. "We found out from her friend at school," Eileen said, "that she was expecting a baby. We were devastated and worried sick about her but, when his wife got to hear of it, she almost went mad. She went down to the canal and threw herself in, and if it hadn't been for her two brothers who went looking for her and dragged her out, there would have been five children left without a mother or a father." She stopped now, just staring down at the floor.

"And it didn't finish there . . ." Patrick said.

Maria got to her feet now and went over to stand by the window. She didn't want to listen now; she didn't want to hear any more. She had heard enough to understand why her mother could never come back to Tullamore to live again. She had heard enough to understand now why her grandmother was the way she was.

Her grandfather shook his head and gave a strange sort of laugh. "The following night, after they'd had a few drinks, her two brothers came up to the house here looking for an address of where they had gone. Of course, we were no wiser than them, but they wouldn't believe it. They thought we were covering up for Anna and Casey." He lifted his eyes to the ceiling and sighed. "Anyway, one word borrowed another – they were volatile fellows, like that son you met tonight – and the next thing the pair of them set about me and Eileen had to run inside and phone for the Guards. A half an hour later we were all sitting in the station in Tullamore."

"If it hadn't been for our solicitor speaking up for us," Eileen said, "we would all have landed up in the court and no doubt the newspapers and everything."

Maria suddenly thought. She turned around now towards them again. "What happened about the baby?" she asked. "Did he get divorced and did they try to get married or anything?"

Her grandmother looked at her, then she smoothed her hands over her greying hair, as though trying to gather herself together. "No – no. We heard nothing from her for two years. We didn't know where they were or anything. And then we got a letter from Anna to say that she was getting married to your father. It seems she lost the baby after she arrived in England. She got some kind of job playing the piano in a hotel and then, a few months later, Casey disappeared again and left her on her own. It seems the people who owned the hotel were good to her and gave her a room and all that, and then she met your father."

"You know the rest of it," her grandfather said. "Anna knew she could never come back here and she didn't want your father to find out the truth, so she told him and you that we didn't approve of her marrying an Italian." He held his hands up. "There's no point in us going over it all again ... it's not going to change anything now."

"She was a young, silly girl," Eileen Donovan said, "but she was never a bad girl. She was more naïve and easily led at that time. She didn't know what she had got herself into with John Casey, and then she never managed to find a way out." She halted. "And then of course Ambrose was born and was very ill, and we all had a lot more on our minds. We knew she was okay and we just thought it was better to let her live her own life over in England since that's what she wanted."

There was a silence in the room and then suddenly there was the sound of shouting and feet running down the hall. Everyone looked startled and, for a moment, Maria thought she was imagining things, as though listening to the accounts of the dramatic events had made her relive them in her head.

And then, the door was flung open and Jude stood there looking at them all.

"It's Ambrose!" he shouted. "What the feck are you all doing down here, leaving him on his own? He's collapsed up in the kitchen. He can't get a breath!" He swung back towards the hallway. "We need to get him into the car and straight into the hospital. If we wait for the ambulance we're going to lose him . . ."

Chapter 45

The snowflakes fell heavier and thicker as Maria and Sister Theresa followed the Donovans' car slowly, through the slippery, winding roads all the way to Tullamore Hospital. Theresa had phoned to warn the casualty department that they were on their way while Jude and Patrick were carrying Ambrose, swaddled in his blankets, out to the car. By the time they arrived at Casualty, there were two doctors and two nurses waiting for them.

Theresa and Maria abandoned the green Morris Minor and ran over to the other car to check how he was.

"He's not great," Patrick said, as the nurses settled Ambrose onto a trolley and covered him with more blankets. "We gave him his inhaler and all the usual things, but he's not great . . ."

And then, when they got inside the doors, the family were asked to stay in the waiting room and Ambrose was wheeled off down a corridor. There were a few other groups of people in the waiting room, but no one any of them knew. They went over to sit at a Formica-topped table in the corner.

When they were settled down, Jude asked, "When did Ambrose's chest start up again?"

"This morning," his mother said. "It was only a bit of a wheeze to start with, but it worsened as the day went on . . . I've never seen it go as quickly as this before. Hopefully when they get the machines on his chest and clear it, he'll come around."

"What was so important," Jude asked, in the same brittle tone he had used back at the house, "that you had to leave him on his own?"

Maria felt her chest tighten and closed her eyes hard to stop herself from crying.

"It was my fault . . ." she started in a quivery voice. "They had to explain something to me that we didn't want Ambrose to hear."

Her grandfather put his arm around her. "Now, you can forget fault and blame," he said, his manner gentle. "If we're going to talk like that, then we have to take the blame for leaving it so long to talk to you." He looked over at Jude. "She had a bit of trouble in Tullamore this afternoon with one of the Casey lads . . . that's what started it all off. Seemingly, he'd had a few drinks and it must have loosened his tongue."

"I thought they were all in Athlone," Jude said. "The family moved years ago."

"One of them works in Salts Factory in Tullamore," Eileen said, her voice flat and emotionless.

Jude's eyes darted from his father to Maria. "And was he very awkward?"

"Very," Sister Theresa said. "But Maria stood her ground and he eventually went."

"So," Jude said, slumping back in his chair, "you all had the big talk when you came back?"

"We did," his father said. "It's all out now. There's nothing else to say about it."

There was another silence and then Maria looked around at the other four faces. "I'm sorry," she said. "I'm so sorry it happened when Ambrose wasn't well . . . I'd no idea how sick he was."

"None of us did," Patrick said. "Sometimes it comes on that quickly it catches you unawares."

"Oh God," Eileen said, her hands coming up to cover her face, "I hope he's all right, I hate to think of the poor soul down there with the doctors on his own. I hope he's not frightened . . ."

Sister Theresa went over to take her hand. "He's a brave boy, Eileen," she said. "He's braver than any one of us."

"I wonder at times does he understand the seriousness of it all," Patrick said quietly.

"Ah, he does . . . and he doesn't," Jude said. "But Sister Theresa's right, he's a brave lad."

There was a lull and then Maria said in a low voice. "It all seems so pointless now. All this stuff about my mother . . . when I think of poor Ambrose, it just seems stupid to have been so upset. It was years ago . . . what does it matter now? The only thing that matters is that Ambrose gets well."

"You're so right," Sister Theresa said, smiling over at her. "Those are wise words. Let the poor souls that are gone rest in peace, and let the rest of us get on with the business of helping one another."

A young blonde nurse came down the corridor, and when she turned in to the waiting room and came towards them Maria was surprised to see it was Cathy, the girl she had met in the cinema. The girl that Jude had said his mother wasn't keen on.

"Mrs and Mrs Donovan?" she said. "The doctors would like a word with you now." She turned her gaze to Maria and said hello to her, and then she looked at Jude. "I'm sorry about Ambrose . . ."

Jude nodded a brief greeting to her, then he said, "Is it all right if I go with them? I'd like to see him too."

She thought for a moment, and then she said, "Yes, I think it will be okay. If it's not, you can wait outside."

They all went down the corridor then, Cathy walking alongside Ambrose's parents and Jude walking behind them on his own.

Sister Theresa reached across the Formica table now and took Maria's hand. "It's been a hard night," she said to her, "but you've done well. You've learned a lot since you arrived, in more ways than one."

A while later the three Donovans came walking back down the corridor with grave faces.

"Ambrose is very bad," Patrick told Maria and Sister

Theresa. "But they're doing all they can for him. They have him on ventilators and oxygen and machines to clear his chest."

"How is he in himself?" Sister Theresa asked.

"He can't talk or anything," Jude said. He gave a weak smile. "And that's always a bad sign with Ambrose."

"We just have to wait," Patrick said. "Wait and pray."

Maria sat still saying nothing. She had been through all this before just a few months ago. If she closed her eyes she could still picture herself sitting in the hospital in Stockport along with Diana. And the worst thing was, she felt almost as sad now with Ambrose as she did with her own father. She didn't know how she would manage if anything happened to him. She just couldn't imagine life in the Donovans' house without his cheery presence. She couldn't imagine life without him at all.

In a few short months, she now realised, she had come to know and love her young uncle very much.

Chapter 46

It was almost midnight when the doctors came to tell them all that Ambrose had turned a corner. A small corner – but there was significant improvement in his condition nonetheless. His chest and lungs had started to clear of the thick mucus that was obstructing his breathing.

"He's not out of the woods yet," the doctor said, "but Ambrose is a fighter. We've seen him this way before and he's pulled through." He looked at the weary five. "I'd advise you all to go home and go to bed now. We've given Ambrose something to help him sleep, so he should be settled overnight."

"You'll ring us if anything changes for the worse?" Eileen Donovan brought her hanky to her mouth.

"The very minute anything changes we'll ring," the doctor said.

Cathy came over to them now. "I'll be with him all the time and I'll make sure you're kept up to date."

"Thank you," Eileen said. "I'll feel easier knowing that."

They made the same slippery journey back home, although a frost had settled down over the snow making it more compacted and slightly easier to drive on. Theresa dropped Maria off at the house and said she would call up first thing in the morning.

They were all exhausted when they finally got into the house and, after a slice of tea and toast, they began to prepare to go to bed. Maria was touched when her grandmother, in the midst of everything, took the time to fill her hot-water bottle for her.

"You'll need this tonight," Eileen said. "Apart from the cold, you need to get a good night's sleep."

She paused and looked at Maria. "You were supposed to come here to be minded after your poor father died, and look at what's happened to you now . . . You'll be wishing to God you'd never laid eyes on any of us."

Maria felt tears welling up. She shook her head. "No, it's quite the opposite . . . Tonight has shown me that I've found what my father wanted for me. Tonight when I saw Ambrose on the trolley I realised how much I love him. It's only been a few months, but knowing him has changed everything. It might sound the sort of dramatic thing a teenager might just say for attention, but I really mean it."

"We know you do," her grandmother said. "You only have to look in your eyes to see you mean it." She then moved and, for the first time, held her granddaughter tightly in her arms. "You're a good girl, Maria. And God bless your father for having the good sense to send you to us."

"I think we all agree with that," Patrick said. "And nobody more than Ambrose!"

After a while, when they moved apart, brushing tears away, Maria went over to her grandfather and Jude and took both their hands. "Whether we all wanted it or not in the beginning, I'm part of this family now, and whatever happens, I'll be here to help look after Ambrose."

Maria woke several times in the night, and each time she vividly remembered the dream she had just come out of. The worst one had been one where she and Stella were walking at the edge of a canal and then, without warning, Stella had just jumped in to the dark, muddy water. Maria had run up and down the bank trying to find her, but eventually had to give up when two tall policemen in uniforms came and took her away. As they drove her away in the car, there was a line of people all waving to her, and when she looked back at them, she could see her father and mother and Ambrose and Franco all laughing and chatting together.

When she woke up after that particular dream, she knew that she had dreamt about Stella because she had crossed her mind a number of times recently, since all the things had come to light about her own mother. The comparisons were frighteningly obvious. She knew without doubt that her friend had been so besotted by Tony that, if he had encouraged her, Stella would have run away with him too. And, like her mother, she too had got herself into a situation where she might easily have been pregnant.

As she lay in the dark working it all out, she realised that while she liked Paul Spencer very much, she was not besotted to the extent she would get into the trouble either her mother or Stella had.

She did not know if this meant she didn't care enough about Paul, or whether she was more old-fashioned and sensible. Time, she knew, would let her know where her feelings lay. For the present, she was more than happy to look forward to seeing him and her other friends in Manchester at Christmas and catching up on all his news.

She had fallen asleep again and it was light when she woke from another dream about her grandmother playing "Morning" on the piano. It was a strange dream, but not so frightening as the one about the canal. She had just turned over when the phone ringing down in the hallway sounded throughout the house. Her heart started to pound and, as she ran across the room to get her dressing-gown and slippers, she was mumbling 'The Memorare' prayer to herself, asking Our Lady to look after Ambrose and not to let him die.

She had just got down to the bottom of the stairs when Jude came towards her.

"It's for you," he said, smiling and pointing down the hallway to where the receiver lay on its side on the table. "It's your friend, Franco, from Manchester."

She didn't know whether to be relieved it wasn't about Ambrose or pleased it was a call from home. "I won't be a minute," she said. "Just in case the hospital might be trying to phone . . ."

Jude winked at her. "As far as I'm concerned, no news from them is good news."

"Hello, Marietta!" Franco said, sounding like his cheery old self. "How are you over there in Ireland? I was talking to your nice uncle and he said you're settled in well."

"I am, thanks, Franco," she told him. "But I'm afraid my other uncle is very, very sick and in hospital, so I can't talk long in case they are trying to phone us."

"I'm so sorry to hear that," he said, "and I will be very quick. I have good news for you, Maria. The house has a buyer, and at a good price. The other news is that the solicitor found a big insurance policy which will give you much more money than we expected, and your father had cleared a lot of his debts this year, so the bills are not as bad as we thought. The accounts show that the restaurant was making a good weekly profit as long as every-thing . . . as long as everything was properly documented."

Maria said nothing. She knew that Franco meant as long as the owner didn't keep taking money out of the till for the betting shop. "That's good, Franco," she said. "That sounds much better than I expected."

"I'm afraid it was just not enough to keep the house, so I hope you're not upset about that?"

"I am sorry to lose it in a way," she said, "but I know it's not sensible for a young girl to run a place that size. I know it's the right thing."

"But," Franco continued, "there is enough money to pay the mortgage off on the house and the mortgage on Leonardo's and clear all the bills that are outstanding."

"What does that mean, Franco?" she said. "Can we keep Leonardo's?"

"Yes . . . yes!"

Maria's heart soared at the news.

"The solicitor and the manager from the bank explained it all to me," Franco said. "Everything was left to you in your father's will, apart from a small amount of money he left me to help with the children growing up." He paused. "I was worried about accepting it at first because I thought it might help you keep the house, but it's not enough to make any difference . . I'm sorry . . ."

"Don't be sorry for anything, Franco!" Maria told him. "You were like his brother, and in the same position you would have done the same. I'm delighted you have something, and I am just so happy about the restaurant."

"Good . . . good," Franco said, his voice full of emotion now. "It means that you will own Leonardo's outright with no mortgage, and will have just enough left to buy a small house in Heaton Moor with no mortgage either. Diana said there are small houses for sale near her and near Mrs Lowry."

"Franco, I haven't thought it all out because I never imagined we could keep anything, but I know I want Leonardo's. You'll run the restaurant for me, won't you? You haven't gone anywhere else, have you?"

There was a silence. "I've been working in the Midland Hotel in Manchester," he said then. "But it's a temporary position until Christmas." His voice suddenly sounded thick with emotion. "After that I would be delighted to open the kitchen again. I would be honoured to do it when all the finances are sorted out."

"You still have the keys, don't you?" she asked.

"Yes, I do."

"You know you can use it for Christmas Day, as usual, and the children can bring all their toys and things?"

"Yes, Diana told me you'd written to her about it. But we'll see you before then and discuss it all. You're coming over in a few days' time, aren't you? Bernice and the children are looking forward to seeing you very much."

Maria paused. "It all depends, Franco," she said. "It all depends on how Ambrose is."

Chapter 47

Christmas Day

Maria, dressed in the new pink mohair jumper that her grand-mother had knitted, sat at one side of the table. Next to her sat Ambrose, resplendent in a red festive jumper with the head of a reindeer on it, which was a gift knitted by Sister Theresa. He was paler and slightly thinner than before, but he was as cheery as ever. Her grandmother and Sister Theresa sat opposite, while Patrick Donovan and Jude sat at the either end, and the roast turkey and the ham reclined in the middle of the table along with the roast potatoes and the vegetables. All of them wore the colourful paper hats that had just been retrieved from the crackers Jude had bought.

"Aren't we lucky this year," Ambrose said, "to have Maria here with us? Who would have thought it a year ago?"

"We are indeed lucky," Sister Theresa said.

Ambrose gave a few cackly laughs, and then he had to stop when he lost his breath and started coughing. He held his hand up before anyone had a chance to speak. "I'm grand," he said, "I'm grand . . ." He took a few minutes to catch his breath and then he started again. "I was only going to say the nurses at the hospital aren't so lucky, because they were all hoping to hold on to me for Christmas. They told me they were hoping I'd keep the

371

ward entertained, but I told them that I was going back home – I told them *au revoir*!"

His mother's eyebrows lifted. "You know you have to go back in the New Year?" she said. "The doctors said you could come home for Christmas and New Year, but they need you back in after that for another week or two."

"I know," he said. "Why do you think I said *au revoir* instead of *salut?*"

His mother looked puzzled. "What are you talking about?"

"*Au revoir* means goodbye *for now.* It means that I will return to the hospital when I'm good and ready." He made a little bowing gesture to the table and they all laughed. He pointed over to the corner now. "I have too many jigsaws to make and too many books to read to be hanging about in the hospital."

Maria bit her lip, trying not to let her feelings get the better of her. She took a deep breath to steady herself. "And what about the Lego?'"

He looked at her solemnly and then he gave her a big grin. "Exactly," he said. "I have far too much to be doing to be wasting time in hospital."

"But you have to mind yourself," Jude said. "And not be talking too much and driving everybody mad."

"Would you listen to who's talking?" Ambrose said. "Even in the hospital you were busy chatting to all the nurses. Especially the blonde one – Cathy, I think her name is."

"She was a nice girl," his mother said. "She was very good the night you were taken in."

"Yes, she was. But did you notice she had to wear specs at times, Mammy?" Ambrose said. "But I think she forgot to put them on when she was looking at Jude."

"Now, now," Jude laughed, "we won't have any sneering at the table. It's Christmas Day."

He caught Maria's eye and they both smiled. He had told her last night all about Cathy, and how his mother hadn't been keen because there had been some scandal about her sister having a baby adopted. His mother felt that their own family had enough for people to talk about without adding more to it. But, after seeing the way she looked after Ambrose, and the professional but kind way she had gone about her job, her attitude seemed to be softening towards her.

Just after dinner when Maria was helping the women with the washing-up and Ambrose was dozing among his cushions, the phone rang and Maria's grandfather called her to say it was her friend, Paul.

"Now, tell him that you'll see him in a couple of days, as soon as we get the flights sorted," Patrick said quietly. "Tell him you'll be over for New Year."

Maria smiled and nodded. "Okay," she said. "I'll tell him if everything is still okay I'll be over."

An hour later, when she was helping Ambrose with his Lego model, the phone rang again. This time it was Diana.

"Is everything okay?" Diana asked. "I wondered if there was any more news."

"Things are just the same," Maria said in a low voice. "Ambrose is doing better than we thought, but he's still very ill. We're just so very lucky he was able to come home for the week or so."

"I'm so glad for him too," Diana said. "He just sounds the loveliest little chap."

"Oh, he is," Maria said. "I absolutely love him."

"Has it been difficult?" Diana asked. "Has it been a very depressing Christmas Day for you?"

"No," Maria said, smiling to herself now as she thought about it.. "Not at all. It's been a lovely Christmas Day. I'm sorry our plans didn't work out, and of course I miss you all but, this year, my place was in Ireland."

"Well, I'm glad it worked out so well for you."

"It has," Maria said, "and all being well, I'll be over in a few days to spend New Year with you, and I'm looking forward to seeing Mrs Lowry and Stella."

"Oh, Maria, that's wonderful," Diana said. "I'm so looking forward to seeing you and having you to stay for a while. And Franco has said if you make it over he'll open the restaurant again on New Year's Eve and we'll have a bit of a party in it."

"It sounds great," Maria said. "I was talking to Paul earlier and he said he hadn't anything planned for New Year, so he might join us too." She halted. "How is Stella? Is she back to her old self?"

Diana paused. "She's better than she was, but she's still not one hundred per cent. She's not as thin as she was but she is still too thin to be healthy. They had to take the keys of the little ballet studio off her, as they found her up practising in the middle of the night again. Apparently she used to do that a lot when she was trying to lose weight. The clinic have said she's not allowed to dance at all now until they feel she's fully recovered."

"Poor Stella," Maria said. "And it's all off with her and Tony. Apparently he just disappeared off to Birmingham without a word."

"I think," Diana said, "you'll find there was more to that than Stella knows. I think her parents gave Tony a little nudge in that direction."

"What do you mean?"

"Her mother said they just gave him a financial offer to move away that he couldn't refuse. Apparently, he's bought into a share of the stables he moved to down in Birmingham."

"Oh, my God!" Maria said, "I can't believe it!"

"Don't ever tell Stella, of course," Diana said. "But I think if he was happy to take their offer, then he wasn't the right person for her."

"I suppose so, when you think of it like that." Maria paused. "How are you, Diana? Are you okay? Are you missing Dad very much?"

"Yes, Maria, there's no point in lying. I still think of him all the time."

"You made such a lovely couple . . ."

"I know we did, and that's what's so difficult. Where will I ever meet anyone like him again?"

"I'm sure there are a lot of nice Italians around . . ."

"Where?" Diana gave a little laugh. "Where am I supposed to bump into a nice Italian man?"

"Maybe in Leonardo's when we reopen it next year. I thought

you might like to help me and Franco with the accounts and maybe the odd night front of house. I'll need somebody there when I come back. I've decided I want to work there – to eventually run the restaurant myself. I have great ideas for it."

"Are you serious?" Diana asked.

"Yes, I am. Very serious."

"What about the travel agent's?"

"That was always a fall-back position because my dad didn't want me being a waitress. I'll do night classes in business studies and restaurant management. It will be the professional job he wanted me to have but, more importantly, it will be the job I love."

"I'm delighted," Diana said, "so delighted I don't know what to say. And we have so much to talk about with the restaurant and working out where you might like to live when you come back."

"I don't know exactly when it will be, it might be in three months, it might be six months . . . it might be a year."

"Why is that? Franco checked with the lawyer, and as long as your grandparents are okay with it, he will be your guardian in England until you are eighteen and fully independent. It won't be long until you're eighteen."

"I know that," Maria said. "That's not the reason. It's Ambrose." She looked back down the hallway. "I'll explain it all to you when I see you in a few days. Give my love to Mrs Lowry and Stella. I'll ring nearer the time to give you the exact details."

"I'm so, so looking forward to seeing you," Diana said. "It will give us both a lovely start to the year."

Maria put the phone down and then she stood for a minute before joining the others. It was lovely to hear from her friends back home and she couldn't wait to see them when she went back. But for this last week, and especially today, this was the right place to be.

The doctors had told them there was every chance it was Ambrose's last Christmas, and nothing in the world was going to make her miss that. There was a chance of some new drug that had recently been approved and was due out in a few months, and there was a machine due to arrive soon that might help clear his chest, but the specialist gave no guarantees. From now on, each episode would bring Ambrose down a little bit further. And a more serious one he might not survive.

Maria hadn't even given Manchester a second thought when she heard he was coming home, and knew he wanted her to be there. Even if he had been kept in hospital, as they feared he might, she still would have stayed in Ireland to visit and be close to him. She was happy with her day-to-day life for the present here with her family in Ireland, and she was happy with the future that looked mapped out for her back in Manchester.

The sound of 'Blue Christmas' suddenly drifted out into the hallway, and Maria knew that Ambrose had asked for the volume on the radio to be turned up so she could hear it. They had both said it was their favourite Christmas song only this morning. She knew he would be hoping it would make her hurry up on the phone and come back to join them.

She smiled now as she walked back towards the kitchen. She wouldn't think any more sad thoughts about Ambrose or her father or her mother. She would not spoil today with the past, and she had learned that there was no point in worrying about the future.

For today she would live in the present. For today she would be grateful to be spending Christmas with Ambrose and her new family in Ireland. The new family that Leo had found for her.

If you enjoyed
Music From Home by Geraldine O'Neill
why not try
Summer's End also published by Poolbeg?
Here's a sneak preview of Chapter One

Summer's End

Geraldine O'Neill

POOLBEG

Chapter 1

January 1966

Lily knew she shouldn't feel happy about going to a funeral, but it was a perfect excuse to get away from college for a while. It would give her time to forget the fool she had made of herself the other night.

After months of being curious about him, she had caught the eye of the young-looking history lecturer across the late-night bar. She had noticed him when he joined the staff at the beginning of term, and was immediately drawn to his smooth caramel-toned skin and beautiful dark eyes. And although she knew his colour and culture would have been too different for some of the girls, it made him all the more interesting to her. She had been disappointed that he wasn't teaching her course and had waited for the chance to get to know him.

They got chatting and he bought her a glass of wine. They were still talking and drinking when the rest of her group had gone back to the student halls.

He told her that he had just finished his PhD in London before moving to Newcastle, then he told her about growing up in what he called the 'fusion culture' in the Seychelles with his English mother and Seychellois father. She listened intently as he talked about the art, music and food, and the colourful festivals.

It was unlike any other conversation she'd had before, and it stirred her curiosity and interest about different people and places.

As they walked back to the student houses in the dark, he asked her about growing up in Scotland. She told him about Rowanhill, the small mining village she grew up in, which was happily served with a train service going in one direction to Glasgow and the other to Edinburgh. She described how she had travelled to the cities to shop and mooch around most weekends since she was thirteen or fourteen. They stood outside chatting for a while and then he invited her into his flat for coffee.

That was when she made the mistake. And she couldn't blame alcohol; she'd only had a couple. The all-day hangover she suffered when she first arrived at college had made her wary of it. She couldn't have imagined how the months of wondering about him would evaporate in just a few minutes. A few humiliating minutes when she realised she was well out of her depth.

And now she was desperate to avoid him.

She pushed the mortifying memories away and thought of her escape. She loved travelling, and the fact she was flying for the very first time was a bonus. And it wasn't as if she knew her father's aunt very well. She would be solemn and commiserating with her close relatives.

Lily Grace held her compact mirror up, studying her face and light-brown hair which still had a few streaks of the blonde she had as a child. She supposed she wasn't bad-looking, but there were times she wished she was taller and more curvaceous. Her second cousins in Ireland would see a big change in her. Her last visit was when she was sixteen. She was twenty now, and in her second year at teacher training college, just over the border in Newcastle-upon-Tyne.

She had applied to the traditional Catholic colleges in Scotland, but the exam points were higher than England. Her careers tutor had advised all the teaching candidates to apply to an English college just in case, so she had chosen Newcastle.

Lily had been interviewed at three different colleges, and when the results came out she had enough points for the Scottish ones, but she opted for Newcastle which had also accepted her. It was far more modern than the others and it was mixed. A religious, all-girls teacher training college held no appeal for her. With four brothers, she was well used to boys, and had attended a mixed secondary school in Hamilton, some ten miles from Rowanhill. Another plus was that she would get to live on a college campus in England, whereas if she stayed closer to home she would have to travel from Rowanhill by train on a daily basis.

There was no contest. She had got a taste of the bigger world at her Newcastle interview and wanted more of it.

Her mother, Mona, on the other hand, had been devastated. "Why on earth are you going away to England, when you could go to a college here?"

"I liked it better," Lily said. "And it's only a few hours' journey from home. It would be the same distance if I went to somewhere north of here like Inverness or Aberdeen."

"But you didn't apply to Inverness," her mother had argued. "And it's not even a Catholic college. Imagine going all the way to England! What will the Parish Priest say?"

Lily shrugged. What did it have to do with him?

"Well, that's lovely," her mother had said. "And it'll be me that has to face him every day." Mona had been the priest's housekeeper for over a decade and found herself in the firing-line if any of her children strayed off the conventional religious path.

"Are you sure?" her father, Pat, had asked her later when they were on their own. "You'll be a good distance away from us."

"I'll be home every six weeks," Lily said. "And I'm absolutely sure."

She had remained firm in her decision when Father Finlay called around, and told him that going to an English college wouldn't change her religious views one bit. She didn't elaborate on the fact that she already disagreed with many things about the Church.

"I find it very odd," the elderly Irish priest had said, "that anyone would want go to England if they didn't have to." He raised his eyes heavenwards. "But then I shouldn't be surprised – you're not the first one in the Grace family to go down a different road."

He was of course referring to Pat's sister who had married a Protestant, and her cousin Kirsty who had caused uproar when she took up with an older man her parents had disapproved of.

While Lily was delighted with her choice and happy to explain to anyone why she had chosen the modern college and fantastic campus, her mother had remained tight-lipped.

A few weeks after Lily left – laden down with a huge case and bags filled with Scottish bread, pies and packets of *Oddfellows* sweets – Pat had noticed a change in his wife. Although Lily phoned her regularly, she stood at the window each morning watching for the postman with letters from Newcastle. And he had to stop her phoning the halls of residence every other day to see how Lily was settling in.

Mona's sad demeanour reminded him of the time when Lily had been seriously ill with polio as a child. Her determination had pulled her through, but the slight weakness it left in her legs had put paid to Lily's plans to be a dancing teacher.

One Friday night he phoned the pay-phone in Lily's student house to check that she was free the following day, and then he told his wife they were going to Newcastle first thing in the morning.

"We're driving to England?" Her hand had flown to her throat. The only holidays they took were to Ireland or one of the nearby seaside towns. "We can't . . . it's too far away."

"It's only a three-hour drive. We'll leave about nine and be there after twelve. And then we'll see her. Isn't that what you want?"

By eight o'clock Mona was sitting with bags full of more bread and pies. By midday, they had found signs for the Northumberland college, and a few minutes later were signing the visitor's book at the Porter's Lodge.

"Well, what do you think?" Lily asked, as she walked around the college campus between her parents, linking both their arms.

"It's beautiful," Mona said, as they stopped to study the circle of immaculate Victorian houses situated around a large green oval of lawn and flower-beds. "England is nothing like I imagined."

Lily had laughed. "This is only a small bit of it, and of course Newcastle isn't the biggest city."

"It's big enough," her mother said.

An hour later, after lunch in the dining-room and two sherries in the Students' Union bar, Lily knew that parents' fears about her had evaporated.

She was now in her second year and she had made the journey

from Newcastle to Rowanhill so many times she no longer gave it any thought. She was delighted to get a break from college, and since it was for a funeral in Ireland she could string it out to nearly a week. Luckily, it was a term when she didn't have any teaching practices, so she wouldn't be letting any school down.

It was wonderful to be able to fit in a quick visit home to Scotland and then fly over to Ireland. She would also have a couple of days back home after the funeral. A great way to fill the last grey week in January. She had arrived home last night, Tuesday, having caught an evening train to Edinburgh, and her father had picked her up at the station and driven her down home to Rowanhill.

The blustery, wet weather and dark mornings added to the excitement. She felt she was cheating it by travelling, instead of looking at it out of the college windows.

Lily had sat up until twelve with her parents and two brothers, drinking tea and catching up on family news and local gossip. She loved her independent life in Newcastle, and she loved teaching – but she also loved coming home to Rowanhill.

She was surprised to discover she was the only female going to the funeral along with her father and two of her brothers: Seán, who was nearly thirty and married with two children, and Declan the youngest of her brothers, who was single and still living at home. Michael and Patrick were too busy with their own families and working in the family taxi and coach business.

"I thought you were coming with us," she said to her mother.

"Oh, I couldn't face it. The thought of going up in an aeroplane terrifies me, and then driving down those dark wee winding lanes would just finish me off. It's bad enough in the summer never mind the heart of winter."

"But it's all right for me to suffer the terrible trip?" Lily said, making big eyes. "Travelling from Newcastle tonight and going straight to Ireland tomorrow afternoon."

"Get away with you!" Mona gave her a sidelong glance and then started to laugh. "There's no need for you to go at all, and well you know it."

Lily's brother Declan winked at her. "Admit it: you just fancied a holiday off college and the chance to fly in a plane."

"No, I feel I should go to the funeral. She's Dad's aunt."

"What's her full name then? First and second."

"It's Mary Grace."

"Rubbish," Declan laughed. "Her name was Grace before she got married. If you know her well enough to go to her funeral, you surely should know her married name."

An indignant look crossed Lily's face for a second – and then Declan winked again and she started to laugh. "Her name doesn't matter, I just think it's nice for some of us to go to represent the Grace side of the family. And anyway, it's ages since *I've* been to Ireland. I've been working every summer while all you boys went over there fishing."

"Well," her father said, "*I'm* delighted that you're coming with us, Lily. And so would my Aunt Mary be, whose second name is Jordan by the way. At least we won't need to worry about having to make chat to people when you're there. You can talk the hind legs off a donkey."

Everybody laughed.

"I'm really excited about flying," Lily said, grinning. "One of the girls at college goes abroad all the time and she was telling me all about the food and the drink they give you."

"It's only Ireland," Pat reminded her. "It's just over an hour in the air, so you won't have time for much."

"How long will we be there?"

"Four to five days. The removal is tomorrow night and the funeral is on Friday. We'll travel back on the Sunday. Seán and I can't leave the lads any longer."

"You're entitled to take time off," Lily said. "You're always working."

"We're needed – we've got a lot of runs on with both the coaches and the taxis."

"Michael and Patrick will manage without you and Seán," Mona told him, "and they can always get someone in if they get busy over the weekend."

"Five days in Offaly at this time of the year will be long enough," Pat said. "And it will give Lily a day or so when we come back home."

Mona didn't argue. There had been times when her husband had gone to Ireland every chance he got. "It won't do Seán any harm having a bit of a break – in fact, he could do with it." A determined look came on her face. "Eileen has a list of jobs waiting from him every evening he gets in from work. She's obsessed with the house being perfect, and everything has to be the latest fashion. She had him fitting wall-lamps after work the other night and, when the screwdriver made a slight mark on the wallpaper, she told him to watch or they would have to repaper the whole room!" She clucked her tongue. "If it's not painting or decorating, he's running her or the kids over to her mother's house. She hardly gives him time to have a bite after work before he's up and running again."

There was a short silence.

Seán and his highly-strung wife was a favourite topic of Mona's. Once she got into her stride, there was no stopping her.

Lily searched for something to say. "What time is the flight?"

"I think it's at two o'clock," her father took his cue. "I have the tickets in the bedroom."

Some eight years ago Pat Grace, who was a bus-driver for the local company, and his two eldest sons Michael and Seán, who were mechanics, had bought a second-hand coach to do runs at the weekend. The business had taken off quickly and, after several big school contracts and a hectic Christmas driving groups into Glasgow and Edinburgh for work nights and pantomimes, they had bought a second coach.

A year or two later they acquired a couple of taxis as well and were busy enough for Patrick and Declan to join them and for Pat to give up his bus-driving job. The boys had always been mad on cars and engines, and between them all they were able to maintain the vehicles themselves which kept them busy between runs.

Pat came back in with the tickets. "Ten past two," he confirmed. "We'll get into Dublin for half three and pick up the hired car. We should be down in Ballygrace in plenty of time for the removal." He looked at Patrick who was driving them to the airport. "We'll have to be gone from the house around eleven to be in plenty of time."

"No problem, the school runs will be well finished."

"I'll be up around nine," Lily said, "and then I'll drop over to Sophie's for half an hour."

"Will you have time?" Mona asked. "Don't leave everything to the last minute as usual. And make sure you pack your good black dress and coat for the funeral."

"Mother –" Lily rolled her eyes, "I'm not a teenager any more, I'm nearly twenty-one years old and will be a trained teacher by next year."

"That doesn't stop you being late. You never change." Mona studied her daughter for a moment and then she laughed and shook her head. "Although I think you have us all wrapped around your little finger. I'll bet you do everything perfectly when you're in college or on teaching practice. You must have done it right, or you wouldn't have got all those high marks."

"Of course I work hard," Lily told her, "but I'm entitled to relax and be myself when I'm at home."

"What you mean is you save your laziness for us," Declan said.

Lily pulled a face at him. "Anyone know what the weather forecast is?"

"Cold and wet here," her mother said. "And though it's not as cold, you can always depend on Ireland to be damper." She paused, studying her daughter's trouser-clad legs. "Are teachers allowed to wear trousers in school in England?"

Lily stifled a groan. Her 'outlandish' clothes – her mother's term – were another bone of contention between herself and her mother. "They're allowed in some schools," she said, gazing down at her polished fingernails, "but not in the ones I've been on teaching practice in. All the students and lecturers wear them in college." She knew the fact that she said 'lecturers' would halt her mother for a moment.

"And what about the mini-skirts you wear? Surely you're not allowed to wear them in school?"

Lily saw Declan sniggering and felt like killing him. "I wear longer skirts when I'm on teaching practice."

"I thought so," Mona said. "As you say, you do everything right when you need to."

Lily decided to get the argument over tonight. "I'm wearing

trousers for travelling over," she said. "Everyone wears them these days."

Her mother pursed her lips together, a sign she was upset.

Lily looked at her now and immediately felt sorry. What was the point of coming home for a few days to spend it arguing over stupid things like clothes? And, although they had different views on things, she loved her mother with all her heart. Lily leaned over and squeezed her hand. "You don't need to worry," she said. "I won't show you up by wearing anything outlandish, and I promise I'll wear the nice dress and coat for the funeral."

Mona looked at her and smiled. "Good girl," she said. "I know I'm a bit old-fashioned, but I know what people are like and I want them to get the right impression of you. It might not seem fair, but teachers do have a responsibility. They're expected to give an example."

Lily suddenly pictured herself with the lecturer the other night and a heaviness descended on her. She knew exactly what her mother would say if she knew. Him being a lecturer and older would be bad enough, but the fact that he was foreign and coloured would be even worse. And her father's reaction would be exactly the same.

She almost shuddered at the thought.

•—◆—•

If you enjoyed this chapter from
Summer's End by Geraldine O'Neill,
why not order the full book online
@ www.poolbeg.com

•—◆—•